alfred HITCHCOCK'S FATAL ATTRACTIONS

Edited by Elana Lore

The Dial Press

Davis Publications, Inc.
380 Lexington Avenue, New York, N.Y. 10017

Grateful acknowledgment is hereby made for permission to reprint the following:

The Knight's Cross Signal Problem by Ernest Bramah; copyright by the Estate of Ernest Bramah Smith; reprinted by permission of A.P. Watt, Ltd. *Murder in Mind* by C.B. Gilford; first published in Alfred Hitchcock's Mystery Magazine; copyright © H.S.D. Publications, Inc., 1971; reprinted by permission of Scott Meredith Literary Agency, Inc. *The Invisible Tomb* by Arthur Porges; first published in Alfred Hitchcock's Mystery Magazine; copyright © 1967 by H.S.D. Publications, Inc.; reprinted by permission of Scott Meredith Literary Agency, Inc. *The Avenging of Ann Leete* by Marjorie Bowen; reprinted by permission of Harold Ober Incorporated; copyright 1928 by Marjorie Bowen. *Just Curious* by James H. Schmitz; first published in Alfred Hitchcock's Mystery Magazine; copyright © H.S.D. Publications, Inc., 1968; reprinted by permission of Scott Meredith Literary Agency, Inc. *The Vultures of Malabar* by Edward D. Hoch; first published in Alfred Hitchcock's Mystery Magazine; copyright © 1980 by Davis Publications, Inc.; reprinted by permission of the author. *A Matter of Gravity* by Randall Garrett; first published in Analog Science Fiction/Science Fact; copyright © 1974 by The Conde Nast Publications, Inc.; reprinted by permission of Blackstone Literary Agency. *August Heat* by W.F. Harvey; copyright by the Estate of W.F. Harvey; reprinted by permission of J.M. Dent & Sons, Ltd. *The Girl Who Found Things* by Henry Slesar; first published in Alfred Hitchcock's Mystery Magazine; copyright © H.S.D. Publications, Inc., 1973; reprinted by permission of the author. *The Return of Max Kearny* by Ron Goulart; copyright © 1981 by Mercury Press, Inc.; reprinted by permission of the author. *Death Trance* by Clayton Matthews; first published in Alfred Hitchcock's Mystery Magazine; copyright © H.S.D. Publications, Inc., 1970; reprinted by permission of the author. *The Healer* by George C. Chesbro; first published in Alfred Hitchcock's Mystery Magazine; copyright © H.S.D. Publications, Inc., 1974; reprinted by permission of the author. *The Monkey's Paw* by W.W. Jacobs; copyright The Estate of W.W. Jacobs; reprinted by permission of The Society of Authors as the literary representative of the Estate of W.W. Jacobs. *Rowena's Brooch* by Donald Olson; first published in Alfred Hitchcock's Mystery Magazine; copyright © H.S.D. Publications, Inc., 1973; reprinted by permission of Blanche C. Gregory, Inc. *Fat Jow and the Manifestations* by Robert Alan Blair; first published in Alfred Hitchcock's Mystery Magazine; copyright © H.S.D. Publications, Inc., 1968; reprinted by permission of Scott Meredith Literary Agency, Inc. *Murder by Dream* by Patrick O'Keeffe; first published in Alfred Hitchcock's Mystery Magazine; copyright © H.S.D. Publications, Inc., 1968; reprinted by permission of Cathleen O'Keeffe. *The Clairvoyant Countess* by Dorothy Gilman; chapters 8-10 from THE CLAIRVOYANT COUNTESS by Dorothy Gilman; copyright © 1975 by Dorothy Gilman Butters; reprinted by permission of Doubleday & Company, Inc. and McIntosh & Otis, Inc. *The Oracle of the Dog* by G.K. Chesterton; reprinted by permission of DODD, MEAD & COMPANY, INC. from THE INCREDULITY OF FATHER BROWN by G.K. Chesterton; copyright 1923, 1924, 1926 by Dodd, Mead & Company, Inc.; copyright renewed 1953 by Oliver Chesterton; also © 1923 by G.K. Chesterton, renewed 1950 by Oliver Chesterton; reprinted by permission of Miss D.E. Collins.

INTRODUCTION

Dear Readers:

Throughout the years, *Alfred Hitchcock's Mystery Magazine* has published many stories of the bizarre, the occult, and the supernatural, and we thought it might be fun, since these kinds of stories are so popular right now, to put some of them, along with some classic stories in the field, together in a collection. Well, here it is, full of clairvoyants, psychic healers, demonologists, poltergeists, and ghosts, plus some things we just knew were strange, but couldn't quite put our finger on. With all these odd things happening between the covers, we'd advise you not to leave this anthology lying around someplace where it might be able to get into mischief while you're not looking.

The stories also range widely over time, from Charles Dickens' classic story about the bagman's uncle, to a recent adventure of Simon Ark, Ed Hoch's unusual detective who claims to be 2000 years old and who, over these many years, seems to have involved himself in a variety of strange happenings in his quest for the Devil.

We hope you enjoy this. We enjoyed putting it together. We'd particularly like to thank Barry Zeman, a member of Mystery Writers of America, for sharing his library of classic mystery and suspense stories with us.

Elana Lore

CONTENTS

The Knight's Cross Signal Problem

by Ernest Bramah

"**L**ouis," exclaimed Mr. Carrados, with the air of genial gaiety that Carlyle had found so incongruous to his conception of a blind man, "you have a mystery somewhere about you! I know it by your step."

Nearly a month had passed since the incident of the false Dionysius had led to the two men meeting. It was now December. Whatever Mr. Carlyle's step might indicate to the inner eye it betokened to the casual observer the manner of a crisp, alert, self-possessed man of business. Carlyle, in truth, betrayed nothing of the pessimism and despondency that had marked him on the earlier occasion.

"You have only yourself to thank that it is a very poor one," he retorted. "If you hadn't held me to a hasty promise—"

"To give me an option on the next case that baffled you, no matter what it was—"

"Just so. The consequence is that you get a very unsatisfactory affair that has no special interest to an amateur and is only baffling because it is—well—"

"Well, baffling?"

"Exactly, Max. Your would-be jest has discovered the proverbial truth. I need hardly tell you that it is only the insoluble that is finally baffling and this is very probably insoluble. You remember the awful smash on the Central and Suburban at Knight's Cross Station a few weeks ago?"

"Yes," replied Carrados, with interest. "I read the whole ghastly details at the time."

"You read?" exclaimed his friend suspiciously.

"I still use the familiar phrases," explained Carrados, with a smile. "As a matter of fact, my secretary reads to me. I mark what I want to hear and when he comes at ten o'clock we clear off the morning papers in no time."

"And how do you know what to mark?" demanded Mr. Carlyle cunningly.

Carrados's right hand, lying idly on the table, moved to a news-paper near. He ran his finger along a column heading, his eyes still turned towards his visitor.

" 'The Money Market. Continued from page 2. British Railways,' " he announced.

"Extraordinary," murmured Carlyle.

"Not very," said Carrados. "If someone dipped a stick in treacle and wrote 'Rats' across a marble slab you would probably be able to distinguish what was there, blindfold."

"Probably," admitted Mr. Carlyle. "At all events we will not test the experiment."

"The difference to you of treacle on a marble background is scarcely greater than that of printers' ink on newspaper to me. But anything smaller than pica I do not read with comfort, and below long primer I cannot read at all. Hence the secretary. Now the accident, Louis."

"The accident: well, you remember all about that. An ordinary Central and Suburban passenger train, non-stop at Knight's Cross, ran past the signal and crashed into a crowded electric train that was just beginning to move out. It was like sending a garden roller down a row of handlights. Two carriages of the electric train were flattened out of existence; the next two were broken up. For the first time on an English railway there was a good stand-up smash be-tween a heavy steam-engine and a train of light cars, and it was 'bad for the coo.' "

"Twenty-seven killed, forty something injured, eight died since," commented Carrados.

"That was bad for the Co.," said Carlyle. "Well, the main fact was plain enough. The heavy train was in the wrong. But was the engine-driver responsible? He claimed, and he claimed vehemently from the first, and he never varied one iota, that he had a 'clear' sig-nal—that is to say, the green light, it being dark. The signalman concerned was equally dogged that he never pulled off the signal—that it was at 'danger' when the accident happened and that it had been for five minutes before. Obviously, they could not both be right."

"Why, Louis?" asked Mr. Carrados smoothly.

"The signal must either have been up or down—red or green."

"Did you ever notice the signals on the Great Northern Railway, Louis?"

"Not particularly. Why?"

"One winterly day, about the year when you and I were concerned in being born, the engine-driver of a Scotch express received the 'clear' from a signal near a little Huntingdon station called Abbots Ripton. He went on and crashed into a goods train and into the thick of the smash a down express mowed its way. Thirteen killed and the usual tale of injured. He was positive that the signal gave him a 'clear'; the signalman was equally confident that he had never pulled it off the 'danger.' Both were right, and yet the signal was in working order. As I said, it was a winterly day; it had been snowing hard and the snow froze and accumulated on the upper edge of the signal arm until its weight bore it down. That is a fact that no fiction writer dare have invented, but to this day every signal on the Great Northern pivots from the center of the arm instead of from the end, in memory of that snowstorm."

"That came out at the inquest, I presume?" said Mr. Carlyle. "We have had the Board of Trade inquiry and the inquest here and no explanation is forthcoming. Everything was in perfect order. It rests between the word of the signalman and the word of the engine-driver—not a jot of direct evidence either way. Which is right?"

"That is what you are going to find out, Louis?" suggested Carrados.

"It is what I am being paid for finding out," admitted Mr. Carlyle frankly. "But so far we are just where the inquest left it, and, between ourselves, I candidly can't see an inch in front of my face in the matter."

"Nor can I," said the blind man, with a rather wry smile. "Never mind. The engine-driver is your client, of course?"

"Yes," admitted Carlyle. "But how the deuce did you know?"

"Let us say that your sympathies are enlisted on his behalf. The jury were inclined to exonerate the signalman, weren't they? What has the company done with your man?"

"Both are suspended. Hutchins, the driver, hears that he may probably be given charge of a lavatory at one of the stations. He is a decent, bluff, short-spoken old chap, with his heart in his work. Just now you'll find him at his worst—bitter and suspicious. The thought of swabbing down a lavatory and taking pennies all day is poisoning him."

"Naturally. Well, there we have honest Hutchins: taciturn, a little touchy perhaps, grown gray in the service of the company, and manifesting quite a bull-dog-like devotion to his favorite 538."

"Why, that actually was the number of his engine—how do you know it?" demanded Carlyle sharply.

"It was mentioned two or three times at the inquest, Louis," replied Carrados mildly.

"And you remembered—with no reason to?"

"You can generally trust a blind man's memory, especially if he has taken the trouble to develop it."

"Then you will remember that Hutchins did not make a very good impression at the time. He was surly and irritable under the ordeal. I want you to see the case from all sides."

"He called the signalman—Mead—a 'lying young dog,' across the room, I believe. Now, Mead, what is he like? You have seen him, of course?"

"Yes. He does not impress me favorably. He is glib, ingratiating, and distinctly 'greasy.' He has a ready answer for everything almost before the question is out of your mouth. He has thought of everything."

"And now you are going to tell me something, Louis," said Carrados encouragingly.

Mr. Carlyle laughed a little to cover an involuntary movement of surprise.

"There is a suggestive line that was not touched at the enquiries," he admitted. "Hutchins has been a saving man all his life, and he has received good wages. Among his class he is regarded as wealthy. I daresay that he has five hundred pounds in the bank. He is a widower with one daughter, a very nice-mannered girl of about twenty. Mead is a young man, and he and the girl are sweethearts—have been informally engaged for some time. But old Hutchins would not hear of it; he seems to have taken a dislike to the signalman from the first, and latterly he had forbidden him to come to his house or his daughter to speak to him."

"Excellent, Louis," cried Carrados in great delight. "We shall clear your man in a blaze of red and green lights yet and hang the glib, 'greasy' signalman from his own signal-post."

"It is a significant fact, seriously?"

"It is absolutely convincing."

"It may have been a slip, a mental lapse on Mead's part which he discovered the moment it was too late, and then, being too cowardly to admit his fault, and having so much at stake, he took care to make detection impossible. It may have been that, but my idea is rather that probably it was neither quite pure accident nor pure design. I can imagine Mead meanly pluming himself over the fact that the life of this man who stands in his way, and whom he must cordially dislike, lies in his power. I can imagine the idea becoming an obsession as he dwells on it. A dozen times with his hand on the lever he lets his mind explore the possibilities of a moment's defection. Then one day he pulls the signal off in sheer bravado—and hastily puts it at danger again. He may have done it once or he may have done it oftener before he was caught in a fatal moment of irresolution. The chances are about even that the engine-driver would be killed. In any case he would be disgraced, for it is easier on the face of it to believe that a man might run past a danger signal in absentmindedness, without noticing it, than that a man should pull off a signal and replace it without being conscious of his actions."

"The fireman was killed. Does your theory involve the certainty of the fireman being killed, Louis?"

"No," said Carlyle. "The fireman is a difficulty, but looking at it from Mead's point of view—whether he has been guilty of an error or a crime—it resolves itself into this: First, the fireman may be killed. Second, he may not notice the signal at all. Third, in any case he will loyally corroborate his driver and the good old jury will discount that."

Carrados smoked thoughtfully, his open, sightless eyes merely appearing to be set in a tranquil gaze across the room.

"It would not be an improbable explanation," he said presently. "Ninety-nine men out of a hundred would say: 'People do not do these things.' But you and I, who have in our different ways studied criminology, know that they sometimes do, or else there would be no curious crimes. What have you done on that line?"

To anyone who could see, Mr. Carlyle's expression conveyed an answer.

"You are behind the scenes, Max. What was there for me to do? Still I must do something for my money. Well, I have had a very close inquiry made confidentially among the men. There might be a whisper of one of them knowing more than had come out—a man restrained by friendship, or enmity, or even grade jealousy. Nothing came of that. Then there was the remote chance that some private person had noticed the signal without attaching any importance to it then, one who would be able to identify it still by something associated with the time. I went over the line myself. Opposite the signal the line on one side is shut in by a high blank wall; on the other side are houses, but coming below the butt-end of a scullery the signal does not happen to be visible from any road or from any window."

"My poor Louis!" said Carrados, in friendly ridicule. "You were at the end of your tether?"

"I was," admitted Carlyle. "And now that you know the sort of job it is I don't suppose that you are keen on wasting your time over it."

"That would hardly be fair, would it?" said Carrados reasonably. "No, Louis, I will take over your honest old driver and your greasy young signalman and your fatal signal that cannot be seen from anywhere."

"But it is an important point for you to remember, Max, that although the signal cannot be seen from the box, if the mechanism had gone wrong, or anyone tampered with the arm, the automatic indicator would at once have told Mead that the green light was showing. Oh, I have gone very thoroughly into the technical points, I assure you."

"I must do so too," commented Mr. Carrados gravely.

"For that matter, if there is anything you want to know, I dare say that I can tell you," suggested his visitor. "It might save your time."

"True," acquiesced Carrados. "I should like to know whether any-one belonging to the houses that bound the line there came of age or got married on the twenty-sixth of November."

Mr. Carlyle looked across curiously at his host.

"I really do not know, Max," he replied, in his crisp, precise way. "What on earth has that got to do with it, may I enquire?"

"The only explanation of the Pont St. Lin swing-bridge disaster of '75 was the reflection of a green bengal light on a cottage window."

Mr. Carlyle smiled his indulgence privately.

"My dear chap, you mustn't let your retentive memory of obscure happenings run away with you," he remarked wisely. "In nine cases out of ten the obvious explanation is the true one. The difficulty, as here, lies in proving it. Now, you would like to see these men?"

"I expect so; in any case, I will see Hutchins first."

"Both live in Holloway. Shall I ask Hutchins to come here to see you—say to-morrow? He is doing nothing."

"No," replied Carrados. "To-morrow I must call on my brokers and my time may be filled up."

"Quite right; you mustn't neglect your own affairs for this—experiment," assented Carlyle.

"Besides, I should prefer to drop in on Hutchins at his own home.

Now, Louis, enough of the honest old man for one night. I have a lovely thing by Eumenes that I want to show you. To-day is—Tuesday. Come to dinner on Sunday and pour the vials of your ridicule on my want of success."

"That's an amiable way of putting it," replied Carlyle. "All right, I will."

Two hours later Carrados was again in his study, apparently, for a wonder, sitting idle. Sometimes he smiled to himself, and once or twice he laughed a little, but for the most part his pleasant, impassive face reflected no emotion and he sat with his useless eyes tranquilly fixed on an unseen distance. It was a fantastic caprice of the man to mock his sightlessness by a parade of light, and under the soft brilliance of a dozen electric brackets the room was as bright as day. At length he stood up and rang the bell.

"I suppose Mr. Greatorex isn't still here by any chance, Parkinson?" he asked, referring to his secretary.

"I think not, sir, but I will ascertain," replied the man.

"Never mind. Go to his room and bring me the last two files of *The Times*. Now"—when he returned—"turn to the earliest you have there. The date?"

"November the second."

"That will do. Find the Money Market; it will be in the Supplement. Now look down the columns until you come to British Railways."

"I have it, sir."

"Central and Suburban. Read the closing price and the change."

"Central and Suburban Ordinary, 66½-67½, fall ⅛. Preferred Ordinary, 81-81½, no change. Deferred Ordinary, 27½-27¾, fall ¼. That is all, sir."

"Now take a paper about a week on. Read the Deferred only."

"27-27¼, no change."

"Another week."

"29½-30, rise ⅝."

"Another."

"31½-32½, rise 1."

"Very good. Now on Tuesday the twenty-seventh November."

"31⅞-32¾, rise ½."

"Yes. The next day."

"24½-23½, fall 9."

"Quite so, Parkinson. There had been an accident, you see."

"Yes, sir. Very unpleasant accident. Jane knows a person whose sister's young man has a cousin who had his arm torn off in it—torn off at the socket, she says, sir. It seems to bring it home to one, sir."

"That is all. Stay—in the paper you have, look down the first money column and see if there is any reference to the Central and Suburban."

"Yes, sir. 'City and Suburbans, which after their late depression on the projected extension of the motor bus service, had been steadily creeping up on the abandonment of the scheme, and as a result of their own excellent traffic returns, suffered a heavy slump through the lamentable accident of Thursday night. The Deferred in particular at one time fell eleven points as it was felt that the possible dividend, with which rumor has of late been busy, was now out of the question.' "

"Yes; that is all. Now you can take the papers back. And let it be a warning to you, Parkinson, not to invest your savings in speculative railway deferreds."

"Yes, sir. Thank you, sir, I will endeavor to remember." He lingered for a moment as he shook the file of papers level. "I may say, sir, that I have my eye on a small block of cottage property at Acton. But even cottage property scarcely seems safe from legislative depredation now, sir."

The next day Mr. Carrados called on his brokers in the city. It is to be presumed that he got through his private business quicker than he expected, for after leaving Austin Friars he continued his journey to Holloway, where he found Hutchins at home and sitting morosely before his kitchen fire. Rightly assuming that his luxuriant car would involve him in a certain amount of public attention in Klondyke Street, the blind man dismissed it some distance from the house, and walked the rest of the way, guided by the almost imperceptible touch of Parkinson's arm.

"Here is a gentleman to see you, father," explained Miss Hutchins, who had come to the door. She divined the relative positions of the two visitors at a glance.

"Then why don't you take him into the parlor?" grumbled the ex-driver. His face was a testimonial of hard work and general sobriety but at the moment one might hazard from his voice and manner that he had been drinking earlier in the day.

"I don't think that the gentleman would be impressed by the difference between our parlor and our kitchen," replied the girl quaintly, "and it is warmer here."

"What's the matter with the parlor now?" demanded her father sourly. "It was good enough for your mother and me. It used to be good enough for you."

"There is nothing the matter with it, nor with the kitchen either." She turned impassively to the two who had followed her along the narrow passage. "Will you go in, sir?"

"I don't want to see no gentleman," cried Hutchins noisily. "Unless"—his manner suddenly changed to one of pitiable anxiety —"unless you're from the Company sir, to—to—"

"No; I have come on Mr. Carlyle's behalf," replied Carrados, walking to a chair as though he moved by a kind of instinct.

Hutchins laughed his wry contempt.

"Mr. Carlyle!" he reiterated; "Mr. Carlyle! Fat lot of good he's been. Why don't he *do* something for his money?"

"He has," replied Carrados, with imperturbable good-humor; "he has sent me. Now, I want to ask you a few questions."

"A few questions?" roared the irate man. "Why, blast it, I have done nothing else but answer questions; I can get enough of that for nixes. Why don't you go and ask Mr. Herbert Ananias Mead your few questions—then you might find out something."

There was a slight movement by the door and Carrados knew that the girl had quietly left the room.

"You saw that, sir?" demanded the father, diverted to a new line of bitterness. "You saw that girl—my own daughter," explained Hutchins.

"I know, but I did not see her. I see nothing. I am blind."

"Blind!" exclaimed the old fellow, sitting up in startled wonderment. "You mean it, sir? You walk all right and you look at me as if you saw me. You're kidding surely."

"No," smiled Carrados. "It's quite right."

"Then it's a funny business, sir—you what are blind expecting to find something that those with their eyes couldn't," ruminated Hutchins sagely.

"There are things that you can't see with your eyes, Hutchins."

"Perhaps you are right, sir. Well, what is it you want to know?"

"Light a cigar first," said the blind man, holding out his case and waiting until the various sounds told him that his host was smoking contentedly. "The train you were driving at the time of the accident was the six-twenty-seven from Notcliff. It stopped everywhere until it reached Lambeth Bridge, the chief London station of your line. There it became something of an express, and leaving Lambeth Bridge at seven-eleven, should not stop again until it fetched Swanstead on Thames, eleven miles out, at seven-thirty-four. Then it stopped on and off from Swanstead to Ingerfield, the terminus of that branch, which it reached at eight-five."

Hutchins nodded, and then, remembering, said: "That's right, sir."

"That was your business all day—running between Notcliff and Ingerfield?"

"Yes, sir. Three journeys up and three down mostly."

"With the same stops on all the down journeys?"

"No. The seven-eleven is the only one that does a run from the Bridge to Swanstead. You see, it is just on the close of the evening rush, as they call it. A good many late business gentlemen living at Swanstead use the seven-eleven regular. The other journeys we stop at every station to Lambeth Bridge, and then here and there beyond."

"There are, of course, other trains doing exactly the same journey—a service, in fact?"

"Yes, sir. About six."

"And do any of those—say, during the rush—do any of those run non-stop from Lambeth to Swanstead?"

Hutchins reflected a moment. All the choler and restlessness had melted out of the man's face. He was again the excellent artisan, slow but capable and self-reliant.

"That I couldn't definitely say, sir. Very few short-distance trains pass the junction, but some of those may. A guide would show us in a minute but I haven't got one."

"Never mind. You said at the inquest that it was no uncommon thing for you to be pulled up at the 'stop' signal east of Knight's Cross Station. How often would that happen—only with the seven-eleven, mind."

"Perhaps three times a week; perhaps twice."

"The accident was on a Thursday. Have you noticed that you were pulled up oftener on a Thursday than on any other day?"

A smile crossed the driver's face at the question.

"You don't happen to live at Swanstead yourself, sir?" he asked in reply.

"No," admitted Carrados. "Why?"

"Well, sir, we were *always* pulled up on Thursday; practically always, you may say. It got to be quite a saying among those who used the train regular; they used to look out for it."

Carrados's sightless eyes had the one quality of concealing emotion supremely. "Oh," he commented softly, "always; and it was quite a saying, was it? And *why* was it always so on Thursday?"

"It had to do with the early closing, I'm told. The suburban traffic was a bit different. By rights we ought to have been set back two minutes for that day, but I suppose it wasn't thought worth while to alter us in the time-table, so we most always had to wait outside Three Deep tunnel for a west-bound electric to make good."

"You were prepared for it then?"

"Yes, sir, I was," said Hutchins, reddening at some recollection, "and very down about it was one of the jury over that. But, mayhap once in three months, I did get through even on a Thursday, and it's not for me to question whether things are right or wrong just because they are not what I may expect. The signals are my orders, sir—stop! go on! and it's for me to obey, as you would a general on the field of battle. What would happen otherwise! It was nonsense what they said about going cautious; and the man who stated it was a barber who didn't know the difference between a 'distance' and a 'stop' signal down to the minute they gave their verdict. My orders, sir, given me by that signal, was 'Go right ahead and keep to your running time!'"

Carrados nodded a soothing assent. "That is all, I think," he remarked.

"All!" exclaimed Hutchins in surprise. "Why, sir, you can't have got much idea of it yet."

"Quite enough. And I know it isn't pleasant for you to be taken along the same ground over and over again."

The man moved awkwardly in his chair and pulled nervously at his grizzled beard.

"You mustn't take any notice of what I said just now, sir," he apologized. "You somehow make me feel that something may come of it; but I've been badgered about and accused and cross-examined from one to another of them these weeks till it's fairly made me bitter against everything. And now they talk of putting me in a lavatory—me that has been with the company for five and forty years and on the foot-plate thirty-two—a man suspected of running past a danger signal."

"You have had a rough time, Hutchins; you will have to exercise your patience a little longer yet," said Carrados sympathetically.

"You think something may come of it, sir? You think you will be able to clear me? Believe me, sir, if you could give me something to look forward to it might save me from—" He pulled himself up and shook his head sorrowfully. "I've been near it," he added simply. Carrados reflected and took his resolution. "To-day is Wednesday. I think you may hope to hear something from your general manager towards the middle of next week."

"Good God, sir! You really mean that?"

"In the interval show your good sense by behaving reasonably. Keep civilly to yourself and don't talk. Above all"—he nodded towards a quart jug that stood on the table between them, an incident that filled the simple-minded engineer with boundless wonder when he recalled it afterwards—"above all, leave that alone."

Hutchins snatched up the vessel and brought it crashing down on the hearthstone, his face shining with a set resolution. "I've done with it, sir. It was the bitterness and despair that drove me to that. Now I can do without it."

The door was hastily opened and Miss Hutchins looked anxiously from her father to the visitors and back again.

"Oh, whatever is the matter?" she exclaimed. "I heard a great crash."

"This gentleman is going to clear me, Meg, my dear," blurted out the old man irrepressibly. "And I've done with the drink forever."

"Hutchins! Hutchins!" said Carrados warningly.

"My daughter, sir; you wouldn't have her not know?" pleaded Hutchins, rather crest-fallen. "It won't go any further."

Carrados laughed quietly to himself as he felt Margaret Hutchins's startled and questioning eyes attempting to read his mind. He shook hands with the engine-driver without further comment, however, and walked out into the commonplace little street under Parkinson's unobtrusive guidance.

"Very nice of Miss Hutchins to go into half-mourning, Parkinson," he remarked as they went along. "Thoughtful, and yet not ostentatious."

"Yes, sir," agreed Parkinson, who had long ceased to wonder at his master's perceptions.

"The Romans, Parkinson, had a saying to the effect that gold carries no smell. That is a pity sometimes. What jewelry did Miss Hutchins wear?"

"Very little, sir. A plain gold brooch representing a merry-thought—the merry-thought of a sparrow, I should say, sir. The only other article was a smooth-backed gun-metal watch, suspended from a gun-metal bow."

"Nothing showy or expensive, eh?"

"Oh dear no, sir. Quite appropriate for a young person of her position."

"Just what I should have expected." He slackened his pace. "We are passing a hoarding, are we not?"

"Yes, sir."

"We will stand here a moment. Read me the letterpress of the poster before us."

"This 'Oxo' one, sir?"

"Yes."

" 'Oxo,' sir."

Carrados was convulsed with silent laughter. Parkinson had infinitely more dignity and conceded merely a tolerant recognition of the ludicrous.

"That was a bad shot, Parkinson," remarked his master when he could speak. "We will try another."

For three minutes, with scrupulous conscientiousness on the part of the reader and every appearance of keen interest on the part of the hearer, there were set forth the particulars of a sale by auction of superfluous timber and builders' material.

"That will do," said Carrados, when the last detail had been reached. "We can be seen from the door of No. 107 still?"

"Yes, sir."

"No indication of anyone coming to us from there?"

"No, sir."

Carrados walked thoughtfully on again. In the Holloway Road they rejoined the waiting motor-car. "Lambeth Bridge Station" was the order the driver received.

From the station the car was sent on home and Parkinson was instructed to take two first-class singles for Richmond, which could be reached by changing at Stafford Road. The "evening rush" had not yet commenced and they had no difficulty in finding an empty carriage when the train came in.

Parkinson was kept busy that journey describing what he saw at various points between Lambeth Bridge and Knight's Cross. For a quarter of a mile Carrados's demands on the eyes and the memory of his remarkable servant were wide and incessant. Then his questions ceased. They had passed the "stop" signal, east of Knight's Cross Station.

The following afternoon they made the return journey as far as Knight's Cross. This time, however, the surroundings failed to interest Carrados. "We are going to look at some rooms," was the information he offered on the subject, and an imperturbable "Yes, sir" had been the extent of Parkinson's comment on the unusual proceeding. After leaving the station they turned sharply along a road that ran parallel with the line, a dull thoroughfare of substantial, elderly houses that were beginning to sink into decrepitude. Here and there a corner residence displayed the brass plate of a professional occupant, but for the most part they were given up to the various branches of second-rate apartment letting.

"The third house after the one with the flagstaff," said Carrados.

Parkinson rang the bell, which was answered by a young servant, who took an early opportunity of assuring them that she was not tidy as it was rather early in the afternoon. She informed Carrados, in reply to his inquiry, that Miss Chubb was at home, and showed them into a melancholy little sitting-room to await her appearance.

"I shall be 'almost' blind here, Parkinson," remarked Carrados, walking about the room. "It saves explanation."

"Very good, sir," replied Parkinson.

Five minutes later, an interval suggesting that Miss Chubb also found it rather early in the afternoon, Carrados was arranging to take rooms for his attendant and himself for the short time that he would be in London, seeing an oculist.

"One bedroom, mine, must face north," he stipulated. "It has to do with the light."

Miss Chubb replied that she quite understood. Some gentlemen, she added, had their requirements, others their fancies. She endeavored to suit all. The bedroom she had in view from the first *did* face north. She would not have known, only the last gentleman, curiously enough, had made the same request.

"A sufferer like myself?" enquired Carrados affably.

Miss Chubb did not think so. In his case she regarded it merely as a fancy. He had said that he could not sleep on any other side. She had had to turn out of her own room to accommodate him, but if one kept an apartment-house one had to be adaptable; and Mr. Ghoosh was certainly very liberal in his ideas.

"Ghoosh? An Indian gentleman, I presume?" hazarded Carrados.

It appeared that Mr. Ghoosh was an Indian. Miss Chubb confided that at first she had been rather perturbed at the idea of taking in "a black man," as she confessed to regarding him. She reiterated, however, that Mr. Ghoosh proved to be "quite the gentleman." Five minutes of affability put Carrados in full possession of Mr. Ghoosh's manner of life and movements—the dates of his arrival and departure, his solitariness and his daily habits.

"This would be the best bedroom," said Miss Chubb.

It was a fair-sized room on the first floor. The window looked out on to the roof of an outbuilding; beyond, the deep cutting of the railway line. Opposite stood the dead wall that Mr. Carlyle had spoken of.

Carrados "looked" round the room with the discriminating glance that sometimes proved so embarrassing to those who knew him.

"I have to take a little daily exercise," he remarked, walking to the window and running his hand up the woodwork. "You will not mind my fixing a 'developer' here, Miss Chubb—a few small screws?"

Miss Chubb thought not. Then she was sure not. Finally she ridiculed the idea of minding with scorn.

"If there is width enough," mused Carrados, spanning the upright critically. "Do you happen to have a wooden foot-rule convenient?"

"Well, to be sure!" exclaimed Miss Chubb, opening a rapid succession of drawers until she produced the required article. "When we did out this room after Mr. Ghoosh, there was this very ruler among the things that he hadn't thought worth taking. This is what you require, sir?"

"Yes," replied Carrados, accepting it, "I think this is exactly what I require." It was a common new white-wood rule, such as one might buy at any small stationer's for a penny. He carelessly took off the width of the upright, reading the figures with a touch; and then continued to run a finger-tip delicately up and down the edges of the instrument.

"Four and seven-eighths," was his unspoken conclusion.

"I hope it will do, sir."

"Admirably," replied Carrados. "But I haven't reached the end of my requirements yet, Miss Chubb."

"No, sir?" said the landlady, feeling that it would be a pleasure to oblige so agreeable a gentleman, "what else might there be?"

"Although I can see very little I like to have a light, but not any kind of light. Gas I cannot do with. Do you think that you would be able to find me an oil lamp?"

"Certainly, sir. I got out a very nice brass lamp that I have specially for Mr. Ghoosh. He read a good deal of an evening and he preferred a lamp."

"That is very convenient. I suppose it is large enough to burn for a whole evening?"

"Yes, indeed. And very particular he was always to have it filled every day."

"A lamp without oil is not very useful," smiled Carrados, following her towards another room, and absent-mindedly slipping the foot-rule into his pocket.

Whatever Parkinson thought of the arrangement of going into second-rate apartments in an obscure street it is to be inferred that his devotion to his master was sufficient to overcome his private emotions as a self-respecting "man." At all events, as they were approaching the station he asked, and without a trace of feeling, whether there were any orders for him with reference to the proposed migration.

"None, Parkinson," replied his master. "We must be satisfied with our present quarters."

"I beg pardon, sir," said Parkinson, with some constraint. "I understood that you had taken the rooms for a week certain."

"I am afraid that Miss Chubb will be under the same impression. Unforeseen circumstances will prevent our going, however. Mr. Greatorex must write to-morrow, enclosing a cheque, with my regrets, and adding a penny for this ruler which I seem to have brought away with me. It, at least, is something for the money."

Parkinson may be excused for not attempting to understand the course of events.

"Here is your train coming in, sir," he merely said.

"We will let it go and wait for another. Is there a signal at either end of the platform?"

"Yes, sir; at the further end."

"Let us walk towards it. Are there any of the porters or officials about here?"

"No, sir; none."

"Take this ruler. I want you to go up the steps—there are steps up the signal, by the way?"

"Yes, sir."

"I want you to measure the glass of the lamp. Do not go up any higher than is necessary, but if you have to stretch be careful not to mark off the measurement with your nail, although the impulse is a natural one. That has been done already."

Parkinson looked apprehensively round and about. Fortunately the part was a dark and unfrequented spot and everyone else was moving towards the exit at the other end of the platform. Fortunately, also, the signal was not a high one.

"As near as I can judge on the rounded surface, the glass is four and seven-eighths across," reported Parkinson.

"Thank you," replied Carrados, returning the measure to his pocket, "four and seven-eighths is quite near enough. Now we will take the next train back."

Sunday evening came, and with it Mr. Carlyle to the Turrets at the appointed hour. He brought to the situation a mind poised for any eventuality and a trenchant eye. As the time went on and the impenetrable Carrados made allusion to the case, Carlyle's manner inclined to a waggish commiseration of his host's position. Actually, he said little, but the crisp precision of his voice when the path lay open to a remark of any significance left little to be said.

It was not until they had finished dinner and returned to the library that Carrados gave the slightest hint of anything unusual being in the air. His first indication of coming events was to remove the key from the outside to the inside of the door.

"What are you doing, Max?" demanded Mr. Carlyle, his curiosity overcoming the indirect attitude.

"You have been very entertaining, Louis," replied his friend, "but Parkinson should be back very soon now and it is as well to be prepared. Do you happen to carry a revolver?"

"Not when I come to dine with you, Max," replied Carlyle, with all the aplomb he could muster. "Is it usual?"

Carrados smiled affectionately at his guest's agile recovery and touched the secret spring of a drawer in an antique bureau by his side. The little hidden receptacle shot smoothly out, disclosing a pair of dull-blued pistols.

"To-night, at all events, it might be prudent," he replied, handing one to Carlyle and putting the other into his own pocket. "Our man may be here at any minute, and we do not know in what temper he will come."

"Our man!" exclaimed Carlyle, craning forward in excitement. "Max! you don't mean to say that you have got Mead to admit it?"

"No one has admitted it," said Carrados. "And it is not Mead."

"Not Mead. . . . Do you mean that Hutchins—?"

"Neither Mead nor Hutchins. The man who tampered with the signal—for Hutchins was right and a green light *was* exhibited—is a young Indian from Bengal. His name is Drishna and he lives at Swanstead."

Mr. Carlyle stared at his friend between sheer surprise and blank incredulity.

"You really mean this, Carrados?" he said.

"My fatal reputation for humor!" smiled Carrados. "If I am wrong, Louis, the next hour will expose it."

"But why—why—why? The colossal villainy, the unparalleled audacity!" Mr. Carlyle lost himself among incredulous superlatives and could only stare.

"Chiefly to get himself out of a disastrous speculation," replied Carrados, answering the question. "If there was another motive—or at least an incentive—which I suspect, doubtless we shall hear of it."

"All the same, Max, I don't think that you have treated me quite fairly," protested Carlyle, getting over his first surprise and passing to a sense of injury. "Here we are and I know nothing, absolutely nothing, of the whole affair."

"We both have our ideas of pleasantry, Louis," replied Carrados genially. "But I dare say you are right and perhaps there is still time to atone." In the fewest possible words he outlined the course of his investigations. "And now you know all that is to be known until Drishna arrives."

"But will he come?" questioned Carlyle doubtfully. "He may be suspicious."

"Yes, he will be suspicious."

"Then he will not come."

"On the contrary, Louis, he will come because my letter will make him suspicious. He *is* coming; otherwise Parkinson would have telephoned me at once and we should have had to take other measures."

"What did you say, Max?" asked Carlyle curiously.

"I wrote that I was anxious to discuss an Indo-Scythian inscription with him, and sent my car in the hope that he would be able to oblige me."

"But is he interested in Indo-Scythian inscriptions?"

"I haven't the faintest idea," admitted Carrados, and Mr. Carlyle was throwing up his hands in despair when the sound of a motorcar wheels softly kissing the gravel surface of the drive outside brought him to his feet.

"By Gad, you are right, Max!" he exclaimed, peeping through the curtains. "There is a man inside."

"Mr. Drishna," announced Parkinson, a minute later.

The visitor came into the room with leisurely self-possession that might have been real or a desperate assumption. He was a slightly built young man of about twenty-five, with black hair and eyes, a

small, carefully trained mustache, and a dark olive skin. His phys-
iognomy was not displeasing, but his expression had a harsh and
supercilious tinge. In attire he erred towards the immaculately
spruce.

"Mr. Carrados?" he said inquiringly.

Carrados, who had risen, bowed slightly without offering his hand.

"This gentleman," he said, indicating his friend, "is Mr. Carlyle,
the celebrated private detective."

The Indian shot a very sharp glance at the object of this description. Then he sat down.

"You wrote me a letter, Mr. Carrados," he remarked, in English
that scarcely betrayed any foreign origin, "a rather curious letter,
I may say. You asked me about an ancient inscription. I know nothing of antiquities; but I thought, as you had sent, that it would be
more courteous if I came and explained this to you."

"That was the object of my letter," replied Carrados.

"You wished to see me?" said Drishna, unable to stand the ordeal
of the silence that Carrados imposed after his remark.

"When you left Miss Chubb's house you left a ruler behind." One
lay on the desk by Carrados and he took it up as he spoke.

"I don't understand what you are talking about," said Drishna
guardedly. "You are making some mistake."

"The ruler was marked at four and seven-eighths inches—the
measure of the glass of the signal lamp outside."

The unfortunate young man was unable to repress a start. His
face lost its healthy tone. Then, with a sudden impulse, he made a
step forward and snatched the object from Carrados's hand.

"If it is mine I have a right to it," he exclaimed, snapping the
ruler in two and throwing it on to the back of the blazing fire. "It
is nothing."

"Pardon me, I did not say that the one you have so impetuously
disposed of was yours. As a matter of fact, it was mine. Yours
is—elsewhere."

"Wherever it is you have no right to it if it is mine," panted
Drishna, with rising excitement. "You are a thief, Mr. Carrados. I
will not stay any longer here."

He jumped up and turned towards the door. Carlyle made a step
forward, but the precaution was unnecessary.

"One moment, Mr. Drishna," interposed Carrados, in his smooth-
est tones. "It is a pity, after you have come so far, to leave without

hearing of my investigations in the neighborhood of Shaftesbury Avenue."

Drishna sat down again.

"As you like," he muttered. "It does not interest me."

"I wanted to obtain a lamp of a certain pattern," continued Carrados. "It seemed to me that the simplest explanation would be to say that I wanted it for a motor-car. Naturally I went to Long Acre. At the first shop I said: 'Wasn't it here that a friend of mine, an Indian gentleman, recently had a lamp made with a green glass that was nearly five inches across?' No, it was not there but they could make me one. At the next shop the same; at the third, and fourth, and so on. Finally my persistence was rewarded. I found the place where the lamp had been made, and at the cost of ordering another I obtained all the details I wanted. It was news to them, the shopman informed me, that in some parts of India green was the danger color and therefore tail lamps had to show a green light. The incident made some impression on him and he would be able to identify their customer—who paid in advance and gave no address—among a thousand of his countrymen. Do I succeed in interesting you, Mr. Drishna?"

"Do you?" replied Drishna, with a languid yawn. "Do I look interested?"

"You must make allowance for my unfortunate blindness," apologized Carrados, with grim irony.

"Blindness!" exclaimed Drishna, dropping his affectation of unconcern as though electrified by the word, "do you mean—really blind—that you do not see me?"

"Alas, no," admitted Carrados.

The Indian withdrew his right hand from his coat pocket and with a tragic gesture flung a heavy revolver down on the table between them.

"I have had you covered all the time, Mr. Carrados, and if I had wished to go and you or your friend had raised a hand to stop me, it would have been at the peril of your lives," he said, in a voice of melancholy triumph. "But what is the use of defying fate, and who successfully evades his destiny? A month ago I went to see one of our people who reads the future and sought to know the course of certain events. 'You need fear no human eye,' was the message given to me. Then she added: 'But when the sightless sees the unseen, make your peace with Yama.' And I thought she spoke of the Great Hereafter!"

"This amounts to an admission of your guilt," exclaimed Mr. Carlyle practically.

"I bow to the decree of fate," replied Drishna. "And it is fitting to the universal irony of existence that a blind man should be the instrument. I don't imagine, Mr. Carlyle," he added maliciously, "that you, with your eyes, would ever have brought that result about."

"You are a very cold-blooded young scoundrel, sir!" retorted Mr. Carlyle. "Good heavens! do you realize that you are responsible for the death of scores of innocent men and women?"

"Do *you* realize, Mr. Carlyle, that you and your Government and your soldiers are responsible for the death of thousands of innocent men and women in my country every day? If England was occupied by the Germans who quartered an army and an administration with their wives and their families and all their expensive paraphernalia on the unfortunate country until the whole nation was reduced to the verge of famine, and the appointment of every new official meant the callous death sentence on a thousand men and women to pay his salary, then if you went to Berlin and wrecked a train you would be hailed a patriot. What Boadicea did and—and Samson, so have I. If they were heroes, so am I."

"Well, upon my word!" cried the highly scandalized Carlyle, "what next! Boadicea was a—er—semi-legendary person, whom we may possibly admire at a distance. Personally, I do not profess to express an opinion. But Samson, I would remind you, is a Biblical character. Samson was mocked as an enemy. You, I do not doubt, have been entertained as a friend."

"And haven't I been mocked and despised and sneered at every day of my life here by your supercilious, superior, empty-headed men?" flashed back Drishna, his eyes leaping into malignity and his voice trembling with sudden passion. "Oh! how I hated them as I passed them in the street and recognized by a thousand petty insults their lordly English contempt for me as an inferior being—a nigger. How I longed with Caligula that a nation had a single neck that I might destroy it at one blow. I loathe you in your complacent hypocrisy, Mr. Carlyle, despise and utterly abominate you from an eminence of superiority that you can never even understand."

"I think we are getting rather away from the point, Mr. Drishna," interposed Carrados, with the impartiality of a judge. "Unless I am misinformed, you are not so ungallant as to include everyone you have met here in your execration?"

"Ah, no," admitted Drishna, descending into a quite ingenuous frankness. "Much as I hate your men I love your women. How is it possible that a nation should be so divided—its men so dull-witted and offensive, its women so quick, sympathetic and capable of appreciating?"

"But a little expensive, too, at times?" suggested Carrados.

Drishna sighed heavily.

"Yes; it is incredible. It is the generosity of their large nature. My allowance, though what most of you would call noble, has proved quite inadequate. I was compelled to borrow money and the interest became overwhelming. Bankruptcy was impracticable because I should have then been recalled by my people, and much as I detest England a certain reason made the thought of leaving it unbearable?"

"Connected with the Arcady Theater?"

"You know? Well, do not let us introduce the lady's name. In order to restore myself I speculated on the Stock Exchange. My credit was good through my father's position and the standing of the firm to which I am attached. I heard on reliable authority, and very early, that the Central and Suburban, and the Deferred especially, was safe to fall heavily, through a motor bus amalgamation that was then a secret. I opened a bear account and sold largely. The shares fell, but only fractionally, and I waited. Then, unfortunately, they began to go up. Adverse forces were at work and rumors were put about. I could not stand the settlement, and in order to carry over an account I was literally compelled to deal temporarily with some securities that were not technically my own property."

"Embezzlement, sir," commented Mr. Carlyle icily. "But what is embezzlement on the top of wholesale murder!"

"That is what it is called. In my case, however, it was only to be temporary. Unfortunately, the rise continued. Then, at the height of my despair, I chanced to be returning to Swanstead rather earlier than usual one evening, and the train was stopped at a certain signal to let another pass. There was conversation in the carriage and I learned certain details. One said that there would be an accident some day, and so forth. In a flash—as by an inspiration—I saw how the circumstance might be turned to account. A bad accident and the shares would certainly fall and my position would be retrieved. I think Mr. Carrados has somehow learned the rest."

"Max," said Mr. Carlyle, with emotion, "is there any reason why you should not send your man for a police officer and have this monster arrested on his own confession without further delay?"

"Pray do so, Mr. Carrados," acquiesced Drishna. "I shall certainly be hanged, but the speech I shall prepare will ring from one end of India to the other; my memory will be venerated as that of a martyr; and the emancipation of my motherland will be hastened by my sacrifice."

"In other words," commented Carrados, "there will be disturbances at half-a-dozen disaffected places, a few unfortunate police will be clubbed to death, and possibly worse things may happen. That does not suit us, Mr. Drishna."

"And how do you propose to prevent it?" asked Drishna, with cool assurance.

"It is very unpleasant being hanged on a dark winter morning; very cold, very friendless, very inhuman. The long trial, the solitude and the confinement, the thoughts of the long sleepless night before, the hangman and the pinioning and the noosing of the rope, are apt to prey on the imagination. Only a very stupid man can take hanging easily."

"What do you want me to do instead, Mr. Carrados?" asked Drishna shrewdly.

Carrados's hand closed on the weapon that still lay on the table between them. Without a word he pushed it across.

"I see," commented Drishna, with a short laugh and a gleaming eye. "Shoot myself and hush it up to suit your purpose. Withhold my message to save the exposures of a trial, and keep the flame from the torch of insurrectionary freedom."

"Also," interposed Carrados mildly, "to save your worthy people a good deal of shame, and to save the lady who is nameless the unpleasant necessity of relinquishing the house and the income which you have just settled on her. She certainly would not then venerate your memory."

"What is that?"

"The transaction which you carried through was based on a felony and could not be upheld. The firm you dealt with will go to the courts, and the money, being directly traceable, will be held forfeit as no good consideration passed."

"Max!" cried Mr. Carlyle hotly, "you are not going to let this scoundrel cheat the gallows after all?"

"The best use you can make of the gallows is to cheat it, Louis," replied Carrados. "Have you ever reflected what human beings will think of us a hundred years hence?"

"Oh, of course I'm not really in favor of hanging," admitted Mr. Carlyle.

"Nobody really is. But we go on hanging. Mr. Drishna is a dangerous animal who for the sake of pacific animals must cease to exist. Let his barbarous exploit pass into oblivion with him. The disadvantages of spreading it broadcast immeasurably outweigh the benefits."

"I have considered," announced Drishna. "I will do as you wish."

"Very well," said Carrados. "Here is some plain notepaper. You had better write a letter to someone saying that the financial difficulties in which you are involved make life unbearable."

"But there are no financial difficulties—now."

"That does not matter in the least. It will be put down to an hallucination and taken as showing the state of your mind."

"But what guarantee have we that he will not escape?" whispered Mr. Carlyle.

"He cannot escape," replied Carrados tranquilly. "His identity is too clear."

"I have no intention of trying to escape," put in Drishna, as he wrote. "You hardly imagine that I have not considered this eventuality, do you?"

"All the same," murmured the ex-lawyer, "I should like to have a jury behind me. It is one thing to execute a man morally; it is another to do it almost literally."

"Is that all right?" asked Drishna, passing across the letter he had written.

Carrados smiled at this tribute to his perception.

"Quite excellent," he replied courteously. "There is a train at nine-forty. Will that suit you?"

Drishna nodded and stood up. Mr. Carlyle had a very uneasy feeling that he ought to do something but could not suggest to himself what.

The next moment he heard his friend heartily thanking the visitor for the assistance he had been in the matter of the Indo-Scythian inscription, as they walked across the hall together. Then a door closed.

"I believe that there is something positively uncanny about Max at times," murmured the perturbed gentleman to himself.

Murder in Mind

by C. B. Gilford

I t began, Cheryl Royce remembered, as a kind of parlor game—a
slightly dangerous game, dealing with the dark unknown, but
it was the danger, and the venture into the unknown, which
made it interesting.

Hypnosis.

"Sure, I can hypnotize people," Arnold Forbes said.

Nobody at the party except the hosts, the Cunninghams, knew
Forbes very well. Naturally, someone challenged him, someone else
begged him for a demonstration, then Liz Cunningham very sweetly
chimed in, "Arnold used to do a nightclub act. Would you like to
show them, Arnold, dear?"

So Arnold Forbes performed. He was a short, chubby fellow, very
jolly; very deceiving. His blue eyes could suddenly transfix one with
a very penetrating, very commanding stare. Somehow, maybe because he thought she was pretty, or maybe because she looked like
a scoffer, an unbeliever, he chose Cheryl Royce.

With Forbes' blue eyes probing into her own, she "went to sleep"
in about thirty seconds. Only she didn't exactly go to sleep. Her
eyelids closed, but she was far from unconscious. She could hear
Forbes' voice quite clearly. "Your eyelids are very heavy . . . your
arms are heavy . . . your entire body is very heavy . . . very relaxed . . . you are drifting down . . . down . . . down . . . into a very
deep sleep . . ."

No, I'm not, she answered silently. *I'm not going to sleep, because
I can hear you. Besides, I know I'm not asleep. I'm sitting in this easy
chair, and everybody is gathered around, and . . .*

Nevertheless, she had to admit that the state she was in was
strange indeed. Her body did feel heavy, and yet almost weightless.
She hadn't wanted to close her eyes, and yet she had closed them.
Now she wanted to open her eyes, and she couldn't.

She was entirely at the hypnotist's mercy. He gave her commands—to read a book, type a letter, drink a glass of water—and

33

she obeyed him, pantomiming the actions, even though she knew perfectly well that the objects weren't there, and even though she resented going through the silly motions. Forbes passed his finger around her wrists, "tying" her to the chair arms, and she couldn't move, even though she knew there was no rope binding her. The game went on and on, and all the while she felt foolish, for being tricked, for being helpless.

Yet when Arnold Forbes wakened her finally, with a snap of his fingers, she laughed and joked about it, playing at being a good sport. Forbes found another victim, and Cheryl drifted off to the sidelines, gratefully out of the limelight.

Wint Marron followed her. Wint was darkly handsome, in his middle thirties, with a pretty blonde wife. Cheryl had attended perhaps three or four parties where the Marrons had been present.

"How did it feel being hypnotized?" Wint asked her.

"It was fun," she said.

"No, it wasn't," he contradicted her. "You hated it. You fought that guy every minute."

She stared at Wint Marron for a moment. "How do you know that?" she demanded.

He smiled, showing his perfect white teeth. "I know a little about hypnosis. One of the things that happens sometimes is that under hypnosis, telepathic powers are sharpened. Maybe you and I are on the same wavelength. Anyway, I saw into your mind all the time you were asleep there. You kept telling Forbes, 'No, I won't do it . . . I don't have a glass of water in my hand . . . you don't have a rope to tie me with.' And you were angry."

"You saw that from the expression on my face," she argued.

He shook his head, still smiling at her. "Your expression was completely serene. Ask anybody." He waited for an answer, but she had none. "It's interesting, don't you think?"

"I don't know . . ."

"Don't worry that I'll be able to read your thoughts all the time. I won't. It doesn't work that way." He had leaned closer. They were all alone. Everybody else was watching Arnold Forbes and his act. "Telepathic powers are sharper while under hypnosis, like I said. But I might catch a random thought of yours some other time. For that matter, you might catch a thought of mine. It usually works in both directions. Like I said, we seem to be on the same wavelength."

"What am I thinking now?" she demanded.

He hesitated, looking straight into her eyes. With an effort, she met his gaze. "You don't like what I've been telling you," he said finally. "You think your privacy has been invaded. The whole thing disturbs you. Now tit for tat. What do you think I'm thinking?"

She didn't want to, but she kept staring back at him. Was she trying to read the expression in his dark brown eyes? Or was she going beyond his eyes . . . to his thoughts? Then she found herself saying, involuntarily, "I think you want to kiss me."

He laughed softly and winked at her. "I don't know what you're using now, honey," he said. "I don't know whether it's telepathy or not. But you're close. Mighty close . . ."

She didn't see Wint Marron again for months. Perhaps she was even, subconsciously, trying to avoid him. During that interval she perhaps thought *about* him a time or two, but she certainly didn't receive any telepathic messages from him, for which she was grateful. And she didn't send him any messages. At least she didn't think she did.

Once, however, she saw Paula Marron, Wint's pretty blonde wife, in a dim corner of a dim cocktail lounge. She was shoulder to shoulder with another man, acting in a way no married woman should act with a man not her husband.

The incident shocked Cheryl, for several reasons. Paula's obvious infidelity, for one, and that she should be unfaithful to a man as attractive as Wint Marron, for another. Wint was handsome, charming, and doing very well in advertising. Why should Paula be dissatisfied?

It was a while after that incident, a month perhaps, that Cheryl first began to get the strange sensations. Sensations . . . she looked for a better word to describe the experiences; forebodings . . . feelings of uneasiness . . . that came to her at odd times and for no apparent reason.

They came for no apparent reason because everything seemed to be going so well in her life. She'd met Alan Richmond, and had almost decided that Alan was her long-awaited dream man. He was tall, lean, pleasant-looking, ambitious, very fond of her, very devoted to her. They'd been going out together frequently; she'd been with Alan when she'd seen Paula Marron in the cocktail lounge. Her life was happy, and there was the promise of even greater happiness.

But there were those queer sensations, the feeling now and then that a threat lurked somewhere. More than that. An emotional response to that threat . . . a vague kind of anger . . . or hatred . . . or jealousy . . .

Jealousy. She could almost laugh at the notion. She had no cause for jealousy. Alan had proposed marriage—she could have him any time she wanted him—and she knew that he didn't go out with other girls. Why on earth should she be jealous where Alan was concerned?

Well, she couldn't be, and she wasn't. She wasn't jealous . . . *she* wasn't jealous . . . why then did she feel . . . ?

The answer came suddenly.

She'd had a difficult day at her job, had begged off going to the movie with Alan. She was tired. She was in bed, in her dark bedroom, falling asleep, perhaps already asleep. When it happened, she came awake with a jolt.

For a sudden, searing, painful moment she wasn't in her bedroom. She was in that dim cocktail lounge. There was Paula Marron sitting in that corner with that stranger, leaning her shoulder against the stranger's shoulder, stroking his chin with her fingertips, whispering into his ear, her lips very close to the ear. Then Paula turned, distracted by something. Paula was full-face, her expression blank for a second, then her eyes widening, her lips parting.

Paula said one word, loud, in a tone of complete surprise. "Wint!"

The vision faded. Cheryl Royce was in the darkness of her bedroom again. The cocktail lounge, the strange man, Paula Marron, had all departed.

What was left, and it was inside Cheryl Royce, was a bursting flame of anger . . . hatred . . . jealousy! Her hands clutched the blanket in a death-grip, her mouth contorted, she stared at the empty air. It was a minute or two before the feeling subsided, and she lay there afterward limp, drained, her skin clammy with perspiration.

She knew then exactly what the experience had been. Wint Marron had discovered his wife in the company of that other man. Wint Marron was insanely angry and jealous. She, Cheryl Royce, knew all that, because she had been there in that cocktail lounge with him. She had read his mind, been inside his mind.

She and Wint Marron were on the same wavelength.

She didn't confide in Alan, or in anyone. She considered trying to find Arnold Forbes, the hypnotist, asking him to help her. She wanted to get off Wint Marron's wavelength. She didn't want to share his thoughts. But she didn't seek out Forbes. The whole business was too ridiculous, too embarrassing—too incredible, in fact.

She didn't want to believe it. It was quite possible, wasn't it, that she'd been dreaming there in her bed? She had once seen Paula Marron in that cocktail lounge, and so she was able to dream about it. The dream had put her, as it were, in Wint Marron's place, but there was an explanation for that too: the power of suggestion. Wint Marron had suggested that they were "on the same wavelength."

So she spoke of the matter to no one, and she was sorry for that.

Just three weeks later, on a Thursday, at dusk, her consciousness sat inside Wint Marron's skull again, looked out through his eyes, felt his emotions, and decided upon an action.

She was alone again, sitting at her dressing table, combing her hair in front of the mirror. Alan was due to pick her up in half an hour. Her thoughts were on Alan, not on Wint Marron, but then they were wrenched violently away from Alan. Her own face disappeared from the mirror. She was looking not into the mirror, but through the windshield of an automobile.

Ahead was a road, dim and shadowy in the dusk; not a road that she recognized. Then, however, she lost awareness of herself completely.

The car was going slowly at first. The road curved. The headlights swept a border of trees that lined the road. The lights were very bright. The trees showed up very distinctly, but not the road. The road was blacktop, dark.

Something appeared in the road . . . or at the edge of it . . . or just at the side of it . . . the right side. Something white, very brilliant in the lights, in great contrast to the blacktop. White, fluttering . . . a woman's dress.

A woman was standing there by the side of the road, as if waiting to be picked up. Yes, to be picked up, because in her right hand she carried a small suitcase. Definitely a suitcase, blue, very bright blue against the whiteness of the dress.

But she was not waiting for the driver of this car. No, because when she saw which car it was, she made a funny little gesture of surprise, throwing up her left hand, the fingers spread wide. The face registered surprise also. The car was close enough now for the driver to see her face.

Paula Marron's face, almost as white as the dress. Framed in yellow-blonde hair. Blue eyes very wide, very blue, as blue as the little suitcase. Emotion in the eyes. Fear.

Emotion in the driver too. Relentless hatred, and soaring triumph. Here was Paula, the hated object, caught in the act. Where were you

going, Paula? I thought if I took your car keys away from you, you'd
have to stay home. But you're waiting for your chauffeur, aren't
you? *Him.* Where are you going with him? For how long? You're
taking the small suitcase, I see. So maybe it's just overnight. Or
maybe not. Maybe you're going for good, and you decided not to
bother to take all those "rags" hanging in your closet. Well, you're
not going anywhere, baby. Not with *him* you aren't!

The car was going faster now. The engine responded to the accelerator with a rasping roar. Paula seemed to comprehend suddenly. She tried to back away, off the road, into the trees. She'd be
safe among the trees. The car couldn't follow her there.

But she wasn't quick enough. She hadn't comprehended soon
enough. She dropped the suitcase, tried to turn and run, but in her
high spike heels she stumbled on the rough gravel along the road.
She wasn't in costume for racing a car, and she seemed to know that
she couldn't win. She turned again toward the car. Her arms
stretched out in a gesture of pleading.

Don't kill me, Wint!

The gesture of the arms changed. They rose, trying to shield that
soft white face from the onrushing metal. The face grew larger,
almost filled the windshield. The red mouth opened wide, and a
scream competed with the roar of the engine, overcoming it for a
moment.

In the same instant there was the impact, so hard that the glass
in the windshield shook. The trees, the whole scene pictured through
the windshield, shuddered as if in an earthquake. The white face
and the white dress sank down out of the picture. The last visible
parts of Paula were her white hands with their long tapered fingers . . . reaching upward . . . begging . . .

The car didn't stop. It went relentlessly forward, the tires protesting as they dug into the gravel at the side of the road. Why was
the ride so bumpy? Why was the woodsy scene in the windshield
jarring up and down? Were the wheels of the car passing over something? Was there an obstacle in the road? Ah . . .

The road smoothed, the jarring ceased. The car swerved back onto
the blacktop, negotiated the curve adroitly . . .

And as it did, the windshield scene faded. Cross-faded rather, into
a face in the mirror. The face of Cheryl Royce, contorted into an
ugly mask of hatred.

Hands went to the face, Cheryl Royce's hands, covering the staring
eyes, desperately trying to shut out the vision. *What did I just see?*

After a long time, the hands lowered, and Cheryl looked at her own face again. The ugly lines had softened, but there were beads of perspiration on her forehead, and her hands were shaking.

She staggered from the dressing table to the phone, managed to dial Alan's number. "I can't go out tonight," she told him in a trembling voice. "I have this terrible headache."

Which was true.

There was nothing in the morning newspaper, but the afternoon edition told the story completely.

Paula Marron, aged 28, apparently had been the victim of a hit-and-run driver. The accident had occurred sometime early last evening, on Morton's Mill Road, almost in front of the Marron home. Mrs. Marron was struck, run over, and then dragged along the road for about thirty feet. She had died, the examining physician said, immediately. There had been no witnesses.

The Marrons lived in a wooded, exurban area of rather expensive houses, each set on five or six acres. The Marron home was several hundred feet from the road, and the road was invisible from it. Mr. Marron, who was at home at the time of the accident, stated that he had not heard any unusual sounds, nor could he explain why his wife was walking along the road at that time of the evening. Police were questioning neighbors, hoping to find someone who had seen the hit-and-run car.

Cheryl Royce read the newspaper account with growing horror. She had really seen Paula Marron die. In a fit of jealousy, her husband had run her down with his own car. He had committed murder. Cheryl had seen him do it. She had practically ridden in the driver's seat with him.

So of course she should go to the police.

Then she stopped, right there on that crowded downtown street where she'd bought the newspaper. What was she going to tell the police? All that stuff about telepathy, thought-transference, mental wavelengths? Could she, Cheryl Royce, who had been in her own apartment at the time of the murder, qualify as a witness? She felt she had to try.

At police headquarters she was eventually allowed to see a detective sergeant named Evatt, who listened frozen-faced to her story.

"You realize, Miss Royce," he said at the end, "we'd have to have more evidence than what you just told me." Evatt was lean, tired-looking, but polite.

"Yes, I know," she told him, "but I thought this might alert you to look for evidence in Wint Marron's direction. Doesn't a car usually get a bent fender or broken headlight or something if it hits a pedestrian? You could tell them to look at Wint Marron's car."

Evatt nodded. "I can pass on the tip," he agreed, but not too convincingly. "Now, you mentioned, in one of these scenes you imagined—excuse me, one of these times you saw into Mr. Marron's mind—you said you saw another man with Mrs. Marron. Who was he?"

"It wasn't anybody I recognized—well, I really didn't look at him. I was looking at Mrs. Marron most of the time, you see."

"It would help," the detective pointed out, "if we knew something about this guy. It would establish a possible motive."

"Yes, I realize that," she said, "but I don't think the man was anybody I know."

"Well, I'll pass the word on to the officers investigating the accident," Evatt promised, and he jotted down her name, address, and telephone number. But he had called the case an "accident," she noticed, not a murder or a homicide.

As she left the detective's tiny office, she thanked him, and then she paused in the doorway. "I could be wrong, of course," she said. She felt forced to make the admission. "It could have been my imagination."

Evatt nodded again. "It could have."

"I'm not accusing Wint Marron of . . ."

Evatt seemed to understand. "If the boys ask Marron any questions or look around," he promised, "your name won't be mentioned."

She left feeling better. She had done what she could. It was up to the police now. If Wint Marron had committed murder, it was their job to bring him to justice, not hers.

She had dinner with Alan that evening. The restaurant was a quiet place, the music soft and unobtrusive, the lights dim. She didn't confide in Alan. He apparently hadn't even read the newspaper, didn't know that Paula Marron was dead.

She was uneasy the entire evening, as if she were trying to think of something, to remember something, and the elusive little fact kept dodging away. Finally, however, after a long time, the message came through.

Cheryl told them. The three words beat in her brain over and over again. *Cheryl told them.*

Then she knew that Wint Marron knew. Either his suspicions had been aroused by a visit from the police and fresh questions asked, or else he was seeing directly into her mind, as she'd seen into his.

She sent Alan home early, spent the rest of the night tossing in bed, unable to sleep. In the morning she called Detective Sergeant Evatt.

"Your story interested the officer in charge," Evatt told her. "He went back to the Marron home. He made an excuse to get into the Marron garage. There were two cars there, neither with any signs of front-end damage. But the car Mr. Marron usually drives is a Jeep. It has an oversize, reinforced front bumper. The officer concedes you could possibly hit someone with that bumper and not get a dent in it. But possibility isn't proof."

"What about the little blue suitcase?" she asked.

"No sign of that."

"Wint Marron could have retrieved it from the scene of the accident," she argued. "There might be blood on it. Though he could have washed it off—or burned the thing . . ."

"Miss Royce," Sergeant Evatt interrupted, "I've also mentioned this matter to the lieutenant. He doesn't seem to think that the kind of evidence you've offered us is really enough to ask for a search warrant. We don't have any real grounds for suspicion. You weren't exactly an eyewitness."

"So you're not going to do anything."

"There isn't anything we can do right now."

"You think that I'm a crackpot?"

"Nobody said that, Miss Royce. But we've followed it through as far as we can go—for now, anyway."

She confided at last in Alan, and Alan scoffed. No, he would not try to sneak into Wint Marron's garage to inspect his Jeep, or into Marron's house to look for a bloody blue suitcase. Perhaps she had received telepathic signals or vibrations from Marron, but if Marron had murdered his wife, that was the business of the police—not his or hers. She was furious.

That was one of the reasons why she left the city. Another reason was that she was frightened of Wint Marron.

She had no logical explanation for her fear. She had already communicated with the police, and Wint knew she had. Therefore, he wouldn't dare do anything violent to her. What could he do, then? Well, he could annoy her, threaten her. She was almost certain that he would. So she wanted to escape, get away, let time pass. Then perhaps she'd stop seeing into Wint Marron's mind. Perhaps then she could forget.

She begged leave of absence from the agency and drove away that afternoon. Nowhere in particular, not in any special direction. Just out of town. To somewhere different.

She ended up, toward sunset, at the Northway Motel in a small town, not more than a village, called Northway. The motel was a typical long building, with the rooms side by side, and space in front of each unit for the guest's car. A restaurant adjoined. She had a sandwich, and when she strolled back to her door, night had fallen and the stars were out. She checked her car again to make sure it was locked, then went inside.

Guessing that she would need them, she took two sleeping tablets, indulged in a long hot shower, propped herself up in bed on the motel's excellent pillows, and tried to read. It was a futile exercise.

Hours passed. She squirmed restlessly in the bed. The book did not interest her. She turned the light out finally, then stared into the darkness.

She couldn't get Wint Marron out of her mind. He knew that she knew—but did he know how much she knew? Surely her mind couldn't be a completely open book to him. Might he even be afraid that she knew more than she actually did? How he had disposed of the blue suitcase, for instance. Or the identity of Paula's companion in that cocktail lounge.

Since she didn't want to share any more of Wint Marron's guilty secrets, could she send him the message that he had nothing further to fear from her, that she was finished playing public-spirited citizen and informing on a murderer? But would he believe her, would he trust her . . . ?

In the darkness of that strange room she suddenly sat upright. He didn't trust her! Wint Marron was saying that to her, right at this moment.

She came near to panic. For she knew something else too. Whether it was telepathy this time, or a kind of animal instinct for the proximity of danger, or whether she had actually heard a small noise, she wasn't sure. But she knew! Wint Marron was there.

She eased out of the bed. In the front wall of her room near the door was a large window, heavily draped. She inched the drape aside to make a small peephole, found a venetian blind, bent down one of the slats.

At first she saw nothing outside. The driveway was fairly well lighted. Her car was there, a hulking lump of shadow.

Then she did hear a noise, this time unmistakable, the scrape of the sole of a shoe on the sidewalk close to her door. A dark shape passed the window, paused beside her car.

A man. Wint Marron. It could be no other. If she clung to any desperate doubt, however, that doubt was erased when the man walked around to the rear of the car and the light fell on his head and shoulders. Cheryl Royce saw Wint Marron's lean, dark, handsome face.

He had followed her. Quite easily, of course, because she had sent him the message. Northway, the Northway Motel.

Now he was interested in her car—making sure it was the right car, and since it was parked there, checking which was the right door, the right room. He was going to do something to the car, or try to enter her room . . . or perhaps simply wait for her to come out.

Panic overwhelmed judgment. She could phone the motel clerk, ask him to call the Northway police. But the police would never believe her. They hadn't before. They wouldn't now. Not until Wint Marron did something, and then it would be too late. Besides, the police were her enemies. Going to the police had caused Wint Marron to fear her, then to pursue her. Her only safety was in convincing Wint that she'd never go to the police again.

But right now, while he was still angry with her, she must escape. How: *Don't plan . . . don't plan,* some part of her brain warned her. *Wint can read your mind, don't you know that? If you plan where you're going, he'll be there waiting for you. So leave your mind blank . . . use instinct . . . act blindly . . . don't panic . . .*

She dressed quickly, feeling in the dark for her clothes. She refused to think. *I'm getting dressed . . . no, I must not even think that,* she reminded herself. *I must think neither about the future nor the present.*

She stood fully dressed now in the middle of the dark room. It was difficult, almost impossible, to keep her mind blank. The apparatus just isn't constructed that way. But she tried.

The room had a rear window also. She had to pull aside the drape and raise the blind. The window itself resisted for a moment, but finally moved upward. There was a small squeak and a groan as it did so, perhaps not audible on the front side of the building. Without hesitation, without considering the problem that she might be seen, avoiding concentration on the matter, Cheryl eased one leg through the opening, then her torso, then the other leg.

She was standing on a grassy lawn. *Where now?* No, she mustn't think. Just act, move.

She heard traffic noises from the highway, out front. Although she had been in bed for some time, the hour still wasn't late. There were people around, no need to be afraid.

She walked past the rear of the motel restaurant. Inside were a waitress and a customer or two, but the place appeared ready to close. No refuge there. Wint could follow her there anyway.

She walked on, trying not even to note her surroundings, trying not to reflect upon the sense images her eyes gathered. Something large loomed in her path: the rear of a truck. She walked around the more shadowed side of it. Not too long a truck. Not a trailer rig.

A man stood near the front end, smoking a cigarette. Maybe the driver. He heard her footsteps, turned to watch her approach. There was no light on his face, only the glowing tip of the cigarette. She stopped close to him.

"Is this your truck?"

Apparently startled, he didn't answer for a moment. "Yes," he said finally.

"Are you going somewhere or staying here?"

"I'm leaving," he said after another hesitation, "just as soon as I finish this cigarette."

"Will you give me a ride?"

The tip of the cigarette glowed more brightly as the truck driver took a long drag. "Where do you want to go?" he asked.

"It doesn't matter."

"Look, I'm going to . . ."

He stared at her, puzzled, but her face was as much in shadow as his. He dropped his cigarette butt on the gravel and didn't bother to grind it out. What he was thinking was as obvious as if he too were on her mental wavelength. He couldn't guess what kind of risk he might be taking, but the proposition was intriguing . . .

"Hop in," he said after a long moment, and opened the door for her.

I've never ridden in this large a truck before, she thought as she climbed into the cab. But then she told her mind to be still. *Don't think words . . . be quiet . . . go to sleep . . . yes, sleep . . . hypnotize yourself.*

The driver climbed in on his own side, started the engine, and the

truck rolled out. Cheryl kept her eyes closed, but in trying so hard
not to, she sensed that they had turned left onto the highway. Did
Wint notice the truck's departure? Maybe not. Surely he couldn't
read her every thought. He needn't know that she was in the truck.

"I don't know whether I should be doing this," the driver was
saying. "You on drugs or something?"

"No, I'm not on drugs."

"You're not the other type. So you must be running away. Who
from? Your husband?"

"No. I'm sorry. I can't explain."

"I may be doing something illegal."

"No, you're not. I guarantee you that."

They drove in silence for a while. Cheryl tried to keep her eyes
closed, not to notice road signs. The driver glanced at her sideways
now and then, she realized. But whatever he might be thinking, she
had less to fear from him than from Wint Marron.

"Is there a car following us?" she asked suddenly.

She regretted the question instantly, because the driver became
alarmed. He glanced at his mirror. "Nobody back there now. Look,
who are you expecting to follow us?"

"Nobody."

"You might be running away from the police."

"I'm not."

"I don't want to get mixed up in anything."

"All you have to do is take me somewhere. Anywhere."

"I'm just going to Jackson Harbor."

She gave a little shriek, and put her fingers in her ears, but it
was too late. The name of their destination pounded in her
brain . . . *Jackson Harbor* . . . she couldn't stop it. And she knew,
she knew absolutely, that the name was vibrating through the ether,
straight back to Northway, back to Wint.

"What's the matter with you?"

"Let me out!" she screamed. "Just let me out!"

"Look, I said I'd take you—"

"Let me out, or I'll jump!" She poised with the door half open.

"Wait a minute. Wait a minute. Let me find a place where I can
get off the pavement."

He'd put the brakes on, and the truck was slowing down, so she
waited. He picked a place finally, and edged off onto the shoulder.
But long before the truck had come to a dead stop, Cheryl had the

door open, had climbed down to the running board. "Thanks," she called back to the man, and jumped.

She landed on her feet, stumbled, but didn't fall. Only then, when she was safe, did she look to see where she was. A road marker loomed in the bright headlights of the truck. Junction . . . K.

Wint will know exactly where I am, she thought. She shouted to the truck driver. She wanted to get back in, but already the engine was roaring and the big rear tires were spitting gravel at her. Before she could catch up with it, the big vehicle had turned back onto the highway. In a moment it had diminished to a pair of taillights, then it was gone completely.

She was left alone, afoot and in darkness, her exact location pin-pointed to Wint Marron as the junction of Road "K" with the main highway.

Her first instinct was to try to hitch another ride, till she realized the possibility that the first car to stop for her might be Wint's. Or maybe he wouldn't stop. Wint had another method of dealing with female hitchhikers who had displeased him.

A pair of headlights came hurtling down the highway toward her. She dropped into the weeds at the side of the road. She lay there until the lights and the car flashed by.

This main road was dangerous: too many cars. She picked herself up out of the weeds and ran in the only direction left open, down Road K.

Wint knew where she was going, of course, for the moment. *Road K* pounded in her mind in the same rhythm as her feet pounded on the gravel. But she would get lost—lost, that was the answer to her problem. If she didn't know where she was, neither would Wint. She would find an even smaller road than this, a dirt road, and follow that. Or simply run across fields or through the woods.

But she hesitated to plunge off into the darkness. She had only a vague idea of the geography of this area. She knew approximately where Northway was. How far toward Jackson Harbor had they gotten? Jackson Harbor was on the lake, of course. But there were other bodies of water in between, as she recalled the map, a couple of small rivers . . . and weren't there marshes or swamps? Quick-sand, maybe?

Was she doing the right thing, running away from civilization, running into a sparsely populated semi-wilderness? Maybe she should have stayed in the truck, stayed with people. But it was too late now.

It was a clear night, with moon and stars. She could see her way along the road. The woods would be dark, though. She couldn't bring herself to leave the road. She'd find that unmarked side road.

But she didn't. Panting, she had to slow to a walk. And then she stopped.

Where did you go, Cheryl?

It was as if the question had been spoken aloud, it was so clear, precise. But she was alone there on the road. She knew, however, exactly where the question had come from.

Wint Marron was standing by the open rear window of her room at the Northway Motel. That had been a mistake, hadn't it, to leave that window open? Wint stood there, and she was with him, looking at the window through Wint's eyes.

Then he climbed inside, and she accompanied him. A flashlight beam searched the room, glided over the walls, lingered for a moment on the empty, mussed bed.

We're communicating, aren't we, Cheryl? Like a voice, speaking to her from within her own brain. *You know I'm here.* There was a long pause. *And I know where you are.*

Was he lying? She closed her eyes and ground her teeth together in a desperate mental effort not to think about the lonely gravel road and the dark woods on either side.

Don't try to hide from me, Cheryl.

She pressed her lips together to smother a gasp.

You hitchhiked, didn't you?

He was groping, guessing. He didn't know as much as he pretended to. She went on trying to keep her mind blank.

You went to the police. I knew that, didn't I, Cheryl? And I found the Northway Motel, didn't I?

He was goading her, trying to panic her. If he succeeded, she would lose control and perhaps betray her whereabouts.

It's your own fault, you know, Cheryl. You butted into a private affair. It was a while before I realized you were butting in. I guess I should have been more careful, because I was the one who discovered that we could share our thoughts. I even mentioned to you that this telepathy thing could run in both directions. It's too bad, though, it turned out the way it did. You're a cute girl, Cheryl. I did want to kiss you that night we met. After I got rid of Paula, and things had settled down a little, I might have looked you up. Yes, it's your fault, Cheryl. Even after Paula, you didn't have to go to the police. You didn't have to turn against me. Not when you and I were so intimate.

*Couldn't you understand? Couldn't you sympathize? Haven't you ever
been jealous? When I saw Paula with that Don Bruno . . .*

She screamed, a short, choked, stifled scream. Don Bruno, not a
very ordinary name. That detective had said that if she could identify
the other man in the case the police would have something to go on.
Now she knew who the other man was—but she didn't want to know!

Cheryl!

He must not have been aware that she hadn't known before. But
now he surely realized the slip he had made. He had given her a
weapon against him, and now he must disarm her, silence her.

She started running again, on the gravel road, Road K. Turn off
into the woods? No, not now. Wint could run through the woods
better than she could. No, she had to stay on the road, find somebody,
find help, find a telephone. It had to be on this road. Going back to
the highway would mean rushing to meet Wint. This was her only
road. This road led somewhere. And when she found that telephone,
she would call Sergeant Evatt, and she would shout to him, "The
man's name is Don Bruno! Locate him! Make him admit that he was
going to pick up Paula Marron who would be carrying a suitcase!
Don Bruno can tell you enough so you can arrest Wint Marron for
murder!"

She ran on. If the rough gravel hurt her feet through the thin
soles of her shoes, she wasn't aware of it. She'd gotten her second
wind now. She could make it. Wint was still miles behind her, getting
into his car, consulting his map, searching for Road K.

She concentrated on not thinking, on not letting her surroundings
impinge upon her senses. *Don't give Wint any clues. Don't give him
any landmarks. Don't let him know if this road is going through
woods or swamps, or by a stream or near a lake. Don't see any of
those things. Just look for one thing. A light. A light that will mean
human habitation.*

How much time passed? In her state of suspended awareness she
didn't know. Minutes . . . miles . . . neither had meant anything.

Until two sensations came to her at exactly the same moment.
One that she welcomed and one that she feared. One from the front
and one from the rear. A sight and a sound.

Up ahead, still distant, she saw it, a mere pinhead of illumination
amid the woodland foliage. And simultaneously, behind her, she
heard the far-off growl of an automobile engine.

She raced that approaching sound. It was coming down Road K,
she knew that, and as it drew nearer she even thought she recognized

it. She'd heard it once before, the evening that Paula Marron was struck down by a hit-and-run driver. Wint was pursuing her in his Jeep, that Jeep with its reinforced front bumper which wouldn't dent when it smashed into a human body.

But the light grew closer too. The road curved and the light swung to a new position, almost straight ahead. A yellow light, growing larger and larger. A porch light? It didn't matter. Any kind of light meant people, safety.

The Jeep engine was loud in her ears now. She thought she could hear too the rasp of its tires on the gravel. But the light loomed brighter and closer too.

She saw other things now. A reflection of the light, a vertical gleaming bar of yellow. On water, a stream or a narrow inlet, and the light was on the far side.

For a dreadful moment she supposed that she was lost, isolated from that help on the other bank. But then the light illuminated—ever so slightly, and off a bit to the left where the road was curving again—*a bridge!*

Not much of a bridge. Wooden. Old. Rickety. But a bridge nevertheless, leading to the other side of the water and to the light.

Behind her—only yards—the roar of the engine and the scream of tires clawing gravel rose together into one deafening crescendo.

Her flying feet touched the first board of the bridge. Then the Jeep's headlights, swinging around that last little curve of the road suddenly illuminated the whole world . . . herself . . . the floor of the bridge . . . the dark shining water just ahead of her outstretched foot . . .

She couldn't stop. It was too late for that. Her foot leaped ahead of her out into space. There was nothing else beneath it, until the black surface of the water rose up to meet her.

Just as she sank into it, rubber tires hit the boards of the bridge and the hurtling Jeep found the same emptiness in front of it. It sailed over Cheryl's head, darkening the sky, just as her head went under water.

In the water then she felt the exploding pressure waves as the metal monster plunged in just beyond her. She bobbed to the surface.

There was nothing there. The sky was empty. The roar was silenced. Nothing but huge ripples, almost waves, spreading out from the spot where the Jeep had disappeared.

Wint!

She blurted his name, silently, inside her brain. But there was no answer, no communication. The connection was cut. The line was dead at the other end.

Yes, dead . . . or dying. She sensed that somehow. Wint Marron's head had hit something hard, like the windshield. Unconscious, helpless, wedged into his seat, he was drowning now.

She swam a stroke or two toward the source of those ripples. "Wint!" she called aloud.

A numbness seized her. A coldness. She became certain of an unalterable fact. Wint was dead.

So she swam back, toward the bridge . . .

Bridge? She looked at the wooden structure in the moonlight. Not a bridge at all. Only a pier.

She shivered then, not at the coldness of the water. She had killed him. She had killed Wint. Had he known differently, he might have been able to stop the Jeep. But her brain had sent him the wrong message. Not pier. Bridge . . .

The Invisible Tomb

by Arthur Porges

Captain Gregg, in common with some other normally hard-headed people, believed that related events tend to occur in triples. Having just struggled through two cases that involved tricky hiding places—first, one involving a ruby; second, a rare book—he was not altogether surprised to confront the problem of a missing body.

It was, naturally, the worst of the sequence. It's easy enough to hide small objects, but to dispose of roughly one hundred pounds of woman, and in a relatively limited space, is another matter; Gregg could hardly believe it. But unless the murderer had somehow carried the remains through twenty miles of suburban streets to what precious little open country—three-cow "ranches" and the like—existed in so densely populated an area, there to be buried in a shallow grave certain to be found, what alternatives were possible? No, Elsa Newman must be in the Newman basement, house, or yard. Only she wasn't, if Gregg knew anything about conducting a search.

In the other two cases, the criminals had found by brilliant ingenuity—one had to give them that much—how small items like a gem and a book could be hidden almost in plain sight, on the *Purloined Letter* principle, and baffle the most competent detective.

Certainly they had fooled Gregg, forcing him to get help, unorthodox, but effective, in order to solve the seemingly impossible puzzles presented by the talented crooks; and now, for the third time, Gregg was driven to seek out his peculiar consultant. He didn't enjoy having to do it, but knew when he was licked.

Julian Morse Trowbridge looked like a dissipated gnome badly hungover from too much fermented toadstool juice, or whatever the species imbibes when on a bender. His vast, pallid face, moist and unhealthy in its flabbiness, was set on a thready neck. As for his torso, that suggested the ultimate "Before" of the most exaggerated advertisement for a physical culture course. But inside the big, bullet-shaped head was a remarkable brain, packed with esoteric knowledge instantly available on call.

Trowbridge had graduated from Harvard at fourteen, and two years later had a PhD in mathematical physics, but his intellect was decades ahead of his emotional balance, so the boy had broken down and fled from the academic world. Now, at fifty, he lived in a ramshackle house full of books, where he acted as a kind of neighborhood Solomon, handing out free, and usually quite good, advice to all those who asked for it.

When Captain Gregg came for the third time in as many months, he found the gnome explaining patiently, in precise and pedantic terms, a theorem in calculus to a pimply boy whose one burning aim was to con the old creep into doing his homework for him.

"Continuity does *not* imply differentiability," Trowbridge assured the young seeker-after-truth. "Remember that, my boy, and all difficulties with this kind of problem will vanish," he added brusquely.

He politely ushered the student to the door and, sighing with relief, turned to Gregg.

"I take it you didn't do him much good," the detective said dryly.

"I fear you are right; the chap simply hasn't the brains for college. It's a dreadful thing to say, but I really think he does not fully grasp the idea of a function. However," with a twinkling glance at Gregg, "you've done fairly well under the same handicap. Your problem, I'm sure, is not mathematical."

"Things happen in threes," the detective said. "Twice I've been to you about stuff hidden where anybody should have been able to find it, and nobody could until Trowbridge showed the way. Well, this time it's a whole body—a woman; height, five-four; weight, ninety-eight. Missing two weeks now; presumed dead—by me—but no body, even though, incredibly, she ought to be hidden right in the house or the smallish yard. If it weren't for the last two cases, I wouldn't dream of her being that handy, but now—"

The gnome sank deeper in the enormous, sagging, musty armchair he favored.

"Ahhh," he sighed happily. Of all the problems brought to him, he most enjoyed puzzling crimes; they added glamor to his emotionally starved existence. Math was fascinating, but too bloodless. "Tell me about it. Who's your suspect, and why?"

"It's a simple case as to motive and probable killer. Leo Newman's the guy. He's big, ugly, bald, has a pot—and a pretty wife. Brought her back from Germany in 1949. She was only sixteen, and obviously wanted to get away from the mess there. Elsa Keller was her name; blonde, very cute, and flirtatious; the kind of wife who invites the mailman in for coffee—or the grocery boy; the phone installer; anything male that's handy. Newman fought with her often, and threatened to kill her. The neighbors heard them going at it.

"Well, two weeks ago she disappeared. People next door say she and Newman were battling again, that she stopped screaming at him very suddenly. Then it was quiet, and stayed that way.

"He claims she ran away, but nobody saw her leave. There's no evidence of her taking bus, train, or plane, and all her clothes are in the house except, possibly, what she was wearing at the time. Now I figure he lost his temper and killed her, maybe not intending to. Then he disposed of the body somehow. But where? There are square miles of tidy little lawns, and then more roomy suburbs, but no place a body could be buried and not found fast. His own house is an old one and quite big, with attics and plenty of crawl spaces; but, hell, Julian, no spot where we couldn't find a woman's corpse. He didn't chop her up, because that *always* leaves traces—blood, tissue, something—the crime lab boys are sure to find.

"That's really the whole bit. She's gone, but couldn't have run off; so she must be dead. But if so, where did he hide her?"

"That depends, I would say," Trowbridge said calmly, "on how ingenious Mr. Leo Newman is. Is he ingenious?"

"In a way. He's handy, that's certain. Has a big shed full of tools, drills, a lathe; welding, soldering, and brazing equipment; concrete mixes; boxes of bolts, nuts, pipes, chains. Obviously he could repair or make a lot of things, but that's not the same as inventing an invisible grave."

"She's not buried in the small yard, of course."

"You just bet not. We probed every square inch. The lawn hasn't been touched."

"How does he behave?"

"Like a guilty man, I'd say. Very uneasy, as if he weren't at all sure he'd fooled us. Insisted she ran off with one of her many lovers, but wasn't angry—just scared. After we'd searched the place for hours, the next day he moved out to a hotel. I wonder why. Why pay rent when you have your own house? I guessed at first he did have her stashed inside somehow, and knew that after a few days in this warm weather it would be . . . well . . . unpleasant and a dead giveaway. But we've been back twice, with warrants, sniffing around, and there's nothing. So you see—" Gregg shrugged.

"I would be inclined to agree," the gnome said, "that there must be some particular significance in his moving out, but without more data it would be foolish to speculate. May I have a dossier, the usual things, to work with?"

"You bet," the detective assured him. He put a large, scabrous briefcase on Trowbridge's desk, which seemed already sagging under dozens of dusty books, each fatter than the next. "You'll find everything inside: Newman's statements; pictures of him and Elsa; photos of house and grounds; miscellaneous information, like his cheapness," Gregg added bitterly. "He must have known we'd go over the house a few more times, so he had all the utilities shut off; no gas, water, or electricity. On a dark day, or at night, we have to use flashlights. If it was winter, we'd freeze. Naturally, our warrants don't entitle us to use Newman's utilities! I suppose it's the only way he can get back at us; can't keep us out, but he can make our work harder."

Trowbridge cocked his great head. "Spite?" he said softly. "I wonder. How very odd!"

"What are you getting at?" Gregg asked quickly. "Did I miss something again?"

"Nothing; nothing," was the hasty reply, "except that your big, burly, bullying kind doesn't usually get spiteful in so womanish a way. I'll have to think about it."

"Give me a ring, as usual, if you come up with an angle," the detective said.

"Of course," the gnome said, reproach in his voice, escorting Gregg to the door.

The call would probably come at three in the morning, the detective knew, but that couldn't be helped. Trowbridge had his own cycles of activity, more like those of some distant planet than of Earth.

Gregg was wrenched from his deepest sleep of the night at four a.m., as it happened. He fumbled for the phone, hopeful but justifiably querulous. Why couldn't Trowbridge have waited another two hours? Then he felt a pang of guilt; after all, the little guy was trying to help in his own way.

"It is I—Julian," the phone announced pedantically.

"That figures," the detective groaned. "Whatchu got?"

"Maybe nothing, but there's a logical inference," one of his pet phrases, "*provided* your conviction that the body wasn't removed from the premises is sound."

"I think it is," Gregg said, wide awake now. "Everything indicates Newman stuck close to the neighborhood up to the time of our search. Just went to his job, did some shopping, and came home. No long drives, judging from the odometer and what his garage says. So let's have your theory."

"I build on the matter of his moving out," the gnome said cautiously. "Did he have the utilities stopped because of leaving, or was his change to a hotel the excuse for cutting them off? That's the vital point."

"What's the point in having no service at the house? We still searched."

"If they were on, and he still living there, you might wonder why no hot water," was the cryptic reply.

"No hot water," Gregg repeated. Then he gulped. "Hey, are you suggesting—no, it can't be! She was small, but there isn't that much space in a heater! It's not all hollow, has a million pipes and fittings."

"Not really. The actual tank is almost big enough, but any pipes are easily burned out with a torch. You did say, and the dossier confirms, that he knows how to use one."

"Sure, but—"

"All right. He removes the top, cleans out the whole cylinder, which your photos of the house show is a biggish one. The few holes for pipes are quickly welded shut, but so that nothing shows on the outside. Not," he added maliciously, "that anybody took much of a look. Then he puts the body inside, welds the top back on, and has a hermetically sealed, metal tomb—in plain sight, but invisible psychologically. The pipes he adds to his junk piles, already full of such stuff. Oh, it's a wild gamble, but he's scared and desperate. If you once overlook the tank, he can wait you out for months until all surveillance stops. Hermetically sealed, remember, a perfect tomb. But no hot water! Hence the hotel. Make sense?"

There was a pregnant silence for some moments, then the detective managed, "Yes, but I won't believe it until we open the thing! Logic is fine, Julian, but so is sanity. Imagine the gall in stashing her right under our noses. That smarts!" He gave a short, barking laugh. "I'll never sleep now; I'm going to check right away."

When the invisible tomb was opened, two hours later, they found the crumpled remains of Elsa Keller Newman.

The Avenging of Ann Leete

by Marjorie Bowen

This is a queer story, the more queer for the interpretation of passions of strong human heat that have been put upon it, and for glimpses of other motives and doings, not, it would seem, human at all.

The whole thing is seen vaguely, brokenly, a snatch here and there; one tells the tale, strangely another exclaims amaze, a third points out a scene, a fourth has a dim memory of a circumstance, a nine-days' (or less) wonder, an old print helps, the name on a mural tablet in a deserted church pinches the heart with a sense of confirmation, and so you have your story. When all is said it remains a queer tale.

It is seventy years odd ago, so dating back from this present year of 1845 you come to nearly midway in the last century, when conditions were vastly different from what they are now.

The scene is in Glasgow, and there are three points from which we start, all leading us to the heart of our tale.

The first is the portrait of a woman that hangs in the parlour of a respectable banker. He believes it to be the likeness of some connexion of his wife's, dead this many a year, but he does not know much about it. Some while ago it was discovered in a lumber-room, and he keeps it for the pallid beauty of the canvas, which is much faded and rubbed.

Since, as a young man, I first had the privilege of my worthy friend's acquaintance, I have always felt a strange interest in this picture; and, in that peculiar way that the imagination will seize on trifles, I was always fascinated by the dress of the lady. This is of dark green, very fine silk; an uncommon colour to use in a portrait, and, perhaps, in a lady's dress. It is very plain, with a little scarf of a striped Roman pattern, and her hair is drawn up over a pillow in the antique mode. Her face is expressionless, yet strange, the upper lip very thin, the lower very full, the light brown eyes set under brows that slant. I cannot tell why this picture was always to me full of such a great attraction, but I used to think of it a vast deal, and often to note, secretly, that never had I chanced to meet in real life, or in any other painting, a lady in a dark green silk dress.

In the corner of the canvas is a little device, put in a diamond as a gentlewoman might bear arms, yet with no pretensions to heraldry, just three little birds, the topmost with a flower in its beak.

It was not so long ago that I came upon the second clue that leads into the story, and that was a mural tablet in an old church near the Rutherglen Road, a church that has lately fallen into disrepute or neglect, for it was deserted and impoverished. But I was assured that a generation ago it had been a most famous place of worship, fashionable and well frequented by the better sort.

The mural tablet was to one "Ann Leete," and there was just the date (seventy-odd years old), given with what seemed a sinister brevity.

And underneath the lettering, lightly cut on the time-stained marble, was the same device as that on the portrait of the lady in the green silk dress.

I was curious enough to make inquiries, but no one seemed to know anything of, or wished to talk about, Ann Leete.

It was all so long ago, I was told, and there was no one now in the parish of the name of Leete.

And all who had been acquainted with the family of Leete seemed to be dead or gone away. The parish register (my curiosity went so far as an inspection of this) yielded me no more information than the mural tablet.

I spoke to my friend the banker, and he said he thought that his wife had had some cousins by the name of Leete, and that there was some tale of a scandal or great misfortune attached to them which was the reason of a sort of ban on their name so that it had never been mentioned.

When I told him I thought the portrait of the lady in the dark green silk might picture a certain Ann Leete he appeared uneasy and even desirous of having the likeness removed, which roused in me the suspicion that he knew something of the name, and that not pleasant. But it seemed to me indelicate and perhaps useless to question him.

It was a year or so after this incident that my business, which was that of silversmith and jeweller, put into my hands a third clue. One of my apprentices came to me with a rare piece of work which had been left at the shop for repair.

It was a thin medal of the purest gold, on which was set in fresh water pearls, rubies and cairngorms the device of the three birds, the plumage being most skilfully wrought in the bright jewels and the flower held by the topmost creature accurately designed in pearls.

It was one of these pearls that was missing, and I had some difficulty in matching its soft lustre.

An elderly lady called for the ornament, the same person who had left it. I saw her myself, and ventured to admire and praise the workmanship of the medal.

"Oh," she said, "it was worked by a very famous jeweller, my great-uncle, and he has a peculiar regard for it—indeed I believe it has never before been out of his possession, but he was so greatly grieved by the loss of the pearl that he would not rest until I offered to take it to be repaired. He is, you will understand," she added with a smile, "a very old man. He must have made that jewellery—why—seventy-odd years ago."

Seventy-odd years ago—that would bring one back to the date on the tablet to Ann Leete, to the period of the portrait.

"I have seen this device before," I remarked, "on the likeness of a lady and on the mural inscription in memory of a certain Ann Leete." Again this name appeared to make an unpleasant impression.

My customer took her packet hastily.

"It is associated with something dreadful," she said quickly. "We do not speak of it—a very old story. I did not know anyone had heard of it—"

"I certainly have not," I assured her. "I came to Glasgow not so long ago, as apprentice to this business of my uncle's which now I own."

"But you have seen a portrait?" she asked.

"Yes, in the house of a friend of mine."

"This is queer. We did not know that any existed. Yet my great-uncle does speak of one—in a green silk dress."

"In a green silk dress," I confirmed.

The lady appeared amazed.

"But it is better to let the matter rest," she decided. "My relative, you will realize, is very old—nearly, sir, a hundred years old, and his wits wander and he tells queer tales. It was all very strange and horrible, but one cannot tell how much my old uncle dreams."

"I should not think to disturb him," I replied.

But my customer hesitated.

"If you know of this portrait—perhaps he should be told; he laments after it so much, and we have always believed it an hallucination—"

She returned the packet containing the medal.

"Perhaps," she added dubiously, "you are interested enough to take this back to my relative yourself and judge what you shall or shall not tell him?"

I eagerly accepted the offer, and the lady gave me the name and residence of the old man who, although possessed of considerable means, had lived for the past fifty years in the greatest seclusion in that lonely part of the town beyond the Rutherglen Road and near to the Green, the once pretty and fashionable resort for youth and pleasure, but now a deserted and desolate region. Here, on the first opportunity, I took my way, and found myself well out into the country, nearly at the river, before I reached the lonely mansion of Eneas Bretton, as the ancient jeweller was called.

A ferocious dog troubled my entrance in the dark, overgrown garden where the black glossy laurels and bays strangled the few flowers, and a grim woman, in an old-fashioned mutch or cap, at length answered my repeated peals at the rusty chain bell.

It was not without considerable trouble that I was admitted into the presence of Mr. Bretton, and only, I think, by the display of the jewel and the refusal to give it into any hands but those of its owner.

The ancient jeweller was seated on a southern terrace that received the faint and fitful rays of the September sun.

He was wrapped in shawls that disguised his natural form, and a fur and leather cap was fastened under his chin.

I had the impression that he had been a fine man, of a vigorous and handsome appearance; even now, in the extreme of decay, he showed a certain grandeur of line and carriage, a certain majestic power in his personality. Though extremely feeble, I did not take him to be imbecile nor greatly wanting in his faculties.

He received me courteously, though obviously ill-used to strangers.

I had, he said, a claim on him as a fellow-craftsman, and he was good enough to commend the fashion in which I had repaired his medal.

This, as soon as he had unwrapped, he fastened to a fine gold chain he drew from his breast, and slipped inside his heavy clothing.

"A pretty trinket," I said, "and of an unusual design."

"I fashioned it myself," he answered, "over seventy years ago. The year before, sir, she died."

"Ann Leete?" I ventured.

The ancient man was not in the least surprised at the use of this name.

"It is a long time since I heard those words with any but my inner ear," he murmured; "to be sure, I grow very old. You'll not remember Ann Leete?" he added wistfully.

"I take it she died before I was born," I answered.

He peered at me.

"Ah, yes, you are still a young man, though your hair is grey."

I noticed now that he wore a small tartan scarf inside his coat and shawl; this fact gave me a peculiar, almost unpleasant shudder.

"I know this about Ann Leete—she had a dark green silk dress. And a Roman or tartan scarf."

He touched the wisp of bright-coloured silk across his chest.

"This is it. She had her likeness taken so—but it was lost."

"It is preserved," I answered. "And I know where it is. I might, if you desired, bring you to a sight of it."

He turned his grand old face to me with a civil inclination of his massive head.

"That would be very courteous of you, sir, and a pleasure to me. You must not think," he added with dignity, "that the lady has forsaken me or that I do not often see her. Indeed, she comes to me more frequently than before. But it would delight me to have the painting of her to console the hours of her absence."

I reflected what his relative had said about the weakness of his wits, and recalled his great age, which one was apt to forget in face of his composure and reasonableness.

He appeared now to doze and to take no further notice of my presence, so I left him.

He had a strange look of lifelessness as he slumbered there in the faintest rays of the cloudy autumn sun.

I reflected how lightly the spirit must dwell in this ancient frame, how easily it must take flight into the past, how soon into eternity.

It did not cost me much persuasion to induce my friend, the banker, to lend me the portrait of Ann Leete, particularly as the canvas had been again sent up to the attics.

"Do *you* know the story?" I asked him.

He replied that he had heard something; that the case had made a great stir at the time; that it was all very confused and amazing, and that he did not desire to discuss the matter.

I hired a carriage and took the canvas to the house of Eneas Bretton.

He was again on the terrace, enjoying with a sort of calm eagerness the last warmth of the failing sun.

His two servants brought in the picture and placed it on a chair at his side.

He gazed at the painted face with the greatest serenity.

"That is she," he said, "but I am glad to think that she looks happier now, sir. She still wears that dark green silk. I never see her in any other garment."

"A beautiful woman," I remarked quietly, not wishing to agitate or disturb his reflections, which were clearly detached from any considerations of time and space.

"I have always thought so," he answered gently, "but I, sir, have peculiar faculties. I saw her, and see her still as a spirit. I loved her as a spirit. Yet our bodily union was necessary for our complete happiness. And in that my darling and I were balked."

"By death?" I suggested, for I knew that the word had no terrors for him.

"By death," he agreed, "who will soon be forced to unite us again."

"But not in the body," I said.

"How, sir, do you know that?" he smiled. "We have but finite minds. I think we have but little conception of the marvellous future."

"Tell me," I urged, "how you lost Ann Leete."

His dim, heavy-lidded, many-wrinkled eyes flickered a glance over me.

"She was murdered," he said.

I could not forbear a shudder.

"That fragile girl!" I exclaimed. My blood had always run cool and thin, and I detested deeds of violence; my even mind could not grasp the idea of the murder of women save as a monstrous enormity.

I looked at the portrait, and it seemed to me that I had always known that it was the likeness of a creature doomed.

"Seventy years ago and more," continued Eneas Bretton, "since when *she has wandered lonely betwixt time and eternity*, waiting for me. But very soon I shall join her, and then, sir, we shall go where there is no recollection of the evil things of this earth."

By degrees he told me the story, not in any clear sequence, nor at any one time, nor without intervals of sleep and pauses of dreaming, nor without assistance from his servants and his great-niece and her husband, who were his frequent visitors.

Yet it was from his own lips and when we were alone together that I learned all that was really vital in the tale.

He required very frequent attendance; although all human passion was at the utmost ebb with him, he had, he said, a kind of regard for me in that I had brought him his lady's portrait, and he told me things of which he had never spoken to any human being before. I say human on purpose because of his intense belief that he was, and always had been, in communication with powers not of this earth.

In these words I put together his tale.

As a young man [said Eneas Bretton] I was healthy, prosperous and happy.

My family had been goldsmiths as long as there was any record of their existence, and I was an enthusiast in this craft, grave, withal, and studious, over-fond of books and meditation. I do not know how or when I first met Ann Leete.

To me she was always there like the sun; I think I have known her all my life, but perhaps my memory fails.

Her father was a lawyer and she an only child, and though her social station was considered superior to mine, I had far more in the way of worldly goods, so there was no earthly obstacle to our union.

The powers of evil, however, fought against us; I had feared this from the first, as our happiness was the complete circle ever hateful to fiends and devils who try to break the mystic symbol.

The mistress of my soul attracted the lustful attention of a young doctor, Rob Patterson, who had a certain false charm of person, not real comeliness, but a trick of colour, of carriage and a fine taste in clothes.

His admiration was whetted by her coldness and his intense dislike of me.

We came to scenes in which he derided me as no gentleman, but a beggarly tradesman, and I scorned him as an idle voluptuary designing a woman's ruin for the crude pleasure of the gratification of fleeting passions.

For the fellow made not even any pretence of being able to support a wife, and was of that rake-helly temperament that made an open mock of matrimony.

Although he was but a medical student, he was of what they call noble birth, and his family, though decayed, possessed considerable social power, so that his bold pursuit of Ann Leete and his insolent flaunting of me had some license, the more so that he did not lack tact and address in his manner and conduct.

Our marriage could have stopped this persecution, or given the right to publicly resent it, but my darling would not leave her father, who was of a melancholy and querulous disposition.

It was shortly before her twenty-first birthday, for which I had made her the jewel I now wear (the device being the crest of her mother's family and one for which she had a great affection), that her father died suddenly. His last thoughts were of her, for he had this very picture painted for her birthday gift. Finding herself thus unprotected and her affairs in some confusion, she declared her intention of retiring to some distant relative in the Highlands until decorum permitted of our marriage.

And upon my opposing myself to this scheme of separation and delay she was pleased to fall out with me, declaring that I was as importunate as Dr. Patterson, and that I, as well as he, should be kept in ignorance of her retreat.

I had, however, great hopes of inducing her to change this resolution, and, it being then fair spring weather, engaged her to walk with me on the Green, beyond the city, to discuss our future.

I was an orphan like herself, and we had now no common meeting-place suitable to her reputation and my respect.

By reason of a pressure of work, to which by temperament and training I was ever attentive, I was a few moments late at the tryst on the Green, which I found, as usual, empty; but it was a lovely afternoon of May, very still and serene, like the smile of satisfied love.

I paced about, looking for my darling.

Although she was in mourning, she had promised me to wear the dark green silk I so admired under her black cloak, and I looked for this colour among the brighter greens of the trees and bushes.

She did not appear, and my heart was chilled with the fear that she was offended with me and therefore would not come, and an even deeper dread that she might, in vexation, have fled to her unknown retreat.

This thought was sending me hot-foot to seek her at her house, when I saw Rob Patterson coming across the close-shaven grass of the Green.

I remember that the cheerful sun seemed to me to be at this moment darkened, not by any natural clouds or mists, but as it is during an eclipse, and that the fresh trees and innocent flowers took on a ghastly and withered look.

It may appear a trivial detail, but I recall so clearly his habit, which was of a luxury beyond his means—fine grey broadcloth with a deep edging of embroidery in gold thread, little suited to his profession.

As he saw me he cocked his hat over his eyes, but took no other notice of my appearance, and I turned away, not being wishful of any encounter with this gentleman while my spirit was in a tumult.

I went at once to my darling's house, and learnt from her maid that she had left home two hours previously.

I do not wish to dwell on this part of my tale—indeed, I could not, it becomes very confused to me.

The salient facts are these—that no one saw Ann Leete in bodily form again.

And no one could account for her disappearance; yet no great comment was aroused by this, because there was no one to take much interest in her, and it was commonly believed that she had disappeared from the importunity of her lovers, the more so as Rob Patterson swore that the day of her disappearance he had had an interview with her in which she had avowed her intention of going where no one could discover her. This, in a fashion, was confirmed by what she had told me, and I was the more inclined to believe it, as my inner senses told me that she was not dead.

Six months of bitter search, of sad uneasiness, that remain in my memory blurred to one pain, and then, one autumn evening, as I came home late and dispirited, I saw her before me in the gloaming, tripping up the street, wearing her dark green silk dress and tartan or Roman scarf.

I did not see her face as she disappeared before I could gain on her, but she held to her side one hand, and between the long fingers I saw the haft of a surgeon's knife.

I knew then that she was dead.

And I knew that Rob Patterson had killed her.

Although it was well known that my family were all ghostseers, to speak in this case was to be laughed at and reprimanded.

I had no single shred of evidence against Dr. Patterson.

But I resolved that I would use what powers I possessed to make him disclose his crime.

And this is how it befell.

In those days, in Glasgow, it was compulsory to attend some place of worship on the Sabbath, the observation of the holy day being enforced with peculiar strictness, and none being allowed to show themselves in any public place during the hours of the church services, and to this end inspectors and overseers were employed to patrol the streets on a Sabbath and take down the names of those who might be found loitering there.

But few were the defaulters, Glasgow on a Sunday being as bare as the Arabian desert.

Rob Patterson and I both attended the church in Rutherglen Road, towards the Green and the river.

And the Sunday after I had seen the phantom of Ann Leete, I changed my usual place and seated myself behind this young man.

My intention was to so work on his spirit as to cause him to make public confession of his crime. And I crouched there behind him with a concentration of hate and fury, forcing my will on his during the whole of the long service.

I noticed he was pale, and that he glanced several times behind him, but he did not change his place or open his lips; but presently his head fell forward on his arms as if he was praying, and I took him to be in a kind of swoon brought on by the resistance of his spirit against mine.

I did not for this cease to pursue him. I was, indeed, as if in an exaltation, and I thought my soul had his soul by the throat, somewhere above our heads, and was shouting out: "Confess! Confess!"

One o'clock struck and he rose with the rest of the congregation, but in a dazed kind of fashion. It was almost side by side that we issued from the church door.

As the stream of people came into the street they were stopped by a little procession that came down the road.

All immediately recognized two of the inspectors employed to search the Sunday streets for defaulters from church attendance, followed by several citizens who appeared to have left their homes in haste and confusion.

These people carried between them a rude bundle which some compassionate hand had covered with a white linen cloth. Below this fell a swathe of dark green silk and the end of a Roman scarf.

I stepped up to the rough bier.

"You have found Ann Leete," I said.

"It is a dead woman," one answered me. "We know not her name."

I did not need to raise the cloth. The congregation was gathering round us, and amongst them was Rob Patterson.

"Tell me, who was her promised husband, how you found her," I said.

And one of the inspectors answered:

"Near here, on the Green, where the wall bounds the grass, we saw, just now, the young surgeon, Rob Patterson, lying on the sward, and put his name in our books, besides approaching him to inquire the reason of his absence from church. But he, without excuse for his offence, rose from the ground, exclaiming: 'I am a miserable man! Look in the water!'

"With that he crossed a stile that leads to the river and disappeared, and we, going down to the water, found the dead woman, deep tangled between the willows and the weeds—"

"And," added the other inspector gravely, "tangled in her clothes is a surgeon's knife."

"Which," said the former speaker, "perhaps Dr. Patterson can explain, since I perceive he is among this congregation—he must have found some quick way round to have got here before us."

Upon this all eyes turned on the surgeon, but more with amaze than reproach.

And he, with a confident air, said:

"It is known to all these good people that I have been in the church the whole of the morning, especially to Eneas Bretton, who sat behind me, and, I dare swear, never took his eyes from me during the whole of the service."

"Ay, your *body* was there," I said.

With that he laughed angrily, and mingling with the crowd passed on his way.

You may believe there was a great stir; the theory put abroad was that Ann Leete had been kept a prisoner in a solitary, ruined hut there was by the river, and then, in fury or fear, slain by her jailer and cast into the river.

To me all this is black. I only know that she was murdered by Rob Patterson.

He was arrested and tried on the circuit.

He there proved, beyond all cavil, that he had been in the church from the beginning of the service to the end of it; his alibi was perfect. But the two inspectors never wavered in their tale of seeing him on the Green, of his self-accusation in his exclamation; he was very well known to them, and they showed his name written in their books.

He was acquitted by the tribunal of man, but a higher power condemned him.

Shortly after he died by his own hand, which God armed and turned against him.

This mystery, as it was called, was never solved to the public satisfaction, but I know that I sent Rob Patterson's soul out of his body to betray his guilt, and to procure my darling Christian burial.

This was the tale Eneas Bretton, that ancient man, told me, on the old terrace, as he sat opposite the picture of Ann Leete.

"You must think what you will," he concluded. "They will tell you that the shock unsettled my wits, or even that I was always crazed. As they would tell you that I dream when I say that I see Ann Leete now, and babble when I talk of my happiness with her for fifty years."

He smiled faintly; a deeper glory than that of the autumn sunshine seemed to rest on him.

"Explain it yourself, sir. *What was it those inspectors saw on the Green?*"

He slightly raised himself in his chair and peered over my shoulder.

"*And what is this*," he asked triumphantly, in the voice of a young man, "*coming towards us now?*"

I rose; I looked over my shoulder.

Through the gloom I saw a dark green silk gown, a woman's form, a pale hand beckoning.

My impulse was to fly from the spot, but a happy sigh from my companion reproved my cowardice. I looked at the ancient man whose whole figure appeared lapped in warm light, and as the apparition of the woman moved into this glow, which seemed too glorious for the fading sunshine, I heard his last breath flow from his body with a glad cry. I had not answered his questions; I never can.

Just Curious

by James H. Schmitz

Roy Litton's apartment was on the eighteenth floor of the Torrell Arms. It was a pleasant place which cost him thirty-two thousand dollars a year. The living room had a wide veranda which served in season as a sun deck. Far below was a great park. Beyond the park, drawn back to a respectful distance from the Torrell Arms, was the rest of the city.

"May I inquire," Roy Litton said to his visitor, "from whom you learned about me?"

The visitor's name was Jean Merriam. She was a slender, expensive brunette, about twenty-seven. She took a card from her handbag and slid it across the table to Litton. "Will that serve as an introduction?" she asked.

Litton studied the words scribbled on the card and smiled. "Yes," he said, "that's quite satisfactory. I know the lady's handwriting well. In what way can I help you?"

"I represent an organization," Jean said, "which does discreet investigative work."

"You're detectives?"

She shrugged, smiled. "We don't refer to ourselves as detectives, but that's the general idea. Conceivably your talents could be very useful to us. I'm here to find out whether you're willing to put them at our disposal from time to time. If you are, I have a test assignment for you. You don't mind, do you?"

Litton rubbed his chin. "You've been told what my standard fee is?"

Jean Merriam opened the handbag again, took out a check and gave it to him. Litton read it carefully, nodded. "Yes," he said, and laid the check on the table beside him. "Ten thousand dollars. You're in the habit of paying such sums out of your personal account?"

"The sum was put in my account yesterday for this purpose."

"Then what do you, or your organization, want me to do?"

"I've been given a description of how you operate, Mr. Litton, but we don't know how accurate the description is. Before we retain you, I'd like you to tell me exactly what you do."

Litton smiled. "I'm willing to tell you as much as I know."

She nodded. "Very well. I'll decide on the basis of what you say whether or not your services might be worth ten thousand dollars to the organization. Once I offer you the assignment and you accept it, we're committed. The check will be yours when the assignment is completed."

"Who will judge when it has been completed?"

"You will," said Jean. "Naturally there will be no further assignments if we're not satisfied with the results of this one. As I said, this is a test. We're gambling. If you're as good as I've been assured you are, the gamble should pay off. Fair enough?"

Litton nodded. "Fair enough, Miss Merriam." He leaned back in his chair. "Well, then—I sometimes call myself a 'sensor' because the word describes my experiences better than any other word I can think of. I'm not specifically a mind reader. I can't predict the future. I don't have second sight. But under certain conditions, I turn into a long-range sensing device with a limited application. I have no theoretical explanation for it. I can only say what happens.

"I work through contact objects; that is, material items which have had a direct and extensive physical connection with the persons I investigate. A frequently worn garment is the obvious example. Eyeglasses would be excellent. I once was able to use an automobile which the subject had driven daily for about ten months. Through some object I seem to become, for a time which varies between approximately three and five minutes, the person in question." Litton smiled. "Naturally I remain here physically, but my awareness is elsewhere.

"Let me emphasize that during this contact period I *am*—or seem to be—the other person. I am not conscious of Roy Litton or of what Roy Litton is doing. I have never heard of him and know nothing of his sensing ability. I am the other person, aware only of what he is aware, doing what he is doing, thinking what he is thinking. If, meanwhile, you were to speak to the body sitting here, touch it, even cause it severe pain—which has been done experimentally—I wouldn't know it. When the time is up, the contact fades and I'm back. Then I know who I am and can recall my experience and report on it. Essentially, that's the process."

Jean Merriam asked, "To what extent do you control the process?"

"I can initiate it or not initiate it. I'm never drawn out of myself unless I intend to be drawn out of myself. That's the extent of my control. Once it begins, the process continues by itself and concludes itself. I have no way of affecting its course."

Jean said reflectively, "I don't wish to alarm you, Mr. Litton. But mightn't you be running the risk of remaining permanently lost in somebody else's personality . . . unable to return to your own?"

Litton laughed. "No. I know definitely that can't happen, though I don't know why. The process simply can't maintain itself for much more than five minutes. On the other hand, it's rarely terminated in less than three."

"You say that during the time of contact you think what the other person thinks and are aware of what he's aware?"

"That's correct."

"Only that? If we employed you to investigate someone in this manner, we usually would need quite specific information. Wouldn't we have to be extremely fortunate if the person happened to think of that particular matter in the short time you shared his mind?"

"No," said Litton. "Conscious thoughts quite normally have thousands of ramifications and shadings the thinker doesn't know about. When the contact dissolves, I retain his impressions and it is primarily these ramifications and shadings I then investigate. It is something like developing a vast number of photographic prints. Usually the information my clients want can be found in those impressions in sufficient detail."

"What if it can't be found?"

"Then I make a second contact. On only one occasion, so far, have I been obliged to make three separate contacts with a subject to satisfy the client's requirements. There is no fee for additional contacts."

Jean Merriam considered a moment. "Very well," she said. She brought a small box from the handbag, opened it, and took out a ring which she handed to Litton. "The person in whom the organization is interested," she said, "was wearing this ring until four weeks ago. Since then it's been in a safe. The safe was opened yesterday and the ring taken from it and placed in this box. Would you consider it a suitable contact object?"

Litton held the ring in his palm an instant before replying. "Eminently suitable!" he said then.

"You can tell by touching such objects?"

"As a rule. If I get no impression, it's a waste of time to proceed. If I get a negative impression, I refuse to proceed."

"A negative impression?"

Litton shrugged. "A feeling of something that repels me. I can't describe it more definitely."

"Does that mean that the personality connected with the object is a repellent one?"

"Not necessarily. I've merged with some quite definitely repellent personalities in the course of this work. That doesn't disturb me. The feeling I speak of is a different one."

"It frightens you?"

"Perhaps." He smiled. "However, in this case there is no such feeling. Have you decided to offer me the assignment?" he asked.

"Yes, I have," Jean Merriam said. "Now then, I've been told nothing about the person connected with the ring. Since very few men could get it on, and very few children would wear a ring of such value, I assume the owner is a woman—but I don't know even that. The reason I've been told nothing is to make sure I'll give you no clues, inadvertently or otherwise." She smiled. "Even if you were a mind reader, you see, you could get no significant information from me. We want to be certain of the authenticity of your talent."

"I understand," Litton said. "But you must know what kind of information your organization wants to gain from the contact?"

Jean nodded. "Yes, of course. We want you to identify the subject by name and tell us where she can be found. The description of the locality should be specific. We also want to learn as much as we can about the subject's background, her present activities and interests, and any people with whom she is closely involved. The more details you can give us about such people, the better. In general, that's it. Does it seem like too difficult an assignment?"

"Not at all," Litton said. "In fact, I'm surprised you want no more. Is that kind of information really worth ten thousand dollars to you?"

"I've been told," Jean said, "that if we get it within the next twenty-four hours, it will be worth a great deal more than ten thousand dollars."

"I see." Litton settled comfortably in the chair, placed his clasped hands around the ring on the table, enclosing it. "Then, if you like, Miss Merriam, I'll now make the contact."

"No special preparations?" she inquired, watching him.

"Not in this case." Litton nodded toward a heavily curtained alcove in the wall on his left. "That's what I call my withdrawal room. When I feel there's reason to expect difficulties in making a contact,

I go in there. Observers can be disturbing under such circumstances. Otherwise, no preparations are necessary."

"What kind of difficulties could you encounter?" Jean asked.

"Mainly, the pull of personalities other than the one I want. A contact object may be valid, but contaminated by associations with other people. Then it's a matter of defining and following the strongest attraction, which is almost always that of the proper owner and our subject. Incidentally, it would be advantageous if you were prepared to record my report."

Jean tapped the handbag. "I'm recording our entire conversation, Mr. Litton."

He didn't seem surprised. "Very many of my clients do," he remarked. "Very well, then, let's begin . . ."

"How long did it take him to dream up this stuff?" Nick Garland asked.

"Four minutes and thirty-two seconds," Jean Merriam said.

Garland shook his head incredulously. He took the transcript she'd made of her recorded visit to Roy Litton's apartment from the desk and leafed through it again. Jean watched him, her face expressionless. Garland was a big gray-haired bear of a man, coldly irritable at present—potentially dangerous.

He laid the papers down, drummed his fingers on the desk. "I still don't want to believe it," he said, "but I guess I'll have to. He hangs on to Caryl Chase's ring for a few minutes, then he can tell you enough about her to fill five typed, single-spaced pages. . . That's what happened?"

Jean nodded. "Yes, that's what happened. He kept pouring out details about the woman as if he'd known her intimately half her life. He didn't hesitate about anything. My impression was that he wasn't guessing about anything. He seemed to know."

Garland grunted. "Max thinks he knew." He looked up at the man standing to the left of the desk. "Fill Jean in, Max. How accurate is Litton?"

Max Jewett said, "On every point we can check out, he's completely accurate."

"What are the points you can check out?" Jean asked.

"The ring belongs to Caryl Chase. She's thirty-two. She's Phil Chase's wife, currently estranged. She's registered at the Hotel Arve, Geneva, Switzerland, having an uneasy off-and-on affair with one William Haskell, British ski nut. He's jealous, and they fight a lot.

Caryl suspects Phil has detectives looking for her, which he does. Her daughter Ellie is hidden away with friends of Caryl's parents in London. Litton's right about the ring. Caryl got it from her grandmother on her twenty-first birthday and wore it since. When she ran out on Phil last month, she took it off and left it in her room safe. Litton's statement, that leaving it was a symbolic break with her past life, makes sense." Jewett shrugged. "That's about it. Her psychoanalyst might be able to check out some of the rest of what you got on tape. We don't have that kind of information."

Garland growled, "We don't need it. We got enough for now."

Jean exchanged a glance with Jewett. "You feel Litton's genuine, Mr. Garland?"

"He's genuine. Only Max and I knew we were going to test him on Caryl. If he couldn't do what he says he does, you wouldn't have got the tape. There's no other way he could know those things about her." Garland's face twisted into a sour grimace. "I thought Max had lost his marbles when he told me it looked like Phleger had got his information from some kind of swami. But that's how it happened. Frank Phleger got Litton to tap my mind something like two or three months ago. He'd need that much time to get set to make his first move."

"How much have you lost?" Jean asked.

He grunted. "Four, five million. I can't say definitely yet. That's not what bothers me." His mouth clamped shut, a pinched angry line. His eyes shifted bleakly down to the desk, grew remote, lost focus.

Jean Merriam watched him silently. Inside that big skull was stored information which seemed sometimes equal to the intelligence files of a central bank. Nick Garland's brain was a strategic computer, a legal library. He was a multimillionaire, a brutal genius, a solitary and cunning king beast in the financial jungle—a jungle he allowed to become barely aware he existed. Behind his secretiveness he remained an unassailable shadow. In the six years Jean had been working for him she'd never before seen him suffer a setback; but if they were right about Litton, this was more than a setback. Garland's mind had been opened, his plans analyzed, his strengths and weaknesses assessed by another solitary king beast—a lesser one, but one who knew exactly how to make the greatest possible use of the information thus gained—and who had begun to do it. So Jean waited and wondered.

"Jean," Garland said at last. His gaze hadn't shifted from the desk.

"Yes?"

"Did Litton buy your story about representing something like a detective agency?"

"He didn't seem to question it," Jean said. "My impression was that he doesn't particularly care who employs him, or for what purpose."

"He'll look into anyone's mind for a price?" It was said like a bitter curse.

"Yes . . . his price. What are you going to do?"

Garland's shoulders shifted irritably. "Max is trying to get a line on Phleger."

Jean glanced questioningly at Jewett. Jewett told her, "Nobody seems to have any idea where Frank Phleger's been for the past three weeks. We assume he dropped out of sight to avoid possible repercussions. The indications are that we're getting rather close to him."

"I see," Jean said uncomfortably. The king beasts avoided rough play as a matter of policy, usually avoided conflict among themselves, but when they met in a duel there were no rules.

"Give that part of it three days," Garland's voice said. She looked around, found him watching her with a trace of what might be irony, back at any rate from whatever brooding trance he'd been sunk in. "Jean, call Litton sometime tomorrow."

"All right."

"Tell him the boss of your detective organization wants an appointment with him. Ten o'clock, three days from now."

She nodded, said carefully, "Litton could become extremely valuable to you, Mr. Garland."

"He could," Garland agreed. "Anyway, I want to watch the swami perform. We'll give him another assignment."

"Am I to accompany you?"

"You'll be there, Jean. So will Max."

"I keep having the most curiously definitive impression," Roy Litton observed, "that I've met you before."

"You have," Garland said amiably.

Litton frowned, shook his head. "It's odd I should have forgotten the occasion!"

"The name's Nick Garland," Garland told him.

Still frowning, Litton stared at him across the table. Then abruptly his face paled. Jean Merriam, watching from behind her employer, saw Litton's eyes shift to her, from her to Max Jewett, and return at last, hesitantly, to Garland's face. Garland nodded wryly.

"I was what you call one of your subjects, Mr. Litton," he said. "I can't give you the exact date, but it should have been between two and three months ago. You remember now?"

Litton shook his head. "No. After such an interval it would be impossible to be definite about it, in any case. I keep no notes and the details of a contact very quickly grow blurred to me." His voice was guarded; he kept his eyes on Garland's. "Still, you seemed familiar to me at once as a person. And your name seems familiar. It's quite possible that you have been, in fact, a contact subject."

"I was," Garland said. "We know that. That's why we're here."

Litton cleared his throat. "Then the story Miss Merriam told me at her first visit wasn't true."

"Not entirely," Garland admitted. "She wasn't representing a detective outfit. She represented me. Otherwise, she told the truth. She was sent here to find out whether you could do what we'd heard you could do. We learned that you could. Mr. Litton, you've cost me a great deal of money. But I'm not too concerned about that now, because, with your assistance, I'll make it back. And I'll make a great deal more besides. You begin to get the picture?"

Relief and wariness mingled for an instant in Litton's expression. "Yes, I believe I do."

"You'll get paid your regular fees, of course," Garland told him. "The fact is, Mr. Litton, you don't charge enough. What you offer is worth more than ten thousand a shot. What you gave Frank Phleger was worth enormously more."

"Frank Phleger?" Litton said.

"The client who paid you to poke around in my mind. No doubt he wouldn't have used his real name. It doesn't matter. Let's get on to your first real assignment for me. Regular terms. This one isn't a test. It's to bring up information I don't have and couldn't get otherwise. All right?"

Litton nodded, smiled. "You have a suitable contact object?"

"We brought something that should do," Garland said. "Max, give Mr. Litton the belt."

Jean Merriam looked back toward Jewett. Garland hadn't told her what Litton's assignment was to be, had given her no specific instructions, but she'd already turned on the recorder in her handbag. Jewett was taking a large plastic envelope from the briefcase he'd laid beside his chair. He came over to the table, put the envelope before Litton, and returned to his place.

"Can you tell me specifically what you want to know concerning this subject?" Litton asked.

"To start with," Garland said, "just give us whatever you can get. I'm interested in general information."

Litton nodded, opened the plastic envelope and took out a man's leather belt with a broad silver buckle. Almost immediately an expression of distaste showed in his face. He put the belt on the table, looked over at Garland.

"Mr. Garland," he said, "Miss Merriam may have told you that on occasion I'm offered a contact object I can't use. Unfortunately, this belt is such an object."

"What do you mean?" Garland asked. "Why can't you use it?"

"I don't know. It may be something about the belt itself, and it may be the person connected with it." Litton brushed the belt with his fingers. "I simply have a very unpleasant feeling about this object. It repels me." He smiled apologetically. "I'm afraid I must refuse to work with it."

"Well, now," Garland said, "I don't like to hear that. You've cost me a lot, you know. I'm willing to overlook it, but I do expect you to be cooperative in return."

Litton glanced at him, swallowed uneasily. "I understand—and I assure you you'll find me cooperative. If you'll give me some other assignment, I assure you—"

"No," Garland said. "No, right now I want information about this particular person, not somebody else. It's too bad if you don't much like to work with the belt, but that's your problem. We went to a lot of trouble to get the belt for you. Let me state this quite clearly, Mr. Litton. You owe me the information, and I think you'd better get it now."

His voice remained even, but the menace in the words was undisguised. The king beast was stepping out from cover; and Jean's palms were suddenly wet. She saw Litton's face whiten.

"I suppose I do owe it to you," Litton said after a moment. He hesitated again. "But this isn't going to be easy."

Garland snorted. "You're getting ten thousand dollars for a few minutes' work!"

"That isn't it. I . . . ." Litton shook his head helplessly, got to his feet. He indicated the curtained alcove at the side of the room. "I'll go in there. At best, this will be a difficult contact to attempt. I can't be additionally distracted by knowing that three people are staring at me."

"You'll get the information?" Garland asked.

Litton looked at him, said sullenly, "I always get the information." He picked up the belt, went to the alcove, and disappeared through the curtains.

Garland turned toward Jean Merriam. "Start timing him," he said.

She nodded, checked her watch. The room went silent, and immediately Jean felt a heavy oppression settle on her. It was almost as if the air had begun to darken around them. Frightened, she thought, *Nick hates that freak. . . Has he decided to kill him?*

She pushed the question away and narrowed her attention to the almost inaudible ticking of the tiny expensive watch. After a while she realized that Garland was looking at her again. She met his eyes, whispered, "Three minutes and ten seconds." He nodded.

There was a sound from within the alcove. It was not particularly loud, but in the stillness it was startling enough to send a new gush of fright through Jean. She told herself some minor piece of furniture, a chair, a small side table, had fallen over, been knocked over on the carpeting. She was trying to think of some reason why Litton should have knocked over a chair in there when the curtains before the alcove were pushed apart. Litton moved slowly out into the room.

He stopped a few feet from the alcove. He appeared dazed, half-stunned, like a man who'd been slugged hard in the head and wasn't sure what had happened. His mouth worked silently, his lips writhing in slow, stiff contortions as if trying to shape words that couldn't be pronounced. Abruptly he started forward. Jean thought for a moment he was returning to the table, but he went past it, pace quickening, on past Garland and herself without glancing at either of them. By then he was almost running, swaying from side to side in long staggering steps, and she realized he was hurrying toward the French doors which stood open on the wide veranda overlooking the park. Neither Garland nor Jewett moved from their chairs, and Jean, unable to speak, twisted around to look after Litton as they were doing. She saw him run across the veranda, strike the hip-high railing without checking, and go on over.

The limousine moved away from the Torrell Arms through the sunlit park, Jewett at the wheel, Garland and Jean Merriam in the back seat. There was no siren wail behind them, no indication of disturbance, nothing to suggest that anyone else was aware that a few minutes ago a man had dropped into the neatly trimmed park shrubbery from the eighteenth floor of the great apartment hotel.

"You could have made use of him," Jean said. "He could have been of more value to you than anyone else in the world. But you intended to kill him from the start, didn't you?"

Garland didn't reply for a moment. Then he said, "I could have made use of him, sure. So could anyone else with ten thousand dollars to spare, or some way to put pressure on him. I don't need somebody like Litton to stay on top. And I don't like the rules changed. When Phleger found Litton, he started changing them. It could happen again. Litton had to be taken out."

"Max could have handled that," Jean said. Her hands had begun to tremble again; she twisted them tightly together around the strap of the handbag. "What did you do to get Litton to kill himself?"

Garland shook his head. "I didn't intend him to kill himself. Max was to take care of him afterward."

"You did something to him."

Garland drew a long sighing breath. "I was just curious," he said. "There's something I wonder about now and then. I thought Litton might be able to tell me, so I gave him the assignment."

"What assignment? He became someone else for three minutes. What happened to him?"

Garland's head turned slowly toward her. She noticed for the first time that his face was almost colorless. "That was Frank Phleger's belt," he said. "Max's boys caught up with him last night. Phleger's been dead for the last eight hours."

The Vultures of Malabar

by Edward D. Hoch

"**I**n Bombay they don't always bury or cremate their dead," Simon Ark said as our plane passed over the sprawling harbor city on India's west coast and came in for a perfect landing at Santa Cruz Airport. "Bodies are sometimes left to be devoured by vultures."

"You can't be serious!" I protested. Visions of corpses in the streets filled my mind. Simon had persuaded me to accompany him to Bombay with the promise that we'd be meeting some of the leaders of India's thriving film industry. Now it seemed more likely we'd be fighting off vultures on their way to an evening meal.

"It's quite true," Simon insisted as our plane taxied to a stop at the ramp. "The Parsis, who came here from Persia, are followers of the Zoroastrian religion. Their religious beliefs forbid both burial and cremation because they defile the sacred elements of earth, fire, and water."

"But *vultures*, Simon?"

"You'll be meeting some of the Parsi community tomorrow, my friend. You can judge for yourself."

We traveled from the airport through the crowded streets of Bombay to the Taj Mahal Intercontinental Hotel, where I'd reserved adjoining rooms for us in the modern wing. It was a great old structure dating from 1903, and somehow it made me think of the years of British rule in India—the benevolent Raj which had faded away with the twilight of empire. I left Simon at the door to his room and wondered once again what I was doing there.

Come to Bombay and meet the movie people, Simon had said, and it had sounded fine at the time. Neptune Books was looking for someone to write an authoritative volume on the Indian film industry for a series of cinema books I was editing. It was an opportunity to do some work while spending a week with Simon. I saw him all too rarely these days, especially since my wife Shelly had taken an active dislike to him.

"The man is an anachronism," she'd insisted one night over dinner. "He claims to be two thousand years old, but he doesn't have to act so much like he's living in the past! This is the twentieth century—almost the twenty-first! We care about inflation and energy and nuclear war, not about confronting the devil or seeking out ghosts or finding a unicorn! If the devil is still around, he probably wears a suit and tie and holds down a nine-to-five job in New York."

"Not in publishing, I hope." I'd learned to take Shelly's occasional outbursts calmly, especially on the subject of Simon Ark.

But in spite of Shelly's outbursts, or partly because of them, here I was in Bombay with Simon, gazing out the hotel window at a world I'd never seen before. A hot dry April breeze blew in off the sea. I knew what had brought me to Bombay, but I still didn't know what had brought Simon Ark here.

After a good night's rest to recover from jet lag, Simon and I boarded a black-and-yellow taxi at the stand outside the hotel. "What are those men doing?" I asked the driver as we pulled away from the curb, pointing to a pair of brightly turbaned natives who seemed to be peering into the ears of passers-by.

The driver, who spoke the careful English of India under the British Empire, explained. "They are kan-saf wallas—professional ear-cleaners. For about six cents in your money they will gently remove wax from the ear, using a small silver spoon, warm mustard oil, and wisps of cotton."

"I guess I've seen everything now," I said.

But Simon was more interested in our destination than in the ear-cleaners. "We'll be meeting with members of the Sanjan family. They are very active in the Bombay film industry, and I believe they'll be of great help to you."

"And to you, Simon? You didn't fly halfway around the world for your health. What is it here you seek?"

"I always seek the same thing, my friend, though it comes in different guises."

"The devil? Evil?"

"Perhaps only human greed. One never knows."

I'd expected the taxi to take us to one of the film studios or perhaps to the Pali Hill region, where many of the top stars had luxurious homes, but the cab circled Back Bay along the main promenade of Marine Drive and approached the wealthy area of high-rise apartments that was Malabar Hill. When I questioned Simon he merely smiled and said, "No movie stars today. That will come later. The Sanjan family are the backers, the moneyed people. They live here."

We took the elevator to the tenth floor. "Welcome, welcome," an elderly man said, opening an apartment door and beckoning us inside.

Simon introduced me and told him of my interest in a book about the Indian film industry. "This is Dilip Sanjan. He knows more about films than any other man in Bombay."

Sanjan was short and vigorous, though I guessed his age to be well into the seventies. He looked toward the living room and a woman came forward. "My wife, Reba," he said. She seemed no more than forty, and her beauty was striking. I was not at all surprised when he added, "Reba was a star in several pictures before we married."

While Reba brought us refreshments Sanjan and Simon settled down to talk. "Simon and I knew each other fifty years ago," the Indian told me. "When this present trouble arose, he was the only person I could turn to. He is an expert on Satanic rites."

I grinned at Simon and asked, "Did he look the same fifty years ago, Mr. Sanjan?"

"The same, yes. A bit older, if anything. What is the secret of your longevity, Simon?"

"Vitamins," Simon replied with a smile. "But let us get to the matter at hand. You have an unusual problem, Dilip." As he spoke, Simon's eyes followed Reba while she moved to open a sliding glass door onto the balcony.

"As I told you on the telephone, my old friend, it concerns the *dakhmas*."

"Explain them to my friend here."

Sanjan turned to me. "We are Parsis, followers of Zoroaster the prophet. Clustered at the top of Malabar Hill are seven circular enclosures, walled but roofless, where our dead are left to be devoured by vultures. These are called *dakhmas*, or towers of silence. There is a double door in the wall of each tower through which a team of four professional pallbearers, clad all in white, carries the body of the deceased. The towers are kept locked and no one else may enter them. The body is laid out naked on a circular stone platform about thirty yards in diameter. The platform slopes gently toward a central pit, and at a later date the pallbearers return to push any remaining bones into the pit."

"Simon told me about the custom," I admitted, repressing a shudder. It was their religion, after all. "Are there still many vultures in Bombay?"

"Enough. We have our reform element, of course, who claim the vulture population is declining and the dead should be cremated. But I can tell you, when a fresh corpse is carried into the *dakhmas* there are usually several dozen of the birds in attendance."

"You speak from personal experience?"

Simon Ark interrupted. "Dilip is a hereditary pallbearer."

The old man bowed slightly in acknowledgment. "As were my father and grandfather before me." He turned his attention to Simon. "The custom has not changed since we talked of it some fifty years ago, Simon. But now something new and troublesome has occurred. Someone is entering the towers for an unauthorized purpose."

"You told me that much on the telephone," Simon said. "But how is this possible? Have the door locks been tampered with?"

"No, they have not. But remember that the seven walled enclosures are open to the sky, and hidden by dense vegetation which grows quite close to the walls. The walls are over twenty feet high, but a person could reach the top by climbing a nearby tree, then lower himself inside on a rope. A rope was found hanging from one of the branches."

"What about the vultures?" I asked.

"They do not bother the living."

Simon leaned forward. "How do you know of this intruder?"

"One of the pallbearers, Vija Rau, went to a *dakhma* a few days ago to push bones into the central pit. He surprised a man inside—a man bent over studying the bones as if he were looking for something significant. He leaped upon Vija, stabbed him in the side, and escaped through the open door."

"Is Vija alive?"

"Yes. He is recovering in hospital."

"I will want to speak with him," Simon said. "What other evidence is there of—"

He was interrupted by a sudden gasp from Reba. She dashed across the room to the balcony, and I caught just a glimpse of a great black-winged bird poised on the railing, then it was gone. Reba let out a shriek. We ran to her side and followed her horrified gaze to the floor of the balcony.

What was lying there I didn't recognize at first. And then I realized that the great black vulture, startled by Reba, had dropped the thing from its beak as it flew away.

It was a human finger.

At the hospital Simon and I waited to see the wounded Vija Rau. I had still not fully recovered from the incident on the Sanjans' balcony, but Simon was inclined to take it in stride. "After all, the vultures are only behaving in their natural manner. No human or animal can ever be criticized for that. The Parsis place the bodies on the *dakhmas* to be devoured, and the vultures do their job. If one occasionally leaves the dinner table with a piece of its meal, who are we to criticize? Dilip tells me this sort of thing has happened before, and I'm sure it will happen again."

"I hope I'm gone from here when it does."

We were admitted to Rau's hospital room.

The Indian was a young man with a ready smile. He sat up in bed to greet us, though his left side still seemed to pain him a bit. "Dilip Sanjan told me you would come," he said, extending a hand. "I will be out of here in a few days. It was a foolish thing."

"A knife wound is never foolish," Simon told him. "The man might have killed you."

"I was so startled to find him in the *dakhma* that I inadvertently blocked his exit. I don't think he meant to harm me—only to escape."

"The doctor says the wound could have been fatal," Simon persisted. "Did you recognize the man?"

"Not by name, but he looked familiar. It was so unreal—as if I were seeing a film."

"Had you ever encountered an intruder there before?"

"Certainly not! The *dakhmas* are sacred places!"

"And there was nothing of value on the bodies?"

The wounded man shook his head. "They are laid out naked for the vultures. No clothing, no jewelry. In the case of Indu, I personally prepared his body, removing his ring and emptying his pockets after the body was delivered to us. He had a few trinkets—a little silver spoon, some gold coins—nothing more."

"And nothing remains in the *dakhmas* but bones?"

"Nothing."

"Who was this Indu person?" Simon asked.

"Indu Sanjan, a younger cousin. There is much intermarriage, and most Parsis are somehow related. Indu did odd jobs for Dilip's son, Dom Sanjan, at the film studio, but they were not especially close."

"Is the Sanjan studio successful?"

Vija Rau shrugged. "It is small."

"What did Indu die of?"

"An auto accident. He was struck by a hit-and-run driver while crossing the street near the Taj Mahal Hotel."

A nurse arrived to cut short our visit, and we said goodbye as she led us out.

"Did you learn anything?" I asked Simon as we reached the street.

"Not a great deal, my friend. It seems likely that Indu Sanjan was murdered by the hit-and-run driver, but that doesn't explain what someone wanted with his bones."

"You think it was for some sort of devil worship?"

Simon merely smiled. "Never invoke the bizarre until you have exhausted the mundane, my friend."

We went next to call on a film distributor who handled the output of Sanjan's studio. His name was Rudyard Chambers, and his traditional British bearing showed little trace of the Indian mother who Simon assured me had borne him. "Simon Ark," he said, repeating the name. "Yes, Dilip has mentioned you."

"I come as a friend of his," Simon assured him. "I am carrying out an investigation on his behalf. But you must realize there are some questions more easily asked an outsider."

"Of course."

"What can you tell me about Dilip's film-making operations?"

"You must realize first of all that Dilip Sanjan is something of an outsider here. The Bombay film industry is almost exclusively Hindu. So much so, in fact, that production of a new motion picture often starts with a sacred Hindu fire ceremony on the set. Sanjan's Parsi community is Zoroastrian, of course, not Hindu—an entirely different religion in a country where religion is still very important. The Parsis have excelled in shipbuilding, commerce, and industry, but there are few of them in the film business. Sanjan's little studio is unique."

"Has there ever been a hint of anything outside the law?"

"Never, to my knowledge. His pictures are small but quite respectable. He employs mainly actors from his own community, though he also sometimes hires Hindus."

Simon seemed satisfied with the information, though I couldn't see that it was leading us anywhere. Chambers saw us to the door and promised to help us in any way he could.

It was late afternoon when we returned to the hotel, and I was startled to see Reba Sanjan waiting for us in the lobby. Her face was drawn and anxious, and my first thought was that something had happened to her husband. But it was not Sanjan she had come about.

"Vija Rau was stabbed to death in his hospital bed!" she told us, so excitably we could barely catch the words. "An hour after you visited him!"

Simon Ark reached out to steady her. "Do they know who did it?"

"No—someone must have slipped past the nurse's desk!"

"Did your husband send you here?"

She nodded. "He blames himself. He says Vija would still be alive if he hadn't summoned you."

Simon took a deep breath. "We must visit the tower of silence where Vija was wounded."

"It will be dark soon—There are no lights—"

"In the morning, then. Can you arrange it?"

"Only the hereditary pallbearers may enter the *dakhmas*."

"I know that." He repeated his question. "Can you arrange it?"

"Only by stealing my husband's key to the locked doors."

"Do it, then, before there are more deaths."

She sighed and nodded. "What time will you be there?"

"Nine o'clock. Meet us at the foot of Malabar Hill."

"That may be difficult. There is a funeral scheduled for that hour." Simon hesitated.

"Vija Rau's," she reminded him.

We dined at the hotel, in a surprisingly westernized setting with authentic French foods and wines. From down the hall came the familiar sounds of a discotheque. "Western culture is found everywhere," I commented with a wry grin.

Old Sanjan had invited us to a studio party and film screening that evening, but he phoned after dinner to say he'd be unable to attend because of Rau's death. He urged us to go without him, saying his son, Dom, was expecting us.

Simon and I arrived around eight. The party was being held on the elaborate roof garden of the studio office building. One could walk among flowers and trees while commanding a striking view of the city's skyline by night. There were perhaps a hundred people at the party, representing a side of Bombay's culture we hadn't seen before. Many of the women were fashionably dressed in western style, though a few wore traditional saris. Some, in what seemed a compromise, wore saris over low-cut strapless gowns.

One girl in her twenties wore a striking arrangement of gold jewelry that hung from her left earlobe. She asked me, "Are you alone?"

"No, I'm with that gentleman in black."

She eyed Simon critically. "Is he a priest?"

"Of a sort," I sipped my drink. "Are you Hindu or Parsi?"

She giggled and pointed to the red *tika* mark in the center of her forehead. "Hindu. I thought everyone knew that! But there are many Parsis here tonight. They are very successful in the business world. Do you know Dom Sanjan?"

"No, I'm a friend of his father." I told her my name.

"I'm Sushi Mahim. Come along and I'll introduce you to Dom."

Sanjan's son was a tall light-skinned Indian in a grey business suit. He was about my age and he shook my hand vigorously. "I have already met Simon Ark," he said in the perfect English to which I'd become accustomed since our arrival. "I hope you enjoy yourself."

"It's too bad your father couldn't attend."

Dom Sanjan nodded sadly. "Two deaths in the family are a terrible blow. Vija Rau was not really related, but he and my father were hereditary pallbearers together."

"The other dead man, Indu Sanjan, worked for you?"

"Occasionally he did odd jobs at the studio. I told Simon I saw the car hit him. I was the first to reach his body. I tried to apply artificial respiration, but it was too late." He glanced at a younger group with some annoyance, moving us away from the noticeably sweet odor of marijuana. "But what brings you to Bombay?"

"I'm the senior editor of a New York publishing house. We're doing a series of books on films around the world and I want to include a volume on the Indian film industry."

"Speak to Sushi here. She is a script girl at the Hindi Studios, the largest in India."

"Is that right?"

"We make nearly two hundred films a year," she answered proudly. "About one-third of India's total output."

"I was thinking Dilip Sanjan might write a book about the Indian film industry."

"But his view is so limited!" she insisted. "He is not Hindu."

"You have a point."

"The Parsis are businessmen, not artists. They barter in diamonds and drillheads—not in dreams."

Simon Ark had moved over to join us. "Very poetic," he told her.

Before she could answer, Dom Sanjan took us both by the arm. "We must go downstairs. The screening is about to begin."

Like most Indian films, it lasted nearly three hours. A complicated plot was broken at frequent intervals by singing and dancing, and the audience seemed to enjoy it. Sushi sat between Simon and me, translating in a low voice when she thought it might be necessary. At the evening's end she promised to put me in touch with a woman at her studio about the book.

On the way back to the hotel, around midnight, I commented, "At least I have a line on an author. But the evening contributed nothing toward your investigation, Simon."

"On the contrary, my friend. It may have contributed a bit."

That was all he would say.

We were out early the following morning, eating a quick breakfast and taking one of the black-and-yellow taxis to the foot of Malabar Hill. As we approached we saw several cars of a funeral procession starting up the winding road.

"Follow along behind," Simon instructed the driver.

When we reached the summit we left the taxi and followed a line of white-clad mourners through the dense vegetation. In the lead were four men carrying a sort of stretcher on which the body was covered by a sheet. In their white shoes, white suits, and white caps, they reminded me of ambulance attendants removing an accident victim to the hospital rather than pallbearers carrying the deceased to his final bizarre resting place.

The procession of mourners paused before a high curving wall almost hidden by the bushes and trees. A key was inserted in the lock of the double metal doors and they swung open. A woman wept and moaned as the pallbearers entered the tower with their burden. Overhead I heard the flapping of wings and glanced up to see great black vultures settling onto the rim of the wall.

After a few moments the pallbearers came out with the sheet folded neatly on the stretcher and the procession started back down the hill. But suddenly Reba Sanjan detached herself from the line of mourners and hurried over to us.

"Here is the key," she whispered, producing it from within the folds of her white sari. "Be careful."

"Which tower was Rau in when he was attacked?" Simon asked.

"The next one along, to the right." Then she was gone, hurrying after the others.

We waited until they were out of sight and then went along the path to the next walled enclosure. From the outside it seemed identical with the first one, though I was glad to see no vultures hovering over this one. They were otherwise occupied for the moment.

"What do you expect to find here, Simon?" I asked.

"The person who stabbed Rau was obviously interrupted. If he feared recognition enough to kill Rau at the hospital, he may have been afraid to return here. Perhaps we may still find what he was seeking."

"What is there but bones? Didn't Sanjan summon you because he believed someone wanted bones for a Satanic rite of some sort?"

"There are easier ways to obtain bones. The evidence here points to something else."

"But the body was naked, Simon! And the vultures eat everything *but* the bones!"

"Let us see, my friend." He fitted the big old key into the lock and turned it. The metal door swung open on squeaky hinges. Simon left the key in the lock and we entered the sacred place.

The morning sun had just cleared the top of the enclosure's far wall, blinding us for an instant with its brilliance. We shielded our eyes and moved slowly around the circular stone platform, carefully avoiding the bone pit at the center. The platform was nearly empty, with only a few scattered bones to serve as reminders of its purpose. I was thankful at least that there was no recent arrival there to greet us. But almost at once, as Simon bent to examine the remaining bones, shadows began to darken the sky.

"Vultures, Simon."

"They think we bring them a repast."

"Aren't they satisfied with the one next door? Let's go!"

"Vultures do not bother the living."

As they swooped low above my head I wasn't so sure. "Maybe they can't tell the difference."

But Simon ignored them and went on with his search. When he'd circled the stone platform he turned his attention to the bone pit itself. The bottom was lined with skulls and bones, probably several feet deep. "You're certainly not going down there, Simon!"

"No, my friend." He glanced at the sky. "But let us wait here a bit."

"For what?"

"Perhaps the sun will do our searching for us."

"The sun?"

"In less than an hour it should be high enough to shine directly into the pit."

"You mean we have to stay here for an hour?"

"Perhaps by that time you'll grow to love the vultures."

"I doubt it."

But we waited. I couldn't imagine what he expected the sun to reveal, but we waited.

"It would not have been too difficult for the mysterious assailant to lower himself on a rope and escape the same way," Simon observed.

"If anyone was crazy enough to want to." I glanced up at the vultures, who had retreated to the top of the wall. "What about the rope the assailant left behind after he stabbed Rau? Is there any clue there?"

"Not according to Dilip Sanjan. It was a common sort of rope, a kind sold everywhere."

I was growing more restless by the minute. "Wouldn't we be better off investigating Rau's murder at the hospital?"

"His murder began here. It only ended at the hospital."

Presently he walked to the edge of the pit to observe the sun's progress on the bleached bones below. "Do you see anything yet?" I asked.

"No," he admitted. "Let us give it five more minutes, until the sun reaches the far side."

"Do you think the intruder might have had a key, like we did?"

"If he had, he wouldn't have needed the rope, would he?"

"I suppose not."

Suddenly Simon gripped my shoulder. "There! Look there!"

I followed his pointing finger, but all I saw was the glimmer of something reflecting the sun. "What is it? A piece of glass?"

Before he could answer, there was a clanging sound behind us. Simon spun around, shouting, "The key!" I dashed to the metal doors, but it was too late. I heard the key turn in the lock.

"Someone's locked us in, Simon!"

"So it seems."

At first we tried shouting and pounding on the doors. Then I boosted Simon up on my shoulders and he attempted to reach the top of the wall. But his groping fingers were several feet short of their goal.

"Can you get a grip?" I asked. Simon felt around, but the old wall was too smooth to provide a hand- or foothold. He came down to the ground again. I settled back beside him. "Who would do this? Rau's killer?"

"No doubt. I should have realized he would return after the funeral to have another search for his treasure."

"What treasure? That bit of glass in the pit?"

"Unless I am mistaken, my friend, that bit of glass is a diamond."

"A diamond! But how did it get here? Sanjan told us the dead were stripped of all clothing and jewelry before being laid out for the vultures."

"And so they are. The diamond—if that's what it is—was inside the body of the dead man."

I stared at him.

"Don't you see, my friend? When Vija Rau told us he surprised his attacker going through the bones of the man Indu, I suspected it had to be because Indu had something inside his body the killer wanted. Last night before the film showing I overheard that young woman Sushi mention that Parsis sometimes dealt in diamonds. That was the first mention of diamonds, but it was enough to give me something to look for."

"What if the vultures have swallowed the diamond—if there was one—or carried it away?"

"Perhaps they have. Indu himself might have swallowed several before he was killed by that car. But I do think at least one of them is down in that bone pit."

"Well, it's nice knowing I'm going to die so close to a diamond," I said.

"You won't die," he assured me.

"No? Then suppose you tell me how we're going to get out of here? We're locked in an enclosure with a solid twenty-foot wall all around, on top of a hill where no one comes and no one could hear if we were to set up a shout. And I'm sure that if we were to fall asleep those vultures would start pecking at us."

"You're needlessly upset," Simon said. "There are at least three ways out of here if you stop to think about it."

"I'll settle for one."

"Very well. Take off your shirt, please, and give it to me."

"My shirt?" I exclaimed and did as he said.

"Now give me your cigarette lighter."

I've virtually stopped smoking but I still carry a lighter. I handed it over and watched as he weighted the shirt with a piece of bone from the platform. Then he flicked the lighter and held the flame to the shirt. It took a moment to catch fire, and another moment before the flames spread, then he handed it quickly to me.

"Your throwing arm is better than mine. Hurl it over the wall. As high as you can."

"But—"

"Quickly!"

I threw the flaming shirt with its bone weight, and watched it clear the wall.

"Are you trying to burn us up before the vultures get at us?"

"I hope so," he replied seriously. "The vegetation seemed quite dry when we were outside."

"Do you think it's catching onto anything out there?"

"If it doesn't, we'll try again with my shirt."

But a wisp of smoke soon appeared above the wall, and we could hear the crackling of dry underbrush. "What if no one comes to our rescue, Simon?" I asked.

"We're perfectly safe in here. The entire hilltop could burn without getting through these walls. But it should bring the fire department before long, and they'll get us out of here. I only hope they're Hindu firemen and not Parsi, or they may not want to enter here."

Simon was right again. The fire department arrived within twenty minutes. And they were Hindu.

Back at the hotel, I dug another shirt out of my suitcase. "What were the other two ways we could have escaped, Simon?"

"There is no time for that now. We still have a murderer to catch."

"Where do we start looking?"

"I would suggest right in front of this hotel, my friend. It was there that Indu was run down by the car, you'll remember."

"I wonder what he was doing there."

"We know that, too, if you will only think about it. He was found with a tiny silver spoon in his pocket, yes?"

"For narcotics?"

"No—for cleaning out ears."

And then I remembered the professional ear-cleaners we'd observed on our arrival, working near the hotel's taxi stand.

We went down to the stand and observed the ear-cleaners for a time. "What do you hope to see, Simon?" I asked.

"Time will tell."

We had used the firemen's ladder to retrieve the diamond from the bone pit at the *dakhma*, and it now rested in Simon's pocket. I knew he was waiting for something or someone, but I couldn't guess what or who. "How do you know it'll happen today?"

"Because he thinks we're still up there, trapped and dying."

"But all I see are passersby having their ears cleaned out."

"An Indian custom, surely. But look at that man there. He's no Indian."

I followed Simon's gaze to a well-dressed man of vaguely Germanic features. The ear-cleaner had pushed aside his long blond hair to get at the ear. "You're right, Simon. It does seem odd."

"More than odd. Come on!"

I followed him across the sidewalk and watched in astonishment as he gripped the hand of the ear-cleaner. "Call a police officer," he said to me. "Quickly!"

But suddenly a familiar figure had materialized at our side. It was Sanjan's son, Dom Sanjan. "What's the trouble here? Can I be of service?"

There was a moment of confusion, with Dom Sanjan reaching his arm toward Simon. Then I saw Simon falling, and heard the screech of brakes. I acted faster than I'd have thought possible, yanking Simon to safety as a car sped past us.

"Never mind me," Simon ordered. "Don't let him get away!"

"Who?"

"Dom Sanjan! He's the man behind these murders!"

The events of the next few hours tumbled over one another. We held Dom Sanjan for the police, and very quickly they also rounded up the ear-cleaner and the Germanic customer and the man who'd been driving the car that almost hit Simon. We were at the police station near our hotel, telling the authorities what we knew, when old Dilip Sanjan arrived with his wife.

"What is this, Simon? Did I summon you halfway around the world to bring disgrace to my family?"

"I am sorry, old friend," Simon told him. "I would have wished it to be otherwise."

"Dom cannot be involved."

"He is very much involved. Sit down and I will tell you."

The old man sat, and Simon began to speak, telling it as he had told the police not an hour earlier. "It was diamonds, it was all for diamonds. A clever smuggling operation involving a pipeline from

South Africa. The Germanic-looking man was a South African, one of several who smuggled the diamonds out of the mines and into India. Their system was next to foolproof. The South African hid the diamonds in his ears, wearing his hair long to further conceal them. Outside our hotel he visited one of the professional ear-cleaners, who removed the diamonds while doing his cleaning. The diamonds were then passed to Dom Sanjan who, I suspect, sent them to their ultimate destination inside film cans shipped from your company."

"I can't believe that!" Dilip protested.

"Let Simon speak," Reba said, resting her hand on his arm.

"But somehow Indu betrayed the gang and started keeping some diamonds for himself and Dom Sanjan had him run down by a car and killed. The diamonds he was carrying were not found, though, and it was not until after the funeral that your son and his cohorts realized Indu had been in the habit of swallowing the gems after removing them from the ears of the smugglers. So one of the gang was sent to search the *dakhma* for the remains of Indu Sanjan. It was while he was looking for diamonds among Indu's bones that Vija Rau surprised him and was stabbed."

"But why was Rau later killed at the hospital?" Reba asked.

"He told me that seeing the intruder crouched among the bones in the *dakhma* was like viewing a film. It seemed that way, I suspect, because the intruder was a young actor who worked with Dom at the studio. He couldn't risk Rau identifying him later. It was this same man who drove the car that killed Indu and almost hit me today."

"It is a good story," Dilip said. "But what evidence is there to implicate my son?"

"He tried to push me in front of the car today when I caught the diamonds being passed. That is enough evidence for the police. For myself, there is the simple fact: the *dakhma* intruder had to know the diamonds were inside Indu when he died and not simply in his pockets. The only person who could have told him that with assurance was your son Dom, who admitted he was the first to reach Indu's body after the accident. He even told of applying artificial respiration—hardly a wise maneuver after a traffic accident when there could be broken bones and internal injuries. But it helped disguise Dom's real purpose while he searched the dead man for the diamonds. I'm sorry, Dilip, there were other things pointing to your son as well."

"Such as?"

"Rau half remembered his assailant from a film and Indu worked at the studio for your son. Dom was the most likely link between the men. You or Reba could not have been involved because then the *dakhma* intruder could have used a key instead of a rope to enter the enclosure and search for the diamonds."

Dilip Sanjan had little more to say, and within the hour his son Dom had confessed to the charges, even admitting he'd been the one to lock us in the *dakhma*.

Later, Reba found us alone and said, "You have brought my husband great sadness, but you have brought him truth as well. It is better for him to know the human greed that defiled our dead than to conjure up demons where none existed."

I saw Sushi's friend the following morning and arranged for the book on Indian films. Then Simon and I flew home from Bombay. Shelly met us at the airport—I didn't tell her about the vultures.

A Matter of Gravity

by Randall Garrett

The death of My Lord Jillbert, Count de la Vexin, was nothing if not spectacular.

His Lordship lived and worked in Castle Gisors, which towers over the town of the same name, the capital of the County of the Vexin, in the eastern part of the Duchy of Normandy. The basic structure of the ancient fortress has been there since the Eleventh Century, although it has been added to and partly rebuilt since.

De la Vexin had succeeded to the County Seat in 1951, and had governed the Vexin wisely and well. He had a son, a daughter, and a hobby.

It was a combination of all these that killed him.

On the night of April 11, 1974, after attending the Mass of Holy Thursday, My Lord of the Vexin ascended the helical stairway that wound itself around the inside of the Red Tower, followed by two trusted sergeants of the Count's Own Guard—who were, in turn, followed by a four-man squad of ordinary guardsmen.

This was My Lord Count's regular procedure when he went to his *sanctum sanctorum* on the top floor of the Red Tower. When he went up there, eighty feet above the flagstoned courtyard, he wanted no interruptions while he attended to his avocation.

At one minute of ten, he entered his private rooms, leaving his guardsmen outside. No one but himself had been authorized to enter the uppermost room of the Red Tower in twenty years.

He dropped the heavy bar after locking the door, completely sealing the room.

Only two people saw him alive again, and then only for a matter of seconds.

Across the wide, flagstoned courtyard from the Red Tower stood St. Martin's Hall, a new addition built in the early Sixteenth Century, as its Ricardian style attested. Its great mullioned windows cast a warm, yellowed light on the courtyard outside; the hall was

95

brightly illuminated from within, and would remain so all night, for there was a vigil at the Altar of Repose in the Lady Chapel.

Inside, a small fire crackled in the enormous fireplace—just enough blaze to take the slight chill from the air of a pleasant spring evening. On the mantelpiece, a large clock swung its pendulum as the minute hand moved inexorably upward to mark the hour of ten.

Lord Gisors, the only son of de la Vexin, poured himself another glass of Xerez. Of average height, his blocky, not unhandsome face was almost a younger replica of his father's, except that he had his mother's near-black hair and dark brown eyes instead of the brown-and-blue combination of his father. He turned from the sideboard, still holding the unstoppered decanter. "Care for another, my dear?"

The girl seated in the big easy chair in front of the fireplace smiled. "Please." With her right hand, she held out her glass, while her left brushed the long fair hair back from her brow. *She looks beautiful*, His Lordship thought.

Lord Gisors poured, then walked back to the sideboard with the decanter. As he put the glass stopple back in, he began: "You mustn't think badly of My Lord Father, Madelaine, even though he is a bit testy at times. He—"

"I know," she interrupted. "I know. He thinks only of the County. Never of individuals."

Frowning slightly, His Lordship came back with his glass and sat down in another easy chair near her. "But he does think of individuals, my love. He must think of every individual in the Vexin—as *I* must when I succeed to the County Seat. He has to take the long view and the broad view, naturally, but he *is* concerned about individuals."

She sipped at her glass of wine, then looked up at him with solemn gray eyes. "Does his concern for individuals include you? Or me? He knows we love each other, but he forbids our marriage, and insists that you marry Lady Evelynne de Saint-Brieuc—in spite of the fact that you do not love her nor she you. Is that concern for the individual or simply the desire to make an advantageous political marriage for you?"

Lord Gisors closed his eyes and held his tongue for a moment. The two of them had been over and over this ground many times; there was nothing new here. He had explained many times that, whereas My Lord the Count could forbid a marriage, he could not force one. Gisors had even reiterated time and again that he could appeal his case for marriage to His Royal Highness of Normandy, and, if that failed, to His Imperial Majesty—but that he would not do so out of deference to his father. His head seemed to ache at the monotony of "time and again."

He had not, of course, mentioned his own plans for marrying Madelaine without all the rigamarole. She might very likely rebel at the notion.

He opened his eyes again. "Be patient, my darling. I can assure you that he will—"

"—Come round to your way of thinking?" she cut in. "Never! The only time the Count de la Vexin will give his consent to our marriage will be when *you* are Count de la Vexin! Your father—"

"*Quiet!*" Lord Gisors said in an imperative undertone. "*My sister.*"

At the far end of the hall, the door to the Lady Chapel had opened and closed. The woman walking toward them with a rather solemn smile on her face was carefully removing her chapel veil as she came down the wide carpeting to the fireplace. She nodded silently to each of them, then said: "Your watch, My Lord Brother. Ten to eleven, remember?"

Lord Gisors finished his wine and stood up with a smile. "Of course, My Lady Beverly. '*Can you not spend one hour with me?*' The Gospel according to Matthew." Tomorrow would be the Friday of the Crucifixion; this, the night before, would be symbolically spent in the Garden of Gethsemane with Our Lord. Gisors looked at the clock. It was the last second before ten.

" '*Father, my hour has come,*' St. John—" Gisors began.

The pendulum swung down.

The clock struck the first note.

"*What the devil was that?*" Lord Gisors yelled.

Outside, there had been a horrendous scream.

In the courtyard itself, a minute or so earlier, two militiamen of the Count's Own had been standing near the wall of St. Martin's Hall. One was the man at post, the other the Sergeant-of-the-Guard, who was making his evening rounds. They exchanged the usual military courtesies. The guardsman reported the state of his post as being quiet; the sergeant thanked him in the proper military manner. Then he said, with a grin: "It's better doing night duty in April than in March, eh, Jaime?"

Guardsman Jaime grinned back. "At least I'm not freezing my nose off, Sergeant Andray." His eyes shifted upward as he saw a gleam of light from the corner of his eye. "Here comes My Lord Count."

Sergeant Andray turned his head to follow Jaime's gaze. He knew that Jaime did not mean that My Lord the Count was actually approaching the post, merely that His Lordship was going into his private room at the top of the Red Tower. It was an occurrence both of them were used to. The Count was irregular in his visits to his private workshop, but his behavior each time was predictable. He made his presence known to those in the courtyard below by the light of his flickering torch showing through the lozenged windows as he approached it from the door of his laboratory.

Then, as he stood on the desk in front of the window to light the gas jet just above the lintel, the flame of the torch rose, lifting out of sight above the window, leaving only a half-halo of light beneath.

Then the routine changed drastically.

Instead of the warm glow of the gaslight, there was an odd, moving flare of white light that seemed to chase itself around the room for a second or two.

Then, suddenly and violently, the leaded, lozenged window burst asunder, splattering glass through the air. Through that shattered window came the twisting figure of My Lord de la Vexin, a scream tearing from his throat as he somersaulted eighty feet to the stone pavement below, his small torch still in his hand, trailing a comet's tail of flame and sparks.

The Count and the courtyard met with fatal violence, and the sudden silence was punctuated only by the tinkling rain of shards of glass still falling from the ruined window above.

At 12:44 that evening, Jaque Toile, Chief Master-at-Arms for the city of Gisors, was waiting at the railroad station with two Sergeants-at-Arms as the train from Rouen pulled into the station.

Chief Jaque's hard eyes scanned the late-night passengers as they alighted from the first-class coaches. There were few of them, and the Chief quickly spotted the trio he was looking for. "Let's go," he said to the sergeants. "That's them."

The three Officers of the King's Peace moved in.

The three men who were their target stepped out of the coach and waited. The first was a tall, brown-haired, handsome man with lean features, wearing the evening dress of an aristocrat; the second was shorter and muscularly tubby, wearing the working dress of a sorcerer; the third was a rather elderly, dried-up-looking fellow with gray hair, who wore pince-nez and the evening dress of a gentleman. On the shoulders of the latter two was embroidered the badge of the Duke of Normandy.

Chief Jaque walked up to the aristocratic-looking gentleman. "My Lord Darcy?"

Lord Darcy, Chief Investigator for His Royal Highness the Duke of Normandy, nodded. "I am. Chief Jaque Toile, I believe?"

"Yes, M'lord."

"My colleagues," said Lord Darcy by way of introduction, "Sean O Lochlainn, Master Sorcerer, Chief Forensic Sorcerer for His Royal Highness; Doctor James Pateley, Chief Forensic Chirurgeon."

The Chief Master-at-Arms acknowledged the introductions, then: "Sergeants Paul and Bertram, M'lord. We have an official carriage waiting, M'lord."

Four minutes later, the carriage was rolling toward Castle Gisors, its coil spring suspension and pneumatic tires making the ride comfortable in spite of the cobblestone streets. After what seemed a long silence, Lord Darcy's voice came smoothly.

"You seem pensive, my dear Chief."

"What? Oh. Yes. Sorry, M'lord. Just thinking."

"That was painfully apparent. May I inquire as to the subject of your thoughts?"

"Don't like cases like this," said Chief Jaque. "Not equipped for 'em. Ghosts, demons, black magic, that sort of thing. I'm not a scientist; I'm a peace officer."

Master Sean's blue eyes lit up with interest. "Ghosts? Demons? Black magic?"

"One moment," Lord Darcy said. "Let us be systematic. The only information we received at Rouen was that de la Vexin had fallen to his death. No details were given us via teleson. Just what did happen, Chief Jaque?"

The Chief Master-at-Arms explained what had happened as pieced together from the reports of the guardsmen on duty, just prior to My Lord de la Vexin's death.

"No question he was dead," the Chief said. "Skull smashed. Neck broken. Guard Sergeant Andray called for an extension fire ladder. Only way to get up into that room. Sent the guard from the courtyard up the stairs to notify the two men on duty at His Lordship's door."

"They hadn't known?" Lord Darcy asked.

Chief Jaque shook his head. "Door's too thick. Too thick to break down in a short time, even. Need an ax. That's why Andray went up the ladder. Climbed in the window and went over to unbar the door. By that time, the door guards were alerted. That's where the funny part comes in."

"Indeed?" murmured Lord Darcy. "Funny in what way?"

"Nobody in the room. Doesn't make sense."

Master Sean thumbed his chin thoughtfully. "If that's the case, Chief Jaque, then he wasn't pushed, eh? Might it be that it was purely an accident? That when he got up on that desk to light the gaslamp, something slipped and he fell accidentally through the window and to his death?"

The Chief Master-at-Arms shook his head. "Not very likely, Master Sorcerer; body was eighteen feet from the wall. Glass splattered even farther." He shook his head again. "Didn't just fall. Not possible. He was pushed."

Dr. Pateley took his pince-nez from his thin nose and looked at them as he polished them with a fine linen handkerchief. "Or *jumped*, perhaps?" he asked in his diffident voice.

The Chief glanced at him sharply. "*Jumped?* You mean suicide?"

"Not necessarily," said the chirurgeon. He glanced up at Lord Darcy. "There are many reasons why a man might jump—eh, My Lord?"

Lord Darcy held back a smile. "Indeed, Doctor. Most astute of you." He looked at Chief Jaque. "Could he have jumped, Chief?"

"Could have. Doesn't make sense, though. Man doesn't commit suicide by jumping through a closed window. Doesn't make sense. A suicide who decides to jump opens the window first. Doesn't just take a flying leap through a pane of glass."

"That's not the point I had in mind," said Dr. Pateley, replacing his glasses carefully. "What if he were trying to get away from something?"

Chief Jaque's eyes widened. "I knew it! Demons!"

Twenty-five minutes later, Master Sean was saying: "Well, Me Lord, whatever it was that killed My Lord Vexin, it was certainly none of Chief Jaque's 'demons,' nor any other form of projected psychic elemental."

Dr. Pateley frowned. "A what?"

"Elemental, my dear Doctor. A projected psychic manifestation symbolized by the four elementary states of matter: solid, liquid, gas, and plasma. Or earth, water, air, and fire, as they used to call them."

Along with Lord Darcy, Master Sean and the chirurgeon were standing in the room in the Red Tower from which the late Count had been ejected so forcibly. Master Sean had prowled around the room with his eyes half closed, his golden *crux ansata* in his right hand, probing everywhere. The others had stood by silently; it is unwise to disturb a magician at work. Then the round little Irish sorcerer had made his pronouncement.

Lord Darcy had not wasted his time in watching Master Sean; he had seen that process too many times to be interested in it. Instead, his keen gray eyes had been carefully surveying the room.

It was a fairly large room, covering the entire top floor of the Fourteenth Century tower except for the small landing at the head of the stairs. The landing was closed off by a heavy, padded walnut door.

Having noted that, Lord Darcy looked at the rest of the large room.

It was square, some twenty by twenty feet, the tower having been built in the old Norman style. There was only the one window in the room; the rest of the walls were covered with shelving and cabinets. Along the length of the west wall ran a shelf some thirty-two inches deep and three feet from the floor; it was obviously used as a worktable, for it was littered with various kinds of glassware, oddly shaped pieces of wood and metal, a couple of balances, and other paraphernalia. The shelves above it contained rows of bottles and jars, each neatly labeled, containing liquids, powders, and crystals of various kinds.

On the south wall, flanking the shattered window, were two sections of shelving full of books. Half the east wall was filled with books, the other half with cabinets. There were more shelves and cabinets flanking the door of the north wall.

Because of the slight breeze that came in chillingly through the broken window, the gas flame in the sconce above it flickered and danced, casting weird shadows over the room and making glittering highlights on the glassware.

The Count's writing desk was set directly beneath the big window, its top flush with the sill. Lord Darcy walked over to the desk, leaned over it and looked down through the smashed window. There had been no unusual evidence there. My Lord the Count had, from all indications, died of a broken neck and a crushed skull, although the autopsy might tell more. A search of the body had revealed nothing of any consequence—but Lord Darcy now carried the key to the late Count's ultraprivate chamber in his pocket.

Below, Chief Jaque and his men were carefully lifting the body from a glittering field of broken glass and putting it into the special carriage of the local chirurgeon. The autopsy would be performed in the morning by Master Sean and Dr. Pateley.

Lord Darcy leaned back and looked up at the gas flame above the window. The Count de la Vexin had come in with his torch, as usual. Climbed up on his desk, as usual. Turned on the gas, as usual. Lit the gas with his torch, as usual. Then—

What?

"Spooky-looking place, eh, Me Lord?" Master Sean said.

His Lordship turned round, putting his back to the window.

"Gloomy, at any rate, my dear Sean. Are there no other gas jets in this room? Ah, yes; I see them. Two on each of the other walls. Evidently the pipes were lengthened when the shelving was put in." He took out his pipe lighter. "Let's see if we can't shed a little more light on the subject." He went around the room carefully and lit the other six lamps. Even inside their glass chimneys, they tended to flicker; the room was better illuminated, but the shadows still danced.

"Ah! And an old-fashioned oil chandelier," Lord Darcy said, looking up. It was a brass glove some fifteen inches in diameter with a ring at the bottom and a wick with a glass chimney on top, suspended by a web of chains and a pulley system that allowed it to be pulled down for refueling and lighting. Even standing on tiptoe, Lord Darcy couldn't reach the ring.

He looked around quickly, then went to the door and opened it.

"Corporal, is there a hook to lower that oil lamp?"

"Blessed if I know, My Lord," said the Corporal of the Guard. "His Lordship never used it, the lamp, I mean. Hasn't been used as long as I know. Doubt if it has any oil in it, even, My Lord."

"I see. Thank you." He closed the door again. "Well, so much for additional illumination. Hm-m-m. Dr. Pateley, you measured the body; how tall was My Lord Count?"

"Five feet six, My Lord."

"That accounts for it, then."

"Accounts for what, My Lord?"

"There are seven gas jets in this room. Six of them are some seven and a half feet from the floor; the seventh, over the window, is nine feet from the floor. Why did he habitually light that one first? Because it is only six and a half feet from the desk top, and he could reach it."

"Then how did he reach the others if he needed more light?" Dr. Pateley asked, adjusting his pince-nez.

Master Sean grinned, but said nothing.

Lord Darcy sighed. "My dear chirurgeon, I honestly think you never look at anything but human bodies, ill, dying, or dead. What do you see over there?" He pointed to the northeast corner of the room.

Dr. Pateley turned. "Oh. A ladder." He looked rather embarrassed. "Certainly. Of course."

"Had it not been here," Lord Darcy said, "I would be quite astonished. How else would he get to his books and . . ."

His voice trailed off. His eyes were still on the ladder. "Hm-m-m. Interesting." He went over to the ladder, tested it, then climbed up it to the ceiling. He bent his head back to look at the ceiling carefully. "Aha. This was the old watchtower." He pushed up with one hand, then with both. Overhead, a two-and-a-half-foot panel swung back on protesting hinges. Lord Darcy climbed on up and hoisted himself through the opening.

He looked around the roof of the tower, which was surrounded by crenellated walls. Then he came back down, closing the panel.

"Nothing up there, apparently, but I'll have to come back by daylight to check again, more thoroughly."

Then, without another word, he moved silently around the room, looking intently at everything but touching nothing. He looked up at the ceiling. "Heavy brass hooks," he murmured. "Why? Oh, of course. To suspend various pieces of his apparatus. Very good."

He had covered almost all the room before he finally came across something that really piqued his interest. He was standing near the door, his eyes searching the floor, when he said: "Aha! And what might this be?"

He knelt down, looked down at the object carefully, then picked it up between thumb and forefinger.

"It looks," said Master Sean, "like a four-inch piece of half-inch cotton rope, Me Lord. Very dirty, too."

His Lordship smiled dryly. "That appears to be exactly what it is, my good Sean. Interesting." He examined it closely.

"I would be obliged, My Lord," said Master Sean in a semi-formal manner, "if you would explain why it is so interesting."

Dr. Pateley merely blinked behind his pince-nez and said nothing.

"You have noticed, my dear Sean," Lord Darcy said, "how immaculately clean this laboratory is. It is well dusted, well cleaned. Everything seems to be in its place. There are no papers scattered about. There are no messy areas. The place is as neat and as well-kept as a cavalry officer's saber." He made a sweeping gesture to take in the whole room.

"It is, Me Lord, but—" Master Sean began.

"Then what, may I ask," His Lordship continued, "is a short piece of dirty rope doing on the floor?"

"I don't know, Me Lord." Master Sean was honestly puzzled. "What is its significance?"

Lord Darcy's smile broadened. "I haven't the foggiest notion in the world, Master Sean. But I have no doubt that there is *some* significance. What it is will await upon further information."

Another dozen minutes of inspection revealed nothing further to Lord Darcy's scrutiny. "Very well," he said, "we'll leave the rest of this until the morrow, when the light's better. Now let us go down and discuss this affair with those concerned. We'll get little sleep tonight, I fear."

Master Sean cleared his throat apologetically. "My Lord, the good chirurgeon and I, not being qualified for interrogating witnesses, had best occupy our time with the autopsy. Eh?"

"Eh? Oh, certainly, if you wish. Yes, of course." This, Lord Darcy thought, is what comes of assuming that others, even one's closest associates, have the same interests as oneself.

Within St. Martin's Hall, the clock on the mantelpiece solemnly struck the quarter-hour. It was fifteen minutes after two on the morning of Good Friday, 12 April 1974.

The Reverend Father Villiers stood near the fireplace, looking up at Lord Darcy. He was not tall—five-six or so—but his lean, compact body had an aura of physical strength about it. He was quick and accurate in his movements, but never seemed jerky or nervous. There was a calm awareness in him that showed spiritual strength as well. He was, Lord Darcy judged, in his forties, with only a faint touch of gray in his hair and mustache. The fine character lines in his handsome face showed strength, kindliness, and a sense of humor. But at the moment he was not smiling; there was a feeling of tragedy in his eyes.

"They are all in the Chapel, My Lord," he was saying in his brisk, pleasant, low tenor. "Lord Gisors, Lady Beverly, the Demoiselle Madelaine, and Sir Roderique MacKenzie."

"Who are the latter pair, Reverend Sir?" Lord Darcy asked.

"Sir Roderique is Captain of the Count's Own Guard. The Demoiselle Madelaine is his daughter."

"I shall not disturb them, Reverend Father," Lord Darcy said. "To seek solace before our Sacramental Lord on His Altar of Repose on this night is the sacrosanct right of every Christian, and should not be abrogated save in dire emergency."

"You don't consider murder an emergency?"

"Before its commission, yes. Not after. What makes you think it was murder, Reverend Father?"

The priest smiled a little. "It wasn't suicide. I spoke to him shortly before he went over to the Red Tower; as a Sensitive, I'd have picked up any suicidal emotions easily. And it could hardly have been an accident; if he'd merely lost his balance and fallen, he'd have landed at the foot of the wall, not eighteen or twenty feet away."

"Eighteen," murmured Lord Darcy.

"*Ergo*—murder," Father Villiers said.

"I agree, Reverend Father," Lord Darcy said. "The theory has been advanced that My Lord Count saw some sort of apparition which so frightened him that he leaped to his death through a closed window rather than face it. What is your opinion?"

"That would be Chief Jaque." The priest shook his head. "Hardly. His late Lordship would not even have sensed the presence of a true psychic apparition, and a phony—a piece of trickery—would have neither fooled nor frightened him."

"He couldn't have perceived a true psychic apparition?"

Father Villiers shook his head once more. "He was an example of that truly rare case, the psychically blind."

Ever since St. Hilary of Walsingham had formulated his analog equations of the Laws of Magic in the late Thirteenth Century, scientific sorcerers had realized that those laws could not be used by everyone. Some had the Talent and some did not. It was no more to be expected that everyone could be a sorcerer or healer or sensitive than to expect everyone to be a musician, a sculptor, or a chirurgeon.

But the inability to play a violin does not mean an inability to enjoy—or *not* enjoy—someone else's playing. One does not have to be a musician to perceive that music exists.

Unless one is tone-deaf.

To use another analogy: There are a few—very few—men and

women who are *totally* color-blind. They are not just slightly crip-
pled, like those who cannot distinguish between red and green; they
see all things in shades of gray. To them, the world is colorless. It
is difficult for such a person to understand why or how three identical
objects, all the same shade of gray, can be identified by someone else
as "red," "blue," and "green." To the totally color-blind, those words
are without referents and are meaningless.

"His late Lordship," the priest said, "had an early desire to go into
the priesthood, to forgo his right to the County Seat in favor of his
younger brother. He could not do so, of course. An un-Talented,
psychically blind man would be as useless to the Church as a color-
blind man would be to the Artist's Guild."

Naturally, Lord Darcy thought, that would not exclude the late
de la Vexin from an executive position in His Imperial Majesty's
Government. One doesn't need magical Talent to run a County ef-
fectively.

For over eight centuries, since the time of Henry II, the Anglo-
French Empire had held its own and expanded. Henry's son, Richard,
after narrowly escaping death from a crossbow bolt in 1199, had
taken firm control of his kingdom and expanded it. At his death in
1219, his nephew Arthur had increased the kingdom's strength even
more. The Great Reform, during the reign of Richard the Great, in
the late Fifteenth Century, had put the Empire on a solid working
basis, using psychic science to establish a society that had been both
stable and progressive for nearly half a millennium.

"Where is My Lord the late Count's younger brother?" Lord Darcy
asked.

"Captain Lord Louis is with the New England Fleet," Father Villiers said. "At present, I believe, stationed at Port Holy Cross on the
coast of Mechicoe."

Well, that eliminates him *as a suspect,* Lord Darcy told himself.
"Tell me, Reverend Father," he said aloud, "do you know anything
about the laboratory His late Lordship maintained on the top floor
of the Red Tower?"

"A laboratory? Is that what it is? No, I didn't know. He went up
there regularly, but I have no idea what he did up there. I assumed
it was some harmless hobby. Wasn't it?"

"It may have been," Lord Darcy admitted. "I have no reason to
believe otherwise. Have you ever been in that room?"

"No; never. Nor, to my knowledge, has anyone else but the Count.
Why?"

"Because," Lord Darcy said thoughtfully, "it is a very odd laboratory. And yet there is no doubt that it *is* some kind of laboratory for scientific research."

Father Villiers touched the cross at his breast. "Odd? How?" Then he dropped his hand and chuckled. "No. Not Black Magic, of course. He didn't believe in magic at all—black, white, purple, green, red, or rainbow. He was a Materialist."

"Oh?"

"An outgrowth of his psychic blindness, you see," the priest explained. "He wanted to be a priest. He was refused. Therefore, he rejected the basis for his refusal. He refused to believe that anything which he could not detect with his own senses existed. He set out to prove the basic tenet of Materialism: 'All phenomena in the Universe can be explained as a result of nonliving forces reacting with nonliving matter.' "

"Yes," said Lord Darcy. "A philosophy which I, as a living being, find difficult to understand, to say nothing of accepting. So that is the purpose of his laboratory—to bring the scientific method to bear on the Theory of Materialism."

"So it would appear, My Lord," said Father Villiers. "Of course, I have not seen His late Lordship's laboratory, but—"

"Who has?" Lord Darcy asked.

The priest shook his head. "No one that I know of. No one."

Lord Darcy glanced at his watch. "Is there anyone else in the Chapel besides the family, Reverend Sir?"

"Several. There is an outer door through which the occupants within the walls can come in directly from the courtyard. And there are four of the Sisters from the convent.

"Then I could slip in unnoticed for an hour of devotion before the Blessed Sacrament at the Altar of Repose?"

"Most assuredly, My Lord; there are people coming and going all the time. But I suggest you use the family entrance, someone is sure to notice."

"Thank you, Reverend Father. At what hour will you celebrate the Mass of the Presanctified?"

"The service begins at eight o'clock."

"And how do I get to this outside door? Through that door and turn to my left, I believe?"

"Exactly, My Lord."

Three minutes later, Lord Darcy was kneeling in the back of the

Chapel, facing the magnificently flowered Altar of Repose, his eyes on the veiled ciborium that stood at its center.

An hour and a quarter after that, he was sound asleep in the room which had been assigned him by the seneschal.

After the abrupt liturgical finale of the Mass of the Presanctified, at a little past ten on Good Friday morning, Lord Darcy and Master Sean stood waiting outside the family entrance of the Chapel. Dr. Pateley had excused himself immediately; he had volunteered to help one of the local men to prepare the late Count's body for the funeral.

"Put things back the way we found 'em, My Lord," was the way he worded it.

Darcy and the stout little Irish sorcerer had placed themselves at the back of the congregation and had come out ahead of the family who were in their reserved pew at the front.

"I trust," murmured His Lordship very softly, "that Almighty God has reserved a special place of punishment for people who commit murder during Holy Week."

"Aye, Me Lord; I know what you mean," Master Sean whispered. "Meself, I enjoy the Three Hours of Sermon on Good Friday—especially by a really good preacher, which Father Villiers is reputed to be. But—'business before pleasure'." He paused, then went on in the same low tone. "D'you expect to clear up the case soon?"

"Before the day is out, I think."

Master Sean looked startled. "You know who did it, then?" He kept his voice down.

"*Who?* Of course. That should be plain. But I need more data on *how* and *why*."

Master Sean blinked. "But you haven't even questioned anyone yet, My Lord."

"No need to, for that. But my case is as yet incomplete."

Master Sean shook his head and chuckled. "Your touch of the Talent, Me Lord."

"You know, my dear Sean, you have almost convinced me that I *do* have a touch of the Talent. How did you put it?"

"Like all great detectives, My Lord, you have the ability to leap from an unjustified assumption to a foregone conclusion without passing through the distance between. Then you back up and fill in." He paused again. "Well, then, who—"

"*Ssst!* Here they come."

Three people had come out of the Chapel: Lord Gisors, Lady Beverly, and the Demoiselle Madelaine MacKenzie.

Master Sean's lips barely moved, and his voice was barely audible as he said: "Wonder where the rest of the Clan MacKenzie went, Me Lord?"

"We'll ask." Both of them knew that Captain Sir Roderique MacKenzie and his son, Sergeant Andray, had been sitting in the family pew with the others.

The three came up the hallway toward the big fireplace in St. Martin's Hall, where Lord Darcy and Master Sean were waiting.

Lord Darcy stepped forward and bowed. "My Lord de la Vexin."

The young man looked startled. "No. My fa—" He stopped. It was the first time anyone had ever addressed him as "Lord de la Vexin." Of course it was only a courtesy title; he would not be the Count of the Vexin until his title had been validated by the King.

Lord Darcy, seeing the young man's confusion, went on: "I am Lord Darcy, My Lord. This is Master Sean. We appreciate the invitation to breakfast that was conveyed to us by your seneschal."

The new Lord de la Vexin had recovered his composure. "Ah, yes. I am pleased to meet you, My Lord. This is my sister, Lady Beverly, and the Demoiselle Madelaine. Come; breakfast should be ready for us immediately." He led the way.

The breakfast was delicious, not sumptuous: small, exquisitely poached *quinelles de poisson*; portions of eggs Boucher; hot cross buns; milk and *café*.

Captain Roderique and Sergeant Andray made their appearance a few minutes before the meal began, followed almost immediately by Father Villiers.

Conversation during breakfast consisted only of small talk, allowing Lord Darcy to observe the others of the party without being obtrusive about it.

De la Vexin still seemed dazed, as though his mind were somewhere else, only partly pulled back by conversation. The Demoiselle Madelaine, blond and beautiful, behaved with decorum, but there was a bright, anticipatory gleam in her eyes that Lord Darcy did not care for. Lady Beverly, some ten years older than her brother, her dark hair faintly tinged with gray at the temples, looked as though she had been born a widow—or a cloistered nun; she was quiet, soft-spoken, and self-effacing, but underneath Lord Darcy detected a firmness and intelligence kept in abeyance. Captain Sir Roderique MacKenzie was perhaps an inch taller than Lord

Darcy—lean, with an upright, square-shouldered posture, a thick light-brown mustache and beard, and a taciturn manner typical of the Franco-Scot. His son was a great deal like him, except that he was smooth-shaven and his hair was lighter, though not as blond as that of his sister Madelaine. Both had an air about them that was not quite either that of the military or that of the Keepers of the King's Peace, but partook of both. They were Guardsmen and showed it.

Father Villiers seemed preoccupied, and Lord Darcy could understand why. The symbolic death of the Lord Jesus and the actual death of the Lord de la Vexin were too closely juxtaposed for the good Father's own spiritual comfort. Being a priest is not an easy life-game to play.

After breakfast, a fruit compote of Spanish oranges was served, followed by more *café*.

The late Count's son cleared his throat. "My lords, ladies, gentlemen," he began. He paused for a movement and swallowed. "Several of you have addressed me as 'de la Vexin.' I would prefer, until this matter is cleared up, to retain my title of Gisors. Uh—if you please." Another pause. He looked at Lord Darcy. "You came here to question us, My Lord?"

Lord Darcy looked utterly guileless. "Not really, Lord Gisors. However, if you should care to discuss the death of His Lordship, it might clear up some of the mysterious circumstances surrounding it. I know that none of you were in that room at the time of the—ah—incident. I am not looking for alibis. But have any of you any conjectures? How did the late Count de la Vexin die?"

Silence fell like a psychic fog, heavy and damp.

Each looked at the others to speak first, and nobody spoke.

"Well," Lord Darcy said after a time, "let's attack it from another direction. Sergeant Andray, of all the people here, you were apparently the only eyewitness. What was your impression of what happened?"

The sergeant blinked, sat up a little straighter, and cleared his throat nervously. "Well, Your Lordship, at a few minutes before ten o'clock, Guardsman Jaime and I were—"

"No, no, Sergeant," Lord Darcy interrupted gently. "Having read the deposition you and Jaime gave to Chief Jaque, I am fully conversant with what you *saw*. I want to know your theories about the *cause* of what you saw."

After a pause, Sergeant Andray said, "It looked to me as if he'd *jumped* through the window, Your Lordship. But I have no idea why he would do such a thing."

"You saw nothing that might have made him jump?"

Sergeant Andray frowned. "The only thing was that ball of light. Paul and I both mentioned it in our reports."

"Yes. 'A ball of yellowish-white light that seemed to dance all over the room for a few seconds, then dropped to the floor and vanished,' you said. Is that right?"

"I should have said, 'dropped *toward* the floor,' Your Lordship. I couldn't have seen it actually hit the floor. Not from that angle."

"Very good, Sergeant! I wondered if you would correct that minor discrepancy, and you have done so to my satisfaction." Lord Darcy thought for a moment. "Now. You then went over to the body, examined it, and determined to your satisfaction that His Lordship was dead. Did you touch him?"

"Only his wrist, to try to find a pulse. There was none, and the angle of his head . . ." He stopped.

"I quite understand. Meanwhile, you had sent Guardsman Jaime for the fire wagon. When it came, you used the extension ladder to go up and unlock the door, to let the other guardsmen in. Was the gaslight still on?"

"No. It had been blown out. I shut off the gas, and then went over and opened the door. There was enough light from the yardlamps for me to see by."

"And you found nothing odd or out of the way?"

"Nothing and nobody, Your Lordship," the sergeant said firmly. "Nor did any of the other guardsmen."

"That's straightforward enough. You searched the room then?"

"Not really searched it. We looked around to see if there was anyone there, using hand torches. But there's no place to hide in that room. We had called the armsmen; when they came, they looked more carefully. Nothing."

"Very well. Now, when I arrived, that gaslight over the window was lit. Who lit it?"

"Chief Master-at-Arms Jaque Toile, Your Lordship."

"I see. Thank you, Sergeant." He looked at the others, one at a time. Their silence seemed interminable. "Lady Beverly, have you anything to add to this discussion?"

Lady Beverly looked at Father Villiers with her calm eyes.

The priest was looking at her. "My advice is to speak, my child. We must get to the bottom of this."

I see, Lord Darcy thought. *There is something here that has been discussed in the confessional. The Reverend Father* cannot *speak—but he can advise* her *to.*

Lady Beverly looked back to Lord Darcy. "You want a theory, My Lord? Very well." There was a terrible sadness in her voice. "His late Lordship, my father, was punished by God for his unbelief. Father Villiers has told me that this could not be so, but"—she closed her eyes—"I greatly fear that it is."

"How so, My Lady?" Darcy asked gently.

"He was a Materialist. He was psychically blind. He denied that others had the God-given gift of the Sight and the Talent. He said it was all pretense, all hogwash. He was closed off to all emotion."

She was no longer looking *at* Lord Darcy; she was looking through and beyond him, as though her eyes were focused somewhere on a far horizon.

"He was not an evil man," she continued without shifting her gaze, "but he was sinful." Suddenly her eyes flickered, and she was looking directly into Lord Darcy's gray eyes. "Do you know that he forbade a wedding between my brother and the Demoiselle Madelaine because he could not see the love between them? He wanted Gisors to marry Evelynne de Saint-Brieuc."

Darcy's eyes moved rapidly to Lord Gisors and Madelaine MacKenzie. "No. I did not know that. How many did?"

It was Captain Sir Roderique who spoke. "We all did, My Lord. He made a point of it. The Count forbade it, and I forbade it. But legally I had no right to forbid my daughter."

"But why did he—"

Lord Darcy's question was cut off abruptly by Lady Beverly.

"Politics, My Lord. And because he could not see true love. So God punished him for his obstinacy. May I be excused, My Lord? I would hear the Three Hours."

Quickly, Father Villiers said: "Would you excuse us both, My Lord?"

"Certainly, Reverend Sir, Lady Beverly," Lord Darcy said, rising. His eyes watched them in silence as they left the room.

Half past noon.

Lord Darcy and Master Sean stood in the courtyard below the Red

Tower gazing at a small sea of broken glass surrounded by a ring of armsmen and guardsmen.

"Well, my dear Sean, what did you think of our little breakfast conversation?"

"Fascinating, Me Lord," said the sorcerer. "I think I'm beginning to see where you're going. Lady Beverly's mind is not exactly straight, is it?"

"Let's put it that she seems to have some weird ideas about God," Lord Darcy said. "Are you ready for this experiment, Master Sean?"

"I am, Me Lord."

"Don't you need an anchor man for this sort of thing?"

Master Sean nodded. "Of course, Me Lord. Chief Jaque is bringing Journeyman Emile, forensic sorcerer for the County. I met him last night; he's a good man; he'll be a Master one day.

"Actually, Me Lord, the spells are quite simple. According to the Law of Contiguity, any piece of a structure remains a part of the structure. We can return it to the last state in which it was still a part of the contiguous whole—completely, if necessary, but you only want to return it to the point *after* the fracture but *before* the dispersal. Doing it isn't difficult; it's holding it in place afterwards. That's why I need an anchor man."

"I'll take my measurements and make my observations as quickly as possible," Lord Darcy promised. "Ah! There they are!"

Master Sean followed His Lordship's gaze toward the main gate of the courtyard. Then, very solemnly, he said: "Ah, yes. One man is wearing the black-and-silver uniform of a chief master-at-arms; the other is wearing the working garb of a journeyman sorcerer. By which I deduce that they are *not* a squad of Imperial Marines."

"Astute of you, my dear Sean; keep working at it. You will become an expert detective on the same day that I become a Master Sorcerer. Chief Jaque and I will go up to the tower room while you and Journeyman Emile work here. Carry on."

Lord Darcy toiled up eight flights of stairs, past several offices, vaguely wishing he were in the castle at Evreux, where the Countess D'Evreux's late brother had installed a steam-powered elevator. *No fool he*, Lord Darcy thought.

At the top landing, an armsman and a guardsman came immediately to attention as His Lordship appeared. He nodded at them. "Good afternoon." With thumb and forefinger he probed his left-hand waistcoat pocket. Then he probed the other. "Is that room locked?" he asked.

The armsman tested it. "Yes, Your Lordship."

"I seem to have mislaid the key. Is there another?"

"There is a duplicate, Your Lordship," said the guardsman, "but it's locked up in Captain Sir Roderique's office. I'll fetch it for you, if you like; it's only two floors down."

"No. No need." Lord Darcy produced the key from his right-hand waistcoat pocket. "I've found it. Thank you, anyway, Guardsman. Chief Jaque will be up in a few minutes."

He unlocked the door, opened it, went in, and closed the door behind him.

Some three minutes later, when Chief Jaque opened the door, he said: "Looking for something, My Lord?"

Lord Darcy was on his knees, searching a cupboard, moving things aside, taking things out. "Yes, my dear Chief; I am looking for the wherewithal to hang a murderer. At first, I thought it more likely it would be in one of the high cupboards, but they contain nothing but glassware. So I decided it must be—ah!" He pulled his head back out of the cupboard and straightened up, still on his knees. From his fingers dangled a six-foot length of ordinary-looking cotton rope.

"Bit scanty to hang a man," Chief Jaque said dubiously.

"For this murderer, it will be quite adequate," said Lord Darcy, standing up. He looked closely at the rope. "If only it—"

He was interrupted by a halloo from below. He went to the shattered remains of the window and looked down. "Yes, Master Sean?" he called.

"We're ready to begin, My Lord," the round little Irish sorcerer shouted up. "Please stand back."

In the courtyard, armsmen and guardsmen stood in a large circle, facing outward from the center, surrounding the fragments from the broken window. Journeyman Emile, a short, lean man with a Parisian accent, had carefully chalked a pale blue line around the area, drawing it three inches behind the bootheels of the surrounding guard.

"It is that I am ready, Master," he said in his atrocious patois.

"Excellent," said Master Sean. "Get the field set up and hold it. I will give you all the strength I can."

"But yes, Master." He opened his symbol-decorated carpetbag—similar to in general, but differing from in detail, Master Sean's own—and took out two mirror-polished silvery wands which were so deeply incised with symbol engraving that they glittered in the early afternoon sunlight. "For the Cattell Effect, it is that it is necessary for the silver, no?"

"It is," agreed Master Sean. "You will be handling the static spells while I take care of the kinetic. Are you ready?"

"I am prepared," Journeyman Emile said. "Proceed." He took his stance just inside the blue-chalked circle, facing the Red Tower and held up his wands in a ninety-degree V.

Master Sean took an insufflator from his own carpetbag and filled it with a previously charged powder. Then, moving carefully around the circle, he puffed out clouds of the powder, which settled gently to the courtyard floor, touching each fragment of glass with at least one grain of the powder.

When he had completed the circle, Master Sean stood in front of Journeyman Emile. He put the insufflator back in his carpetbag and took out a short, eighteen-inch wand of pale yellow crystal, with which he inscribed a symbol in the air.

The Cattell Effect began to manifest itself.

Slowly at first, then more rapidly, the fragments from the shattered window began to move.

Like a reverse cascade in slow motion, they lifted and gathered themselves together, a myriad of sparkling shards moving upward, fountaining glitteringly toward the empty window casement eighty feet above. There was a tinkling like fairy bells as occasional fragments struck each other on the way up as they had struck on the way down.

Only the superb discipline of the armsmen and guardsmen kept them from turning to see.

Up, up, went the bits and pieces, like sharp-edged raindrops falling toward the sky.

At the empty opening, they coalesced and came together to form a window—that was not quite a window. It bulged.

Inside the late Count's upper room, Lord Darcy watched the flying fragments return whence they had come. When the stasis was achieved, Lord Darcy glanced at the Chief Master-at-Arms.

"Come, my dear Jaque; we must not tax our sorcerers more than necessary." He walked over to the window, followed by the Chief Armsman.

The lozenged window was neither a shattered wreckage nor a complete whole. It bulged outward curiously, each piece almost touching its neighbor, but not fitted closely to it. The leading between the lozenges was stretched and twisted outward, as if the whole window had been punched from within by a gigantic fist and had stopped stretching at the last moment.

"Not quite sure I understand this," said Chief Jaque.

"This is the way the window was a fraction of a second after His Lordship, the late Count, struck it. At that time, it was pushed outward and broken, but the fragments had yet to shatter. I direct your attention to the central portion of the window."

The Chief Master-at-Arms took in the scene with keen eyes. "See what you mean. Like a mold, a casting. There's the chin—the chest—the belly—the knees."

"Exactly. Now try to get yourself into a position such that you would make an impression like that," Lord Darcy said.

The Chief grinned. "Don't need to. Obvious. Calves bent back at the knees. Head bent back so the chin hit first. Chest and belly hit first." He narrowed his eyes. "Didn't jump out; didn't fall out. Pushed from behind—violently."

"Precisely so. Excellent, Chief Jaque. Now let us make our measurements as rapidly and as accurately as possible," Lord Darcy said, "being careful not to touch that inherently unstable structure. If we do, we're likely to get badly cut hands when the whole thing collapses."

Below, in the courtyard, an unmoving tableau presented itself. Armsmen and guardsmen stood at parade rest, while the two sorcerers stood like unmoving statues, their eyes and minds on the window above, their wands held precisely and confidently.

Minute after minute went by, and the strain was beginning to tell. Then Lord Darcy's voice came: "Anytime you're ready, Master Sean!"

Without moving, Master Sean said sharply, "Sergeant! Get your men well back! Move 'em!"

The Sergeant-at-Arms called out orders, and both armsmen and guardsmen rapidly moved back toward the main gate. Then they turned to watch.

The magicians released control. The powerful forces which had held up the glass shards no longer obtained, and gravity took over. There was an avalanche, a waterfall of sparkling shards. They slid and tumbled down the stone wall with a great and joyous noise and subsided into a heap at the foot of the Red Tower.

The display had not been as spectacular as the reconstruction of the window had been, but it was quite satisfactory to the armsmen and guardsmen.

A few minutes later, Master Sean toiled his way up the stairs and entered the late Count's laboratory.

"Ah! Master Sean," said Lord Darcy, "Where is Journeyman Emile?"

The Irish sorcerer's smile was a little wan. "He's headed home, My Lord. That's exhaustin' work, and he hasn't trained for it as I have."

"I trust you conveyed to him my compliments. That was a marvelous piece of work the two of you did."

"Thank you, My Lord. I gave Journeyman Emile my personal compliments and assured him of yours. Did you get what you wanted, My Lord?"

"I did, indeed. There is but one more thing. A simple test, but I'm sure it will be most enlightening. First, I will call your attention to those two five-gallon carboys which Chief Jaque and I have just discovered in one of the lower cupboards."

The carboys, which had been lifted up to the worktable, stood side by side, labels showing. One of them, with scarcely half an inch of pale yellowish liquid in it, was labeled *Concentrated Aqueous Spirit of Niter*. The other, half full of a clear, oily-looking liquid, was *Concentrated Oil of Vitriol*.

"I suppose you knew you'd find 'em, Me Lord?" Master Sean said.

"I didn't *know*; I merely suspected. But their presence certainly strengthens my case. Do they suggest anything to you?"

Master Sean shrugged. "I know what they are, My Lord, but I'm not a specialist in the Khemic Arts."

"Nor am I." Lord Darcy took out his pipe and thumbed tobacco into it. "But an Officer of the King's Justice should be widely read enough to be a jack-of-all-trades, at least in theory. Do you know what happens when a mixture of those acids is added to common cotton?"

"No—wait." Master Sean frowned, then shook his head. "I've read it somewhere, but—the details won't come."

"You get nitrated cotton," Lord Darcy said.

Chief Jaque coughed delicately. "Well, what does *that* do, Your Lordship?"

"I think I can show you," His Lordship said with a rather mysterious smile. From his wallet, he took the four-inch piece of blackened rope he had found near the door the evening before. Then he picked up the six-foot piece of clean rope he had found half an hour before. Using his sharp pocketknife, he cut a small piece from the end of each and put them on the lab table about eighteen inches from each other. "Chief Jaque, take these long pieces and put them on the desk, well away from here. I shouldn't want to lose *all* my evidence. Thank you. Now watch."

He lit each bit with his pipe lighter. They both flared in a sudden hissing burst of yellow-white flame and were gone, leaving no trace. Lord Darcy calmly lit his pipe.

Master Sean's eyes lit up. "Aaa-*hah!*"

Chief Jaque said: "The demon!"

"Precisely, my dear Chief. Now we must go down and talk to the rest of the *dramatis personae.*"

As they went back down the stairs, Master Sean said: "But why was the short piece covered with dirt, my Lord?"

"Not dirt, my dear Sean; lampblack."

"Lampblack? But why?"

"To render it invisible, of course."

"You are not preaching the Three Hours, Reverend Father?" Lord Darcy asked with a raised eyebrow.

"No, My Lord," Father Villiers replied. "I am just a little too upset. Besides, I thought my presence here might be required. Father Dubois very kindly agreed to come over from the monastery and take my place."

Clouds had come, shortly after noon, to obliterate the bright morning sun, and a damp chill had enveloped the castle. The chill was being offset by the fire in the great fireplace in St. Martin's Hall, but to the ten people seated on sofas and chairs around the fireplace, there seemed to be a different sort of chill in the huge room.

The three MacKenzies, father, son, and daughter, sat together on one sofa, saying nothing, their eyes moving around, but always coming back to Lord Darcy. Lady Beverly sat alone near the fire, her eyes watching the flames unseeingly. Master Sean and Dr. Pateley were talking in very low tones on the opposite side of the fireplace. Chief Jaque stood stolidly in front of the mullioned window, watching the entire room without seeming to do so.

On the mantelpiece, the big clock swung its pendulum with muffled clicks.

Lord Gisors rose from his seat and came toward the sideboard where Lord Darcy and Father Villiers were talking.

"Excuse me, Lord Darcy, Father." He paused and cleared his throat a little, then looked at the priest. "We're all a little nervous, Reverend Sir. I know it's Good Friday, but would it be wrong to—er—to ask if anyone wants a glass of Xerez?"

"Of course not, my son. We are all suffering with Our Lord this day, and may suffer more, but I do not think He would frown upon our use of a stiff dose of medicinal palliative. Certainly Our Lord did not. According to St. John, He said, 'I thirst,' and they held up to Him a sponge soaked in wine. After He had received it, He said, 'It is accomplished.' " Father Villiers stopped.

" 'And gave up His spirit,' " Lord Gisors quoted glumly.

"Exactly," said the priest firmly. "But by Easter Day His spirit had returned, and the only casualty among the faithful that weekend was Judas. I'll have a brandy, myself."

Only Lady Beverly and Chief Jaque refused refreshment—each for a different reason. When the drinks were about half gone, Lord Darcy walked casually to the fireplace and faced them all.

"We have a vexing problem before us. We must show how the late Count de la Vexin met his death. With the cooperation of all of you, I think we can do it. First, we have to dispense with the notion that there was any Black Magic involved in the death of His Lordship. Master Sean?"

The Irishman rolled Xerez around on his tongue and swallowed before answering. "Me Lords, ladies, and gentlemen, having thoroughly given the situation every scientific test, I would be willing to state in His Majesty's Court of Justice that, by whatever means His Lordship the Count was killed, there was no trace of any magic, black *or* white, involved. Not in any capacity by anyone."

Lady Beverly's eyes blazed suddenly. "By no *human* agency, I suppose you mean?" Her voice was low, intense.

"Aye, Me Lady," Master Sean agreed.

"But what of the punishment of God? Or the evil works of Satan?"

A silence hung in the air. After a moment, Master Sean said: "I think I'll let the Reverend Father answer that one."

Father Villiers steepled his fingers. "My child, God punishes transgressors in many ways—usually through the purgatorial torture of conscience, or, if the conscience is weak, by the reaction of the sinner's fellow men to his evildoing. The Devil, in hope that the sinner may die before he has a chance to repent, may use various methods of driving them to self-destruction.

"But you cannot ascribe an act like this to *both* God and Satan. There is, furthermore, no evidence whatever that your late father was so great a sinner that God would have resorted to such drastic punishment, nor that the Devil feared of His Lordship's relenting in the near future of such minor sins as he may have committed.

"In any case, *neither God nor the Devil disposes of a man by grabbing him by the scruff of the neck and the seat of the pants and throwing him through a window!*

"Execution by defenestration, my child, is a peculiarly human act."

Lady Beverly bowed her head and said nothing.

Again a moment of silence, broken by Lord Darcy.

"My Lord Gisors, assuming that your father was killed by purely physical means, can you suggest how it might have been done?"

Lord Gisors, who had been at the sidetable pouring himself another drink, turned slowly around. "Yes, Lord Darcy. I can," he said thoughtfully.

Lord Darcy raised his left eyebrow again. "Indeed? Pray elucidate, My Lord."

Lord Gisors lifted his right index finger. "My father was pushed out that window. Correct?" His voice was shaking a little.

"Correct," Lord Darcy acknowledged.

"Then, by God, somebody had to push him out! I don't know who, I don't know how! But there had to be someone in there to do it!" He took another swallow of his drink and then went on in a somewhat calmer voice. "Look at it this way. Someone was in there waiting for him. My father came in, walked toward the window, got up on his desk, and that someone, whoever he was, ran up behind him and pushed him out. I don't know who or why, but that's what *had* to have happened! You're the Duke's Investigator. You find out what happened and who did it. But don't try to put it on any of us, My Lord, because none of us was anywhere near that room when it happened!"

He finished his drink in one swallow and poured another.

Lord Darcy spoke quietly. "Assuming your hypothesis is true, My Lord, how did the killer get into the room, and how did he get out?" Without waiting for an answer from Lord Gisors, Lord Darcy looked at Captain Sir Roderique. "Have you any suggestions, Sir Roderique?"

The old guardsman scowled. "I don't know. The laboratory was locked at all times, and always guarded when His Lordship was in there. But it wasn't especially guarded when Lord Jillbert was gone. He didn't go in often—not more than once or twice a week. The room wasn't particularly guarded the rest of the time. Anyone with a key could have got in. Someone could have stolen the key from My Lord de la Vexin and had a duplicate made."

"Highly unlikely," Lord Darcy said. "His Lordship wanted no one in that room but himself. On the other hand, my dear Captain, *you* have a duplicate."

Roderique's face seemed to turn purple. He came suddenly to his feet, looking down at Lord Darcy. "Are you accusing *me?*"

Darcy lifted a hand, palm outward. "Not yet, my dear Captain; perhaps not ever. Let us continue with our discussion without permitting our emotions to boil over." The Captain of the Guard sat down slowly without taking his eyes from Lord Darcy's face.

"I assure you, My Lord," the captain said, "that no other duplicate has ever been made from the key in my possession, and that the key has never been out of my possession."

"I believe you, Captain; I never said that any duplicate was made from *your* key. But let us make a hypothesis.

"Let us assume," Lord Darcy continued, "that the killer *did* have a duplicate key. Very well. What happened then?" He looked at Sergeant Andray. "Give us your opinion, Sergeant."

Andray frowned as though concentration on the problem was just a little beyond his capabilities. His handsome features seemed to be unsure of themselves. "Well—uh—well, My Lord, this is—I mean—well, if it were me—" He licked his lips again and looked at his wine glass. "Well, now, My Lord, supposing there were someone hidden inside the room, waiting for My Lord Count. Hm-m-m. His Lordship comes in and climbs up on the desk. Then the killer would have run forward and pushed him out. Yes. That's the only way it could have happened, isn't it?"

"Then how did he get out of the room afterward, Sergeant? You have told us that there was no one in the room when you went in through the window, and that the guardsmen outside found no one in the room after you let them in. The room was under guard all that time, was it not?"

"Yes, My Lord, it was."

"Then how did the killer get out?"

The Sergeant blinked. "Well, My Lord, the only other way out is through the trapdoor to the roof. He might have gone out that way."

Lord Darcy shook his head slowly. "Impossible. I looked at that rooftop carefully this morning. There is no sign that anyone has been up there for some time. Besides, how would he get down? The tower was surrounded by guardsmen who would have seen anyone trying to go down ninety feet on a rope, and there is hardly any other way. At any rate, he would have been seen. And he could hardly have come down the stairs; the interior was full of the Guard." His Lordship's eyes shifted suddenly. "Do you have any suggestions, Demoiselle Madelaine?"

She looked up at him with her round blue eyes. "No, My Lord. I know nothing about such things. It still seems like magic to me."

More silence.

Well, that's enough of this, Lord Darcy thought. *Now we go on to the final phase.*

"Does anyone else have a suggestion?" Apparently, no one did. "Very well, then; perhaps you would like to know my theory of how the killer—a very solid and human killer—got in and out of that room without being seen. Better than merely telling you, I shall demonstrate. Shall we repair to the late Count's *sanctum sanctorum?* Come."

There was a peculiar mixture of reluctance and avidity in the general feeling of those present, but they rose without objection and followed Lord Darcy across the courtyard to the Red Tower and up the long stairway to the late Count's room.

"Now," said Lord Darcy after they were all in the room, "I want all of you to obey my instructions exactly. Otherwise, someone is likely to get hurt. I am sorry there are no chairs in this room—evidently My Lord de la Vexin liked to work on his feet—so you will have to stand. Be so good as to stand over against the east wall. That's it. Thank you."

He took the five-inch brass key from his waistcoat pocket, then went over to the door and closed it. "The door was locked, so." *Click.* "And barred, so." *Thump.*

He repocketed the key and turned to face the others. "There, now. That's approximately the way things were after Lord de la Vexin locked himself in his laboratory for the last time. Except, of course, for the condition of that ruined window." He gestured toward the casement, empty now save for broken shards of glass and leading around the edges.

He looked all around the room, side to side and up and down. "No, it still isn't right, is it? Well, that can soon be adjusted properly. Firstly, we'll need to get that unused oil lamp down. Yonder ladder is a full two feet short to reach a ten-foot beam. There are no chairs or stools. A thorough search has shown that the long-handled hook which is the usual accouterment for such a lamp is nowhere in the room. Dear me! What shall we do?"

Most of the others were looking at Lord Darcy as though he had suddenly become simple-minded, but Master Sean smiled inwardly. He knew that His Lordship's blithering was to a purpose.

"Well! What have we here?" Lord Darcy was looking at the brass key in his hand as if he had never seen it before. "Hm-m-m, the end which engages the lock wards should make an excellent hook. Let us see."

Standing directly beneath the brass globe, he jumped up and accurately hooked the brass ring with the key. Then he lowered the big lamp down.

"What is this? It comes down quite easily! It balances the counterweight to a nicety. How odd! Can it be that it is not empty after all?" He took off the glass chimney, put it on the worktable of the east wall, went back and took out the wickholder. "Bless my soul! It is quite brimful of fuel."

He screwed the wickholder back in and lowered the whole lamp to the fullest extent of the pulley chain. It was hardly more than an inch off the floor. Then he grabbed the chain firmly with both hands and lifted. The lamp came up off the floor, but the chain above Lord Darcy's hands went limp and did not move upward. "Ah! The ratchet lock works perfectly. The counterweight cannot raise the lamp unless one pulls the chain down a little bit and then releases it slowly. Excellent." He lowered the lamp back down.

"Now comes the difficult part. That lamp is quite heavy." Lord Darcy smiled. "But, fortunately, we can use the ladder for this."

He brought the ladder over to the locked and barred door, bracing it against the wall over the lintel. Then his audience watched in stunned silence as he picked up the heavy lamp, carried it over to the ladder, climbed up, and hooked the chain over one of the apparatus hooks that the Count had fastened at many places in the ceiling.

"There, now," he said, descending the ladder. He looked up at the resulting configuration. The lamp chain now stretched almost horizontally from its supporting beam to the heavy hook in the ceiling

over the door. "You will notice," said His Lordship, "that the supporting beam for the lamp is not in the exact center of the room. It
is two feet nearer the window than it is to the door. The center of
the beam is eleven feet from the door, nine feet from the window."

"What *are* you talking about?" Lady Beverly burst out suddenly.
"What has all this to do with—"

"*If you please*, My Lady!" Lord Darcy cut her off sharply. Then,
more calmly. "Restrain yourself, I pray. All will become clear when
I have finished."

Good Lord, he thought to himself, *it should be plain to the veriest
dunce.*

Aloud, he said, "We are not through yet. The rope, Master Sean."

Without a word, Master Sean O Lochlainn opened his big symbol-
decorated carpetbag and took from it a coil of cotton rope; he gave
it to Lord Darcy.

"This is plain, ordinary cotton rope," His Lordship said. "But it
is not quite long enough. The other bit of rope, if you please, my
dear Sean."

The sorcerer handed him another foot-long piece of rope that
looked exactly like the coil he already held.

Using a fisherman's knot, Lord Darcy tied the two together.

He climbed up on the late Count's desk and tied the end of the
rope to another hook above the gaslight—the end with the tied-on
extra piece. Then he turned and threw the coil of rope across the
room to the foot of the ladder. He went back across the room and
climbed the ladder again, taking with him the other end of the rope.

Working carefully, he tied the rope to the chain link just above
the lamp, then, taking the chain off the hook, he looped the rope
over the hook so that it supported the lamp.

He climbed back down the ladder and pointed. "As you see, the
lamp is now supported solely by the rope, which is fastened at the
hook above the gaslamp over the window, stretches across the room,
and is looped over the hook above the door to support the weight."

By this time, they all understood. There was tenseness in the
room.

"I said," continued Lord Darcy, "that the rope I have used is ordinary cotton. So it is, except for that last additional foot which is
tied above the gaslamp. That last foot is not ordinary cotton, but of
specially treated cotton which is called nitred or nitrated cotton. It
burns extremely rapidly. In the original death trap, the entire rope

was made of that substance, but there was not enough left for me to use in this demonstration.

"As you will notice, the end which supports the lamp is several inches too long, after the knot was tied. The person who set this trap very tidily cut off the excess and then failed to pick up the discarded end. Well, we all make mistakes, don't we?"

Lord Darcy stood dramatically in the center of the room. "I want you all to imagine what it was like in this room last night. Dark—or nearly so. There is only the dim illumination from the courtyard lamps below." He picked up an unlit torch from the workbench a few feet away, then went to the door.

"My Lord Count has just come in. He has closed, locked, and barred the door. He has a torch in his hand." Lord Darcy lit the torch with his pipe lighter.

"Now, he walks across the room, to light the gaslamp above the window, as is his wont." Lord Darcy acted out his words.

"He climbs up on his desk. He turns on the gas valve. He lifts his torch to light the gas."

The gas jet shot a yellow flame several inches high. It touched the nitrated cotton rope above it. The rope flared into hissing flame.

Lord Darcy leaped aside and bounced to the floor, well away from the desk.

On the opposite side of the room, the heavy lamp was suddenly released from its hold. Like some airborne juggernaut, it swung ponderously along the arc of its chain. At the bottom of that arc, it grazed the floor with the brass ring. Then it swung up and—as anyone could see—would have smashed the window, had it still been there. Then it swung back.

Everyone in the room watched the lamp pendulum back and forth, dragging the cotton rope behind it. The nitrated section had long since vanished in flame.

Lord Darcy stood on the east side of the room, with the pendulum scything the air between himself and the others.

"Thus you see how the late Count de la Vexin came to his death. The arc this thing cuts would have struck him just below the shoul-der-blades. Naturally, it would not have swung so long as now, having been considerably slowed by its impact with the Count's body." He walked over, grabbed the chain, and fought the pendulum to a standstill.

They all stared fascinated at the deadly weight which now swung in a modest two-inch wobble.

The young Lord Gisors lifted his head with a jerk and stared straight into Lord Darcy's eyes. "Surely my father would have seen that white rope, Darcy."

"Not if it were covered with lampblack—which it was."

Lord Gisors narrowed his eyes. "Oh, fine. So that's the end of it, eh? With the lamp hanging there, almost touching the floor. Then—*will you explain how it got back up to where it belongs?*"

"Certainly," said Lord Darcy.

He walked over to the lamp, removed the length of cotton rope, pulled gently on the chain to unlock the ratchet, and eased the lamp up. After it left his outstretched hand, it moved on up quietly to its accustomed place.

"Like that," said Lord Darcy blandly. "Except, of course, that the glass chimney was replaced first. And the rope did not need to be removed, since it had all been burnt up."

Before anyone else could speak, Father Villiers said: "Just a moment, My Lord. If someone had done that, he would have had to have been in this room—seconds after the death. But there is no way in or out of this room except the door—which was guarded—and the door to the roof, which you have said was not used. There is no other way in or out of this room."

Lord Darcy smiled. "Oh, but there is, Reverend Father."

The priest looked blank.

"The way My Lord de la Vexin took," Lord Darcy said gently.

Surely they understand now, Lord Darcy thought. He broke the silence by saying: "The lamp was down. There was no one in this room. Then someone climbed in through the window via the fire ladder, raised the lamp again, and—

"*Chief Jaque!*" Lord Darcy shouted.

But he was a fraction of a second too late.

Sergeant Andray had drawn a concealed sidearm. Chief Jaque was just a little too late getting his own gun out.

There was the sudden ear-shattering shock of a heavy-caliber pistol firing in a closed room, and Chief Jaque went down with a bullet in him.

Lord Darcy's hand darted toward the pistol at his own hip, but before it could clear the holster, Captain Sir Roderique leaped toward his son.

"*You fool! You—*" His voice was agonized.

He grabbed the sergeant's wrist, twisted it up.

There came a second shattering blast.

Sir Roderique fell backwards; the bullet had gone in under his chin and taken the top of his head off.

Sergeant Andray screamed.

Then he spun around, leaped to the top of the desk, and flung himself out the window, still screaming.

The scream lasted just a bit over two second before Sergeant Andray was permanently silenced by the courtyard below.

The celebrations of Holy Saturday were over. Easter Season had officially begun. The bells were still ringing in the tower of the Cathedral of St. Ouen in the city of Rouen, the capital of the Duchy of Normandy.

His Royal Highness, Richard, Duke of Normandy, leaned back in his chair and smiled across the cozy fireplace at his Chief Investigator. Both of them were holding warming glasses of fine Champagne brandy.

His Highness had just finished reading Lord Darcy's report.

"I see, My Lord," he said. "After the trap had been set and triggered—after the late de la Vexin had been propelled through the window to his death—Sergeant Andray went up the fire ladder alone, raised the lamp back to its usual position, and then opened the barred door to allow in the other guardsmen. The fox concealing himself among the hounds."

"Precisely, Your Highness. And you see the motive."

His Highness the Duke, younger brother of His Imperial Majesty, King John IV, was blond, blue-eyed, and handsome like all the Plantagenets, but at this moment there was a faint frown upon his forehead.

"The motive was obvious from the beginning, My Lord," he said. "I can see that Sergeant Andray wanted to get rid of My Lord de la Vexin in order to clear the way for a marriage which would be beneficial to his sister—and, of course, to the rest of the family. But your written report is incomplete." He tapped the sheaf of papers in his hand.

"I fear, Your Highness," Lord Darcy said carefully, "that it must remain forever incomplete.

Prince Richard leaned back and sighed. "Very well, Darcy. Give it to me orally. Off the record, as usual."

"As you command, Your Highness," Lord Darcy said, refilling his glass.

"Young Andray must be blamed for the murder. The evidence I

have can go no further, now that both he and his father are dead. Chief Jaque, who will easily recover from the bullet wound in his shoulder, has no more evidence than I have.

"Captain Sir Roderique will be buried with military honors, since eyewitnesses can and will say that he tried to stop his son from shooting me. Further hypotheses now would merely raise a discussion that could never be resolved.

"But it was not Sergeant Andray who set the trap. Only Captain Sir Roderique had access to the key that unlocked the laboratory. Only he could have gone up there and set the death trap that killed the late Count."

"Then why," the Prince asked, "did he try to stop his son?"

"Because, Your Highness," Lord Darcy replied, "he did not think I had enough evidence to convict. He was trying to stop young Andray from making a fool of himself by giving the whole thing away. Andray had panicked—which I had hoped he would, but not, I must admit, to that extent.

"He killed his father, who had plotted the whole thing, and, seeing what he had done, went into a suicidal hysteria which resulted in his death. I am sorry for that, Your Highness."

"Not your fault, Darcy. What about the Demoiselle Madelaine?"

Lord Darcy sipped at his brandy. "She was the prime mover, of course. She instigated the whole thing—subtly. No way to prove it. But Lord Gisors sees through her now. He will wed the lady his father quite properly chose for him."

"I see," said the Prince. "You told him the truth?"

"I spoke to him, Your Highness," Lord Darcy said. "But he already knew the truth."

"Then the matter is settled." His Highness straightened up in his chair. "Now, about those notebooks you brought back with you. What do they mean?"

"They are the late Count's scientific-materialistic notes on his researches for the past twenty years, Your Highness. They represent two decades of hard research."

"But—really, Darcy. Research on Materialism? Of what use could they possibly be?"

"Your Highness, the Laws of Magic tell us how the mind of man can influence the material universe. But the universe is more than the mind of man can possibly encompass. The mind of God may keep the planets and the stars in their courses, but, if so, then He has laws by which He abides."

Lord Darcy finished his brandy. "There are more things in this universe than the mind of man, Your Highness, and there are laws which govern them. Someday, those notebooks may be invaluable."

August Heat

by W. F. Harvey

I have had what I believe to be the most remarkable day in my life, and while the events are still fresh in my mind, I wish to put them down on paper as clearly as possible.

Let me say at the outset that my name is James Clarence Withencroft.

I am forty years old, in perfect health, never having known a day's illness.

By profession I am an artist, not a very successful one, but I earn enough money by my black-and-white work to satisfy my necessary wants.

My only near relative, a sister, died five years ago, so that I am independent.

I breakfasted this morning at nine, and after glancing through the morning paper I lighted my pipe and proceeded to let my mind wander in the hope that I might chance upon some subject for my pencil.

The room, though door and windows were open, was oppressively hot, and I had just made up my mind that the coolest and most comfortable place in the neighbourhood would be the deep end of the public swimming bath, when the idea came.

I began to draw. So intent was I on my work that I left my lunch untouched, only stopping work when the clock of St. Jude's struck four.

The final result, for a hurried sketch, was, I felt sure, the best thing I had done.

It showed a criminal in the dock immediately after the judge had pronounced sentence. The man was fat—enormously fat. The flesh hung in rolls about his chin; it creased his huge, stumpy neck. He was clean shaven (perhaps I should say a few days before he must have been clean shaven) and almost bald. He stood in the dock, his short, clumsy fingers clasping the rail, looking straight in front of

130

him. The feeling that his expression conveyed was not so much one of horror as of utter, absolute collapse.

There seemed nothing in the man strong enough to sustain that mountain of flesh.

I rolled up the sketch, and without quite knowing why, placed it in my pocket. Then with the rare sense of happiness which the knowledge of a good thing well done gives, I left the house.

I believe that I set out with the idea of calling upon Trenton, for I remember walking along Lytton Street and turning to the right along Gilchrist Road at the bottom of the hill where the men were at work on the new tram lines.

From there onwards I have only the vaguest recollection of where I went. The one thing of which I was fully conscious was the awful heat, that came up from the dusty asphalt pavement as an almost palpable wave. I longed for the thunder promised by the great banks of copper-coloured cloud that hung low over the western sky.

I must have walked five or six miles, when a small boy roused me from my reverie by asking the time.

It was twenty minutes to seven.

When he left me I began to take stock of my bearings. I found myself standing before a gate that led into a yard bordered by a strip of thirsty earth, where there were flowers, purple stock and scarlet geranium. Above the entrance was a board with the inscription—

CHS. ATKINSON. MONUMENTAL MASON.
WORKER IN ENGLISH AND ITALIAN MARBLES.

From the yard itself came a cheery whistle, the noise of hammer blows, and the cold sound of steel meeting stone.

A sudden impulse made me enter.

A man was sitting with his back towards me, busy at work on a slab of curiously veined marble. He turned round as he heard my steps and I stopped short.

It was the man I had been drawing, whose portrait lay in my pocket.

He sat there, huge and elephantine, the sweat pouring from his scalp, which he wiped with a red silk handkerchief. But though the face was the same, the expression was absolutely different.

He greeted me smiling, as if we were old friends, and shook my hand.

I apologised for my intrusion.

"Everything is hot and glary outside," I said. "This seems an oasis in the wilderness."

"I don't know about the oasis," he replied, "but it certainly is hot, as hot as hell. Take a seat, sir!"

He pointed to the end of the gravestone on which he was at work, and I sat down.

"That's a beautiful stone you've got hold of," I said.

He shook his head. "In a way it is," he answered; "the surface here is as fine as anything you could wish, but there's a big flaw at the back, though I don't expect you'd ever notice it. I could never make really a good job of a bit of marble like that. It would be all right in a summer like this; it wouldn't mind the blasted heat. But wait till the winter comes. There's nothing quite like frost to find out the weak points in stone."

"Then what's it for?" I asked.

The man burst out laughing.

"You'd hardly believe me if I was to tell you it's for an exhibition, but it's the truth. Artists have exhibitions: so do grocers and butchers; we have them too. All the latest little things in headstones, you know."

He went on to talk of marbles, which sort best withstood wind and rain, and which were easiest to work; then of his garden and a new sort of carnation he had bought. At the end of every other minute he would drop his tools, wipe his shining head, and curse the heat.

I said little, for 1 felt uneasy. There was something unnatural, uncanny, in meeting this man.

I tried at first to persuade myself that I had seen him before, that his face, unknown to me, had found a place in some out-of-the-way corner of my memory, but I knew that I was practising little more than a plausible piece of self-deception.

Mr. Atkinson finished his work, spat on the ground, and got up with a sigh of relief.

"There! What do you think of that?" he said, with an air of evident pride.

The inscription which I read for the first time was this—

SACRED TO THE MEMORY

OF

JAMES CLARENCE WITHENCROFT

BORN JAN. 18TH, 1860.

HE PASSED AWAY VERY SUDDENLY
ON AUGUST 20TH, 190—
"In the midst of life we are in death."

For some time I sat in silence. Then a cold shudder ran down my spine. I asked him where he had seen the name.

"Oh, I didn't see it anywhere," replied Mr. Atkinson. "I wanted some name, and I put down the first that came into my head. Why do you want to know?"

"It's a strange coincidence, but it happens to be mine."

He gave a long, low whistle.

"And the dates?"

"I can only answer for one of them, and that's correct."

"It's a rum go!" he said.

But he knew less than I did. I told him of my morning's work. I took the sketch from my pocket and showed it to him. As he looked, the expression of his face altered until it became more and more like that of the man I had drawn.

"And it was only the day before yesterday," he said, "that I told Maria there were no such things as ghosts!"

Neither of us had seen a ghost, but I knew what he meant.

"You probably heard my name," I said.

"And you must have seen me somewhere and have forgotten it! Were you at Clacton-on-Sea last July?"

I had never been to Clacton in my life. We were silent for some time. We were both looking at the same thing, the two dates on the gravestone, and one was right.

"Come inside and have some supper," said Mr. Atkinson.

His wife is a cheerful little woman, with the flaky red cheeks of the country-bred. Her husband introduced me as a friend of his who was an artist. The result was unfortunate, for after the sardines and watercress had been removed, she brought out a Doré Bible, and I had to sit and express my admiration for nearly half an hour.

I went outside, and found Atkinson sitting on the gravestone smoking.

We resumed the conversation at the point we had left off.

"You must excuse my asking," I said, "but do you know of anything you've done for which you could be put on trial?"

He shook his head.

"I'm not a bankrupt, the business is prosperous enough. Three years ago I gave turkeys to some of the guardians at Christmas, but

that's all I can think of. And they were small ones, too," he added
as an afterthought.

He got up, fetched a can from the porch, and began to water the
flowers. "Twice a day regular in the hot weather," he said, "and then
the heat sometimes gets the better of the delicate ones. And ferns,
good-Lord! they could never stand it. Where do you live?"

I told him my address. It would take an hour's quick walk to get
back home.

"It's like this," he said. "We'll look at the matter straight. If you
go back home tonight, you take your chance of accidents. A cart
may run over you, and there's always banana skins and orange peel,
to say nothing of falling ladders."

He spoke of the improbable with an intense seriousness that would
have been laughable six hours before. But I did not laugh.

"The best thing we can do," he continued, "is for you to stay here
till twelve o'clock. We'll go upstairs and smoke; it may be cooler
inside."

To my surprise I agreed.

We are sitting now in a long, low room beneath the eaves. Atkinson has sent his wife to bed. He himself is busy sharpening some
tools at a little oilstone, smoking one of my cigars the while.

The air seems charged with thunder. I am writing this at a shaky
table before the open window. The leg is cracked, and Atkinson, who
seems a handy man with his tools, is going to mend it as soon as he
has finished putting an edge on his chisel.

It is after eleven now. I shall be gone in less than an hour.

But the heat is stifling.

It is enough to send a man mad.

The Girl Who Found Things

by Henry Slesar

I t was dark by the time Lucas stopped his taxi in the driveway of the Wheeler home and lumbered up the path to the front entrance. He still wore his heavy boots, despite the spring thaw; his mackinaw and knitted cap were reminders of the hard winter that had come and gone.

When Geraldine Wheeler opened the door, wearing her light-weight traveling suit, she shivered at the sight of him. "Come in," she said crisply. "My trunk is inside."

Lucas went through the foyer to the stairway, knowing his way around the house, accustomed to its rich, dark textures and somber furnishings; he was Medvale's only taxi driver. He found the heavy black trunk at the foot of the stairs, and hoisted it on his back. "That all the luggage, Miss Wheeler?"

"That's all, I've sent the rest ahead to the ship. Good heavens, Lucas, aren't you *hot* in that outfit?" She opened a drawer and rummaged through it. "I've probably forgotten a million things. Gas, electricity, phone ... Fireplace! Lucas, would you check it for me, please?"

"Yes, Miss," Lucas said. He went into the living room, past the white-shrouded furniture. There were some glowing embers among the blackened stumps, and he snuffed them out with a poker.

A moment later the woman entered, pulling on long silken gloves. "All right," she said breathlessly. "I guess that's all. We can go now."

"Yes, Miss," Lucas said.

She turned her back and he came up behind her, still holding the poker. He made a noise, either a sob or a grunt, as he raised the ash-coated iron and struck her squarely in the back of the head. Her knees buckled, and she sank to the carpet in an ungraceful fall. Lucas never doubted that she had died instantly, because he had once killed an ailing shorthorn bull with a blow no greater. He tried to act as calmly now. He put the poker back into the fireplace, purifying it among the hot coals. Then he went to his victim and examined her wound. It was ugly, but there was no blood.

He picked up the light body without effort and went through the screen door of the kitchen and out into the back yard, straight to the thickly wooded acreage that surrounded the Wheeler estate. When he found an appropriate place for Geraldine Wheeler's grave, he went to the toolshed for a spade and shovel.

It was spring, but the ground was hard. He was stripped of mackinaw and cap when he was finished. For the first time in months, since the icy winter began, Lucas was warm.

April had lived up to its moist reputation; there was mud on the roads and pools of black water in the driveway. When the big white car came to a halt, its metal skirt was clotted with Medvale's red clay. Rowena, David Wheeler's wife, didn't leave the car, but waited with an impatient frown until her husband helped her out. She put her high heels into the mud, and clucked in vexation.

David smiled, smiled charmingly, forgiving the mud, the rain, and his wife's bad temper. "Come on, it's not so bad," he said. "Only a few steps." He heard the front door open, and saw his Aunt Faith waving to them. "There's the old gypsy now," he said happily. "Now remember what I told you, darling, when she starts talking about spooks and séances, you just keep a straight face."

"I'll try," Rowena said dryly.

There was affectionate collision between David and his aunt at the doorway; he put his arms around her sizable circumference and pressed his patrician nose to her plump cheek.

"David, my handsome boy! I'm so glad to see you!"

"It's wonderful seeing you, Aunt Faith!"

They were inside before David introduced the two women. David and Rowena had been married in Virginia two years ago, but Aunt Faith never stirred beyond the borders of Medvale County.

The old woman gave Rowena a glowing look of inspection. "Oh, my dear, you're beautiful," she said. "David, you beast, how could you keep her all to yourself?"

He laughed, and coats were shed, and they went into the living room together. There, the cheerfulness of the moment was dissipated. A man was standing by the fireplace smoking a cigarette in nervous puffs, and David was reminded of the grim purpose of the reunion.

"Lieutenant Reese," Aunt Faith said, "this is my nephew, David, and his wife."

Reese was a balding man, with blurred and melancholy features. He shook David's hand solemnly. "Sorry we have to meet this way," he said. "But then, I always seem to meet people when they're in trouble. Of course, I've known Mrs. Demerest for some time."

"Lieutenant Reese has been a wonderful help with my charity work," Aunt Faith said. "And he's been such a comfort since . . . this awful thing happened."

David looked around the room. "It's been years since I was here. Wonder if I remember where the liquor's kept?"

"I'm afraid there is none," Reese said. "There wasn't any when we came in to search the place some weeks ago, when Miss Wheeler first disappeared."

There was a moment's silence. David broke it with, "Well, I've got a bottle in the car."

"Not now, Mr. Wheeler. As a matter of fact, I'd appreciate it if you and I could have a word alone."

Aunt Faith went to Rowena's side. "I'll tell you what. Why don't you and I go upstairs, and I'll show you your room?"

"That would be fine," Rowena said.

"I can even show you the room where David was born, and his old nursery. Wouldn't you like that?"

"That would be lovely," Rowena said flatly.

When they were alone, Reese said, "How long have you been away from Medvale, Mr. Wheeler?"

"Oh, maybe ten years. I've been back here on visits, of course. Once when my father died, four years ago. As you know, our family's business is down south."

"Yes, I knew. You and your sister—"

"My half sister."

"Yes," Reese said. "You and your half sister, you were the only proprietors of the mill, weren't you?"

"That's right."

"But you did most of the managing, I gather. When your parents died, Miss Wheeler kept the estate, and you went to Virginia to manage the mill. That's how it was, right?"

"That's how it was," David said.

"Successfully, would you say?"

David sat in a wing chair, and stretched his long legs. "Lieutenant, I'm going to save you a great deal of time. Geraldine and I didn't get along. We saw as little of each other as both could arrange, and that was *very* little."

Reese cleared his throat. "Thank you for being frank."

"I can even guess your next question, Lieutenant. You'd like to know when I saw Geraldine last."

"When did you?"

"Three months ago, in Virginia. On her semiannual visit to the mill."

"But you were in Medvale after that, weren't you?"

"Yes. I came up to see Geraldine in March on a matter of some importance. As my aunt probably told you, Geraldine refused to see me at that time."

"What was the purpose of that visit?"

"Purely business. I wanted Geraldine to approve a bank loan I wished to make to purchase new equipment. She was against it, wouldn't even discuss it. So I left and returned to Virginia."

"And you never saw her again?"

"Never," David said. He smiled, smiled engagingly, and got to his feet. "I don't care if you're a teetotaler like my aunt, Lieutenant, I've *got* to have that drink."

He went toward the front hall, but paused at the doorway. "In case you're wondering," he said lightly, "I have no idea where Geraldine is, Lieutenant. No idea at all."

Rowena and Aunt Faith didn't come downstairs until an hour later, after the lieutenant had left. Aunt Faith looked like she had been sleeping; Rowena had changed into a sweater and gray skirt. In the living room, they found David, a half-empty bottle of Scotch, and a dying fire.

"Well?" Aunt Faith said. "Was he very bothersome?"

"Not at all," David said. "You look lovely, Rowena."

"I'd like a drink, David."

"Yes, of course." He made one for her, and teased Aunt Faith about her abstinence. She didn't seem to mind. She wanted to talk, about Geraldine.

"I just can't understand it," she said. "Nobody can, not the police, not anybody. She was all set for that Caribbean trip, some of her bags were already on the ship. You remember Lucas, the cab driver? He came out here to pick her up and take her to the station, but she wasn't here. She wasn't anywhere."

"I suppose the police have checked the usual sources?"

"Everything. Hospitals, morgues, everywhere. Lieutenant Reese says almost anything could have happened to her. She might have been robbed and murdered; she might have lost her memory; she might even have—" Aunt Faith blushed. "Well, this I'd *never* believe, but Lieutenant Reese says she might have disappeared deliberately—with some *man*."

Rowena had been at the window, drinking quietly. "I know what happened," she said.

David looked at her sharply.

"She just left. She just walked out of this gloomy old house and this crawly little town. She was sick of living alone. Sick of a whole town waiting for her to get married. She was tired of worrying about looms and loans and debentures. She was sick of being herself. That's how a woman can get."

She reached for the bottle, and David held her wrist. "Don't," he said. "You haven't eaten all day."

"Let me go," Rowena said softly.

He smiled, and let her go.

"I think the lieutenant was right," Rowena said. "I think there was a man, Auntie. Some vulgar type. Maybe a coal digger or a truck driver, somebody without any *charm* at all." She raised her glass in David's direction. "No charm at all."

Aunt Faith stood up, her plump cheeks mottled. "David, I have an idea—about how we can find Geraldine, I mean. I'm certain of it."

"Really?"

"But you're not going to agree with me. You're going to give me that nice smile of yours and you're going to humor me. But whether you approve or not, David, I'm going to ask Iris Lloyd where Geraldine is."

David's eyebrows made an arc. "Ask who?"

"Iris Lloyd," Aunt Faith said firmly. "Now don't tell me you've never heard of that child. There was a story in the papers about her only two months ago, and heaven knows I've mentioned her in my letters a dozen times."

"I remember," Rowena said, coming forward. "She's the one who's . . . psychic or something. Some sort of orphan?"

"Iris is a ward of the state, a resident at the Medvale Home for Girls. I've been vice-chairman of the place for donkey's years, so I know all about it. She's sixteen and amazing, David, absolutely uncanny!"

"I see." He hid an amused smile behind his glass. "And what makes Iris such a phenomenon?"

"She's a seer, David, a genuine clairvoyant. I've told you about this Count Louis Hamon, the one who called himself Cheiro the Great? Of course, he's dead now, he died in 1936, but he was gifted in the same way Iris is. He could just *look* at a person's mark and know the most astounding things—"

"Wait a minute. You really think this foundling can tell us where Geraldine is? Through some kind of séance?"

"She's not a medium. I suppose you could call her a *finder*. She seems to have the ability to *find* things that are lost. People, too."

"How does she do it, Mrs. Demerest?" Rowena asked.

"I can't say. I'm not sure Iris can either. The gift hasn't made her happy, poor child—such talents rarely do. For a while, it seemed like nothing more than a parlor trick. There was a Sister Theresa at the Home, a rather befuddled old lady who was always misplacing her thimble or what-have-you, and each time Iris was able to find it—even in the unlikeliest places."

David chuckled. "Sometimes kids *hide* things in the unlikeliest places. Couldn't she be some sort of prankster?"

"But there was more," Aunt Faith said gravely. "One day, the Home had a picnic at Crompton Lake. They discovered that an eight-year-old girl named Dorothea was missing. They couldn't find her, until Iris Lloyd began screaming."

"Screaming . . .?" Rowena said.

"These insights cause her great pain. But she was able to describe the place where they would find Dorothea; a small natural cave, where Dorothea was found only half-alive from a bad fall she had taken."

Rowena shivered.

"You were right," David said pleasantly. "I can't agree with you, Auntie. I don't go along with this spirit business; let's leave it up to the police."

Aunt Faith sighed. "I knew you'd feel that way. But I have to do this, David. I've arranged with the Home to have Iris spend some time with us, to become acquainted with the . . . aura of Geraldine that's still in the house."

"Are you serious? You've asked that girl *here*?"

"I knew you wouldn't be pleased. But the police can't find Geraldine, they haven't turned up a clue. Iris can."

"I won't have it," he said tightly. "I'm sorry, Auntie, but the whole thing is ridiculous."

"You can't stop me. I was only hoping that you would cooperate." She looked at Rowena, her eyes softening. "You understand me, my dear. I know you do."

Rowena hesitated, then touched the old woman's hands. "I do, Mrs. Demerest." She looked at David with a curious smile. "And I'd like nothing better than to meet Iris."

Ivy failed to soften the Medvale Home's cold stone substance and ugly lines. It had been built in an era that equated orphanages with penal institutions, and its effect upon David was depressing.

The head of the institution, Sister Clothilde, entered her office, sat down briskly, and folded her hands. "I don't have to tell you that I'm against this, Mrs. Demerest," she said. "I think it's completely wrong to encourage Iris in these delusions of hers."

Aunt Faith seemed cowed by the woman; her reply was timid. "Delusions, Sister? It's a gift of God."

"If this . . . ability of Iris' has any spiritual origin, I'm afraid it's from quite another place. Not that I admit there *is* a gift."

David turned on his most charming smile, but Sister Clothilde seemed immune to it.

"I'm glad to see I have an ally," he said. "I've been telling my aunt that it's all nonsense—"

Sister Clothilde bristled. "It's true that Iris has done some remarkable things which we're at a loss to explain. But I'm hoping she'll outgrow this—whatever it is, and be just a normal, happy girl. As she is now—"

"Is she very unhappy?" Aunt Faith asked sadly.

"She's undisciplined, you might even say wild. In less than two years, when she's of legal age, we'll be forced to release her from the Home, and we'd very much like to send her away a better person than she is now."

"But you *are* letting us have her, Sister? She can come home with us?"

"Did you think my poor objections carried any weight, Mrs. Demerest?"

A moment later, Iris Lloyd was brought in.

She was a girl in the pony stage, long gawky arms and legs protruding from a smock dress that had been washed out of all color and starched out of all shape. Her stringy hair was either dirty blonde or just dirty; David guessed the latter. She had a flat-footed walk, and kept twisting her arms. She kept her eyes lowered as Sister Bertha brought her forward.

"Iris," Sister Clothilde said, "you know Mrs. Demerest. And this is her nephew, Mr. Wheeler."

Iris nodded. Then, in a flash almost too sudden to be observed, her eyes came up and stabbed them with such an intensity of either hostility or malice that David almost made his surprise audible. No one else, however, seemed to have noticed.

"You remember me, Iris," Aunt Faith said. "I've been coming here at least once a year to see all you girls."

"Yes, Mrs. Demerest," Iris whispered.

"The directors have been good enough to let us take you home with us for a while. We need your help, Iris. We want you to see if you can help us find someone who is lost."

"Yes, Mrs. Demerest," she answered serenely. "I'd like to come home with you. I'd like to help you find Miss Wheeler."

"Then you know about my poor niece, Iris?"

Sister Clothilde clucked. "The Secret Service couldn't have secrets here, Mrs. Demerest. You know how girls are."

David cleared his throat and stood up. "I guess we can get started any time. If Miss Lloyd has her bags ready . . ."

Iris gave him a quick smile at that, but Sister Clothilde wiped it off with, "Please call her Iris, Mr. Wheeler. Remember that you're still dealing with a child."

When Iris' bags were in the trunk compartment, she climbed between David and his aunt in the front seat, and watched with interest as David turned the key in the ignition.

"Say," she said, "you wouldn't have a cigarette, would you?"

"Why, Iris!" Aunt Faith gasped.

She grinned. "Never mind," she said lightly. "Just never mind." Then she closed her eyes, and began to hum. She hummed to herself all the way to the Wheeler house.

David drove into town that afternoon, carrying a long list of groceries and sundries that Aunt Faith deemed necessary for the care and feeding of a sixteen-year-old girl.

He was coming out of the Medvale Supermarket when he saw Lucas Mitchell's battered black taxicab rolling slowly down the back slope of the parking lot. He frowned and walked quickly to his own car, but as he put the groceries in the rear, he saw Lucas' cab stop beside him.

"Hello, Mr. Wheeler," Lucas said, leaning out the window.

"Hello, Lucas. How's business?"

"Could I talk to you a minute, Mr. Wheeler?"

"No," David said. He went around front and climbed into the driver's seat. He fumbled in his pocket for the key, and the sight of Lucas leaving his cab made it seem much more difficult to find.

"I've got to talk to you, Mr. Wheeler."

"Not here," David said. "Not here and not now, Lucas."

"It's important. I want to ask you something."

"For the love of Mike," David said, gritting his teeth. He found the key at last, and shoved it into the slit on the dashboard. "Get out of the way, Lucas, I can't stop now."

"That girl, Mr. Wheeler. Is it true about the girl?"

"What girl?"

"That Iris Lloyd. She does funny things, that one. I'm afraid of her, Mr. Wheeler, I'm afraid she'll find out what we did."

"Get out of the way!" David shouted. He turned the key, and stomped the accelerator to make the engine roar a threat. Lucas moved away, bewildered, and David backed the car out sharply and drove off.

He got home to find Rowena pacing the living room. Her agitation served to quiet his own. "What's wrong?" he said.

"I wouldn't know for sure. Better ask your aunt."

"Where is she?"

"In her room, lying down. All I know is she went up to see if dear little Iris was awake, and they had some kind of scene. I caught only a few of the words, but I'll tell you one thing, that girl has the vocabulary of a longshoreman."

David grunted. "Well, it'll knock some sense into Aunt Faith. I'll go up to see her, and tell her I'll take that little psychic delinquent back where she came from—"

"I wouldn't bother her now, she's not feeling well."

"Then I'll see the little monster. Where is she?"

"Next door to us, in Geraldine's room."

At the door, he lifted his hand to knock, but the door was flung open before his knuckles touched wood.

Iris looked out, her hair tumbled over one eye. Her mouth went from petulant to sultry, and she put her hands on the shapeless uniform where her hips should be.

"Hello, handsome," she said. "Auntie says you went shopping for me."

"What have you been up to?" He walked in and closed the door. "My aunt isn't a well woman, Iris, and we won't put up with any bad behavior. Now, what happened here?"

She shrugged, and walked back to the bed. "Nothing," she said sullenly. "I found a butt in an ash tray and was taking a drag when she walked in. You'd think I was burning the house down the way she yelled."

"I heard you did some fancy yelling yourself. Is that what the Sisters taught you?"

"They didn't teach me anything worthwhile."

Suddenly, Iris changed; face, posture, everything. In an astonishing transformation, she was a child again.

"I'm sorry," she whimpered. "I'm awfully sorry, Mr. Wheeler. I didn't mean to do anything wrong."

He stared at her, baffled, not knowing how to take the alteration of personality. Then he realized that the door had opened behind him, and that Aunt Faith had entered.

Iris fell on the bed and began to sob, and with four long strides, Aunt Faith crossed the room and put her plump arms around her in maternal sympathy.

"There, there," she crooned, "it's all right, Iris. I know you didn't mean what you said, it's the Gift that makes you this way. And don't worry about what I asked you to do. You take your time about Geraldine, take as long as you like."

"Oh, but I *want* to help!" Iris said fervently. "I really do, Aunt Faith." She stood up, her face animated. "I can *feel* your niece in this house. I can almost hear her—whispering to me—telling me where she is!"

"You can?" Aunt Faith said in awe. "Really and truly?"

"Almost, almost!" Iris said, spinning in an awkward dance. She twirled in front of a closet, and opened the door; there were still half a dozen hangers of clothing inside. "These are *her* clothes. Oh, they're so beautiful! She must have looked beautiful in them!"

David snorted. "Has Iris ever seen a photo of Geraldine?"

The girl took out a gold lamé evening gown and held it in her arms. "Oh, it's so lovely! I can *feel* her in this dress, I can just *feel* her!" She looked at Aunt Faith with wild happiness. "I just know I'm going to be able to help you!"

"Bless you," Aunt Faith said. Her eyes were damp.

Iris was on her best behavior for the rest of the day; her mood extended all the way through dinner. It was an uncomfortable meal for everyone except the girl. She asked to leave the table before coffee was served, and went upstairs.

When the maid cleared the dining table, they went to the living room, and David said, "Aunt Faith, I think this is a terrible mistake."

"Mistake, David? Explain that."

"This polite act of Iris'. Can't you see it's a pose?"

The woman stiffened. "You're wrong. You don't understand psychic personalities. It wasn't *her* swearing at me, David, it was this demon that possesses her. The same spirit that gives her the gift of insight."

Rowena laughed. "It's probably the spirit of an old sailor, judging from the language. Frankly, Aunt Faith, to me she seems like an ordinary little girl."

"You'll see," Aunt Faith said stubbornly. "You just wait and see how ordinary she is."

As if to prove Aunt Faith's contention, Iris came downstairs twenty minutes later wearing Geraldine Wheeler's gold lamé gown. Her face had been smeared with an overdose of makeup, and her stringy hair clumsily tied in an upsweep that refused to stay up. David and Rowena gawked at the spectacle, but Aunt Faith was only mildly perturbed.

"Iris, dear," she said, "what have you done?"

She minced into the center of the room. She hadn't changed her flat-heeled shoes, and the effect of her attempted gracefulness was almost comic; but David didn't laugh.

"Get upstairs and change," he said tightly. "You've no right to wear my sister's clothes."

Her face fell in disappointment and she looked at Aunt Faith. "Oh, Aunt Faith!" she wailed. "You know what I told you! I *have* to wear your niece's clothes, to feel her . . . aura!"

"Aura, my foot!" David said.

She stared at him, stunned. Then she fell into the wing chair by the fireplace and sobbed. Aunt Faith quickly repeated her ministrations of that afternoon, and chided David.

"You shouldn't have said that!" she said angrily. "The poor girl is trying to help us, David, and you're spoiling it!"

"Sorry," he said wryly. "I guess I'm just not a believer, Aunt Faith."

"You won't even give her a chance!"

Aunt Faith waited until Iris' sobs quieted, her face thoughtful. Then she leaned close to the girl's ear. "Iris, listen to me. You remember those things you did at the Home? The way you found things for Sister Theresa?"

Iris blinked away the remainder of her tears. "Yes."

"Do you think you could do that again, Iris? Right now, for us?"

"I—I don't know. I could try."

"Will you let her try, David?"

"I don't know what you mean."

"I want you to hide something, or name some object you've lost or misplaced, perhaps somewhere in this house."

"This is silly. It's a parlor game—"

"David!"

He frowned. "All right, have it your own way. How do we play this little game of hide-and-seek?"

Rowena said, "David, what about the cat?"

"The cat?"

"You remember. You once told me about a wool kitten you used to have as a child. You said you lost it somewhere in the house when you were five, and you were so unhappy about it that you wouldn't eat for days."

"That's preposterous. That's thirty years ago—"

"All the better," Aunt Faith said. "All the better, David." She turned to the girl. "Do you think you can find it, Iris? Could you find David's cloth kitten?"

"I'm not sure. I'm never sure, Aunt Faith."

"Just try, Iris. We won't blame you if you fail. It might have been thrown out ages ago, but try anyway."

The girl sat up, and put her face in her hands.

"David," Aunt Faith whispered, "put out the light."

David turned off the one table lamp that lit the room. The flames of the fireplace animated their shadows.

"Try, Iris," Aunt Faith encouraged.

The clock on the mantelpiece revealed its loud tick. Then Iris dropped her hands limply into her lap, and she leaned against the high back of the wing chair with a long, troubled sigh.

"It's a trance," Aunt Faith whispered. "You see it, David, you must see it. The girl is in a genuine trance."

"I wouldn't know," David said.

Iris' eyes were closed, and her lips were moving. There were drops of spittle at the corners of her mouth.

"What's she saying?" Rowena said. "I can't hear her."

"Wait! You must wait!" Aunt Faith cautioned.

Iris' voice became audible. "Hot," she said. "Oh, it's so hot . . . so hot . . ." She squirmed in the chair, and her fingers tugged at the neckline of the evening dress. "So hot back here!" she said loudly. "Oh, please! Oh, please! Kitty is hot! Kitty is hot!"

Then Iris screamed, and David jumped to his feet. Rowena came to his side and clutched his arm.

"It's nothing!" David said. "Can't you see it's an act?"

"Hush, please!" Aunt Faith said. "The girl is in pain!"

Iris moaned and thrashed in the chair. There were beads of perspiration on her forehead now, and her squirming, twisting body had all the aspects of a soul in hell-fire.

"Hot! Hot!" she shrieked. "Behind the stove! Oh please, oh please, oh please . . . so hot . . . kitty so hot . . ." Then she sagged in the chair and groaned.

Aunt Faith rushed to her side and picked up the thin wrists. She rubbed them vigorously, and said, "You heard her, David, you heard it for yourself. Can you doubt the girl now?"

"I didn't hear anything. A lot of screams and moans and gibberish about heat. What's it supposed to mean?"

"You *are* a stubborn fool! Why, the kitten's behind the stove, of course, where you probably stuffed it when you were a little brat of a boy!"

Rowena tugged his arm. "We could find out, couldn't we? Is the same stove still in the kitchen?"

"I suppose so. There's some kind of electronic oven, too, but they've never moved the old iron monster, far as I know."

"Let's look, David, please!" Rowena urged.

Iris was coming awake. She blinked and opened her eyes, and looked at their watching faces. "Is it there?" she said. "Is it where I said it was? Behind the stove in the kitchen?"

"We haven't looked yet," David said.

"Then look," Aunt Faith commanded.

They looked, Rowena and David, and it was there, a dust-covered cloth kitten, browned and almost destroyed by three decades of heat and decay; but it was there.

David clutched the old plaything in his fist, and his face went white. Rowena looked at him sadly, and thought he was suffering the pangs of nostalgia, but he wasn't. He was suffering from fear.

In the beginning of May, the rains vanished and were replaced by a succession of sunlit days. Iris Lloyd began to spend most of her time outdoors, communing with nature or her own cryptic thoughts.

That was where David found her one midweek afternoon, lying on the grass amid a tangle of daisies. She was dissecting one in an ancient ritual.

"Well," David said, "what's the answer?"

She smiled coyly, and threw the disfigured daisy away. "You tell me, Uncle David."

"Cut out the Uncle David stuff." He bent down to pick up the mutilated flower, and plucked off the remaining petals. "Loves me not," he said.

"Who? Your wife?" She smirked at him boldly. "You can't fool me, Uncle David. I know all about it."

He started to turn away, but she caught his ankle. "Don't go away. I want to talk."

He came back and squatted down to her level. "Look, what's the story with you, Iris? You've been here over a week and you haven't done anything about—well, you know what. This is just a great big picnic for you, isn't it?"

"Sure it is," she said. "You think I want to go back to that sticky Home? It's better here." She lay back on the grass. "No uniforms. No six a.m. prayers. None of that junk they call food . . ." She grinned. "And a lot nicer company."

"I suppose I should say thank you."

"There's nothing you can say I don't know already." She tittered. "Did you forget? I'm psychic."

"Is it really true, Iris," he said casually, "or is it some kind of trick? I mean, these things you do."

"I'll show you if it's a trick." She covered her eyes with both hands. "Your wife hates you," she said. "She thinks you're rotten. You weren't even married a year when you started running around with other women. You never even went to the mill, not more'n once or twice a month, that was how *you* ran the business. All *you* knew how to do was spend the money."

David's face had grown progressively paler during her recitation. Now he grabbed her thin forearm. "You little brat! You're not psychic! You're an eavesdropper!"

"Let go of my arm!"

"Your room is right next door. You've been listening!"

"All right!" she squealed. "You think I could help hearing you two arguing?"

He released her wrist. She rubbed it ruefully, and then laughed, deciding it was funny. Suddenly she flung herself at him and kissed him on the mouth, clutching him with her thin, strong fingers.

He pushed her away, amazed. "What do you think you're doing?" he said roughly. "You dumb kid!"

"I'm not a kid!" she said. "I'm almost seventeen!"

"You were sixteen three months ago!"

"I'm a woman!" Iris shrieked. "But you're not even a man!" She struck him a blow on the chest with a balled fist, and it knocked the breath out of him. Then she turned and ran down the hill toward the house.

He returned home through the back of the estate and entered the kitchen. Aunt Faith was giving Hattie some silverware-cleaning instructions at the kitchen table. She looked up and said, "Did you call for a taxi, David?"

"Taxi? No, why should I?"

"I don't know. But Lucas' cab is in the driveway; he said he was waiting for you."

Lucas climbed out of the cab at David's approach. He peeled off the knitted cap and pressed it against his stomach.

"What do you want, Lucas?"

"To talk, Mr. Wheeler, like I said last week."

David climbed into the rear seat. "All right," he said, "drive someplace. We can talk while you're driving."

"Yes, sir."

Lucas didn't speak again until they were out of sight of the estate; then he said, "I did what you told me, Mr. Wheeler, 'zactly like you said. I hit her clean, she didn't hurt a bit, no blood. Just like an old steer she went down, Mr. Wheeler."

"All right," David said harshly. "I don't want to hear about it anymore, Lucas, I'm satisfied. You should be, too. You got your money, now forget about it."

"I picked her up," Lucas said dreamily. "I took her out in the woods, like you said, and I dug deep, deep as I could. The ground was awful hard then, Mr. Wheeler, it was a lot of work. I smoothed it over real good, ain't nobody could guess what was there. Nobody . . . except—"

"Is it that girl? Is that what's bothering you?"

"I heard awful funny things about her, Mr. Wheeler. About her findin' things, findin' that little kid what fell near Crompton Lake. She's got funny eyes. Maybe she can see right into that woman's grave . . ."

"Stop the car, Lucas!"

Lucas put his heavy foot on the brake.

"Iris Lloyd won't find her," David said, teeth clenched. "Nobody will. You've got to stop worrying about it. The more you worry, the more you'll give yourself away."

"But she's right behind the house, Mr. Wheeler! She's so close, right in the woods . . ."

"You've got to forget it, Lucas, like it never happened. My sister's disappeared, and she's not coming back. As for the girl, let me worry about her."

He clapped Lucas' shoulder in what was meant to be reassurance, but his touch made Lucas stiffen.

"Now, take me home," David said.

He worried about Iris for another five days, but she seemed to have forgotten the purpose of her stay completely. She was a house guest, a replacement for the missing Geraldine, and Aunt Faith's patience seemed inexhaustible as she waited for the psychic miracle to happen.

The next Thursday night, in their bedroom, Rowena caught David's eyes in the vanity mirror and started to say something about the mill.

"Shut up," he said pleasantly. "Don't say another word. I've found out that Iris can hear every nasty little quarrel in this room, so let's declare a truce."

"She doesn't have to eavesdrop, does she? Can't she read minds?" She swiveled around to face him. "Well, she's not the only clairvoyant around here. I can read her mind, too."

"Oh?"

"It's easy," Rowena said bitterly. "I can read every wicked thought in her head, every time she looks at you. I'm surprised you haven't noticed."

"She's a child, for heaven's sake."

"She's in love with you."

He snorted, and went to his bed.

"You're her Sir Galahad," she said mockingly. "You're going to rescue her from that evil castle where they're holding her prisoner. Didn't you know that . . .?"

"Go to sleep, Rowena."

"Of course, there's still one minor obstruction to her plans. A small matter of your wife. But then, I've never been much of a hindrance to your romances, have I?"

"I've asked you for a truce," he said.

She laughed. "You're a pacifist, David, that's part of your famous charm. That's why you came up here in March, wasn't it? To make a truce with Geraldine?"

"I came here on business."

"Yes, I know. To keep Geraldine from sending you to prison, wasn't that the business?"

"You don't know anything about it."

"I have eyes, David. Not like Iris Lloyd, but eyes. I know you were taking money from the mill, too much of it. Geraldine knew it, too. How much time did she give you to make up the loss?"

David thought of himself as a man without a temper, but he found one now, and lost it just as quickly. "Not another word, you hear? I don't want to hear another word!"

He lay awake for the next hour, his eyes staring sightlessly into the dark of the room.

He was still awake when he heard the shuffle of feet in the corridor outside. He sat up, listening, and heard the quiet click of a latching door.

He got out of bed and put on his robe and slippers. There was a patch of moonlight on his wife's pillow; Rowena was asleep. He went noiselessly to the door and opened it.

Iris Lloyd, in a nightdress, was walking slowly down the stairway to the ground floor, her blonde head rigid on her shoulders, moving with the mechanical grace of the somnambulist.

At the end of the hall, Aunt Faith opened her door and peered out, wide-eyed. "Is that you, David?"

"It's Iris," David said.

Aunt Faith came into the hallway, tying her housecoat around her middle, her hands shaking. David tried to restrain her from following the girl, but his aunt was stubborn.

They paused at the landing. Iris, her eyes open and unblinking, was moving frenetically around the front hall.

"What did I forget?" the girl mumbled. "What did I forget?"

Aunt Faith reached for David's arm.

"You're late," Iris said, facing the front door. "It's time we were going . . ." She whirled and seemed to be looking straight at her spectators, without seeing them.

"We have to be going!" she said, almost tearfully. "Oh, please get my luggage. I'm so nervous. I'm so afraid . . ."

"It's a trance," Aunt Faith whispered, squeezing his hand. "Oh, David, this may be it!"

"What did I forget?" Iris quavered. "Gas, electricity, phone, fireplace . . . Is the fireplace still lit? *Oh!*" She sobbed suddenly, and put her face in her hands.

David took a step toward her, and Aunt Faith said, "Don't! Don't waken her!"

Now Iris was walking, a phantom in the loose gown, toward the back of the house. She went to the kitchen, and opened the screen door.

"She's going outside!" David said. "We can't let her—"

"Leave her alone, David! Please, leave her alone!"

Iris stepped outside into the back yard, following a path of moonlight that trailed into the dark woods.

"Iris!" David shouted. "*Iris!*"

"No!" Aunt Faith cried. "Don't waken her! You mustn't!"

"You want that girl to catch pneumonia?" David said furiously. "Are you crazy? Iris!" he shouted again.

She stopped at the sound of her name, turned, and the eyes went from nothingness to bewilderment. Then, as David's arms enclosed her, she screamed and struck at him. He fought to drag her back to the house, pinning her arms to her side. She was sobbing bitterly by the time he had her indoors.

Aunt Faith fluttered about her with tearful cries. "Oh, how could you do that, David?" she groaned. "You know you shouldn't waken a sleepwalker, you know that!"

"I wasn't going to let that child catch her death of cold! That would be a fine thing to tell the Sisters, wouldn't it, Auntie? That we let their little girl die of pneumonia?"

Iris had quieted, her head still cradled in her arms. Now she looked up, and studied their strained faces. "Aunt Faith . . ."

"Are you all right, Iris?"

There was still a remnant of the sleepwalker's distant look in her round eyes. "Yes," she said. "Yes, I'm all right. I think I'm ready now, Aunt Faith. I can do it now."

"Do it now? You mean . . . tell us where Geraldine is?"

"I can try, Aunt Faith."

The old woman straightened up, her manner transformed. "We must call Lieutenant Reese, David. Right now. He'll want to hear anything Iris says."

"Reese? It's after two in the morning!"

"He'll come," Aunt Faith said grimly. "I know he will. I'll telephone him myself; you take Iris to her room."

David helped the girl up the stairs, frowning at the closeness with which she clung to his side. Her manner was meek. She fell on her bed, her eyes closed. Then the eyes opened, and she smiled at him. "You're scared," she said.

He swallowed hard, because it was true. "I'm sending you back," he said hoarsely. "I'm not letting you stay in this house another day. You're more trouble than you're worth, just like Sister Clothilde said."

"Is that the reason, David?"

She began to laugh. Her laughter angered him, and he sat beside her and clamped his hand over her mouth.

"Shut up!" he said. "Shut up, you little fool!"

She stopped laughing. Her eyes, over the fingers of his hand, penetrated his. He put his arm to his side.

Iris leaned toward him. "David," she said sensuously, "I won't give you away. Not if you don't want me to."

"You don't know what you're talking about," he said uncertainly. "You're a fraud."

"Am I? You don't believe that."

She leaned closer still. He grabbed her with brutal suddenness and kissed her mouth. She moved against him, moaning, her thin fingers plucking at the lapel of his robe.

When they parted, he wiped his mouth in disgust and said, "What part of hell did you come from, anyway?"

"David," she said dreamily, "you'll take me away from that place, won't you? You won't let me go back there, will you?"

"You're crazy! You know I'm married—"

"That doesn't matter. You can divorce that woman, David. You don't love her anyway, do you?"

The door opened. Rowena, imperious in her nightgown, looked at them with mixed anger and disdain.

"Get out of here!" Iris shrieked. "I don't want you in my room!"

"Rowena—" David turned to her.

His wife said, "I just came in to tell you something, David. You were right about the walls between these rooms."

"I hate you!" Iris shouted. "David hates you, too! Tell her, David, why don't you tell her?"

"Yes," Rowena said. "Why don't you, David? It's the only thing you haven't done so far."

He looked back and forth between them, the hot-eyed young girl in the heavy flannel nightdress; the cool-eyed woman in silk, waiting to be answered, asking for injury.

"Damn you both!" he muttered. Then he brushed past Rowena and went out.

Lieutenant Reese still seemed half-asleep; the stray hairs on his balding scalp were ruffled, and his clothes had the appearance of having been put on hastily. Rowena, still in nightclothes, sat by the window, apparently disinterested. Aunt Faith was at the fireplace, coaxing the embers into flames.

Iris sat in the wing chair, her hands clasped in her lap, her expression enigmatic.

When the fire started, Aunt Faith said, "We can begin any time. David, would you turn out the lamp?"

David made himself a drink before he dimmed the lights, and then went over to the chair opposite Iris.

Aunt Faith said, "Are you ready, my child?"

Iris, white-lipped, nodded.

David caught her eyes before they shut in the beginning of the trance. They seemed to recognize his unspoken, plaintive question, but they gave no hint of a reply.

Then they were silent. The silence lasted for a hundred ticks of the mantelpiece clock.

Gradually Iris Lloyd began to rock from side to side in the chair, and her lips moved.

"It's starting," Aunt Faith whispered. "It's starting . . ."

Iris began to moan. She made sounds of torment, and twisted her young body in an ecstasy of anguish. Her mouth fell open, and she gasped; the spittle frothed at the corners and spilled onto her chin.

"You've got to stop this," David said, his voice shaking. "The girl's having a fit."

Lieutenant Reese looked alarmed. "Mrs. Demerest, don't you think—"

"Please!" Aunt Faith said. "It's only the trance. You've seen it before, David, you know—"

Iris cried out.

Reese stood. "Maybe Mr. Wheeler's right. The girl might do herself some harm, Mrs. Demerest—"

"No, no! You must wait!"

Then Iris screamed, in such a mounting cadence of terror that the glass of the room trembled in sympathetic vibration, and Rowena put her hands over her ears.

"*Aunt Faith! Aunt Faith!*" Iris shrieked. "I'm here! I'm here, Aunt Faith, come and find me! Help me, Aunt Faith, it's dark! So dark! Oh, won't somebody help me?"

"Where are you?" Aunt Faith cried, the tears flooding her cheeks. "Oh, Geraldine, my poor darling, where are you?"

"Oh, help me! Help, please!" Iris writhed and twisted in the chair. "It's so dark, I'm so afraid! Aunt Faith! Do you hear me? Do you hear me?"

"We hear you! We hear you, darling!" Aunt Faith sobbed. "Tell us where you are! Tell us!"

Iris lifted herself from the chair, screamed again, and fell back in a fit of weeping. A few moments later, the heaving of her breast subsided, and her eyes opened slowly.

David tried to go to her, but Lieutenant Reese intervened. "One moment, Mr. Wheeler."

Reese went to his knees, and put his thumb on the girl's pulse. With his other hand, he widened her right eye and stared at the pupil. "Can you hear me, Iris? Are you all right?"

"Yes, sir, everything."

"Do you know where Geraldine Wheeler is?"

She looked at the circle of faces, and then paused at David's.

His eyes pleaded.

"Yes," Iris whispered.

"Where is she, Iris?"

Iris' gaze went distant. "Someplace far away. A place with ships. The sun is shining there. I saw hills, and green trees . . . I heard bells ringing in the streets . . ."

Reese turned to the others, to match his own bewilderment with theirs.

"A place with ships . . . Does that mean anything to you?"

There was no reply.

"It's a city," Iris said. "It's far away . . ."

"Across the ocean, Iris? Is that where Geraldine is?"

"No! Not across the ocean. Someplace here, in America, where there are ships. I saw a bay, and a bridge and blue water . . ."

"San Francisco!" Rowena said. "I'm sure she means San Francisco, Lieutenant."

"Iris," Reese said sternly. "You've got to be certain of this, we can't chase all over the country. Was it San Francisco? Is that where you saw Geraldine?"

"Yes!" Iris said. "Now I know. There were trolleys in the streets, funny trolleys going uphill . . . It's San Francisco. She's in San Francisco!"

Reese got to his feet, and scratched the back of his neck. "Well, who knows?" he said. "It's as good a guess as I've heard. Has Geraldine ever been in San Francisco before?"

"Never," Aunt Faith said. "Why would she go there, David?"

"I don't know," David grinned. He went over to Iris and patted her shoulder. "But that's where Iris says she is, and I guess the spirits know what they're talking about. Right, Iris?"

She turned her head aside. "I want to go home," she said. "I want Mother Clothilde . . ." Then she began to cry, softly, like a child.

It was spring, but the day felt summery. When David and Aunt Faith returned from the Medvale Home for Girls, the old woman looked out of the car window, but the countryside charm failed to enliven her mood.

"Come on, you old gypsy," David laughed, "your little clairvoyant was a huge success. Now all the police have to do is find Geraldine in San Francisco—if she hasn't taken a boat to the South Seas by now."

"I don't understand it," Aunt Faith said. "It's not like Geraldine to run away without a word. Why did she do it?"

"I don't know," David replied.

Later that day he drove into town. When he saw Lucas standing at the depot beside his black taxi, he pulled up and climbed out, the smile wide on his face. "Hello, Lucas. How's the taxi business?"

"Could be better." Lucas searched his face. "You got any news for me, Mr. Wheeler?"

"Maybe I do. Suppose we step into your office."

He clapped his hand on Lucas' shoulder, and Lucas preceded him into the depot office. He closed the door carefully, and told the cabman to sit down.

"It's all over," David said. "I've just come from the Medvale Home for Girls. We took Iris Lloyd back."

Lucas released a sigh from deep in his burly chest. "Then she didn't know? She didn't know where the—that woman was?"

"She didn't know, Lucas."

The cabman leaned back, and squeezed the palms of his hand together. "Then I did the right thing. I knew it was the right thing, Mr. Wheeler, but I didn't want to tell you."

"Right thing? What do you mean?"

Lucas looked up with glowing eyes, narrowed by what he might have thought was cunning. "I figured that girl could tell if the body was buried right outside the house. But she'd never find it if it was someplace else. Ain't that right? Someplace far away?"

A spasm took David by the throat. He hurled himself at Lucas and grabbed the collar of his wool jacket.

"What are you talking about? What do you mean, someplace else?" Lucas was too frightened to answer. "What did you do?" David shouted.

"I was afraid you'd be sore," Lucas whimpered. "I didn't want to tell you. I went out in the woods one night last week and dug up that woman's body. I put it in that trunk of hers, Mr. Wheeler, and I sent it by train, far away as I could get it. Farthest place I know, Mr. Wheeler. That's why Iris Lloyd couldn't find it. It's too far away now."

"Where? Where, you moron? San Francisco?"

Lucas mumbled his terror, and then nodded his shaggy head.

The baggagemaster listened intently to the questions of the two plainclothesmen, shrugged when they showed him the photograph of the woman, and then led them to the Unclaimed Baggage room in the rear of the terminal. When he pointed to the trunk that bore the initials G.W., the two men exchanged looks, and then walked slowly toward it. They broke open the lock, and lifted the lid.

Three thousand miles away, Iris Lloyd sat up in the narrow dormitory bed and gasped into the darkness, wondering what strange dream had broken her untroubled sleep.

The Return of Max Kearny

by Ron Goulart

At just a minute short of midnight the bathtub started screaming again.

On his side of the fourposter the big, bear-shaped man clenched his paw-like fists and feigned deep untroubled sleep. On the opposite side his lovely blonde wife sat bolt upright, her frilly diminutive nightie twisting around her smooth body, and gave him a punch in the kidneys.

"Oh, shoot. There it is all over again," said Tinkle Snowden. The moonlight knifing into the second-floor bedroom made her deeply tan skin shimmer in a highly provocative way.

Still huddled in one of his hibernating poses, Boswell Snowden bit his tongue and waited for the pain in his lower back to subside.

"This is really gross, Boz," said Tinkle, full lips next to his shaggy ear. "A bathtub that wails like a banshee is . . . gross."

"Hum?" He faked a mumbled yawn.

"What sort of impression must we be making on the other people who live here in Hollow Hills Circle?" She placed an icy hand on his naked shoulder. "Our bathtub screams, our furnace chuckles like a madman, our . . . what the heck is that?"

Down the hall the toilet had begun yodeling.

"Houses make noises at night," said Snowden.

Tinkle said, "It's not just noises, Boz, as you know darn well."

"You're not used to being on the ground so much," suggested her husband, trying not to hear the awesome noises rolling down the hall from the bathroom.

"Well, no, I never heard a biffy yodeling when I was a flight attendant for TransAm Airways, no." She swung one long handsome leg over the bed edge. "I'm going to march right down to the john and—"

"Listen, some things you ought not to fool with, hon."

"No darn bathtub's going to spoil my . . . oh, ugh!"

He lumbered into a sitting position. "What now?"

"I just stepped in something horrible and slimy. It's all over the bedchamber floor," his wife said. "Oh, how gross . . . it's blood. Our lovely rug's awash with blood, Boz."

"Probably only a leaking faucet." He elbowed over to Tinkle's side of the bed to stare down at the dark floor.

"What sort of faucet would leak blood?"

"Moonlight plays strange tricks on your eyes," suggested Snowden, striving to put a soothing note into his rumbling voice. "That stuff looks more like chocolate than blood to me anyway."

"Well, it's not fun putting your bare foot down in lukewarm chocolate either," she said. "And where'd gallons of it come leaking from?"

"Oh, there has to be a simple explanation."

"Heck, that's what you always say," she complained, making a tentative swipe at her toes with her forefinger. "One would think, Boz, that you, of all people, the nation's leading author of supernatural fiction, would—"

"I'm not exactly the leading writer of weird stuff," he corrected. "There are three guys ahead of me."

"But *Curse of the Demon* has been number nine on the darn *New York Times* list for weeks and weeks."

"Meaning eight books are ahead of us."

"But it's been optioned by Mecca-Universal for a six-figure advance," persisted Tinkle. "On top of which you're dead sure to win the Grisly Award from the Occult Writers of America at the banquet at the Biltmore in New York City next—"

"That's Ghastly, not Grisly."

"Well, grisly or ghastly, you ought to believe in a real occult phenomenon when it happens right smack . . . darn, that is so blood." She'd clicked on her frill-shaded bedside lamp.

Her fingertip was red-smeared. The bedroom carpet, usually a sedate buff color, was now a soggy crimson across most of its four hundred square feet.

"Aw, looks more like rusty water to me."

"Rusty water? You could use this stuff to give sick people transfusions, Boz," his wife said. "I'd like to see you phone up Burt Nostradamus the plumber and tell him you've got twenty gallons or so of blood spilled on the rug and you think a rusty faucet did—"

"We won't be using Nostradamus anymore."

"Simply because he wanted to interview you?" Tinkle continued to study her fingertip. "Personally I think it's darn admirable that

he doesn't want to be a plumber all his life and aspires to become
a writer of—"

"Your average plumber in this part of Connecticut makes more
money than 97 percent of the freelance writers in the country," said
Snowden. "Furthermore, Nostradamus writes for the *National Intruder*, which ain't my idea of the main current in American—"

"It'd be nice publicity for you, Boz."

"Sure, *Crazed Author Plagued by Real Life Horrors!* I don't need
that sort of publicity, honey."

"Before you had this fantastic success with *Curse of the Demon*,
Boz, before you'd gotten that $100,000 advance from Usher House
Books for the hardcover and the $230,000 from Midget Books for the
paperback, before we'd met when you took that TransAm flight out
of Hollywood to talk turkey with the movie moguls, back then you'd
have jumped at—"

"Exactly. Now I don't need cheap publicity. Turn off the damn
light."

"The bathtub is still screaming. Boz, this has been happening
almost every night for the past three weeks," persisted Tinkle. "This
house has to be haunted or possessed. I bet it's the site of a long-
forgotten murder."

"This house is not even a year old."

"You absolutely have to find out what is wrong, what evil force
holds our house in its sway."

"Ignore it," he advised, rubbing at his beard and then pretending
to assume a ready-to-sleep position.

"You keep saying that and it keeps getting worse. First it was
only an occasional maniacal laugh in the middle of the night or a
few drops of blood forming on a wall." She paused to take a breath.
"The whole dreadful process is accelerating. I really believe this
horrible house wants to drive me goofy, the same way the mansion
in *Curse of the Demon* did to poor Alice."

"Alicia," he corrected.

"Well, whatever. It's a silly name for a girl. Boz, maybe we ought
to move before the house destroys—"

"I've been writing professionally for eleven years, Tinkle," he said,
rising up on one shaggy elbow. "I'm nearly thirty-eight and this is
my first real taste of success. This damn house represents something
to me, a goal I've reached. No one is going to take it away or scare
me into . . . never mind. Let's go to sleep."

"What do you mean no one? Do you know what's behind these ghostly manifestations?"

He waited a few seconds before answering, "No."

The screaming was waning, growing weak. So was the yodeling.

"What about the blood?" asked Tinkle.

"It'll be gone by morning."

She punched him in the side. "See? You *do* believe it's supernatural. Real blood wouldn't possibly go away just—"

"If you're not in the mood for going to sleep, what say we make love?"

"With the house full of demons and goblins and lord knows what else?" Shivering, Tinkle folded her arms across her breasts.

Her husband turned his massive back on her, soon began producing snoring sounds.

"I think we're not the only ones," Tinkle said after a moment.

"What?"

"Not the only ones with a haunted house. Nobody's said anything directly to me, yet I suspect . . . well, it's possible all the houses in the circle are haunted," she replied. "Isn't that a really gross possibility? Something really terrible must've happened here a long time ago."

"More recently than that," murmured Snowden into his pillow.

The smell of sulfur awakened Max Kearny seconds before his bedside clock commenced bonging in impossibly loud and sepulchral tones. The brimstone scent was a familiar, though not recently experienced one. Wide awake, he hopped out of bed and made his way across the unfamiliar moonlit room. As he reached his trousers on the wicker armchair where he'd tossed them, an unearthly wailing came drifting up from the patio below.

Pants in hand, Max sprinted to a window.

There was a dark figure crouched next to the barbecue pit. Ducked low, it went scurrying away into the shadowy brush beyond the flagstones.

Max narrowed one eye. Turning away from the window, he tugged his pants on. "I think I see the real reason I'm a house guest," he said to himself. He shed the pajama top he'd been sleeping in, pulled on a rugby shirt, and moved to the doorway.

He was a middle-sized man, slim and forty-one. He wore his grey-spattered black hair in a sort of shaggy crewcut.

Three steps into the upstairs hall and he stepped in something warm and slick, went sliding and skidding.

He hit the balustrade, teetered on the brink of plummeting over into the yawning stairwell. Saving himself, he pushed back and stopped when he was leaning against the wall.

"That you out there, Max?" called a female voice.

"Yeah, it is." He wiped two fingers across his bare sole. "So you can come on out."

The other bedroom door opened and a plump red-haired woman in a terry robe peered out. "Can't sleep, huh?"

A thin-faced man, his sandy blond hair sleep-tousled, looked out over the redhead. "Nightmare, Max?"

Inspecting his fingers, Max said, "Blood."

"Wake up," urged the red-haired woman, "you're still dream—"

"C'mon, Nita," said Max as he wiped his hand on a pocket tissue. "I don't mind being conned now and then, but it can cease now."

"Sometimes when you mix pills and booze," suggested Nita McNulty, eyes not meeting his, "it causes . . . oh, hell, we do love you, Max, and we're sorry Jillian didn't come East with you on this trip. And we're happy you're our house guest while your advertising work keeps you back here."

"You're one of our favorite California people," picked up her husband, "and I miss you more than almost any other friend we left out there when we moved to Connecticut six years ago and I went to work for *Muck* magazine."

"But?" supplied Max.

"Let's go downstairs into the living room," suggested Nita. "I'll brew a pot of coffee and . . . oh, you're into herb teas now, aren't you."

"I can forgo beverages of any kind, if you give me an explanation."

"Downstairs," said Gil McNulty, coming out into the hallway and taking hold of Max's arm. "Safer . . . that is, easier to chat down there."

"Watch out," warned his wife. "Don't step in the blood."

"Ah, so you folks do see it, too."

Wrapping her yellow robe more tightly around her wide body, Nita led the way down the stairs.

Before any of them reached the ground floor, the upstairs toilet started yodeling.

Max was the only one who flinched. Noticing, he asked, "This happens regularly?"

"Most nights," answered Gil, yawning. He'd pulled khaki slacks on over his paisley pajamas, giving himself makeshift anklets. "Around midnight or thereabouts."

"We're sort of used to it."

When they were settled in the living room, Gil said, "We would've invited you out for this weekend anyway, Max."

"Sure, I know." He glanced up at the ceiling.

A glistening black patch was forming on the white plaster; some thick black liquid was oozing through.

"The houses here in Hollow Hills Circle are all good houses, well-built, all ten of them." Nita was watching the growing black puddle. "Working for the Hollow Hills Realty Agency I could be a mite prejudiced, since I have to sell them. But, honestly, Max, there is nothing technically wrong with any of the ten. What's been happening isn't due to shoddy materials or faulty construction."

"No, that wouldn't account for blood-curdling wails and corridors of blood," he said, remembering to sip his peppermint tea.

"I told you he'd be sympathetic," said Gil across to his wife.

Nita held her mug of coffee tightly in both plump freckled hands. "Part of the problem, Max, is my being responsible for the selling of the particular houses. They go for $200,000, which is a damn good price for this part of Connecticut. Little over an hour from New York City, really wonderful shopping mall only a few minutes downhill, brand-new middle school and a whole new high school complex planned for—"

"Spiel," mentioned her husband.

"Yes, I'm sorry. Anyhow, Max, I have four more yet to sell. That's $800,000 worth of houses and my commission will be . . . quite nice."

"But something is wrong with one of the houses, with this one?"

Gil gave a bitter laugh. "If it were only this one."

Sitting up and putting his cup on the glass coffee table, Max said, "You mean people are experiencing similar stuff in other houses in the circle?"

"In all of them," Nita replied, staring sadly into her coffee.

The black splotch in the ceiling began to drip.

Max rose, crossed to where the drops were hitting the rug, and probed with a finger. "Some kind of foul-smelling sludge."

"It always disappears in an hour or two," said Gil.

"How long has all this been going on?"

"Nearly three weeks," answered Gil. "At first there were only small things. Odd gurgles from the pipes, modest little drippings.

We had our friend Burt Nostradamus the plumber in to check out most of the early complaints. Thing is, it's been growing increasingly worse. Now we also get screams, wails and howlings."

"Blood dripping in big puddles, toilets glowing in the dark, little fuzzy creatures lurking under tables. . . . Oh, Max, you must realize how awful things like this will affect the property values."

"Every single resident of the circle has complained?"

"That's right, every . . . well, no," said Nita, thoughtful. "For some reason the Snowdens haven't uttered a negative word. Which is odd, considering."

"He's Boswell Snowden," added Gil.

Max said, "Guy who wrote *Curse of the Demon?*"

"The same," replied his friend. "This ought to be right up his alley, but he and his nifty . . . well, she is pretty attractive, Nita, don't scowl . . . he and his wife are acting as though nothing is wrong."

"Acting?"

"I've done a couple of midnight prowls," said Gil, "while the . . . manifestations were in full swing. I'm just about certain every damn house in Hollow Hills Circle is suffering from the same sort of haunting or whatever. That includes the Snowden place as well as the homes Nita hasn't even sold yet."

"I'll never sell them," she sighed. "The poor people I conned into buying into this beautiful spot are barely speaking to me now; we all know if something isn't done soon, some of them will try to unload. For a lot less than they paid."

"So far, to anticipate your next possible question, Max, we haven't gone to the local cops," Gil told him. "Because, frankly, I don't see any way this could be a prank or vandalism. We could maybe ask some sort of environmental agency to come in and make a study, except this is unlike any contamination I've ever investigated. And on *Muck* I've investigated plenty of cases."

"Nobody else has gone for outside help?" Max tried his tea again.

"The Snowdens won't admit they're being tormented; the Milmans are away in Europe and have been since before this mess started," explained Nita. "As for the rest of them, the Steffansons, the Silvas and the Sanhammels, they—"

"All afraid," took up Gil. "See, they don't want to be laughed at or have the circle turn into a damn tourist attraction. Besides which, should word get around this area's contaminated by spooks or devils or whatever, well, Nita's right . . . the property values'd plummet,

Max. The housing market is lousy enough without adding a super-natural element."

"You can't keep something like this quiet forever, though," said Nita. "Little rumors are already leaking, and if something isn't done soon, darn soon, it could really turn out terrible for all of us."

"When you phoned that you were in New York to supervise the filming of some commercials for . . . what was the product?"

"*Slurp!*," he replied. "Instant soup in a plastic mug. Our slogan is, 'I'd rather *Slurp!* than eat!' Which brings me to an important point, folks. I am, in real everyday life, a full-fledged advertising person. When we were all chums out in San Francisco years back, I worked for someone else. The past four years and more, I've been president of Kearny & Associates, with an annual billing of $27,000,000. Jillian and I, along with Stephanie, live a fairly afflu-ent life in the wilds of Marin County, and so . . . well, I haven't done any occult detective work for years. Far as that's concerned, I'm retired."

"You did such brilliant work," said Gil. "I was always writing your exploits up when I was with the *Chronicle*. That invisible antiporn group and the guy with the haunted TV set and the ly-canthrope who turned into an elephant on national holidays and the suburban gnome who—"

"Decade and more ago," reminded Max as he stood.

The black spot was fading, the toilet had grown silent.

"If this whole area goes under, it'll be awful," said Nita. "Not just because of the financial thing, but because of the brave families who've settled here, Max, put down roots, fought against all sorts of—"

"C'mon, you make us sound like something out of a John Jakes saga," said her husband. "Really, though, Max, we'd appreciate some help from you."

He was gazing out at the moonlit front acre. Turning to face his old friends, Max said, "Okay, I'll come out of retirement."

Gil said, "Great!"

"You're lovely," said Nita, coming over to hug him.

"For a couple days anyway," he added.

The young woman on the 10-speed bicycle said, "You're Max Kearny."

Nodding, Max kept on running. "And you're a neighbor of the McNultys."

The dark blonde said, settling into a speed which kept her beside him on the early-morning lane, "I'm Kate Tillman, my husband is Bronco Sanhammel."

"Used to play . . . football, didn't he?"

"That's him," she said. "Reason I'm Tillman and he's Sanhammel is I believe a woman ought to maintain her identity in marriage. Bronco doesn't exactly agree, but he's too busy at Malfunctions to argue."

"What sort of malfunctions?"

"No, it's the name of a company, Malfunction Studies International. A research organization based over in Stamford. They study companies and institutions and explain why they're screwed up. Lots of clients these days. Your wife didn't hold on to her own name."

"No, she foolishly abandoned it years ago. How'd you know?"

"Read a frothy piece on you two in *People* last year. Do you find advertising a compromising trade?"

"A compromise with starvation." As far as Max could recall, the half page of copy in *People* hadn't mentioned his one-time ghost-breaking sideline. "I'd like to come over and talk to you and your husband sometime today. A sort of research thing I'm—"

"Bronco's in Ethiopia," Kate told him. "Looking into a donut factory that's been turning them out square instead of round. We're both individuals, though, and I can talk to you while he's away. Do you always wheeze like this when you jog?"

"Only on the fifth and final mile," Max admitted.

The young woman was frowning, studying him out of the corner of her eyes. "How old are you?"

"Forty-one."

"That explains it, I'm twenty-nine. We come from different generations."

"Is that still going around, generation gap?"

Kate's frown deepened. "I'm trying to remember something else about you. Something from when I was a kid."

"Way back in the dim and distant sixties?"

Her head bobbed in affirmation. "It was in some strange and sleazy magazine Uncle Alfie used to get. . . . Right! You were a ghost detective, an occult investigator."

"According to Nita and Gil, I still am."

Downhill loomed the landscaped entryway to Hollow Hills Circle.

"Then I very much do want to talk to you, Max," she said. "You don't mind if I call you Max right off?"

"I expect such familiarity from your generation."

"You're teasing but I'm serious," she said. "Why don't you drop in for breakfast now? I'm a vegetarian, so I can't offer you ham and sausage or any other dreadful traditional Sunday breakfast fare. We can talk, though, about . . ."

"About what?"

"The hauntings."

Max sat on the brick front porch of the Tillman-Sanhammel colonial, watching a carrion crow circle a nearby wooded area and aware of various thumpings coming from inside the house. A scruffy terrier cut across the vast front lawn, pausing to gruff once at him.

"Okay, all shipshape. You can come on in," invited Kate from the now open front door.

Stretching up, his left knee making a creaking, Max went into the cool, spotless living room, which was furnished with stark functional furniture and tropical plants. There were bookcases built into one wall, and he noticed, while following her through to the kitchen, a gap of about two feet on the otherwise crowded shelves. "How long have you lived here?"

"I suppose that was an old-fashioned stereotyped female thing to do," said Kate over her shoulder. "Tidying up before letting you in."

"Warms the heart of us senior citizens."

The kitchen was yellow, black and white, as angularly furnished as the living room.

Nodding at a square yellow table, Kate said, "What were you asking, Max?"

"How long you and Bronco have lived here in Hollow Hills."

"Oh, just a bit over two months," she said. "Before that we had a place over in Weston, but when Bronco got promoted to Assistant Foul-Up Field Research Man, we decided to move up the ladder a rung or two. Not that I'm into status."

"Did you hear about this area through someone?"

She placed a glass teakettle on an electric burner of the stark black stove. "Rose hip or Red Zinger tea?"

"Dealer's choice."

Kate reached up and took a box of rose hip tea from a cabinet shelf. Her navy-blue jersey hiked, showing a smooth stretch of tan back. "Matter of fact, we knew some of the people who were already living here," she said, busying herself with getting out two teabags and dropping them into a fat black teapot. "Actually I knew Boz Snowden and he'd spoken highly of Hollow Hills Circle."

"You're friends of the Snowdens?"

"Not exactly. I used to be Boz's typist." She turned, leaned against a counter. "He had a small place in Weston, too, before the tremendous success of *Curse of the Demon*."

"You type the manuscript on that?"

Kate lifted the whistling kettle off the heat. "Yes, a good part of it," she answered as she poured steaming water into the teapot. "How do soy pancakes sound? As the main course? Along with hash-brown rutabagas?"

"Yum-yum."

"I suppose, depending on the mass food business for your livelihood, you have to pretend to enjoy eating garbage."

"It's required, yes. Garbage, sewage, all sorts of other unspeakable stuff. That's what they pay me for." He took the cup of tea she handed him. "You ready now to talk about the unusual things that've been going on hereabouts?"

Bending from the waist, bare back flashing again, she took a black mixing bowl from a low shelf. "Everyone has been bothered by strange things, Max, all the houses," Kate said. "Strange noises during the witching hour, occult manifestations, ghostly material-izations."

"What do you think causes it all?"

She faced him again, bowl clutched to her chest. "I haven't done as much digging into local history as I'd like," she said. "I do know, though, that centuries ago there was some kind of devil-worshipping cult that flourished in these parts, Max. It seems most likely that what we're experiencing is some sort of residual evil, a kind of supernatural toxic waste that's built up."

"What do you and your husband intend to do?"

Kate fetched two eggs from the squat yellow refrigerator. "Oh, Bronco isn't here enough to be much bothered. And, as you may recall, when he played pro ball they dubbed him the Salinas Stoic." She broke two eggs into the bowl. "Gibbering bathtubs and blood dripping from doorknobs doesn't much faze him. I guess we'll just sit it out. Sometimes, from what I've heard, these ghostly things end as suddenly as they began."

"In Boz Snowden's book it took two cardinals, a bishop and a psychic investigator to exorcise the demon who'd been dwelling in that old mansion on the Long Island Sound."

Kate sniffed. "That's fiction, Max." Picking up a mixing spoon, she began working on the contents of the bowl.

The white wallphone rang.

She caught it on the second ring. "Yes?" Kate paused, listening. "I can't talk to you now. . . . It doesn't sound as though you have anything new to say to me anyway. . . . Oh, really? I . . . I'll phone you later." She hung up carefully. "Relatives, even distant ones, can be a pain."

Max eased to his feet. "Can I wash up someplace before breakfast?"

"Downstairs bathroom's through the living room and along the hall on your right."

"Thanks." On his way there, Max stopped in the stark living room to take a look at the gap on the bookshelf.

Shaved, showered and wearing old tennis shoes and denim slacks, Max cut across a grassy acre between the houses which ringed, informally, the circle. The sun was nearly at its midday mark in the clear blue sky.

On the close-cropped lawn directly in front of the Snowden house a long, tanned young woman in a fawn-colored bikini was spread-eagled on an air-cushion. Near her fluffy blonde head a tiny transistor radio was gurgling.

At the sound of Max's sneakers on the gravel path leading to the front door, the blonde sat up. "Are you coming over to complain?"

He shook his head. "I'm Max Kearny, staying with the McNultys for a few—"

"Boz, my gifted husband, is very class-conscious. He's got the dopey notion sunbathing annoys people and that I ought to do it out back in the privacy of our patio, except the sun's better out front this time of day. It isn't, besides, that I'm mother naked or indecent. He's Boswell Snowden, author of *Curse of the Demon*. It's a best seller."

"I know." Max approached Tinkle Snowden across the bright grass. "Reason I dropped over, Nita McNulty, in her capacity as a real estate agent, has asked me to check out some complaints she's been getting. Always anxious to keep all the residents of the circle as content as—"

"Complaints, maybe, about spooky noises?"

Halting, Max squatted at the edge of the polka-dot air mattress. "Have you been suffering from such disturbances, Mrs. Snowden?"

". . . climbing right up to the top of the charts, baby . . ." murmured the tiny radio.

"I guess you could say so. I mean, golly, the bathtub screams like a hooty owl, the toilet sounds like there's a fat man drowning in it, and . . . well, well, and how do you like Connecticut, Mr. Kearny?"

"Hum?"

"Nix, nix." She hunched one bare shoulder at her colonial-style house, then whispered, "The electric typewriter's stopped clacking. He's probably watching us. From his studio."

"Does he read lips?"

"Boz has a wide range of unusual talents. I don't know, but he doesn't want me to admit we've been having any trouble with our house."

"Does he now? I'd have thought, since this is exactly the sort of thing he writes about in his novels, that he'd be eager to—"

"Heyo!" The front door flapped open, and while it was still quivering, the huge bearded Snowden emerged to stand squinting on the front porch. "What are you selling, buddy?"

"*Slurp!*" called Max. "But not to you. I'm a guest of the McNultys. Nita's asked me to—"

"No comment." Snowden came lumbering down across the lawn, a ballpoint pen gripped between his teeth.

"Nita's very anxious to make certain the folks residing here are trouble-free and—"

"No comment," replied the bearlike author. "I can emphasize that with a poke in the snoot."

"Boz, don't beat up Mr. Kearny." Tinkle hopped up. "He's much dinkier than you."

"Kearny? Kearny? I read about you someplace, saw a picture."

"No doubt in *People*. About my wife and me, and my advertising agency."

"Naw, this was when I was a kid and first got hooked on the supernatural . . ." His thick shaggy eyebrows tilted toward each other. "Yeah, you used to be a ghost breaker, a demon buster, an occult busybody."

"In my vanished youth," said Max. "Right now I'm just doing Nita a favor by—"

"We have nothing to say, Kearny." Snowden raised a shaggy fist.

"But, Boz, maybe we ought to—"

"Shut your yap," advised her husband.

"If you are suffering from any sort of occult manifestations, the publicity from that could only help your—"

"You're going to suffer from a busted snoz if you don't haul ass out of here."

"Really?" Max remained facing the larger man.

After a second Snowden dropped his fist. "Tinkle's right, I can't smack a wimp like you."

Grinning at them, Max said, "If either of you change your mind, I'm staying at the McNultys through Tuesday." He walked away.

"Nice meeting you, Mr. Kearny," called Tinkle.

Max leaned his elbows on the metal patio table, studying the notes he'd scribbled on the pages of a yellow legal tablet after talking with all the beleaguered residents of the circle, shuffling through the maps and floorplans Nita'd provided. "Demonic possession . . . some sort of residual evil . . . an unsolved murder in the past . . . none of the above?"

Pipes and wrenches rattled. "Courting the muse?"

Glancing up, Max beheld a man in a tan suit at the edge of the flagstone patio, a tool chest dangling in one hand. "You must be Burt Nostradamus," he said, pushing back in his deck chair.

Nostradamus was tall and lean, wearing dark glasses. "The village plumber." He came over and sat opposite Max unbidden. "Yet in my heart dwell deeper yearnings."

"Toward me?"

"I'm alluding to my dream of being some day a full-time professional writer," the plumber explained. "The ambition first struck me one chill winter's eve some years since while I labored to unearth the frozen pipe leading to the Hungerfords' cesspool. Flurries of snow assailed my slim frame, making white smudges across the black slate of the night. 'Nostradamus,' I exclaimed at that moment of insight, 'there is more to life than dibbing into cesspools in the middle of the night.' From that day I was dedicated to becoming an author."

"How've you been doing?"

"Thus far I've sold seven articles to the *National Intruder*," the plumber said, smiling faintly with pride. "I know I could get a full page in there if only Boz Snowden would cooperate."

"You want to interview him?"

"This yarn is big enough to hit maybe even the wire services. If, that is, I can persuade Snowden to speak frankly and openly with me."

"This all has something to do with the strange midnight happenings?"

The gaunt plumber dropped his toolkit with a thunking rattle. "I know of your work in the field of occult investigation, Mr. Kearny," he said in a confiding tone. "When I was but a small lad I read of your daring exploits in the very pages of the *Intruder*. Little did I dream that some fine day my own work would be gracing those selfsame pages, or that I'd meet such a—"

"You're around the Circle a lot, aren't you?"

"More than some realize," replied the plumber. "In the interest of gathering material, I've been paying nocturnal visits. Indeed, I was here last night when the demonic manifestations occurred. Perhaps you noticed me, being more perceptive than the rest, as I moved hither and yon on the track of the unknown."

"Were you out here on the patio?"

Nostradamus nodded. "It's risky being out in the open when this devilish work is going on, yet for a story—"

"What about the empty house two houses to the left of us? You been in there?"

Shaking his head, the plumber said, "Not since we installed the plumbing some time since. Why? You don't think a fellow occult investigator would stoop to housebreaking on the side."

Max said, "What's your theory as to what's behind this all?"

"Boswell Snowden's novel is a runaway best seller, yet he writes little better than I do," said the plumber. "His earlier novels, all of which I've read, are much worse even. Poorly plotted, filled with trite conventionalities and stilted prose. They did not sell."

"*Curse of the Demon* is pretty well written."

"The explanation is childishly simple, Mr. Kearny," said Nostradamus, leaning. "In order to insure himself a better prose style and to guarantee impressive sales, I am certain what Snowden did. He did what greedy and ambitious men have done through the ages, entered into a pact with the devil."

"You have any proof?"

"Nothing concrete, no," admitted the gaunt plumber. "Yet, from all I've seen and heard here during the grim watches of the night, I know I am right. As soon as I can prove my case, then have I got a story for the *Intruder*."

"What about all the things that are happening to the other houses?"

"Side effects," said the plumber, sitting back.

Phone on his lap and receiver to his ear, Max sat alone in the McNulty living room and watched the twilight come sweeping slowly across Hollow Hills Circle.

"Hello?"

"We have a collect call from the Bowery, New York," he said. "A Mr. Maxwell Kearny, Jr. claims, as far as we can make out from his babbling, that he is your common-law spouse. Will you accept charges?"

"Oh, him. No, toss him back into his gutter and mention I'm on the brink of running away with the college boy who comes and seeds the lawn."

Max said, "Otherwise how are things, Jill?"

Jillian Kearny said, "Stephanie got a homer and a double today."

"Admirable. Is she still the only girl in the Little League?"

"The only one on the Mill Valley Brewers. She's out at practice this very moment, so you can't talk to her. Did you buy her something?"

"It's in my suitcase."

"How are Nita and—"

"Listen, Jill, there's something going on here."

"Such as?"

He told her.

When he'd concluded she asked, "What's this Kate Tillman look like?"

"Oh, your usual long-legged blonde, beautiful and highly intelligent. Just like most wives in Fairfield County," he answered. "Little dinky auburn-haired ladies in their waning thirties they turn back at the border."

Jillian said, "You're investigating this whole frumus, huh?"

"Apparently so."

"Couldn't stay retired."

"Nope."

"So what do you think is afoot?"

"Somebody's summoned up a demon," he said. "All the manifestations point to that."

"Sounds like, yes," she agreed. "Which prompts me to suggest you go easy, Max."

Pushing aside the three library books on the coffee table, he moved the legal tablet into writing range. "Listen, Jill, all of my occult reference books and manuscripts are still up in the attic, aren't they?"

"I bumped into them only last night when I was hunting for Stephanie's bingo game, which she had a sudden wild urge to play."

"Can you pop up there and copy off a few of the strongest spells for getting rid of a demon?"

"Sure. Are we talking about a demon summoned to aid somebody?"

"No," he said, "one brought forth to get revenge."

A soft night rain was falling. Max zipped up his windbreaker, went edging along beside the McNulty house. He carried an unlit flashlight in his hand.

He waited in the bushes, watching the empty, rain-slick road which curved around the circle. After a few damp moments, he jogged across a slanting lawn, ran along a white driveway and, slowing, approached one of the unoccupied houses.

Moving along close to the side of the house, he halted near the window of the den. As he'd anticipated, there was a flickering light inside.

His watch face wasn't in the mood to glow, so he had to squint to make out the time. Three minutes in front of midnight.

He crept around to the rear of the house, let himself in by way of the kitchen door he'd left open during his afternoon visit.

The part of the house he'd entered still smelled of fresh paint and new wood. As he walked, silently, toward the den, though, new odors hit him. The smells of brimstone, sweet strong incense, damp earth, decay. Not your usual suburban household scents.

The whole house began to shudder.

Windows rattled, floors creaked.

It was like being directly over a quake.

From the den came a woman's voice. "You've got to go back!"

There was a rumbling, rasping laugh. "The gate has been opened! I am unleashed."

"Yes, but you were only supposed to do one simple thing and then go back . . . home."

Again the awful booming laughter.

All the pipes in the empty house began to shriek. Strange gurglings commenced underfoot. All the toilets were chortling.

"You haven't even succeeded in doing what I summoned you for. You've been making all sorts of annoying trouble for innocent people. It's stubborn and . . . mean-minded."

"You should have reckoned on that when you allowed Morax into this world again."

"I looked up another new spell, and this one'll bottle you up again."

Another evil laugh. "Your magic is not strong enough to stop me, foolish wench."

In the den Kate Tillman began, a shade nervously, to recite a spell in Latin.

Max was standing quietly next to the oddly glowing doorway. He shook his head. "Outmoded spell, not a chance of working."

"I heed it not! It has no effect!" roared Morax. "Now I'll once again torment your fellows."

"I really wish you'd go away. This hasn't worked out at all. He's even more stubborn than you."

"There is no way to stop me now. Each night at this enchanted hour I shall return to have my way."

"That's another thing, you keep doing these silly things to people. Can't you zero in on him, give him a real scare. I wouldn't mind your messing up the rest of us if—"

"Morax does as he pleases. None can stop such an all powerful demon!"

"Correction." Max crossed the threshold, unfolding a sheet of yellow paper from his pocket. "This is a very effective spell, worked out by a demonologist working in tandem with a computer. Been tested on a lot tougher demons than you, always works."

Crouched just outside the magic circle, face illuminated by the flickering flames of the ring of votive candles, was Kate. A patch of smooth tan skin showed between the top of her white slacks and her green jersey. A hand pressed to her left breast, she was staring at the demon who stood within the circle.

He was impressive. Over nine feet high, muddy green in color, covered with dry scales, his growling mouth packed with needle-like teeth. His bulging eyes glowed with an unsettling yellow light.

"Impotent fool!" he warned Max. "I will visit numerous annoyances upon you."

Clearing his throat, Max said, "Okay, here we go. Zimimar, Gorson, Agares, Leraie, Zenophilus," he read slowly and carefully.

"Bah, this has no . . . I do feel decidedly. . . ." Morax brought his terrible clawed paws up to his scaly face. "Gar . . ."

"Wierus, Pinel, Belphegor," continued Max.

The demon was panting, snarling, spewing greenish smoke from his mouth and ears.

Max kept on reciting the spell.

Morax shook, huddled in on himself, began to fade. Another moment and he was gone, even the smell of him.

The candles sputtered and died, the house was silent again.

Folding up the spell and slipping it away, Max crossed and touched Kate's shoulder. "I'll see you home."

Taking his hand, she got to her feet. "I . . . I wrote that book, you know."

"*Curse of the Demon.* Yeah, I figured that out," he said, as he guided her to the doorway. "After comparing his earlier works with it."

"I was so dumb, I signed some wretched agreement with Boz that gave him 90 percent of all the profits and 100 percent of the credit," she said. "Demonology has always been a hobby of mine. I did a really splendid job on that book. Thing is, I was timid and figured I needed someone like Boz Snowden to help me break into print."

They left through the back door. "So when he moved here, you followed. Deciding to go after a bigger share of the money the book's earning."

"Yes, although Bronco doesn't know that part of it," she said. "He's off in Ethiopia and Portugal and such places, never even knew I did the damn book."

"When you confronted Boz Snowden, he wouldn't give in?"

The rain was falling harder. Max put his arm around her slim shoulders.

"He simply threatened me, wouldn't listen at all," she said. "He's pretty vain; I think he's convinced himself that *Curse* wasn't a collaboration at all and that the book is entirely his. Well, I can get pretty mad and I decided to fix him good. The reason *Curse* is so good, Max, is because I really believe in demonology. And, damn it, it works."

"Somewhat too well."

"I summoned up Morax, that was easy, and ordered him to plague Snowden," she explained. "Except the demon started plaguing the whole area, all the houses. I suppose, giving him the benefit of the doubt, it's difficult to zero in on a small target. When I realized what was going on, I tried to send him off. Except, as you saw, I couldn't control Morax. He kept coming back night after night to play his pranks. On top of which, Boz has been very stubborn and, even though I told him the weird happenings were happening because he'd cheated me, he hasn't given in. All in all, it's been an awful mess."

"Your library of occult literature isn't broad enough for you to fool around with this sort of thing."

"How'd you know about my—"

"You hid the books in the hall closet this morning before you'd let me in the house," he replied. "I found 'em when I went to wash my hands."

"I should have expected that, you being a detective."

"Why'd you use the empty house as a base?"

"I didn't want to summon up a demon in our own place," she said as they neared her home. "There might have been a mess, and Bronco is very fastidious. How'd you know I'd been using that particular place?"

"I went through all the houses today, even the unoccupied ones. The remains of your magic circle showed on the floor," he told her. "My guess was we had a demon who'd gotten out of hand and that you'd be going back each night to try to keep him from reappearing."

"I'm sorry, more or less, that Morax made trouble for all the Circle people," Kate said, moving free of him and climbing to her front door. "But I'm not at all sorry about Boz Snowden. I'd still like to put a few more curses on him."

Max said, "I know a good literary attorney in Manhattan. Suppose we go in and talk to him tomorrow."

"You mean I ought to use legal means instead of supernatural to get what's rightfully mine?"

"Slower but sometimes more effective."

She shrugged, resigned. "Well, since demons turned out to be so unreliable, I may as well go to the law."

"I'll be driving into Manhattan tomorrow; you can come along."

"I'll do that." She opened the door. "Can I offer you a cup of tea?"

He hesitated before answering, "You can."

Death Trance

by Clayton Matthews

G regory Zeno picked up the buzzing house phone. "Yes?"

"Mr. Zeno? There's a young lady down here, Miss Anne Thomas. She claims an appointment."

"Yes. Please send Miss Thomas right up."

Zeno was a slight, slender man of thirty-five, with hair white as sun-bleached bone, a round face as innocent as a cherub's, and eyes a pale gray with a sleepy look about them. He left the study, crossed down the long living room, and was at the door, waiting, when the bell rang.

The girl to whom he opened the door was tall, golden, with green eyes and a good figure, in her early twenties. She struck Zeno as a vital person, but at the moment she seemed to be under rigid control, a shadow of apprehension behind her eyes.

"Miss Thomas? Please come in."

She stepped inside, and Zeno closed the door. He saw her looking around with quickening interest, but he was accustomed to people being impressed by his apartment in the high-rise area of Westwood. It was expensively furnished, ultramodern with clean, stark lines and in simple, basic colors, except for a few pictures on the walls, like vivid splashes of paint.

Zeno knew that most people associated the occult with another century, expecting darkness and shadow, furniture decorated with cabalistic signs, perhaps even creaking doors and unswept cobwebs, and so were disconcerted when confronted with living quarters as modern as a space rocket's functional furnishings.

Her inspection finished, Anne Thomas gave him a single flashing glance, but said nothing.

Zeno motioned. "Shall we go into my study?"

The study was more in keeping. Three walls were lined with books on the occult, the psychic, the mysterious. There was even a crystal ball on a pedestal in one corner, a contemptuous gift from a medium Zeno had exposed for a fraud.

Zeno seated the girl across from his desk and asked, "A drink, Miss Thomas? Perhaps a glass of sherry?"

"No, Mr. Zeno, thank you."

Zeno sat behind his desk. "What can I do for you?"

"Well, I . . ." She hesitated, moistening her lips with her tongue, then blurted, "My stepfather is trying to get my mother to kill herself!"

Zeno frowned. "I'm sorry to hear that, of course, but why come to me? I'm not a private detective, not in the usual sense. I only take cases involving the occult."

"But you don't understand! This *is* in your field. My mother believes in mediums, spirits, things like that. My stepfather caters to this. He has brought a medium around who claims communication with my dead father's spirit, and this spirit wants Mother to join him on the other side. Now do you see?"

"Who is this medium?"

"A woman named Madame Tora. Do you know her?"

"No, but that doesn't mean anything."

"Well, she is something else! Mr. Zeno, are any of these mediums authentic?"

Zeno said cautiously, "Let's just say it hasn't been proved to my satisfaction either way. I've found several to be frauds, yet that doesn't mean there aren't any authentic mediums."

"This one must be a fake. She must be! There's something else, you see. My father was killed two years ago in a fall from the roof of our house. It was ruled an accident. But this voice that's supposed to be my father's says someone pushed him over, but he doesn't know who. Mother thinks she may have done it. Did you ever hear such nonsense?"

"It isn't nonsense if your mother believes it. Does she?"

"She's beginning to. But she wouldn't hurt a fly, much less push Dad off a roof. If anybody did it, it was my stepfather."

"Do you have any reason to suspect him?"

"Well, Dad left Mother well off and Darrin—that's my stepfather, Darrin Woods—was hanging around Mother before Dad was . . . before Dad died."

"It's not unusual for children to dislike stepfathers."

"Oh, I don't like him! Heavens, no! But I'm sure he married Mother for her money. If she kills herself, he'll have it all. If he can manage that, couldn't he have killed my father?"

"I'm hardly in a position to give an opinion."

"But if you take the case . . . *Will* you take the case?"

Zeno scrubbed a hand down across his face, then reached a sudden decision. "Yes, I'll see what I can do."

Anne's face lit up. Then she leaned forward to say tensely, "There's a . . . sitting at the house tonight. You can come, see what this Madame Tora is all about. I'm home from college for the summer. I'll tell them you're a . . . Oh, a college instructor interested in parapsychology."

"That sounds fine, Anne. What time?"

"The sitting starts at eight."

"I'll be there."

He escorted her out, then returned to stare somberly out the study window. He knew why he had taken on her problem. Of course it seemed an interesting case, the sort that always intrigued him, but that wasn't the whole of it. The similarity between her mother's situation and Zeno's own mother was uncanny, a little frightening.

Zeno had been ten when his father was killed in a hunting accident. For three years thereafter, his grieving mother went from medium to medium seeking contact with her dead husband. Finally she found one who helped her communicate. Either that, or the medium was an ingenious fraud, and the voice purported to be that of Zeno's father had begged his wife to join him on the other side until she had finally killed herself.

From that day forward, Zeno's interest in the occult mounted until, in the end, he became an investigator into psychic phenomena, always searching for concrete proof of the existence of spirits. So far, as he had told Anne, he had uncovered a number of fake mediums, yet he had not resolved the question to his own satisfaction. Until he did, he would never know whether or not his mother's suicide had been the result of a fraud practiced on her.

It was easy to see how Anne's father could have been killed by a fall from the roof. The house was in the Hollywood hills, up one of the old canyons, perched like a gray, medieval castle on the lip of a bluff, a straight drop of several hundred feet to the floor of the canyon.

"He fell from here," Anne said in a subdued voice, "or was pushed."

The roof of the building was flat, with a three-foot parapet around the edge. There was a sort of garden on the roof, with potted shrubs and trees, chairs and a table with an umbrella.

Zeno had been a little early and Anne, watching for him, had taken him up on the roof.

"I suppose it's possible to fall off but it wouldn't be easy," he said. "Not with that wall to fall over."

"Well, you see . . ." Anne shifted her feet uncomfortably, avoiding his gaze. Then she blurted, "Dad drank. He often sat up here alone at night, drinking—as he was that night. The autopsy showed he'd consumed quite a bit. It was decided he was drunk and stumbled over."

"One thing puzzles me, Anne. You said your mother is afraid she may have pushed him over. Doesn't she *know*?"

"She isn't sure, not positively." Again she looked away. "She drank too, you see. Then, I mean. They weren't getting along well. They'd been quarreling for some time. What about, I'm not sure. Maybe about Darrin hanging around Mother. She was supposed to be downstairs asleep at the time. But the thing is, she used to get up and wander around when she'd been drinking and not remember a thing later." She faced him defiantly. "I guess you think we're a weird family, Mr. Zeno."

"I never judge people, Anne," Zeno said gently. "At least, not until all the evidence is in."

His gaze went past her to a man who was striding briskly toward them. He was on the far side of fifty, slender, tanned, and had black hair with a distinguished peppering of gray. He was quite handsome and beautifully dressed.

Anne had turned at the sound of approaching footsteps. Her face became an expressionless mask.

"My dear, the sitting is about to begin," the newcomer said in a rich voice that matched his appearance.

"This is the instructor I told you about, Gregory Zeno. Mr. Zeno, this is my stepfather, Darrin Woods."

The man's handshake was firm. "We're always delighted to have someone join us who's truly interested in the occult."

"Oh, I'm interested," Zeno said. "Very interested."

"Then shall we go down?"

Woods extended his arm to Anne. She ignored it and strode on ahead.

The seance was held in a room on the first floor. Apparently it had once been a study. Now, it was bare of furniture except for a round dinette table and a half dozen chairs ringing it.

There were two women sitting at the table.

Helen Woods, Anne's mother, was in her late forties, with brown eyes and brown hair. There was an ethereal quality about her, her skin almost translucent, as though she already hovered on the threshold of the other world. She responded not at all when Anne introduced Zeno, and he doubted she was even aware of his presence. She reminded him of a drug addict waiting impatiently for a fix. From past experience with such situations, he knew this wasn't as fanciful as it seemed.

Madame Tora was somewhat of a surprise. Many mediums that Zeno had encountered were often physically unattractive, but not Madame Tora. She was about thirty, with a cloud of hair the color of rust, a provocative face, and she wore a green mini-dress to match her eyes. She eyed him closely, but accepted his presence without comment.

Zeno was seated at the table between Anne and Madame Tora. Woods dimmed the lights, blindfolded Madame Tora with a silk scarf, then sat directly across from Zeno. They linked hands all the way around the table.

Madame Tora tilted her head back. In a moment her breathing quickened, became a harsh, rasping sound in the room. Her head rolled on her neck. She grew more and more agitated. Then she said, "Fredrick? Are you there, Fredrick?"

"Fredrick is her spirit control," Anne whispered in Zeno's ear, "or so she claims."

Zeno nodded without taking his gaze from the medium.

Now a deep male voice issued from the medium's lips, "Yes, Madame Tora. This is Fredrick."

"Is someone with you, Fredrick? Someone who wishes to communicate?"

"Yes, someone who . . ."

As Zeno watched, the cords in Madame Tora's throat tautened like steel cables, and the male voice coming from her changed subtly. "Helen, are you there, darling? This is Keith."

Zeno saw a quiver go through Helen Woods, and she said hoarsely, "Yes, Keith, I'm here."

Zeno looked at her. She sat rigidly, eyes wide and staring at the medium. Zeno's glance moved on to Woods. He, also, was looking at the medium with a fixed stare.

The thought passed through Zeno's mind that they could both be in a state bordering on a hypnotic trance. That could mean that

Woods was equally convinced of Madame Tora's authenticity. Or it could mean . . .

"Helen, have you decided?"

"No, Keith. Not yet. I—"

"There isn't a great deal of time, Helen. Soon I may move on to another plane. And if that happens, we will not be able to—" The voice began to fade.

"Keith! Don't go! Not yet!"

"Good-bye, Helen. Good-bye, my darling . . ." The voice faded and was gone.

"No!" Helen Woods tore her hand from Darrin's grasp and leaped to her feet. "Keith, wait! Please wait!"

Madame Tora slumped, arms hanging loosely at her sides, head bent over the chair back. Helen Woods collapsed, head in her hands on the table, sobbing wildly. Zeno stood up and went to her, but her husband jumped up, pushing Zeno aside. "Don't touch her! I'll take care of her."

The woman seemed only half-conscious as Woods helped her from the room. Zeno stared after them, a thought nudging his mind. Anne touched his arm, and he looked around. Madame Tora had roused and was briskly preparing to depart, ignoring them as though they didn't exist.

Anne started to leave and Zeno followed her, neither speaking on their way up to the roof. It was full dark now, the air refreshing.

Anne took out a cigarette and leaned back against the parapet. He struck a match for her.

She expelled smoke and said, "Well?"

"If you want to know if she's a fraud, I'm not prepared to answer that. She could be a ventriloquist. She could be a good voice mimic. She could be many things, even a true medium. But that's not the important thing."

"Then what is, for heaven's sake?"

"Your mother's guilt, real or imagined. Has she ever been hypnotized?"

Anne looked perplexed. "Mother? Hypnotized? Not that I know about. What does that have to do with anything?"

"I'm not sure." He stared thoughtfully down at the lights in the canyon below.

"I think they're having an affair, Darrin and that Madame Tora," Anne said with unexpected venom. "I think he's promised to marry her if Mother dies."

"People recall things under hypnosis, things they've forgotten ever doing, things their minds have blanked out for one reason or another," Zeno said, pointedly ignoring her remark. "Do you think your mother would consent?"

"He'll be opposed, I know, but I'm sure I can talk her into it. Do you think it will work?"

"It might, if she's a good hypnotic subject, and I think she is, from watching her tonight. But there's one thing you should take into consideration, Anne."

"What's that?"

"There's always the possibility she's guilty. If she is, it'll probably come out."

"I'm willing to take that chance and I'm sure Mother is, too."

The hypnotic session also took place in the former study. The hypnotist was one Zeno had used before. Zeno was himself a good amateur hypnotist, but he thought this too important to trust to amateurs. To be effective, a hypnotist must practice intense concentration and Zeno wanted his attention free for something else.

Madame Tora had asked to be present. Anne had balked at this, but it suited Zeno's purpose to have the medium there.

Zeno had given the hypnotist certain instructions. The chairs were arranged so that Woods and his wife were side by side, the others somewhat apart. When everyone was seated, the hypnotist took up a stance in front of them. He was a distinguished-looking man, with a shock of gray hair and a rich, resonant voice.

"Now I want you to relax completely, let every muscle go slack, and concentrate on the sound of my voice. Make your mind as blank as a clean sheet of paper and think of nothing but the sound of my voice . . ."

Zeno had warned Anne as to what to expect, had told her to think of something exciting that had recently happened to her, concentrate on anything but the hypnotist's voice. Zeno had a strong suspicion that Madame Tora didn't need any warning.

"Now you are completely relaxed," the hypnotist intoned. "Close your eyes. You are getting sleepy, very sleepy. You are thinking sleep . . ."

Zeno's surmise had been correct. Helen Woods was a good hypnotic subject. She was going under. But even more to Zeno's satisfaction, he noted that Woods also had his eyes closed, his head and hands hanging limply.

After a little, the hypnotist said in a sharper tone, "Helen, extend

your arm straight out. That's fine. Now it is rigid as an iron bar.
You cannot bend it. You *cannot* bend it! Now . . . try to bend it,
Helen."

The woman's efforts to bend the arm were clearly visible, but try
as she would, she couldn't lower it.

"Good, Helen. That's fine. You may lower it. Now, Helen, we are
going back two years, back to the evening of your first husband's
death. Do you remember that evening, Helen?"

A low, moaning sound came from Helen Woods. "Yes . . . I remember . . ."

"Were you with him on the roof at the time of his death?"

She was silent.

"Were you *with* him, Helen?"

"No . . . I was in bed. Asleep. I'd had too much to drink."

"You were *not* on the roof with him at the time?"

"No, no! In bed!"

"You didn't push him over the edge?" The hypnotist's voice curled
at her like a lash.

"No, no . . . I was . . ." Helen Woods was laboring, her face shiny
with sweat. "I was in bed . . . Asleep, asleep."

Anne stirred by Zeno's side, murmuring in protest. Zeno clamped
his hand around her wrist and held her still.

"All right, Helen." The hypnotist's voice became gentler. "You
will relax now. You will go deeper into sleep, deeper . . ."

The lines of strain left the woman's face, and she slumped down
in the chair, limp as a rag doll.

The hypnotist turned to Woods, who was in a trance apparently
as deep as his wife's. "Darrin, do you hear me?"

"Yes . . . I hear you."

The hypnotist picked up the man's right hand. "Your right hand
is numb, Darrin. Do you understand? It is numb. You cannot feel
a thing."

The hypnotist took a needle from his pocket and pricked Woods'
thumb. He didn't flinch or cry out. A drop of blood oozed from the
thumb. The hypnotist wiped away the blood and let the hand fall.

"Darrin, look toward the door."

Woods brought his head around and stared at the closed door.

"There is a man just entering. Do you see him?"

"I . . . Yes, I see him."

"He is a policeman, Darrin."

Woods became noticeably agitated. "A policeman?"

"Yes, Darrin, a plainclothes detective. He is here to question you about the death of Keith Thomas." The hypnotist made his voice stern. "You are to answer his questions truthfully."

A cry came from Madame Tora. "Darrin, don't be a fool! There's no one there! No cop, nobody!" She jumped up and ran toward Woods.

Zeno had been prepared. He stepped into her path and seized her arm. "Now, Madame, you don't want to interfere. And why should you be concerned if Mr. Woods thinks a policeman is present? Do you have something to hide?" He watched her closely.

She paled, eyes widening. "Of course not! I just don't like to see him made a fool of."

"But that's the name of the game, isn't it? The hypnotic subject doing and saying things he wouldn't otherwise?"

She recoiled from him as though he'd hissed at her like a venomous snake, and resumed her seat without another word.

"Darrin, were you on the roof the night Keith Thomas died?" the hypnotist asked.

Woods twitched, as though from a delayed reaction to the pin prick, but he didn't speak.

"Darrin, did you push him off the roof?"

"I . . ."

Another cry came from Madame Tora. This time she broke for the door. Again Zeno had anticipated her. He caught her three steps from the door.

"What's your hurry, Madame?"

"Let me go!" She tried to pull loose.

"Are you afraid of what he might tell us? Are you implicated in some way?"

"I'm implicated in nothing! If he tells you I am, he's lying! He pushed that man off the roof! I didn't know about it until long afterwards. He said . . ." The words spilled from her in a flood. "He said all I had to do was . . ." She broke down completely, hands over her face, shoulders heaving.

Zeno led her gently back to the chair. "Anne, you'd better call the police now."

As the police started to take Madame Tora away, Anne stopped them with a gesture. "Madame Tora, my father's voice . . . Was that . . . ?"

Madame Tora had recovered some of her aplomb. She said haughtily, "You dare ask that of *me*? Are you insinuating that I am a fraud?"

Gathering the shreds of her dignity around her like a tattered cloak, she swept from the room, leading the policemen instead of being led.

Zeno and Anne were left alone. Woods had been awakened from his trance and taken away earlier. Zeno had taped the session on a small recorder and had played it back for the police and Anne's mother, who had dissolved into hysterics and fled to her bedroom.

Anne shivered, hugging herself. She said violently, "I hate this place! I'm getting Mother out of here."

By unspoken agreement, they mounted the stairs to the roof.

"Mr. Zeno, did he push my father off the roof?"

"It appears quite likely, Anne."

"Will they convict him?"

"The odds are good, especially since Madame Tora let the cat out."

"But can they use what you taped?"

"Not in court, no. But by playing your stepfather against Madame Tora and using the tape, I think they'll get a confession."

"Would he have confessed if the hypnotist had kept on?"

Zeno shook his head. "Not likely. If that were so, the police would use hypnosis all the time. There are many misconceptions about hypnosis. It's almost impossible to force someone to do something against his will."

"But he seemed to believe there was a policeman in the room."

"A susceptible subject, which your stepfather is, can be made to believe many things but not *do* them against the dictates of the subconscious. For instance, there are cases on record of people jumping to their death while in a hypnotic trance by being told a ten-story window is the door to another room. Yet, if they were told the window *was* a window and ordered to step out, they wouldn't do it."

"Yet Madame Tora believed he was going to confess."

Zeno smiled. "That's what I had hoped."

Anne was silent for a moment before she said in a low voice, "Mr. Zeno, do you think . . . ?" She shivered again. "We still don't know for sure if Madame Tora's a fraud, if my father's voice . . ."

Zeno said thoughtfully, "No, we don't know that for sure, do we?"

The Healer

by George C. Chesbro

The man waiting for me in my downtown office looked like a movie star who didn't want to be recognized. After he took off his hat, dark glasses and leather maxi-coat he still looked like a movie star. He also looked like a certain famous Southern senator.

"Dr. Frederickson," he said, extending a large, sinewy hand. "I've been doing so much reading about you in the past few days, I feel I already know you. I must say it's a distinct pleasure. I'm Bill Younger."

"Senator," I said, shaking the hand and motioning him toward the chair in front of my desk. I had a sudden, mad flash that the senator might be looking for a new campaign gimmick, like an endorsement from a dwarf criminologist-college professor-private detective. Those are the kinds of mad flashes you get when you're a dwarf criminologist-college professor-private detective. I went around to the other side of the desk. Younger, with his boyish, forty-five-year-old face and full head of brown, modishly-cut hair, looked good. Except for the fear in his eyes he might have been ready to step into a television studio. "Why the background check, Senator?"

He half-smiled. "I used to take my daughter to see you perform when you were with the circus."

"That was a long time ago, Senator." It was six years. It seemed a hundred.

The smile faded. "You're famous. I wanted to see if you were also discreet. My sources tell me your credentials are impeccable. You seem to have a penchant for unusual cases."

"Unusual cases seem to have a penchant for me. You'd be amazed how few people feel the need for a dwarf private detective."

Younger didn't seem to be listening. "You've heard of Esteban Morales?"

I said I hadn't. The senator seemed surprised. "I was away for the summer," I added.

The senator nodded absently, then rose and began to pace back and forth in front of the desk. The activity seemed to relax him. "Esteban is one of my constituents, so I'm quite familiar with his work. He's a healer."

"A doctor?"

"No, not a doctor. A psychic healer. He heals with his hands. His mind." He cast a quick look in my direction to gauge my reaction. He must have been satisfied with what he saw because he went on. "There are a number of good psychic healers in this country. Those who are familiar with this kind of phenomenon consider Esteban the best although his work does not receive much publicity. There are considerable . . . pressures."

"Why did you assume I'd heard of him?"

"He spent the past summer at the university where you teach. He'd agreed to participate in a research project."

"What kind of research project?"

"I'm not sure. It was something in microbiology. I think a Dr. Mason was heading the project."

I nodded. Janet Mason is a friend of mine.

"The project was never finished," Younger continued. "Esteban is now in jail awaiting trial for murder." He added almost parenthetically, "Your brother was the arresting officer."

I was beginning to get the notion that it was more than my natural dwarf charm that had attracted Senator Younger. "Who is this Esteban Morales accused of killing?"

"A physician by the name of Robert Edmonston."

"Why?"

The senator suddenly stopped pacing and planted his hands firmly on top of my desk. He seemed extremely agitated. "The papers reported that Edmonston filed a complaint against Esteban. Practicing medicine without a license. The police think Esteban killed him because of it."

"They'd need more than thoughts to book him."

"They . . . found Esteban in the office with the body. Edmonston had been dead only a few minutes. His throat had been cut with a knife they found dissolving in a vial of acid." The first words had come hard for Younger. The rest came easier. "If charges had been filed against Esteban, it wouldn't have been the first time. These are the things Esteban has to put up with. He's always taken the enmity of the medical establishment in stride. Esteban is not a killer—he's a healer. He couldn't kill anyone!" He suddenly straight-

ened up, then slumped into the chair behind him. "I'm sorry," he
said quietly. "I must seem overwrought."

"How do you feel I can help you, Senator?"

"You must clear Esteban," Younger said. His voice was steady
but intense. "Either prove he didn't do it, or that someone else did."

I looked at him to see if he might, just possibly, be joking. He
wasn't. "That's a pretty tall order, Senator. And it could get expensive. On the other hand, you've got the whole New York City Police
Department set up to do that work for free."

The senator shook his head. "I want one man—you—to devote
himself to nothing but this case. You work at the university. You
have contacts. You may be able to find out something the police
couldn't, or didn't care to look for. After all, the police have other
things besides Esteban's case to occupy their attention."

"I wouldn't argue with that."

"This is *most* important to me, Dr. Frederickson," the senator said,
jabbing his finger in the air for emphasis. "I will double your usual
fee."

"That won't be nec—"

"At the least, I must have access to Esteban if you fail. Perhaps
your brother could arrange that. I am willing to donate ten thousand
dollars to any cause your brother deems worthy."

"Hold on, Senator. Overwrought or not, I wouldn't mention that
kind of arrangement to Garth. He might interpret it as a bribe offer.
Very embarrassing."

"It *will* be a bribe offer!"

I thought about that for a few seconds, then said, "You certainly
do a lot for your constituents, Senator. I'm surprised you're not
President."

I must have sounded snide. The flesh on the senator's face
blanched bone-white, then filled with blood. His eyes flashed. Still,
somewhere in their depths, the fear remained. His words came out
in a forced whisper. "If Esteban Morales is not released, my daughter
will die."

I felt a chill, and wasn't sure whether it was because I believed
him or because of the possibility that a United States senator and
presidential hopeful was a madman. I settled for something in between and tried to regulate my tone of voice accordingly. "I don't
understand, Senator."

"Really? I thought I was making myself perfectly clear. My daughter's life is totally dependent on Esteban Morales." He took a deep

breath. "My daughter Linda has cystic fibrosis, Dr. Frederickson. As you may know, medical doctors consider cystic fibrosis incurable. The normal pattern is for a sufferer to die in his or her early teens—usually from pulmonary complications. Esteban has been treating my daughter all her life, and she is now twenty-four. But Linda needs him again. Her lungs are filling with fluid."

I was beginning to understand how the medical establishment might get a little nervous at Esteban Morales' activities, and a psychic warning light was flashing in my brain. Senator or no, this didn't sound like the kind of case in which I liked to get involved. If Morales were a hoaxer—or a killer—I had no desire to be the bearer of bad tidings to a man with the senator's emotional investment.

"How does Morales treat your daughter? With drugs?"

Younger shook his head. "He just . . . *touches* her. He moves his hands up and down her body. Sometimes he looks like he's in a trance, but he isn't. It's . . . very hard to explain. You have to see him do it."

"How much does he charge for these treatments?"

The senator looked surprised. "Esteban doesn't charge anything. Most psychic healers—the real ones—won't take money. They feel it interferes with whatever it is they do." He laughed shortly, without humor. "Esteban prefers to live simply, off Social Security, a pension check and a few gifts—small ones—from his friends. He's a retired metal shop foreman."

Esteban Morales didn't exactly fit the mental picture I'd drawn of him, and my picture of the senator was still hazy. "Senator," I said, tapping my fingers lightly on the desk, "why don't you hold a press conference and describe what you feel Esteban Morales has done for your daughter? It could do you more good than hiring a private detective. Coming from you, I guarantee it will get the police moving."

Younger smiled thinly. "Or get me locked up in Bellevue. At the least I would be voted out of office, perhaps recalled. My state is in the so-called Bible Belt, and there would be a great deal of misunderstanding. Esteban is not a religious man in my constituents' sense of the word. He does not claim to receive his powers from God. Even if he did, it wouldn't make much difference." The smile got thinner. "I've found that most religious people prefer their miracles well-aged. You'll forgive me if I sound selfish, but I would like to try to save Linda's life without demolishing my career. If all else fails, I will hold a press conference. Will you take the job?"

I told him I'd see what I could find out.

It looked like a large, photographic negative. In its center was a dark outline of a hand with the fingers outstretched. The tips of the fingers were surrounded by waves of color, pink, red and violet, undulating outward to a distance of an inch or two from the hand itself. The effect was oddly beautiful and very mysterious.

"What the hell is it?"

"It's a Kirlian photograph," Dr. Janet Mason said. She seemed pleased with my reaction. "The technique is named after a Russian who invented it about thirty years ago. The Russians, by the way, are far ahead of us in this field."

I looked at her. Janet Mason is a handsome woman in her early fifties. Her shiny gray hair was drawn back into a severe bun, highlighting the fine features of her face. You didn't need a special technique to be aware of her sex appeal. She is a tough-minded scientist who, rumor has it, had gone through a long string of lab-assistant lovers. Her work left her little time for anything else. Janet Mason has been liberated a long time. I like her.

"Uh, what field?"

"Psychic research: healing, ESP, clairvoyance, that sort of thing. Kirlian photography, for example, purports to record what is known as the human *aura*, part of the energy that all living things radiate. The technique itself is quite simple. You put an individual into a circuit with an unexposed photographic plate and have the person touch the plate with some part of his body." She pointed to the print I was holding. "That's what you end up with."

"Morales'?"

"Mine. That's an 'average' aura, if you will." She reached into the drawer of her desk and took out another set of photographs. She looked through them, then handed one to me. "This is Esteban's."

I glanced at the print. It looked the same as the first one, and I told her so.

"That's Esteban at rest, you might say. He's not thinking about healing." She handed me another photograph. "Here he is with his batteries charged."

The print startled me. The bands of color were erupting out from the fingers, especially the index and middle fingers. The apogee of the waves was somewhere off the print; they looked like sun storms.

"You won't find that in the others," Janet continued. "With most people, thinking about healing makes very little difference."

"So what does it mean?"

She smiled disarmingly. "Mongo, I'm a scientist. I deal in facts. The fact of the matter is that Esteban Morales takes one hell of a Kirlian photograph. The implication is that he can literally radiate extra amounts of energy at will."

"Do you think he can actually heal people?"

She took a long time to answer. "There's no doubt in *my* mind that he can," she said at last. I considered it a rather startling confession. "And he's not dealing with psychosomatic disorders. Esteban has been involved in other research projects, at different universities. In one, a strip of skin was removed surgically from the backs of monkeys. The monkeys were divided into two groups. Esteban simply handled the monkeys in one group. Those monkeys healed twice as fast as the ones he didn't handle." She smiled wanly. "Plants are supposed to grow faster when he waters them."

"What did you have him working on?"

"Enzymes," Janet said with a hint of pride. "The perfect research model; no personalities involved. You see, enzymes are the basic chemicals of the body. If Esteban could heal, the reasoning went, he should be able to affect pure enzymes. He can."

"The results were good?"

She laughed lightly. "Spectacular. Irradiated—'injured'—enzymes break down at specific rates in certain chemical solutions. The less damaged they are, the slower their rate of breakdown. What we did was to take test tubes full of enzymes—supplied by a commercial lab—and irradiate them. Then we gave Esteban half of the samples to handle. The samples he handled broke down at a statistically significant *lesser* rate than the ones he didn't handle." She paused again, then said, "Ninety-nine and nine-tenths percent of the population can't affect the enzymes one way or the other. On the other hand, a very few people can make the enzymes break down *faster*."

" 'Negative' healers?"

"Right. Pretty hairy, huh?"

I laughed. "It's incredible. Why haven't I heard anything about it? I mean, here's a man who may be able to heal people with his hands and nobody's heard of him. I would think Morales would make headlines in every newspaper in the country."

Janet gave me the kind of smile I suspected she normally reserved for some particularly naive student. "It's next to impossible just to get funding for this kind of research, what's more, publicity. Psychic healing is thought of as, well, *occult*."

"You mean like acupuncture?"

It was Janet's turn to laugh. "You make my point. You know how long it took Western scientists and doctors to get around to taking acupuncture seriously. Psychic healing just doesn't fit into the currently accepted pattern of scientific thinking. When you do get a study done, none of the journals want to publish it."

"I understand that Dr. Edmonston filed a complaint against Morales. Is that true?"

"That's what the police said. I have no reason to doubt it. Edmonston was never happy about his part in the project. Now I'm beginning to wonder about Dr. Johnson. I'm still waiting for his anecdotal reports."

"What project? What reports? What Dr. Johnson?"

Janet looked surprised. "You don't know about that?"

"I got all my information from my client. Obviously, he didn't know. Was there some kind of tie-in between Morales and Edmonston?"

"I would say so." She replaced the Kirlian photographs in her desk drawer. "We actually needed Esteban only about an hour or so a day, when he handled samples. The rest of the time we were involved in computer analysis. We decided it might be interesting to see what Esteban could do with some real patients, under medical supervision. We wanted to get a physician's point of view. We put some feelers out into the medical community and got a cold shoulder—except for Dr. Johnson, who incidentally happened to be Robert Edmonston's partner. I get the impression the two of them had a big argument over using Esteban, and Rolfe Johnson eventually won. We worked out a plan where Esteban would go to their offices after finishing here. They would refer certain patients—who volunteered—to him. These particular patients were in no immediate danger, but they would eventually require hospitalization. These patients would report how they felt to Edmonston and Johnson after their sessions with Esteban. The two doctors would then make up anecdotal reports. Not very scientific, but we thought it might make an interesting footnote to the main study."

"And you haven't seen these reports?"

"No. I think Dr. Johnson is stalling."

"Why would he do that after he agreed to participate in the project?"

"I don't know. Maybe he's had second thoughts after the murder. Or maybe he's simply afraid his colleagues will laugh at him."

I wondered. It still seemed a curious shift in attitude. It also occurred to me that I would like to see the list of patients that had been referred to Morales. It just might contain the name of someone with a motive to kill Edmonston—and try to pin it on Esteban Morales. "Tell me some more about Edmonston and Johnson," I said. "You mentioned the fact they were partners."

Janet took a cigarette from her purse and I supplied a match. She studied me through a cloud of smoke. "Is this confidential?"

"If you say so."

"Johnson and Edmonston were very much into the modern big-business aspect of medicine. It's what a lot of doctors are doing these days: labs, ancillary patient centers, private, profit-making hospitals. Dr. Johnson's skills seemed to be more in the area of administration of their enterprises. As a matter of fact, he'd be about the last person I'd expect to be interested in psychic healing. There were rumors to the effect they were going public in a few months."

"Doctors go public?"

"Sure. They build up a network of the types of facilities I mentioned, incorporate, then sell stocks."

"How'd they get along?"

"Who knows? I assume they got along as well as any other business partners. They were different, though."

"How so?"

"Edmonston was the older of the two men. I suspect he was attracted to Johnson because of Johnson's ideas in the areas I mentioned. Edmonston was rumored to be a good doctor, but he was brooding. No sense of humor. Johnson had a lighter, happy-go-lucky side. Obviously, he was also the more adventurous of the two."

"What was the basis of Edmonston's complaint?"

"Dr. Edmonston claimed that Esteban was giving his patients drugs."

I thought about that. It certainly didn't fit in with what the senator had told me. "Janet, doesn't it strike you as odd that two doctors like Johnson and Edmonston would agree to work with a psychic healer? Aside from philosophic differences, they sound like busy men."

"Oh, yes. I really can't explain Dr. Johnson's enthusiasm. As I told you, Dr. Edmonston was against the project from the beginning. He didn't want to waste his time on what he considered to be superstitious nonsense." She paused, then added, "He must have given off some bad vibrations."

"Why do you say that?"

"I'm not sure. Toward the end of the experiment something was affecting Esteban's concentration. He wasn't getting the same results he had earlier. And before you ask, I don't know why he was upset. I broached the subject once and he made it clear he didn't want to discuss it."

"Do you think he killed Edmonston?"

She laughed shortly, without humor. "Uh-uh, Mongo. That's your department. I deal in enzymes; they're much simpler than people."

"C'mon, Janet. You spent an entire summer working with him. He must have left some kind of impression. Do you think Esteban Morales is the kind of man who would slit somebody's throat?"

She looked at me a long time. Finally she said, "Esteban Morales is probably the gentlest, most loving person I've ever met. And that's all you're going to get from me. Except that I wish you luck."

I nodded my thanks, then rose and started for the door.

"Mongo?"

I turned with my hand on the doorknob. Janet was now sitting on the edge of her desk, exposing a generous portion of her very shapely legs. They were the best looking fifty-year-old legs I'd ever seen—and on a very pretty woman.

"You have to come and see me more often," she continued evenly. "I don't have that many dwarf colleagues."

I winked broadly. "See you, kid."

"Of course I was curious," Dr. Rolfe Johnson said. "That's why I was so anxious to participate in the project in the first place. I like to consider myself open-minded."

I studied Johnson. He was a boyish thirty-seven, outrageously good-looking, with Nordic blue eyes and a full head of blond hair. I was impressed by his enthusiasm, somewhat puzzled by his agreeing to see me within twenty minutes of my phone call. For a busy doctor-businessman he seemed very free with his time—or very anxious to nail the lid on Esteban Morales. He was just a little too eager to please me.

"Dr. Edmonston wasn't?"

Johnson cleared his throat. "Well, I didn't mean that. Robert was a . . . traditionalist. You will find that most doctors are just not that

curious. He considered working with Mr. Morales an unnecessary
drain on our time. I thought it was worth it."

"Why? What was in it for you?"

He looked slightly hurt. "I considered it a purely scientific inquiry.
After all, no doctor ever actually *heals* anyone. Nor does any medicine. The body heals itself, and all any doctor can do is to try to
stimulate the body to do its job. From his advance publicity, Esteban
Morales was a man who could do that without benefit of drugs or
scalpels. I wanted to see if it were true."

"Was it?"

Johnson snorted. "Of course not. It was all mumbo jumbo. Oh, he
certainly had a psychosomatic effect on some people—but they had
to believe in him. From what I could see, the effects of what he was
doing were at most ephemeral, and extremely short-lived. I suppose
that's why he panicked."

"Panicked?"

Johnson's eyebrows lifted. "The police haven't told you?"

"I'm running ahead of myself. I haven't talked to the police yet.
I assume you're talking about the drugs Morales is supposed to have
administered."

"Oh, not *supposed* to. I *saw* him, and it was reported to me by the
patient."

"What patient?"

He clucked his tongue. "Surely you can appreciate the fact that
I can't give out patients' names."

"Sure. You told Edmonston?"

"It was his patient. And he insisted on filing the complaint himself." He shook his head. "Dr. Mason would have been doing everyone
a favor if she hadn't insisted on having the university bail him out."

"Uh-huh. Can you tell me what happened the night Dr. Edmonston
died? What you know?"

He thought about it for a while. At least he looked like he was
thinking about it. "Dr. Edmonston and I always met on Thursday
nights. There were records to be kept, decisions to be made, and
there just wasn't enough time during the week. On that night I was
a few minutes late." He shook his head. "Those few minutes may
have cost Robert his life."

"Maybe. What was Morales doing there?"

"I'm sure I don't know. Obviously, he was enraged with Robert.
He must have found out about the Thursday night meeting while

he was working with us, and decided that would be a good time to kill Dr. Edmonston."

"But if he knew about the meetings, he'd know you'd be there."

Johnson glanced impatiently at his watch. "I am not privy to what went on in Esteban Morales' mind. After all, as you must know, he is almost completely illiterate. A stupid man. Perhaps he simply wasn't thinking straight . . . if he ever does." He rose abruptly. "I'm afraid I've given you all the time I can afford. I've talked to you in the interests of obtaining justice for Dr. Edmonston. I hoped you would see that you were wasting your time investigating the matter."

The interview was obviously over.

Johnson's story stunk. The problem was how to get someone else to sniff around it. With a prime suspect like Morales in the net, the New York police weren't about to complicate matters for themselves before they had to, meaning before the senator either got Morales a good lawyer or laid his own career on the line. My job was to prevent that necessity, which meant, at the least, getting Morales out on bail. To do that I was going to have to start raising some doubts.

It was time to talk to Morales.

I stopped off at a drive-in for dinner, took out three hamburgers and a chocolate milk shake intended as a bribe for my outrageously oversized brother. The food wasn't enough. A half hour later, after threats, shouts and appeals to familial loyalty, I was transformed from a dwarf private detective to a dwarf lawyer and taken to see Esteban Morales. The guard assigned to me thought it was funny as hell.

Esteban Morales looked like an abandoned extra from *Viva Zapata*. He wore a battered, broad-brimmed straw hat to cover a full head of long, matted gray hair. He wore shapeless corduroy pants and a bulky, torn red sweater. Squatting down on the cell's dirty cot, his back to the wall, he looked forlorn and lonely. He looked up as I entered. His eyes were a deep, wet brown. Something moved in their depths as he looked at me. Whatever it was—curiosity, perhaps—quickly passed.

I went over to him and held out my hand. "Hello, Mr. Morales. My name is Bob Frederickson. My friends call me Mongo."

Morales shook my hand. For an old man, his grip was surprisingly firm. "Glad to meet you, Mr. Mongo," he said in a thickly accented voice. "You lawyer?"

"No. A private detective. I'd like to try to help you."

"Who hire you?"

"A friend of yours." I mouthed the word "senator" so the guard wouldn't hear me. Morales' eyes lit up. "Your friend feels that his daughter needs you. I'm going to try to get you out, at least on bail."

Morales lifted his large hands slowly and studied the palms. I remembered Janet Mason's Kirlian photographs; I wondered what mysterious force was in those hands, and what its source was. "I help Linda if I can get to see her," he said quietly. "I must touch." He suddenly looked up. "I no kill anybody, Mr. Mongo. I never hurt anybody."

"What happened that night?"

The hands pressed together, dropped between his knees. "Dr. Edmonston no like me. I can tell that. He think I phony. Still he let me help his patients, and I grateful to him for that."

"Do you think you actually helped any of them?"

Morales smiled disarmingly, like a child who has done something of which he is proud. "I know I did. And the patients, they know. They tell me, and they tell Dr. Edmonston and Dr. Johnson."

"Did you give drugs to anybody?"

"No, Mr. Mongo." He lifted his hands. "My power is here, in my hands. All drugs bad for body."

"Why do you think Dr. Edmonston said you did?"

He shook his head in obvious bewilderment. "One day the police pick me up at university. They say I under arrest for pretending to be doctor. I no understand. Dr. Mason get me out. Then I get message same day—"

"A Thursday?"

"I think so. The message say that Dr. Edmonston want to see me that night at 7:30. I want to know why he mad at me so I decide to go. I come in and find him dead. Somebody cut throat. Dr. Johnson come in a few minutes later. He think I do it. He call police . . ." His voice trailed off, punctuated by a gesture that included the cell, and the unseen world outside. It was an elegant gesture.

"How did you get into the office, Esteban?"

"The lights are on and door open. When nobody answer knock I walk in."

I nodded. Esteban Morales was either a monumental acting talent or a man impossible not to believe. "Do you have any idea why Dr. Edmonston wanted to talk to you?"

"No, Mr. Mongo. I thought maybe he sorry he call police."

"How do you do what you do, Esteban?" The question was meant to surprise him. It didn't. He simply smiled.

"You think I play tricks, Mr. Mongo?"

"What I think doesn't matter."

"Then why you ask?"

"I'm curious."

"Then I answer." Again he lifted his hands, stared at them. "The body make music, Mr. Mongo. A healthy body make good music. I can hear through my hands. A sick body make bad music. My hands . . . I can make music good, make it sound like I know it should." He paused, shook his head. "Not easy to explain, Mr. Mongo."

"Why were you upset near the end of the project, Esteban?"

"Who told you I upset?"

"Dr. Mason. She said you were having a difficult time affecting the enzymes."

He took a long time to answer. "I don't think it right to talk about it."

"Talk about what, Esteban? How can I help you if you won't level with me?"

"I know many things about people, but I don't speak about them," he said almost to himself. "What make me unhappy have nothing to do with my trouble."

"Why don't you let me decide that?"

Again, it took him a long time to answer. "I guess it no make difference any longer."

"*What* doesn't make a difference any longer, Esteban?"

He looked up at me. "Dr. Edmonston was dying. Of cancer."

"Dr. Edmonston told you that?"

"Oh, no. Dr. Edmonston no tell anyone. He not want anyone to know. But I know."

"How, Esteban? How did you know?"

He pointed to his eyes. "I see, Mr. Mongo. I see the aura. Dr. Edmonston's aura brown-black. Flicker. He dying of cancer. I know he have five, maybe six more months to live." He lowered his eyes and shook his head. "I tell him I know. I tell him I want to help. He get very mad at me. He tell me to mind my own business. That upset me. It upset me to be around people in pain who no want my help."

My mouth was suddenly very dry. I swallowed hard. "You say you *saw* this aura?" I remembered the Kirlian photographs Janet Mason had shown me and I could feel a prickling at the back of my neck.

"Yes," Morales said simply. "I see aura."

"Can you see *anybody's* aura?" I had raised my voice a few notches so that the guard could hear. I shot a quick glance in his direction. He was smirking, which meant we were coming in loud and clear. That was good . . . maybe.

"Usually. Mostly I see sick people's aura, because that what I look for."

"Can you see mine?" I asked.

His eyes slowly came up and met mine. They held. It was a moment of unexpected, embarrassing intimacy, and I knew what he was going to say before he said it.

Esteban Morales didn't smile. "I can see yours, Mr. Mongo," he said softly.

He was going to say something else but I cut him off. I was feeling a little light-headed and I wanted to get the next part of the production over as quickly as possible. I could sympathize with Dr. Edmonston.

I pressed the guard and he reluctantly admitted he'd overheard the last part of our conversation. Then I asked him to get Garth.

Garth arrived looking suspicious. Garth always looks suspicious when I send for him. He nodded briefly at Esteban, then looked at me. "What's up, Mongo?"

"I just want you to sit here for a minute and listen to something."

"Mongo, I've got *reports!*"

I ignored him and he leaned back against the bars of the cell and began to tap his foot impatiently. I turned to Esteban Morales. "Esteban," I said quietly, "will you tell my brother what an aura is?"

Morales described the human aura and I followed up by describing the Kirlian photographs Janet Mason had shown me: what they were, and what they purported to show. Garth's foot continued its monotonous tapping. Once he glanced at his watch.

"Esteban," I said, "how does my brother look? I mean his aura."

"Oh, he fine," Esteban said, puzzled. "Aura a good, healthy pink."

"What about me?"

Morales dropped his eyes and shook his head mutely.

The foot-tapping in the corner had stopped. Suddenly Garth was beside me, gripping my arm. "Mongo, what the hell is this all about?"

"Just listen, Garth. I need a witness." I took a deep breath, then started in again on Morales. "Esteban," I whispered, "I asked you a question. Can you see my aura? Damn it, if you can, say so! I may be able to help you. If you can see my aura you have to say so!"

Esteban Morales slowly lifted his head. His eyes were filled with pain. "I cannot help you, Mr. Mongo."

Garth gripped my arm even tighter. "Mongo—"

"I'm all right, Garth. Esteban, tell me what it is you see."

The healer took a long, shuddering breath. "You are dying, Mr. Mongo. Your mind is sharp, but your body is—" He gestured toward me. "Your body is the way it is. It is the same inside. I cannot change that. I cannot help. I am sorry."

"Don't be," I said. I was caught between conflicting emotions, exultation at coming up a winner and bitterness at what Morales' statement was costing me. I decided to spin the wheel again. "Can you tell about how many years I have left, Esteban?"

"Five," Morales said in a choked voice. "Maybe six or seven. Why you make me say these things?"

I spun on Garth. I hoped I had my smile on straight. "Well, brother, how does Esteban's opinion compare with the medical authorities'?"

Garth shook his head. His voice was hollow. "Your clients get a lot for their money, Mongo."

"How about getting hold of a lawyer and arranging a bail hearing for Esteban. Like tomorrow?"

"I can get a public defender in here, Mongo," Garth said in the same tone. "But you haven't proved anything."

"Was there an autopsy done on Edmonston?"

"Yeah. The report is probably filed away by now. What about it?"

"Well, that autopsy will show that Edmonston was dying of cancer, and I can prove that Esteban knew it. I just gave you a demonstration of what he can do."

"It still doesn't prove anything," Garth said tightly. "Mongo, I wish it did."

"All I want is Esteban out on bail—and the cops dusting a few more corners. All I want to show is that Esteban knew Edmonston was dying, fast. It wouldn't have made any sense for Esteban to kill him. And I think I can bring in a surprise character witness. A heavy. Will you talk to the judge?"

"Yeah, I'll talk to the judge." Again, Garth gripped my arm. "You sure you're all right? You're white as chalk."

"I'm all right. Hell, we're all dying, aren't we?" My laugh turned short and bitter. "When you've been dying as long as I have, you get used to it. I need a phone."

I didn't wait for an answer. I walked quickly out of the cell and used the first phone I found to call the senator. Then I hurried outside and lit a cigarette. It tasted lousy.

Two days later Garth popped his head into my office. "He confessed. I thought you'd want to know."

I pushed aside the criminology lecture on which I'd been working. "Who confessed?"

Garth came in and closed the door. "Johnson, of course. He came into his office this morning and found us searching through his records. He just managed to ask to see the warrant before he folded. Told the whole story twice, once for us and once for the DA. What an amateur!"

I was vaguely surprised to find myself monumentally disinterested. My job had been finished the day before when the senator and I had walked in a back door of the courthouse to meet with Garth and the sitting judge. Forty-five minutes later Esteban Morales had been out on bail and on his way to meet with Linda Younger. Rolfe Johnson had been my prime suspect five minutes after I'd begun to talk to him, and there'd been no doubt in my mind that the police would nail him, once they decided to go to the bother.

"What was his motive?" I asked.

"Johnson's forte was business. No question about it. He just couldn't cut it as a murderer ... or a doctor. He had at least a dozen malpractice suits filed against him. Edmonston was getting tired of having a flunky as a partner. Johnson was becoming an increasing embarrassment and was hurting the medical side of the business. Patients, after all, are the bottom line. Edmonston had the original practice and a controlling interest in their corporation. He was going to cut Johnson adrift, and Johnson found out about it.

"Johnson, with all his troubles, knew that he was finished if Edmonston dissolved the partnership. When Dr. Mason told him about Morales, Johnson had a notion that he just might be able to use the situation to his own advantage. After all, what better patsy than an illiterate psychic healer?"

"Johnson sent the message to Esteban, didn't he?"

"Sure. First, he admitted lying to Edmonston about Esteban giving drugs to one of Edmonston's patients, then he told how he maneuvered Edmonston into filing a complaint. He figured the university would bail Esteban out, and a motive would have been established. It wasn't much, but Johnson didn't figure he needed much. After all, he assumed Esteban was crazy and that any jury would know he was crazy. He picked his day, then left a message in the name of Edmonston for Esteban to come to the offices that night. He asked Edmonston to come forty-five minutes early, and he killed him, then waited for Esteban to show up to take the rap. Pretty crude, but then Johnson isn't that imaginative."

"Didn't the feedback from the patients give him any pause?"

Garth laughed. "From what I can gather from his statement, Johnson never paid any attention to the reports. Edmonston did most of the interviewing."

"There seems to be a touch of irony there," I said dryly.

"There seems to be. Well, I've got a car running downstairs. Like I said, I thought you'd want to know."

"Thanks, Garth."

He paused with his hand on the knob and looked at me for a long time. I knew we were thinking about the same thing, words spoken in a jail cell, a very private family secret shared by two brothers. For a moment I was afraid he was going to say something that would embarrass both of us. He didn't.

"See you," Garth said.

"See you."

The Monkey's Paw

by W. W. Jacobs

Without, the night was cold and wet, but in the small parlour of Laburnum Villa the blinds were drawn and the fire burned brightly. Father and son were at chess; the former, who possessed ideas about the game involving radical changes, putting his king into such sharp and unnecessary perils that it even provoked comment from the white-haired old lady knitting placidly by the fire.

"Hark at the wind," said Mr. White, who, having seen a fatal mistake after it was too late, was amiably desirous of preventing his son from seeing it.

"I'm listening," said the latter, grimly surveying the board as he stretched out his hand. "Check."

"I should hardly think that he'd come tonight," said his father, with his hand poised over the board.

"Mate," replied the son.

"That's the worst of living so far out," bawled Mr. White, with sudden and unlooked-for violence; "of all the beastly, slushy, out-of-the-way places to live in, this is the worst. Path's a bog, and the road's a torrent. I don't know what people are thinking about. I suppose because only two houses in the road are let, they think it doesn't matter."

"Never mind, dear," said his wife soothingly; "perhaps you'll win the next one."

Mr. White looked up sharply, just in time to intercept a knowing glance between mother and son. The words died away on his lips, and he hid a guilty grin in his thin grey beard.

"There he is," said Herbert White, as the gate banged to loudly and heavy footsteps came toward the door.

The old man rose with hospitable haste, and opening the door, was heard condoling with the new arrival. The new arrival also condoled with himself, so that Mrs. White said, "Tut, tut!" and coughed gently as her husband entered the room, followed by a tall, burly man, beady of eye and rubicund of visage.

"Sergeant-Major Morris," he said, introducing him.

The sergeant-major shook hands, and taking the proffered seat by the fire, watched contentedly while his host got out whisky and tumblers and stood a small copper kettle on the fire.

At the third glass his eyes got brighter, and he began to talk, the little family circle regarding with eager interest this visitor from distant parts, as he squared his broad shoulders in the chair, and spoke of wild scenes and doughty deeds; of wars and plagues, and strange peoples.

"Twenty-one years of it," said Mr. White, nodding at his wife and son. "When he went away he was a slip of a youth in the warehouse. Now look at him."

"He don't look to have taken much harm," said Mrs. White politely.

"I'd like to go to India myself," said the old man, "just to look round a bit, you know."

"Better where you are," said the sergeant-major, shaking his head. He put down the empty glass, and sighing softly, shook it again.

"I should like to see those old temples and fakirs and jugglers," said the old man. "What was that you started telling me the other day about a monkey's paw or something, Morris?"

"Nothing," said the soldier hastily. "Leastways nothing worth hearing."

"Monkey's paw?" said Mrs. White curiously.

"Well, it's just a bit of what you might call magic, perhaps," said the sergeant-major off-handedly.

His three listeners leaned forward eagerly. The visitor absent-mindedly put his empty glass to his lips and then set it down again. His host filled it for him.

"To look at," said the sergeant-major, fumbling in his pocket, "it's just an ordinary little paw, dried to a mummy."

He took something out of his pocket and proffered it. Mrs. White drew back with a grimace, but her son, taking it, examined it curiously.

"And what is there special about it?" inquired Mr. White as he took it from his son, and having examined it, placed it upon the table.

"It had a spell put on it by an old fakir," said the sergeant-major, "a very holy man. He wanted to show that fate ruled people's lives, and that those who interfered with it did so to their sorrow. He put a spell on it so that three separate men could each have three wishes from it."

His manner was so impressive that his hearers were conscious that their light laughter jarred somewhat.

"Well, why don't you have three, sir?" said Herbert White cleverly.

The soldier regarded him in the way that middle age is wont to regard presumptuous youth. "I have," he said quietly, and his blotchy face whitened.

"And did you really have the three wishes granted?" asked Mrs. White.

"I did," said the sergeant-major, and his glass tapped against his strong teeth.

"And has anybody else wished?" persisted the old lady.

"The first man had his three wishes. Yes," was the reply; "I don't know what the first two were, but the third was for death. That's how I got the paw."

His tones were so grave that a hush fell upon the group.

"If you've had your three wishes, it's no good to you now, then, Morris," said the old man at last. "What do you keep it for?"

The soldier shook his head. "Fancy, I suppose," he said slowly. "I did have some idea of selling it, but I don't think I will. It has caused enough mischief already. Besides, people won't buy. They think it's a fairy tale, some of them; and those who do think anything of it want to try it first and pay me afterward."

"If you could have another three wishes," said the old man, eyeing him keenly, "would you have them?"

"I don't know," said the other. "I don't know."

He took the paw, and dangling it between his forefinger and thumb, suddenly threw it upon the fire. White, with a slight cry, stooped down and snatched it off.

"Better let it burn," said the soldier solemnly.

"If you don't want it, Morris," said the other, "give it to me."

"I won't," said his friend doggedly. "I threw it on the fire. If you keep it, don't blame me for what happens. Pitch it on the fire again like a sensible man."

The other shook his head and examined his new possession closely. "How do you do it?" he inquired.

"Hold it up in your right hand and wish aloud," said the sergeant-major, "but I warn you of the consequences."

"Sounds like the *Arabian Nights*," said Mrs. White, as she rose

and began to set the supper. "Don't you think you might wish for
four pairs of hands for me?"

Her husband drew the talisman from his pocket, and then all
three burst into laughter as the sergeant-major, with a look of alarm
on his face, caught him by the arm.

"If you must wish," he said gruffly, "wish for something sensible."

Mr. White dropped it back in his pocket, and placing chairs, motioned his friend to the table. In the business of supper the talisman
was partly forgotten, and afterward the three sat listening in an
enthralled fashion to a second installment of the soldier's adventures
in India.

"If the tale about the monkey's paw is not more truthful than
those he has been telling us," said Herbert, as the door closed behind
their guest, just in time to catch the last train, "we shan't make
much out of it."

"Did you give him anything for it, father?" inquired Mrs. White,
regarding her husband closely.

"A trifle," said he, colouring slightly. "He didn't want it, but I
made him take it. And he pressed me again to throw it away."

"Likely," said Herbert, with pretended horror. "Why, we're going
to be rich, and famous, and happy. Wish to be an emperor, father,
to begin with; then you can't be henpecked."

He darted round the table, pursued by the maligned Mrs. White
armed with an antimacassar.

Mr. White took the paw from his pocket and eyed it dubiously.
"I don't know what to wish for, and that's a fact," he said slowly.
"It seems to me I've got all I want."

"If you only cleared the house, you'd be quite happy, wouldn't
you!" said Herbert, with his hand on his shoulder. "Well, wish for
two hundred pounds, then; that'll just do it."

His father, smiling shamefacedly at his own credulity, held up the
talisman, as his son, with a solemn face, somewhat marred by a
wink at his mother, sat down at the piano and struck a few impressive chords.

"I wish for two hundred pounds," said the old man distinctly.

A fine crash from the piano greeted the words, interrupted by a
shuddering cry from the old man. His wife and son ran toward him.

"It moved," he cried, with a glance of disgust at the object as it
lay on the floor. "As I wished, it twisted in my hand like a snake."

"Well, I don't see the money," said his son, as he picked it up and
placed it on the table, "and I bet I never shall."

"It must have been your fancy, father," said his wife, regarding him anxiously.

He shook his head. "Never mind, though; there's no harm done, but it gave me a shock all the same."

They sat down by the fire again while the two men finished their pipes. Outside, the wind was higher than ever, and the old man started nervously at the sound of a door banging upstairs. A silence unusual and depressing settled upon all three, which lasted until the old couple rose to retire for the night.

"I expect you'll find the cash tied up in a big bag in the middle of your bed," said Herbert, as he bade them good night, "and something horrible squatting up on top of the wardrobe watching you as you pocket your ill-gotten gains."

He sat alone in the darkness, gazing at the dying fire, and seeing faces in it. The last face was so horrible and so simian that he gazed at it in amazement. It got so vivid that, with a little uneasy laugh, he felt on the table for a glass containing a little water to throw over it. His hand grasped the monkey's paw, and with a little shiver he wiped his hand on his coat and went up to bed.

II

In the brightness of the wintry sun next morning as it streamed over the breakfast table he laughed at his fears. There was an air of prosaic wholesomeness about the room which it had lacked on the previous night, and the dirty, shrivelled little paw was pitched on the side-board with a carelessness which betokened no great belief in its virtues.

"I suppose all old soldiers are the same," said Mrs. White. "The idea of our listening to such nonsense! How could wishes be granted in these days? And if they could, how could two hundred pounds hurt you, father?"

"Might drop on his head from the sky," said the frivolous Herbert.

"Morris said the things happened so naturally," said his father, "that you might if you so wished attribute it to coincidence."

"Well, don't break into the money before I come back," said Herbert as he rose from the table. "I'm afraid it'll turn you into a mean, avaricious man, and we shall have to disown you."

His mother laughed, and following him to the door, watched him down the road; and returning to the breakfast table, was very happy at the expense of her husband's credulity. All of which did not prevent her from scurrying to the door at the postman's knock, nor prevent her from referring somewhat shortly to retired sergeant-majors of bibulous habits when she found that the post brought a tailor's bill.

"Herbert will have some more of his funny remarks, I expect, when he comes home," she said, as they sat at dinner.

"I dare say," said Mr. White, pouring himself out some beer; "but for all that, the thing moved in my hand; that I'll swear to."

"You thought it did," said the old lady soothingly.

"I say it did," replied the other. "There was no thought about it; I had just—What's the matter?"

His wife made no reply. She was watching the mysterious movements of a man outside, who, peering in an undecided fashion at the house, appeared to be trying to make up his mind to enter. In mental connection with the two hundred pounds, she noticed that the stranger was well dressed, and wore a silk hat of glossy newness. Three times he paused at the gate, and then walked on again. The fourth time he stood with his hand upon it, and then with sudden resolution flung it open and walked up the path. Mrs. White at the same moment placed her hands behind her, and hurriedly unfastening the strings of her apron, put that useful article of apparel beneath the cushion of her chair.

She brought the stranger, who seemed ill at ease, into the room. He gazed at her furtively, and listened in a preoccupied fashion as the old lady apologized for the appearance of the room, and her husband's coat, a garment which he usually reserved for the garden. She then waited as patiently as her sex would permit, for him to broach his business, but he was at first strangely silent.

"I—was asked to call," he said at last, and stooped and picked a piece of cotton from his trousers. "I come from 'Maw and Meggins.'"

The old lady started. "Is anything the matter?" she asked breathlessly. "Has anything happened to Herbert? What is it? What is it?"

Her husband interposed. "There, there, mother," he said hastily. "Sit down, and don't jump to conclusions. You've not brought bad news, I'm sure, sir;" and he eyed the other wistfully.

"I'm sorry—" began the visitor.

"Is he hurt?" demanded the mother wildly.

The visitor bowed in assent. "Badly hurt," he said quietly, "but he is not in any pain."

"Oh, thank God!" said the old woman, clasping her hands. "Thank God for that! Thank—"

She broke off suddenly as the sinister meaning of the assurance dawned upon her, and she saw the awful confirmation of her fears in the other's averted face. She caught her breath, and turning to her slower-witted husband, laid her trembling old hand upon his. There was a long silence.

"He was caught in the machinery," said the visitor at length in a low voice.

"Caught in the machinery," repeated Mr. White, in a dazed fashion, "yes."

He sat staring blankly out at the window, and taking his wife's hand between his own, pressed it as he had been wont to do in their old courting days nearly forty years before.

"He was the only one left to us," he said, turning gently to the visitor. "It is hard."

The other coughed, and rising, walked slowly to the window. "The firm wished me to convey their sincere sympathy with you in your great loss," he said, without looking round. "I beg that you will understand I am only their servant and merely obeying orders."

There was no reply; the old woman's face was white, her eyes staring, and her breath inaudible; on the husband's face was a look such as his friend the sergeant might have carried into his first action.

"I was to say that Maw and Meggins disclaim all responsibility," continued the other. "They admit no liability at all, but in consideration of your son's services, they wish to present you with a certain sum as compensation."

Mr. White dropped his wife's hand, and rising to his feet, gazed with a look of horror at his visitor. His dry lips shaped the words, "How much?"

"Two hundred pounds," was the answer.

Unconscious of his wife's shriek, the old man smiled faintly, put out his hands like a sightless man, and dropped, a senseless heap, to the floor.

III

In the huge new cemetery, some two miles distant, the old people buried their dead, and came back to the house steeped in shadow and silence. It was all over so quickly that at first they could hardly realise it, and remained in a state of expectation as though of something else to happen—something else which was to lighten this load, too heavy for old hearts to bear.

But the days passed, and expectation gave place to resignation—the hopeless resignation of the old, sometimes miscalled apathy. Sometimes they hardly exchanged a word, for now they had nothing to talk about, and their days were long to weariness.

It was about a week after, that the old man, waking suddenly in the night, stretched out his hand and found himself alone. The room was in darkness, and the sound of subdued weeping came from the window. He raised himself in bed and listened.

"Come back," he said tenderly. "You will be cold."

"It is colder for my son," said the old woman, and wept afresh.

The sound of her sobs died away on his ears. The bed was warm, and his eyes heavy with sleep. He dozed fitfully, and then slept until a sudden wild cry from his wife awoke him with a start.

"The paw!" she cried wildly. "The monkey's paw!"

He started up in alarm. "Where? Where is it? What's the matter?"

She came stumbling across the room toward him. "I want it," she said quietly. "You've not destroyed it?"

"It's in the parlour, on the bracket," he replied, marvelling. "Why?"

She cried and laughed together, and bending over, kissed his cheek.

"I only just thought of it," she said hysterically. "Why didn't I think of it before? Why didn't *you* think of it?"

"Think of what?" he questioned.

"The other two wishes," she replied rapidly. "We've only had one."

"Was not that enough?" he demanded fiercely.

"No," she cried triumphantly; "we'll have one more. Go down and get it quickly, and wish our boy alive again."

The man sat up in bed and flung the bedclothes from his quaking limbs. "Good God, you are mad!" he cried, aghast.

"Get it," she panted; "get it quickly, and wish—Oh, my boy, my boy!"

Her husband struck a match and lit the candle. "Get back to bed," he said unsteadily. "You don't know what you are saying."

"We had the first wish granted," said the old woman feverishly; "why not the second?"

"A coincidence," stammered the old man.

"Go and get it and wish," cried his wife, quivering with excitement.

The old man turned and regarded her, and his voice shook. "He has been dead ten days, and besides he—I would not tell you else, but—I could only recognize him by his clothing. If he was too terrible for you to see then, how now?"

"Bring him back," cried the old woman, and dragged him toward the door. "Do you think I fear the child I have nursed?"

He went down in the darkness, and felt his way to the parlour, and then to the mantelpiece. The talisman was in its place, and a horrible fear that the unspoken wish might bring his mutilated son before him ere he could escape from the room seized upon him, and he caught his breath as he found that he had lost the direction of the door. His brow cold with sweat, he felt his way round the table, and groped along the wall until he found himself in the small passage with the unwholesome thing in his hand.

Even his wife's face seemed changed as he entered the room. It was white and expectant, and to his fears seemed to have an unnatural look upon it. He was afraid of her.

"*Wish!*" she cried, in a strong voice.

"It is foolish and wicked," he faltered.

"*Wish!*" repeated his wife.

He raised his hand. "I wish my son alive again."

The talisman fell to the floor, and he regarded it fearfully. Then he sank trembling into a chair as the old woman, with burning eyes, walked to the window and raised the blind.

He sat until he was chilled with the cold, glancing occasionally at the figure of the old woman peering through the window. The candle-end, which had burned below the rim of the china candlestick, was throwing pulsating shadows on the ceiling and walls, until, with a flicker larger than the rest, it expired. The old man, with an unspeakable sense of relief at the failure of the talisman, crept back to his bed, and a minute or two afterward the old woman came silently and apathetically beside him.

Neither spoke, but lay silently listening to the ticking of the clock. A stair creaked, and a squeaky mouse scurried noisily through the wall. The darkness was oppressive, and after lying for some time screwing up his courage, he took the box of matches, and striking one, went downstairs for a candle.

At the foot of the stairs the match went out, and he paused to strike another; and at the same moment a knock, so quiet and stealthy as to be scarcely audible, sounded on the front door.

The matches fell from his hand and spilled in the passage. He
stood motionless, his breath suspended until the knock was repeated.
Then he turned and fled swiftly back to his room, and closed the
door behind him. A third knock sounded through the house.

"*What's that?*" cried the old woman, starting up.

"A rat," said the old man in shaking tones—"a rat. It passed me
on the stairs."

His wife sat up in bed listening. A loud knock resounded through
the house.

"It's Herbert!" she screamed. "It's Herbert!"

She ran to the door, but her husband was before her, and catching
her by the arm, held her tightly.

"What are you going to do?" he whispered hoarsely.

"It's my boy; it's Herbert!" she cried, struggling mechanically. "I
forgot it was two miles away. What are you holding me for? Let go.
I must open the door."

"For God's sake don't let it in," cried the old man, trembling.

"You're afraid of your own son," she cried, struggling. "Let me go.
I'm coming, Herbert; I'm coming."

There was another knock, and another. The old woman with a
sudden wrench broke free and ran from the room. Her husband
followed to the landing, and called after her appealingly as she
hurried downstairs. He heard the chain rattle back and the bottom
bolt drawn slowly and stiffly from the socket. Then the old woman's
voice, strained and panting.

"The bolt," she cried loudly. "Come down. I can't reach it."

But her husband was on his hands and knees groping wildly on
the floor in search of the paw. If he could only find it before the
thing outside got in. A perfect fusillade of knocks reverberated
through the house, and he heard the scraping of a chair as his wife
put it down in the passage against the door. He heard the creaking
of the bolt as it came slowly back, and at the same moment he found
the monkey's paw, and frantically breathed his third and last wish.

The knocking ceased suddenly, although the echoes of it were still
in the house. He heard the chair drawn back, and the door opened.
A cold wind rushed up the staircase, and a long loud wail of disappointment and misery from his wife gave him courage to run down
to her side, and then to the gate beyond. The street lamp flickering
opposite shone on a quiet and deserted road.

Rowena's Brooch

by Donald Olson

The invitations to Clementine Beal's dinner party carried an intriguing phrase: *Group Reading by Mr. Willie Bruneau.* As Clementine had never offered anything less conventional than bridge at her dinner parties it caused a ripple of interest among the invited, and when it was learned that Rowena Telford was to be one of the guests the ripple became a tidal wave.

Everyone in town knew Rowena Telford. Widow of the late Chandler Telford (latest, in fact, of three husbands Rowena had survived), she was a local legend. Thirty years earlier, as Ruby Ditzler, she had left town a sprightly young widow and made a name for herself on Broadway. She had returned to town only six months before Clementine's party and taken up residence in the old Ditzler mansion left to her by her first husband. Here she lived in Garboesque seclusion, seldom seen on the streets and only occasionally glimpsed, in dark glasses and concealing hat, at one of the better shops or cinemas. Every hostess in town had tried to lure her into the social arena, but not until now had she been tempted forth. Clementine was ecstatic. Rowena Telford and Willie Bruneau! The event had to be a dazzling success.

Willie Bruneau was a psychic just beginning to attain a degree of celebrity that was as yet primarily local, although stories of his readings for a certain best-selling novelist and for a familiar TV personality had begun to make his name more widely known. Only recently had he begun accepting invitations for group readings in the homes of the well-to-do, where he did not shrink from accepting monetary tributes to his psychic prowess, tributes that, so far, had been far more modest than Willie himself.

Stories about him became town gossip. Everyone soon heard about the fabulously wealthy old lady in New York who had taken him to Hawaii for six months out of gratitude for his having saved her life; he had "seen" her nephew greasing the stairs of her mansion in hopes of causing a fatal accident. Another relative had tried to

215

poison her with chocolates; Willie had "seen" this, too. With such tales circulating, which some people were churlish enough to suggest had been started by Willie himself, his legend was bound to grow.

Unfortunately, Clementine's evening got off to a bad start. When she announced, over dessert, that Mr. Bruneau would be joining them later, Rowena Telford was the only one around the table who expressed displeasure.

"I'd rather play cards," she said flatly.

After a moment's panic, Clementine smoothed over the awkwardness. "You'll adore Willie, my dear. Everyone does. Later, if you wish, we'll have a rubber of bridge, just to unwind. Seriously, I understand he's very good."

"Psychics—or fortune-tellers, if you want to call a spade a spade—are never *good*," retorted Rowena in her most devastating theatrical manner. "At best they're merely clever."

"Oh, I'm sure you're right about *most* of them, darling."

"I've met the best of them. They're all ninety-nine percent show biz and one percent psychic."

"Ah, but that one percent!"

Nevertheless, Rowena was a good sport about it. When Willie Bruneau made his entrance, she observed with only the most discreet look of satisfaction the universal dismay of her fellow guests. Willie looked one hundred percent show biz. He was short and plumpish, with a rose-petal complexion, gold-rimmed glasses, flirtatious eyes, a sleek black toupee styled in bangs and ringlets; he wore a plum-colored velour pullover, black silk slacks, and snakeskin shoes. He was, furthermore, as glibly facetious as the most experienced con artist.

Yet, once the initial shock was over, this all had the curious effect of soothing rather than exciting skepticism. Such hocus-pocus eyes and razzle-dazzle garb would only be flaunted, one felt sure, by someone as sincere as a child; and this is what eventually came through, a childlike lack of guile that soon had everyone hanging upon his words. He had a flair for the telling anecdote and he wasn't the least daunted by the elegance of the group for which he'd been invited to read. Nor was anyone left in doubt that he had actually read for those celebrities, when he could recount such juicily authentic-sounding bits of gossip about them, speaking with wry compassion of the lady columnist's singular obsession with violet candles and revealing, as if it were already public knowledge, details of the lady novelist's drinking problem.

Rowena Telford was not so rude as to refrain from listening, but she listened with the polite, frosty scorn of the nonbeliever. Nor did she refuse to join the group in the serious business following the preliminary chitchat. Willie instructed the hostess in the placing of the chairs and seating of the guests. Only one dim lamp was left burning.

Taking his place at the round table, Willie removed his gold-rimmed glasses and placed upon his nose a pair of Ben Franklin spectacles with smoked transparent lenses.

Besides the medium, Clementine Beal, and Rowena Telford, the party included Dolly and Della Treff, Fred Zinsel, John Carlyle, Paul Campbell, and Steven and Penelope St. James.

Willie kept talking in the same gossipy tone of voice, and then abruptly, in mid-sentence, his head snapped back, one could actually hear a vertebra crack, and his voice became more highly pitched.

No one could say he was not good—or at least very clever. Instead of the generalities of the ordinary parlor psychic, Willie spoke with a specificity and candor that enthralled his audience.

"Someone at this table is negotiating a divorce. Don't go through with it, dear. That man is dying. There's a lot of phlegm, isn't there? You might even say he's already dead. You know what I mean, dear. Don't blame me. It's not my fault. I only tell what I see. The raft is drifting away from shore. Death, my dear, always death. Now, I don't want you to think I'm mercenary, but you'd be far better off sticking with him till the end. There's a lot of property involved. Besides, you're going to be a great comfort to him in the last six weeks. He's insanely jealous and he knows about P. But you're in no real danger from him, darling. Now, someone at this table is very fond of horses. But whatever you do, don't go riding with a man named Gene . . ."

He didn't pause once, never stumbled, never gave the impression he was repeating something he'd rehearsed. It was all urbane, fluent, chattily confidential, and thus the effect all the more harrowing. When the lights were turned up, no one cared in the first few moments to look directly into his neighbor's eyes.

It was Rowena Telford who broke the spell: "*Now* can we play cards?"

Clementine gave a sigh. "Splendid idea, dear. Willie, I can't thank you enough. You were marvelous. But then, why should I *thank* you? I'm sure some of your remarks were aimed at me . . . No, don't tell me! Now, I know you don't charge a fee for demonstrating your gift, but you can't possibly object if we express our delight by—"

She was cut off by a shriek from Rowena: "My brooch! It's gone!"

Dead silence reigned. Everyone stared at her. Her hands were skimming over her clothes. They had all noticed the brooch, of course; several had admired it: a wreath of diamonds around a huge star ruby. A search was undertaken.

"When did you last notice it?" Clementine asked her.

"I don't know. It was simply there. I never thought about it."

Della Treff said, "I'm quite positive you had it when we came in from the dining room."

"Then it must be in your clothes, or around your chair." Clementine's voice had a mousy note of alarm.

The search was concentrated in that area, and again Rowena felt about her person. No sign of the brooch.

By now the company was visibly uneasy, especially the two men who had flanked Rowena at the table during the reading.

When no trace could be found of the missing brooch, Rowena became indifferent. "Don't worry, it'll show up. It has to be here."

Clementine was in the worst position possible for a hostess: if she dismissed the matter she would be doing her guest of honor an injustice, and if she pressed the search to its limits she would insult each of her other guests. The poor woman was distraught.

"It's quite costly," said Rowena, "but not something to ruin your evening over. Please don't fuss." She shot an ambiguous look at her hostess. "It's been fun, darling. But now I must say good night."

Clementine looked helplessly from Rowena to her other guests. Willie Bruneau, looking exhausted from the strain of the reading, had sipped a glass of sherry while the search was going on.

It was the lawyer, Carlyle, who finally said what all of them had known must be said: "Forgive me. We can all see what a spot our hostess is in because of this little mischance. I, for one, insist upon being searched before leaving this house."

Rowena replied coldly. "Don't be absurd. I'm certainly not suggesting anyone stole my brooch. It's here and will be found. Let's just forget it."

Carlyle shook his head. "I'd rather not leave the house under a cloud of guilt. If one of you fellows will step into the next room with me, I insist on being searched."

"And so do I." Willie Bruneau's voice was still languid with fatigue and laced with humor, as if it were all a huge joke. "I'm more or less the only outsider among you."

"Well, I didn't take it," spoke up Dolly Treff, sparkling with her own collection of gems. "I drooled over it, but I'm no thief. I agree with these gentlemen, though. Don't you, Della? The logical thing is to be searched before leaving."

Now all clamored to be searched.

Rowena looked very cross. "I won't permit it. I know none of you are thieves."

Carlyle spoke with deference but determination. "Please, Mrs. Telford. No one objects to being searched. It's the only way to clear the air. Of course, if it's to mean anything, we must *all* submit to being searched. Including you."

Rowena gave him a withering look. "As if I would steal my own brooch!"

"Will you allow yourself to be searched along with the rest of us?"

"No!"

Rowena's anger came suddenly but fiercely. The others looked at her with growing suspicion.

"But you must see what that implies."

"What it implies, my good man, is that *I* haven't a guilty conscience at all," Rowena fumed.

"Quite the opposite, I should say. It's been apparent, Mrs. Telford, that you have no faith in Mr. Bruneau's gift. Well and good. I'm not a believer myself. But I'm willing to keep an open mind. And I don't at all object to being entertained in the process—as I was. But what you're obviously trying to plant in our minds is the belief that Mr. Bruneau is not only a faker but a thief as well—or the accomplice of one. Mr. Bruneau has agreed to be searched. So has everyone else, except you. What other conclusion can we draw but that you've faked a theft in order to impugn this man's character?"

This put Rowena into a stammering fury. "You're talking rubbish and you know it. One of you in this room needs a scapegoat. You should appreciate my volunteering for the role. Surely you must see that if we're all searched and none of us has the brooch, it would prove only that someone is a most clever thief. Don't you suppose that whoever stole it would expect to be searched? I'm letting you all off the hook. No applause?" She turned to Clementine, who looked ready to bawl in the shambles of her evening. "I'm so sorry, my dear. I should never have worn the silly brooch. Good night." Rowena stalked out.

Universal relief greeted her departure.

"What a shabby stunt!" cried Della Treff. "Just because she didn't believe in Mr. Bruneau she didn't have to make him out to be a thief."

This was the substance of most of the remarks, but of course Rowena Telford was a legend of eccentricity. What else could one expect from her?

"She was in the theater for years," said Dolly. "I suppose she hates being upstaged even now."

From the sofa where he reclined, sipping another glass of sherry, Willie Bruneau intervened. "You're all being more than kind to me and less than kind to that poor lady."

They all looked at him.

"If I were in your shoes," said Carlyle, "I don't think I should be quite so charitable."

"Her motives were entirely pure. You've misjudged her."

Clementine looked puzzled. "Are you saying she *didn't* steal the brooch herself?"

"Precisely."

Now there was general consternation. "Then you mean to say one of us *did* swipe it?"

"Not at all. It's here in this room."

"Impossible. It's been searched."

"Not that thoroughly, Mr. Carlyle. Please be kind enough to remove those flowers from that bowl. I think you'll find the brooch at the bottom of it. It's deep. Better roll up your sleeve."

Carlyle did as he was asked, reached down into the bowl and fished out the brooch. The discovery was greeted with an outburst of wonder.

"But how on earth did you *know*?" cried Dolly.

"Because I saw him remove the brooch from her dress and hide it there."

Again, tension. "Saw who?"

"Her second husband." Bruneau smiled. "The spirit of her second husband, you understand. He always hated that brooch because Ditzler, her first husband, had given it to her. She was very fond of it and insisted on wearing it. He would always remove it and hide it from her. I feel sure she knew what had happened to it here tonight, though she would never have said so. She's profoundly psychic herself, even if she won't admit it. It frightens her. She can't cope with anything—unworldly."

Clementine was stricken. "Poor Rowena. She thinks we all believe she did it deliberately, to discredit you. Would you all mind if I left at once and took it to her, with sincere apologies from all of us?"

"Please let me," Willie said. "I may be able to help her. *This* may show her the way."

Thus did Willie Bruneau and Rowena Telford become the hero and heroine of the evening. They would have drunk to their success had Rowena had anything suitable in the house to offer the medium, who found her sitting in what had been the maid's tiny room on the third floor of the mansion, sipping a soft drink and munching a cheese sandwich.

"So how much did they cough up, Willie, dear?"

"Eighty-five bucks."

She held out her hand and he counted out her share.

"There'll be more next time," she promised him. "I may be broke, honey, but I've got the two things you need most right now: contacts and charisma. And as long as nobody knows I'm broke, we can both cash in on them."

He smiled modestly. "You won't be broke for long."

His self-assurance, that air of mystic tranquillity, soothed whatever doubts she still might have had that their association would be mutually beneficial. She had noticed that air about him the first time they met, quite by accident, in the air terminal lounge in Newark.

He drew the brooch from his pocket. "I can't tell them apart."

"I can." She took the real brooch out of her purse. "A hunk of jewelry and an old house. Three marriages, and they're all I've got to show for them. Where did you hide it?"

"In the flowerpot."

"First time in my life I really enjoyed acting. And I intend to keep hustling, sweetie. I'm sick of living in this dinky room and eating sandwiches. It's not my style." She looked shrewdly reflective. "That Carlyle's a smart cookie, you know that? Ugly, but loaded. Willie, before you go—"

"No."

"Please."

"Absolutely not."

She sighed. "Did they really swallow the business about my second husband's spirit hiding the brooch?"

"If they didn't, they were too well-bred to laugh." He looked at her as if, for all her sophistication, she were still a child. "It doesn't matter, actually, if they believe or don't believe. To a psychic, my dear, all that counts is one small but very essential fact of human nature."

"And what's that?"

"There is no such thing as a skeptic who doesn't *want* to believe."

Rowena wasn't sure if Willie was ninety percent show biz and ten percent psychic, or the other way around. Maybe he himself didn't know to what degree his prophetic capacity was genuine.

He got up to go. She put her hand on his arm. "Please. You promised."

"Darling, not now. I'm exhausted. You've no idea now much it takes out of me."

"But I've got to know, Willie. I won't sleep a wink tonight."

Grudgingly, he sank back into the chair. "Oh, very well, Rowena, if you're going to nag. But I don't promise anything. When I'm tired, nothing's likely to come through. So don't blame me."

She clapped her hands together like a little girl who had been promised a glimpse of Santa Claus. "I want to know if I'll see him again. If we're going to become *very* good friends. Mr. John Carlyle and I."

Willie tried to relax, threw back his head until he heard the little snap in his neck. His tone changed. He began to speak.

Rowena listened.

Fat Jow and the Manifestations

by Robert Alan Blair

A spasm of panicking terror chilled him out of the depths of sleep. For several suffocating heartbeats he dared not open his eyes lest this dank, buried sensation of encompassing moist earth prove reality instead of illusion. Again? This was not the first time in recent weeks.

To mind sprang thought of Ng Chak, of the other unmourned unknowns who supposedly slept beneath the cellar floor of the Baxter mansion which was now converted into apartments.

By effort of will Fat Jow forced open his eyes, to discover with an explosive release of breath that the night appeared normal. The mirrored walls of the former ballroom radiated a comforting glow from the street lamp outside. Sleep gone, he sat up on the edge of the couch.

From the dark bedroom at the rear came a soft whimper as the child Hsiang Yuen stirred in sleep. Fat Jow had initiated this sleeping arrangement since his grand-nephew's arrival; a boy needs a room of his own.

He tiptoed to the bedroom doorway, to be reassured by the child's regular breathing. A dream, perhaps; that it had coincided with his own waking interested him. Had he too dreamed? His sleep had been sound. He returned to sit upon the couch, smiled slightly. Fears and uncertainties are magnified out of proportion in the silent midnight hours—yet the disquieting feeling was not entirely dispelled.

A tinkling drew his eyes toward the ceiling, where the crystal chandelier was quivering visibly, its teardrop pendants alive with reflected specks of light. This was no earth tremor, so common through the year in San Francisco, for only the chandelier moved—not the room.

The tinkling faded, the dancing lights gentled; then an abrupt crash in the room brought him tensely standing. His worn leather rocker had fallen, beside it a table and broken crockery lamp. His apartment door, which he had locked before retiring, burst inward

223

as from a violent kick, but he saw no one in the dimness of the foyer beyond.

A corresponding bang across the foyer, a series of crashes and screams from his landlady's apartment, goaded Fat Jow from his trance. Hurriedly he put on robe and slippers, ventured out into the foyer. Down the shadowy lightwell echoed the voices of alarmed tenants from the balconied landings of the upper floors.

A man's voice rose over the rest: "Who screamed?"

From the darkness of Adah Baxter's apartment she rushed, spectral in white nightdress, her white hair unbound and flying. Her customary regal dignity abandoned, she clung wordlessly to Fat Jow, a head shorter than she. From her apartment sounded a final smashing of glass—and no more.

"A mild quake," offered Fat Jow, in explanation to the voices above. "I think it has passed."

Adah Baxter whispered fiercely to him, "You and I know that was no quake!"

A woman called down, "Is anything wrong, Miss Baxter?"

She looked fearfully back toward her apartment. "No . . . really," she quavered. "I was . . . frightened, that's all." In a rapid undertone to Fat Jow, she added, "I can't go back in there. May I come in with you for a while?"

Wearily he gestured toward his door. "Sleep is quite far from these eyes," he said. He reached in past her and switched on the chandelier.

Adah Baxter paused at sight of his tipped furniture. "It—it was in here, too?"

"It appeared to begin in here," he said, righting table and rocker and kicking the pieces of the lamp aside, "then passed into your apartment . . . through two locked doors."

"Oh, dear!" She dropped limply into the rocker. "The child! Have you seen to the child? The poor thing must be terrified."

He listened at the bedroom doorway, softly pulled the door shut. "Nothing disturbs Hsiang Yuen," he said with indulgent pride, taxing imagination to define an area of excellence. He pulled the blanket from the couch and placed it about her shoulders.

"It wasn't what I'd thought," she said desolately.

"What had you thought?"

"That it was those real-estate people, trying to scare me into selling the house. I wish it were—I'd rather be mad than scared—but this wasn't that, was it?"

"It is questionable," said Fat Jow.

She hugged her shoulders and swayed. "I guess I've been waiting for something like this."

Fat Jow sat on the couch, frowned at the floor. "Do you pretend to know?"

"Well, don't you?"

"I try to believe this matter of your former tenants to be all a misunderstanding, but I find it difficult. If they *are* in the cellar . . ."

"But I told you . . ." Adah Baxter looked out through his open apartment door into the foyer. "I wonder which one of them it was?" she mused.

He asked uncomfortably. "How many?"

"Good gracious, who counts? They go back over a period of sixty-some years. My memory's not what it used to be."

"Were they all . . . oriental gentlemen?"

"Oh my, no. Only the last two . . . or was it three? I'd had such bad luck with occidentals that I thought orientals would be more dependable, if you know what I mean. But it didn't work."

"One does not choose dependable traits," observed Fat Jow, "by a person's accident of origin. Every nation has produced its poets—and its madmen. Besides the noises, Miss Baxter, did you happen to feel also a great fear?"

"Yes, after the noises started."

"Have there been other manifestations before now?"

"No!" It was a new thought. "Isn't it strange they've waited all this time?"

"Perhaps we grasp the obvious answer because it is easier," he said with faint hope.

"But how can we know?" she wailed. "When will it come again?"

"Whatever it is, it would not seem malevolent. It has not offered to harm us." He would not perturb her further by telling her of his other broken sleeps. "Let us assess the damage in your apartment."

Hesitantly she followed him across the foyer, gaining confidence when he turned on the lights.

The oil portrait of her father lay facedown on the hearth rug, the copper samovar in which she brewed her singular tea lying beside it among the scattered fire tools. By the door to her room a throw rug had been curled back, a small chair upset. In her room they found the window shattered outward, fragments in the flower border below.

Giving the buried tenants a more suitable interment must only draw official attention and, despite her lethal leanings, Fat Jow entertained an affection for Adah Baxter so would not see her come to harm. The Walking Woman, sweeping grandly through the city in picture hat and long black gown, was to be preserved as jealously as any cherished landmark.

"I should like your permission," said Fat Jow, "to consult an expert in these matters."

"If it will do any good," she said fervently, "go right ahead."

He moved toward the door. "Do you wish me to remain?"

"I'll be fine, thanks."

Fat Jow bowed himself out.

The Buddhist Temple on Pacific was built with contributions of money, material and labor, not only from Buddhists but also from persons of every faith and no faith throughout the Bay Area. Its austerely functional lines show the heady new flavor imparted to Buddhist tradition by transplantation from Asia to America.

Fat Jow sought through the peripheral chambers of the temple, found his young friend, the novitiate, at study in the library. Catching his eye from the doorway, he beckoned him into the passage.

"If you have not yet enjoyed the midday meal," said Fat Jow, "please join me."

Kwan Ho stretched his stiff muscles. "Knowing you, I'd say there was more than hospitality behind this."

"You are the only person I know who makes a serious study of parapsychology."

"At last!" laughed Kwan Ho. "My two semesters at Duke University pay off, a free lunch."

Over dishes of Wandering Dragon in the relaxed atmosphere of a restaurant on Grand Avenue, Fat Jow related the midnight occurrences.

Kwan How interrupted: "That's the second time you've mentioned buried tenants. Your symbolism escapes me."

"No symbolism." Fat Jow looked about them, lowered his voice. "You will hold this in confidence?"

"If that's what you want."

"There are some buried tenants in the cellar . . . I think. I have never been certain, nor wish to be. One must, however, give Miss Baxter credit for selectivity. She chooses for this honor only those who reveal themselves to be after her hidden hoard of currency. And she is relatively humane; her potion has a gentle soporific effect."

Forgetting to eat, Kwan Ho stared at him. "You're dead serious."

"Yes. The Walking Woman is rather unusual."

"But the police . . ."

"She promptly reports each demise to the police, as it occurs, but such is her nostalgic reputation that they fondly disbelieve her. They think it is all in her mind, as indeed it may be, since the vanished opportunists who have attempted to victimize her are not of a sort to have family or friends eager to trace them."

"But *you* don't think it's all in her mind, do you?"

"No. She may be an habitual killer, but Adah Baxter is as rational as you or I."

Kwan Ho grunted. "Everyone to his hobby."

"If there be such a thing as infestation by spirits, will your skill enable you to banish them?"

Kwan Ho scratched his head. "These days, one is less and less inclined to look for the occult behind phenomena like this. Often it turns out to be loose floorboards, rattling pipes, rubbing branches, or mice."

"I am sure we may eliminate these."

"So am I. When you'd had a chance to look at things in the light of day, did you get any ideas?"

Fat Jow nodded slowly. "Two possibilities, neither of which satisfies: the one, because no unscrupulous real-estate developer could have produced these effects from outside the house; and the other, because I am reluctant to accept a supernatural explanation."

Kwan Ho winced. "Supernatural has become a bad word. Today's abnormal or paranormal may be tomorrow's commonplace. If phenomena conform to standards or laws of their own, they ought to take their place *in* nature, not beyond it. Frankly, only one part of your whole picture, that cold feeling of terror, might be blamed indirectly on your friends in the cellar. But moving solid objects is something else, established experimentally in the laboratory; telekinesis, used by an agent who's very much alive. Before there was much formal study in the field, it was called a poltergeist. I'd want to go over the site before I offered any theory, though."

"This," said Fat Jow, beaming, "is exactly what I had hoped you would say."

Early the following Saturday, while Adah Baxter was absent on her daily circuit through North Beach and Chinatown, Kwan Ho came. Preferring to work without distraction of company or conversation, he prowled house and grounds alone, missing nothing.

After nearly an hour he rejoined Fat Jow in his apartment. Absently he stalked in, stood just inside the closed door. Manner and voice were awed: "I counted sixteen cement patches in that cellar floor. Do you suppose . . ." He made no attempt to finish the sentence.

Fat Jow leaned back in his rocker and studied the chandelier. "The less I know with certainty, the less I am troubled. What have you to report?"

"I'm not one of your true ESPers, understand, but I can detect a signal here and there, if I put my mind to it." Kwan Ho hesitated, rubbed the back of his neck. "I don't like to give you something more to worry about, but the strongest signals I get are right here in this room."

Surprised and uncomfortable, Fat Jow asked, "And not down cellar?"

"None there. As a layman, you're conditioned by a long heritage of superstition to attribute powers to the remains of the deceased. Instead, the effects are felt at the scene of the decease itself. The event leaves its mark on the surroundings, sort of soaks into the woodwork."

Fat Jow glanced about restlessly. "Then relocation of the remains would accomplish nothing?"

"Probably not. About the only way to get rid of the signals is to destroy the building."

Fat Jow disliked what he was hearing. "Must we then live with these signals?"

Kwan Ho walked slowly around the room, pausing now and again as if listening. "There are actually two types of phenomena here, like a double set of signals, one amplifying the other, combining forces in a pretty good show. The residual effects of a past event are limited; they can only create a mood, or a vague illusion, and there they stop; but something else is influencing them, bringing them out into the open." He stopped in the middle of the room, thrust hands into trouser pockets. "Our knowledge of the forces involved is sketchy, but telekinesis is usually connected with a disturbed child lashing out at the offending world through his subconscious, while he's asleep."

Fat Jow stiffened in the rocker, eyes piercing the younger man. "Did you know about the child?"

"You didn't say there was a child."

"My grand-nephew from China lives with me." Fat Jow moved to the window to look out toward the vacant lot at the corner, where the neighboring children were playing. "His parents are dead, and the Reds released him to me."

Kwan Ho threw out his arms. "There you are! Why didn't you say so? If anybody's got an excuse to be disturbed, he has."

Fat Jow turned. "Hsiang Yuen is an excellent child, obedient and well-mannered."

"That's the worst kind; he's hiding something. You've got a Chinese poltergeist on your hands. You'd better find out what's bugging the kid, before he brings the roof down around your ears. He could, you know."

"Can you not learn this?"

"You're closer to him. I came to diagnose some phenomena, not to psychoanalyze the kid who's causing them. If you think it's beyond you, take him to a doctor."

Fat Jow said coldly, "There is no fault in his mind."

"Didn't say there was. But before this is over you may need professional help."

"How may one so small," asked Fat Jow sadly, "harbor anything but small problems?"

"Small? Uprooted from the only homeland he knows, trying to adjust to a radically different society—it's been too much for him to swallow in one gulp."

"But he has adapted, swiftly and admirably. He plays with the others, he attends the nursery school—"

"Regimentation!" said Kwan Ho, snapping his fingers. "What would you expect? Naturally it reminds him of life in Red China, and doesn't fit in with the rest of his concept of America."

"Your logic aspires to the profundity of youth. The wounds of childhood may strike deep, but they heal rapidly and are soon forgotten. I would seek simpler and more immediate causes."

Kwan Ho shrugged and turned to leave. "Good luck! You may look a long time."

Alone again, Fat Jow retreated to the familiar embrace of his rocker and regarded himself in a mirrored panel.

Hsiang Yuen had settled readily and, Fat Jow thought, contentedly, into his new environment. Had not Fat Jow, concerned lest the child feel restricted by the conservative ways of an old man, followed the excellent advice of Mrs. Yick, the social worker from the neighborhood center, and sent him to her nursery school? She spoke knowingly of peer-group and parallel mental-emotional levels, of creative play and self-expression, of group therapy and healthy psychological development. This was a new world to Fat Jow as well as to Hsiang Yuen . . . and occasionally frightening.

How had he matured to manhood without any grasp of these values? Preparing a child for his place in modern society seemed an overwhelming responsibility.

When Hsiang Yuen returned from play, Fat Jow beckoned him to his side. The child came solemnly and silently. He seldom smiled, for his short years had been less than happy. His father, a Red Army captain, had been killed by anti-Maoists on the streets of Canton; his mother, a minor Party official, had died of illness within the year. Alone and apprehensive, he had flown the Pacific to the land of the Yankee imperialist enemy, to join his great-uncle whom he had never seen. Dutifully he stood before Fat Jow, hands clasped at his waist, eyes directed above, at the crystal chandelier.

"Come nearer," said Fat Jow, extending his hand.

Shyly Hsiang Yuen accepted his hand, climbed into his lap, leaned against the warmth of the old man. Fat Jow rested one arm lightly about the small shoulders. "Do you like living here with me?"

"Yes, Uncle." The child's eyes remained upon the chandelier. "Does it sparkle at night too, when the lights are out?"

Fat Jow sighed. Patience . . . a child's attention is elusive, often ethereal, but follows its own reasoning. "A little," he replied, "but at night there is only the streetlight for it to reflect. Perhaps there is something you do not like? Something you would want changed?"

After a thoughtful pause, Hsiang Yuen's eyes wandered from the chandelier to the bedroom door. "No, Uncle."

"I am sure there is something. Is it the nursery school?"

The child pondered, slowly formed an opinion. "I do not like Mrs. Yick," he said experimentally.

"Nonsense. Mrs. Yick is kind and wise, and she knows what is best for children who will soon be attending the elementary school." He could not confess that he too did not much like Mrs. Yick.

In a pleading note, the small round face tilted wistfully up at him. "Uncle, at first you took me with you to the herb shop. Why do you now send me away?"

"I do not send you away—" began Fat Jow, but his words died. Was Kwan Ho right? "You will be spending many years in school," he argued. "It is better that you know what it is like."

Hsiang Yuen eyed him reproachfully, pushed down off his lap. "I liked the herb shop better," he grumbled, shuffling toward the room.

Fat Jow let the child accompany him to the herb shop on Monday. He set him to small tasks, saw him respond with professional devotion. Hsiang Yuen listened to the talk, watched Fat Jow's skillful fingers at their diverse functions. Toward the end of the day, Fat Jow felt that this was right, that the young absorb interest and learn from the old. Was not this the child's own choice?

Not unexpectedly, Mrs. Yick appeared late Wednesday afternoon as they were about to close the shop. From within the doorway she surveyed the scene with disapproval. She was as tall and as heavy as Fat Jow, her level gaze fortified by authoritarian dark-rimmed spectacles. "This child is not ill," she charged. "You are keeping him away deliberately."

"It is his wish," said Fat Jow. "He is happier here. I cannot deny him."

"You deny him far more by indulging his whim, by depriving him of the school environment. His formal enrollment will then be the more difficult, that is certain."

Fat Jow shook his head, knowing the futility of explaining his true motive to someone like Mrs. Yick. He said sullenly, "I know what the child likes, and what he does not."

"He is better spending his days among those of his own generation," insisted Mrs. Yick; "not here, among the trappings of a primitive, outmoded craft."

He returned angrily, "The old is not to be discarded simply because it is old; it retains much of significance for the world of today." He waved about the shop. "Were this a restaurant or laundry, would your objection be as strong? Why do you focus upon my profession? Many Chinese-American children grow up in the business establishments of their parents."

"This is the Twentieth Century. Witchcraft and shamanism are being rooted out of civilized society, but they die hard."

Fat Jow drew himself up to his full five feet. "Traditional Chinese medicine is an ancient and honored art, requiring long years of study and operative techniques as delicate as those of any surgeon."

Mrs. Yick folded her plump arms in her immovable way. "The Health Department could put you out of business for dispensing drugs without a license."

He held up a finger. "Ah, since you mention this particular agency—" he started toward the wall-telephone, "—allow me to call the University of California Medical Center, where a distinguished faculty member—"

"Wait," she said with mingled uncertainty and curiosity. "What have you to do with them? I should expect you to stay away from there."

He turned back. "I have had the honor of working with them. When conventional courses of treatment have failed, as with advanced arthritis in the elderly, my friend has consulted me."

She whispered, "He . . . calls *you*?"

"Many medical men scoff, as do you; but others, like this man, who is a figure of national stature in the field of orthopedic surgery, look with scientific detachment upon traditional Chinese medicine. They cannot do less than the Chinese Reds. These most pragmatic of people permit it and actively support it."

"And you have been able to help?"

"Twice he approved acupuncture, and his patients responded favorably."

She shuddered. "Sticking needles in people! It sounds barbaric."

"There is relatively little pain. The needles are placed with meticulous care, to avoid sensory areas. It is an exact science, Mrs. Yick. A child might do worse in his choice of career."

"I hardly know what to say," said Mrs. Yick, slightly subdued. "I understand much now that I did not before." Her voice firmed. "But I still think Hsiang Yuen needs a school environment."

Fat Jow looked down at Hsiang Yuen, a rapt listener. "It is your life we juggle so blithely. Would you feel better about going to Mrs. Yick's if you spent part of the week here with me?"

Hsiang Yuen brightened, and the beginnings of a smile tugged at the corners of his mouth. "I think I would like that," he said.

"A compromise?" Fat Jow asked Mrs. Yick.

"A compromise," she said, smiling now.

Mrs. Yick then drove them home through the evening traffic, across Nob Hill. Wednesday was gone, and the child had his half-week at the herb shop; he would appear at the nursery school in the morning.

Fat Jow knew a relaxing sense of accomplishment—and the nights were serene. After two weeks had passed without incident he began to hope that he had divined Hsiang Yuen's unsettling problem—if, indeed, such had been the cause of the manifestations. Professional help had not been required.

They were partly into a third week when Fat Jow awoke shivering, cold through chest and shoulders. It was a simple physical cold, because he had become uncovered. This in itself was not unusual but as consciousness returned, he found that the blanket and sheet, with a gentle steady motion, were creeping down over the foot of the couch. He hauled back upon them without effect, for they moved with a force beyond his strength and weight. He released them, and they landed in a heap on the floor.

He sat up, perplexed, unsure of his next move. This decision was taken from him when slowly the couch tilted from back to front, and he scurried to a safe distance to avoid its toppling over upon him; but when he was away, it settled back into position as if content to have dislodged him.

Wavering now between fear and frustration, Fat Jow put on robe and slippers. Another wakeful night was indicated. He approached the couch, stopped when it moved again.

The apartment door banged open, and he awaited the corresponding bang from Adah Baxter's door ... but nothing. Cautiously he emerged into the foyer, peered into the shadows, then upward, where a tiny creaking and scraping from the top of the lightwell recalled to him Kwan Ho's words: ". . . before he brings the roof down around your ears."

The stained-glass dome, three stories up, spanned most of the foyer. Discretion prompted Fat Jow to step back into the comparative shelter of his doorway. The century-old house was forever giving voice to its infirmities, but Fat Jow was not an adventurous person, especially not after midnight.

With an abrupt tiny tinkle that was immediately swallowed in the vastness of the foyer, a single triangular piece of stained glass fell and shattered upon the parquet floor. Had his door been closed, he would not have heard it. He waited motionless fully ten minutes, but nothing more happened, and no one came.

Why a single small piece? It would seem that the night's foray had been abandoned when hardly begun.

Grimly he turned and strode through his apartment to the bedroom; an understanding with Hsiang Yuen was overdue. Without hesitation he switched on the overhead bedroom light. Let the child wake.

Anger drained away. The bed was empty, and Fat Jow was the sole occupant of the room. Unbelieving, he groped over the tumbled bedclothes, knelt to look under the bed, inspected the closet, the screened window, the bathroom. He dashed back to the open apartment door, ready to arouse the household, but he paused, hand on knob, looked toward the couch. The covers were again in place, drawn up to cover the small form of Hsiang Yuen, genuinely and soundly asleep.

Fat Jow looked down upon the child, then took himself quietly into the bedroom. He awoke to brilliant morning, refreshed and in good humor, for the bed was more comfortable than the couch.

Hsiang Yuen was standing by his side, tousled and bare-footed, smiling broadly. "I was in there when I woke," he announced with happy wonder. "The crystals make little rainbows when the sun strikes them."

Fat Jow drew him to sit beside him. "And you like that."

"Thank you, Uncle."

"But I did not—" Fat Jow decided to let it pass. "Why did you not tell me from the beginning that you wished to sleep upon the couch?"

Hsiang Yuen's smile lessened. "I was ashamed."

"Ashamed? Of expressing a little preference?"

"No, Uncle . . . of being afraid of the dark."

Fat Jow, suppressing a smile, nodded gravely. He understood more than he wished to imply. "It is nothing of which to be ashamed. At your age, I was the same."

Small problems require small solutions.

Murder by Dream

by Patrick O'Keeffe

My cousin Janice first told me about her strange flower dreams one afternoon on our way home from high school. As we passed the florist next to Sitwell's drug store, she remarked dolefully, "I'm going to hear of a death in the family."

"What makes you say that?"

"I dreamed of flowers last night, and every time I dream of them I always get news of a death in the family soon afterward, on one side or the other."

"Maybe a coincidence or two," I suggested.

"It's been happening for the past few years. I've never known it to be wrong."

Next day a telegram brought word from San Francisco that Grandma Barrow had passed away. Six months later my father died of a heart attack, and Janice told me that she had dreamed of flowers the night before.

His untimely death was the cause of my going to sea. Mother was a semi-invalid, and I had neither the competence nor the desire to take over my father's wholesale paint business. My ambitions lay in radio, and if ather had lived I would have gone to college and studied radio engineering. The business was sold and, putting my few years of amateur-radio experience to professional use, I passed for a radio-telegraph operator's license and took the first opening aboard ship. On my salary I managed to keep mother in our home and put a little aside for future college fees.

I used to see Janice between voyages, since she lived only a few blocks away, and during that seagoing period I happened to be at home prior to the deaths of Uncle Charlie, Aunt Laura, and cousin Joe's wife, who was killed in a plane collision. On each occasion Janice told me that she had had her usual flowers dream. I was at sea when Grandpa Barrow died, and also when cousin George drowned, but Janice mentioned in her letters that she had dreamed of flowers preceding the news of each death.

Until Janice met Bob, I think I was the only one in whom she confided about her flower dreams, for we were like brother and sister, each of us being an only child. She was reluctant to tell anyone else in or connected with the family, for fear of creating anxiety when she had the dream, especially if some member happened to be sick. The only person I mentioned them to was a Jesuit missionary we once had as an intransit passenger to Panama. I told him about the dreams during a chat on preternatural and supernatural phenomena and manifestations.

"Do you think Janice's dreams have any meaning or purpose?" I asked.

He was a large, elderly man with a venerable brown beard that swept a wide chest as he shook his head dubiously.

"If they were of divine origin their meaning or design would perhaps be less obscure, more easily interpreted. I see none in your cousin's dreams. We must never forget, though, that dreams may be of evil origin. Satan seeks souls in ways other than by pact. As long as we don't allow dreams to influence us, don't make a superstition of them, they are powerless to harm us."

When I repeated the Jesuit's words to Janice, she said, "I'm naturally upset each time I have the dream, waiting to see who has died. I can't help being affected like that."

"You believe in the dream, so that amounts to making a superstition of it," I said.

"But Phil, it's never been wrong. I can't help but believe in it. I don't see how just believing it will come true can harm me."

"I don't either," I said. Nevertheless, I had an uneasy feeling about her dreams. There was something unnatural in them. I wished she did not have them.

It was about a year later that Janice and Bob made their honeymoon cruise. Janice had met Bob when the firm he worked for audited the books at the bank soon after Janice had taken a job in the Trust Department. Janice brought him home for supper that same weekend, so rapidly had they discovered each other, and within a year they were married. They agreed on a summer honeymoon cruise, and Janice wanted it to be with me. I was then chief radio officer of the new Crescent liner running to Bermuda, the Leeward Islands and down to Trinidad.

Southbound, we had a full passenger list, roughly a hundred and fifty. Janice and Bob would have been no less happy if the ship had been empty, for all they wanted was each other's company. However, they did not act the inseparable newlyweds, but gave more than their share of time toward helping others to enjoy the cruise by taking part in all the games and competitions. Bob, who was something of an acrobat and liked to show off his talent, won first prize on amateur night; Janice placed second in the bridge tournament. To all on board they were Janice and Bob rather than Mr. and Mrs. Blake. Scarcely anyone could fail to be charmed by Janice on sight, with her friendly round face and warm dark eyes; and no one glancing from her to Bob's cheerful smooth-skinned face and head of tossed light hair ever needed to wonder what she saw in him.

Nothing happened to mar Janice's enjoyment of the cruise until it was more than half over and we were returning north among the islands. Janice and Bob used to take part in the usual evening dancing for a while, and then Janice would help to make up a foursome at bridge. Bob was a rabid poker fan, with little taste for bridge, and southbound he had managed to get up an odd game or two with husbands whose wives had not already drafted them for the bridge tables. In Trinidad, however, a number of oilmen from the Venezuelan fields joined the ship as passengers to New York. Flush with vacation pay, and poker their chief evening pastime, they were exactly what Bob would have ordered.

The bridge games generally ended in the lounge toward midnight, but the poker sessions in the smoking-room sometimes lasted until the early hours of the morning, although Bob usually quit soon after Janice had looked in on her way to their cabin. Once, it was almost two o'clock before he appeared, saying that he was well ahead and didn't like to quit without giving the others a chance to win some of it back. Janice laughingly told him that the next time he came home late, she would be the outraged wife and lock him out.

The next night, when it was almost two-thirty and Bob had not yet come in, Janice got out of bed and bolted the door, and then lay down again and resumed reading a ship's library novel in anticipation of some fun at Bob's expense when he found himself locked out.

Bob, however, was long in coming, and Janice fell asleep with the book in her hands and the bed light on. It was after seven when she awoke. Her first thought was of Bob. She was puzzled that he had not aroused her. Although she was a sound sleeper, a knock or two on the door would have wakened her. She concluded that Bob, finding the door locked and her apparently asleep, had chosen not to disturb her and had perhaps gone to one of the oilmen's cabins to sleep on a settee.

Then suddenly she was terror-stricken. During the night she had dreamed of flowers. She had seen them in a vase in a window. She turned out at once and dressed, frantically hoping that Bob would come in any minute and start washing and shaving for breakfast. By the time the first gong sounded, he was still absent. Janice hurried out on deck, clinging to a hope that Bob was sleeping late in one of the poker players' cabins. She saw a group of the oilmen chatting by the rails on the promenade deck. She rushed up to them and asked where Bob was. They did not know, nor had he slept in any of their cabins.

Janice turned to other passengers. None had seen Bob that morning. Janice came running up to the radio room in stark panic.

"Something's happened to Bob," she moaned.

I got her calmed down, and she told me about her dream and that Bob was missing.

"He's probably keeping out of sight somewhere to pay you back for locking him out," I said.

That was really wishful thinking, but it wasn't without good grounds. Janice and Bob had played pranks on each other during the cruise, as when Bob put sand in Janice's bed and she had responded by getting the bedroom steward to shut off the water when Bob was soaped up under the shower.

"He'll have to show his face this forenoon," I said. "There's a boat and fire drill at ten o'clock."

Bob was missing from boat drill. Janice came running to the radio room again, almost hysterical.

"He must have fallen overboard," she wailed.

"Not a chance in this weather," I told her. "He's hiding somewhere. Wait here till I come back."

I left her with the third radio officer and went straight to the captain's quarters, desperately hoping I was right about Bob. Old Blagdon decided that if it was all a joke on Bob's part, it was more than time to end it. He had Bob paged over the loudspeakers. There was no response. The captain ordered the chief officer to make a quick search of the ship. He summoned one of the oilmen to his office. The oilman told us that the poker game had ended soon after four o'clock, but that Bob had dropped out around three-thirty and gone to his cabin.

"He didn't sleep in it," the captain said. "He's missing."

The oilman, a skinny, sunbrowned Oklahoman in khaki shorts, looked concerned. After a moment's thought, he asked, "Do you know if his wife locked him out of their cabin last night?"

I answered him. "Yes. She did it in fun."

"Then maybe that's it. He told us she'd said she would next time he stayed out late, but he said he knew a way to fool her. His idea was to lower himself down the ship's side from the rails and slide feet first through the bathroom porthole. He said he'd already given it half a try when she wasn't around and had found it easy enough. He meant to walk in on her, leaving her to wonder how he'd managed it. We thought it a pretty risky stunt, even for a double-jointed guy like him. I guess he must have slipped, or something."

If the oilman's guess was correct, then Bob had been overboard for nearly eight hours up to that moment. Yet he was a powerful swimmer, and if he conserved his strength, he could keep afloat in that warm, calm sea for many hours to come. On the dark side were the possibilities that he might have injured himself against the hull as he slipped, or perhaps he had got foul of the propellers. Sharks prowled those waters too.

Captain Blagdon decided that the prospects of finding Bob still afloat were good enough to warrant turning the ship back. He was a hardheaded old seagull in some ways, but he had a human streak running through him like a blue strand in a manila rope. I believe he would have put the ship about solely out of sympathy for Janice, even if he had felt there was no hope of finding Bob. He did not even wait for the chief officer's report on the ship search, which proved negative.

I hurried back to the radio room, where Janice sat waiting for me in her gay cruise blouse and pink shorts but with anguish in her dark eyes. When I broke the news to her, she moaned, "My dream!" and collapsed.

I sent for the ship's doctor and a stewardess, and when Janice recovered I went below with them to her cabin. Before he left, the doctor gave her a tranquilizer. After he'd gone, Janice cried piteously to me:

"It's all my fault. I'll never see Bob again."

It was Bob I blamed to myself. The row of portholes to Section "C" cabins was just below the rails on the port side. To worm in through one of them a man merely had to climb over the rails, grasp the lowest one, and lower his legs to the opening, thrust them in and slide through feet first, shifting his hand grip from the rail down to the edge of the fishplate and letting go as soon as his shoulders were safely inside. The ship not being air-conditioned, the ports were kept open in tropical waters.

I had known of more than one steward to slip into a cabin that way for some passenger who had lost his key when another one was not immediately available, but only in port and on the offshore side where nothing worse than a ducking was risked, and never at sea, during darkness and with the ship under way. Bob must have been crazy.

It was still light when we approached the vicinity of what was estimated to have been the ship's position at the time that Bob dropped overboard. There was no shortage of lookouts. Passengers in all kinds of bright cruise regalia lined the rails on both sides, although the merriment had been suspended when the orchestra had put aside the instruments with the first word that Bob was missing overboard. I posted myself high up on the radar mast.

The conditions for sighting a man in the water were favorable. The sea was unrippled, as if glassed over, gray at that late hour of the day. Yet while a man's head would stand out like a dark polka dot at close hand, from even a short distance it could be as inconspicuous as a bubble.

With the approximate position of Bob's likely whereabouts as a center, Captain Blagdon cruised in widening circles until long after dark, with searchlights and spotlights waving beams from the bridge like the feelers of some lost marine monster. Not so much as a piece of driftwood or ship garbage was sighted. Gloom spread over the entire ship, and when Captain Blagdon swung her back to her original course, even the most carping among the passengers would have conceded that the captain had done his utmost. It was like turning away from a new grave.

Captain Blagdon, however, was not without hope, and he went below with me to Janice's cabin to try to instill it in Janice. She had not stirred out on deck during the search, convinced that her dream had arisen from Bob's death. She had changed into a dark dress with a black belt.

"You mustn't give up hope for a long while yet," the captain said. "Bob may very well have been picked up by some vessel. If it's a small one with no radio, you won't hear from Bob until she calls at her next port, and that may be halfway round the world."

But Janice only wept, and when the captain had gone, she sobbed to me, "I could have told him about my dream, but he wouldn't have understood it as you and I do."

"I don't understand it your way, Janice. It could mean someone else in the family and not Bob. It could be wrong, too, and not mean a death, not anyone's death."

"Phil, in your heart you don't mean that. You're trying to be kind, like everyone else, trying to pacify me with false hope."

"I do mean it, and it's not false hope. You can't see it because you're making a superstition of your dream. It's harming you, blinding you to reason."

"I can't suffer any worse harm."

I could make no impression on Janice. She mourned Bob as dead. She kept to her cabin all next day, scarcely touching the tempting trays brought by the stewardesses, refusing to let in passengers wishing to show their sympathy and express their hopes for Bob's safety. I spent most of my spare time with her. Between fits of weeping she lay motionless on the bed or sat in a chair and gazed fixedly at the bolt on the closed door. At intervals she would moan, "Why did I do it? Why couldn't I have seen what would happen to him?"

Before I turned in late that evening, I went down to Janice's cabin again. There was a tray of untouched food on the dresser, the coffee now cold. I had hardly closed the door before Janice cried:

"Oh, Phil, I can't go on living without Bob."

I had no fear that Janice, as a devout Catholic, would damn her soul for all eternity by taking her own life. "Janice," I pleaded, "don't go on brooding and starving yourself. You'll bring on a nervous breakdown, and wouldn't that be a fine state for Bob to find you in?"

"Please don't torture me, Phil. I'll never see Bob again in this world. Phil, I'm losing my mind."

There was a strange look in Janice's sunken and red-rimmed eyes, and it frightened me. Perhaps she was really going out of her mind. I felt desperate, helpless. The faintest hope that Bob was still alive might help to keep her mind in balance until the first shock had passed, even though the hope turned out to be false; but it was impossible to force it past the barrier of her dream. It seemed to me that the only thing able to save Janice's sanity would be word that Bob had been picked up, and it would have to come soon.

Before I left I said, "Janice, try to get a good night's sleep. You need it badly. There may be good news for you tomorrow."

She lay on the bed, staring up at the deckhead, and did not seem to hear me, but she answered my "Good night, Janice," as I closed the door.

About seven o'clock next morning I received a radiogram that threw me into wild joy. It was from Bob. He had been picked up by an auxiliary trading schooner, without radio. He had been unable to get word to us until the vessel had berthed in San Juan.

I did not stop to ring for the bellboy. I rushed below to deliver the message myself. I knocked on Janice's door. I knocked again, louder. There was no response. Thinking that Janice might finally have fallen into heavy sleep, I opened the door and peered inside.

There was no sign of Janice. The bathroom door was open; I called out, but there was no response. Thinking hopefully that Janice was at last beginning to recover from her crushing grief and had gone up on deck, I was about to withdraw when I spotted the envelope. It was wedged between the mirror above the little dressing-table and the bulkhead. The sight of it chilled the joy in my heart—Janice missing, a note left behind. I stepped inside and read the name on the envelope, ship stationery. It was mine. I was stricken with anguish by the note inside.

"Good-bye, dear Phil. I've gone to join Bob. Lovingly, Janice."

Janice had placed a chair under the bathroom porthole to stand on. She had not only set out to join Bob, but had also chosen the same point of departure. I knew it would be futile to have the ship turned back a second time. Janice could not swim.

Possibly a Satanic chuckle followed Janice as she started on her last journey. Her dream had not foreshadowed news of Bob's death but of her own, and in diabolical fashion had brought it about. I prayed that the Recording Angel would mercifully be able to write, "While of unsound mind." To me, no less than if Janice had been driven by human agency into committing her last act, it was murder.

The Clairvoyant Countess

by Dorothy Gilman

"**W**hat's this?" asked Lieutenant Pruden, stopping in at Madame Karitska's one evening on his way home after a long day on the street. He had just discovered that Madame Karitska had two guests, one of them Gavin O'Connell, a student from St. Bonaventure's School, the other a very Establishment-type middle-aged man in a well-cut business suit.

Madame Karitska put a finger to her lips and gestured him to follow her to the center of the room. Lieutenant Pruden could make no sense of what he saw. Neither Gavin nor the stranger appeared even aware of his arrival: in front of each lay a book, and they were staring with enormous concentration at their respective half-open volumes.

And suddenly as he watched a strange thing happened: a page of Gavin's book slowly lifted and turned. There were no windows open: there were no hands touching the pages, and yet the page had turned.

"I did it," crowed Gavin gleefully. "Hey, Jonesy, I did it!"

"Mr. Faber-Jones, this is Lieutenant Pruden," broke in Madame Karitska. "Yes, you did it, Gavin. Capital! But Mr. Faber-Jones also had some success, I notice."

"Kind of you," said Faber-Jones, getting to his feet. "Only pushed the page halfway, though, and frankly I'm exhausted."

"Me too," admitted Gavin. "Hi, Lieutenant Pruden!"

"What have I interrupted?" asked Pruden curiously.

"A practice session," Gavin told him eagerly. "It's great meeting Mr. Faber-Jones, you know, he has the gift too."

"Oh? But what have you been practicing?"

"Concentration," said Madame Karitska. "The moving of mountains by the use of the mind. In this case, the lifting of a page in a book by sheer concentration of psychic energies. The pages can turn—you saw it yourself."

"Incredible," said Pruden.

"You can't just say 'Move!' to the pages either," put in Gavin. "You have to lift them with concentrated *thought*, and boy it's rough. It's fun too, though. You ought to try it."

Pruden's laugh was short and doubting.

"You find it unbelievable?" inquired Madame Karitska.

"I don't know," said Pruden, frowning. "I might have six days ago but—"

"But what?" asked Faber-Jones, sinking into the couch, obviously tired and ready for diversion.

"Do not say a word," said Madame Karitska, "until I bring out the Turkish coffee I've brewed, with a glass of milk for Gavin." When she had returned and distributed refreshments she sat down and inserted a cigarette into a long holder. "Now tell us what has placed a crack in your imperviousness."

Pruden said, "I'd really like to know: you believe the mind has such intensity, such power?"

"But of course," she said, amused. "We use only a fraction of its power, we use only a tiny amount of ourselves."

"But for instance," Pruden said, picking his words carefully, "do you believe a man can simply announce that he's going to die, be in perfect health and—just die?"

Madame Karitska smiled faintly. "So many diseases are psychosomatic, it happens oftener than you think. I have seen people turn their faces from life, their will to live gone. It may take months or years but they die."

He shook his head. "I mean something much faster than that—death in a matter of days."

"Ah," said Madame Karitska, "now that is very interesting. You have met such a situation? You must have met such a situation or you would not be speaking of this?"

He said ruefully, "I'm still not accustomed to having my mind browsed through, but yes, I've met such a situation. Heard about it, at least. The patrolman on the block, Bill Kane, has been puzzling over it for days. It seems a man named Arturo Mendez died about two weeks ago. On a Wednesday he told his brother Luis that he would die before the week was out, and on the following Tuesday night he died."

"Did they not call a doctor?"

"On Monday they called an ambulance and he was taken to the hospital. The doctors found nothing organically wrong with him, but the following night he was dead."

"Did they perform an autopsy?"

Pruden nodded. "He died quite literally of a heart stoppage but there was nothing wrong with his heart either."

"Then it was precognition," put in Gavin eagerly. "He knew something was going to happen ahead of time."

"No—no, I think not," Madame Karitska said, and with an intent glance at Pruden, "There is more?"

He nodded. "Yesterday Bill Kane told me that Arturo's brother Luis won't get out of bed now. He's settled his debts, paid his landlady a week's rent in advance, and told her that he'll be dead by Monday morning."

"And this is Friday night," mused Madame Karitska. "I wonder . . . where do they live, Lieutenant?"

"Three blocks away on Fifth Street, in the Puerto Rican section."

She nodded. "I will go there tomorrow, I would like to see this."

Pruden shook his head. "It's not a good section for gringos, as they call us. Very few speak English, and Luis only a little. Do you speak Spanish?"

"No," said Madame Karitska, "but there is communication without speech." She added thoughtfully, "This is very interesting to me. There are yogis in the East, of course, who can stop breathing at will, but neither of your two men is a yogi; there must be very powerful forces involved here. It is the invisible at work, and I am a student of the invisible." She glanced abruptly at her watch and said, "It's time, Gavin." To Pruden she explained, "Mr. Faber-Jones has brought over a portable television so that we can see John Painter make his debut on the 'Tommy Tompkins Show.'"

"Someone you know?" asked Pruden as Gavin jumped up to turn on the set.

"A protégé of Mr. Faber-Jones."

Faber-Jones looked at her reproachfully. "We both know whose protégé he really is, Madame Karitska."

"Nonsense," she told him, "you're growing quite fond of him and you know it, especially since he stopped wearing tennis sneakers."

"He only exchanged them for calfskin boots and a sequin jump suit," put in Faber-Jones dryly. "A very expensive sequin jump suit too, I might add."

"Hey, that sounds cool," broke in Gavin. "You think I could meet him sometime?"

"Sssh," said Madame Karitska, touching his shoulder and pointing to the television screen on which a glowing sequinned figure had

appeared, guitar in hand, to sit on a stool in front of the cameras.
Faber-Jones turned up the volume just as the song began:

"Once in old Atlantis
I loved a lady pure . . .
And then the waters rose . . ."

"It's already number two on the charts," Faber-Jones told Pruden
in an aside. "My Pisces Company cut the platter."

"Oh?" said Pruden, blinking, and gave Faber-Jones a startled
second glance.

On the following morning Madame Karitska had an appointment
at nine o'clock, and when her client had left she placed a sign on
her door that read BACK AT 12. She then set out for Fifth Street,
which she had always enjoyed on her walks around the city because
so much of its life was lived without concealment on the street.
Today was no exception: the sun was summer-hot and before Madame Karitska had even reached Fifth Street she could hear its music.
At this hour flamenco dominated, and then as she rounded the corner
she was met by John Painter's "Once in Old Atlantis" pouring out
of the Caballeros Social Club across the street.

Madame Karitska picked her way along the crowded sidewalk.
Street vendors chanted and shouted, and young men armed with
lugs and wrenches peered into the hoods of old cars or lay under
them with only sandaled feet showing. Several old men huddled
over a game spread out on empty orange crates, and one family of
four were unself-consciously eating early lunch at a card table on
the sidewalk. Every stair and porch was occupied by people of vary-
ing ages taking the sun with the enthusiasm of any Miami Beach
sun lounger. It was noisy, but it was more alive than Walnut Street
could ever be.

As Madame Karitska approached number 203 a uniformed policeman came out of a store across the street, saw her, and waved.
Crossing to her side he said, "You must be the lady Lieutenant
Pruden said would be coming around ten to see Luis. I've been
watching for you. I'm Bill Kane."

They shook hands. "I told his landlady I'd be bringing you over,"
he added. "Her name's Mrs. Malone."

"Malone!" said Madame Karitska, amused. "Lieutenant Pruden
was certain no one would speak English here."

"The lieutenant's not a patrolman, he only drives through in a car," Kane said forgivingly. "Mrs. Malone's been here for years, runs a very tight boardinghouse. This area," he said, pointing, "runs ten blocks down to the river. Used to be Irish, now it's Puerto Rican."

He stopped in front of a narrow clapboard house painted a dull brown. Narrow wooden steps led up to a narrow front porch made narrower by two windows with starched lace curtains and a heavy wooden door with a peephole. Patrolman Kane rang, and after an interval they heard approaching footsteps inside. The door swung open and a large woman with round pink cheeks and black hair confronted them. Her face softened when she saw Bill Kane. "Well, now, so it's you," she said, beaming at them both. "I didn't even have time to take off my apron, I was that busy baking, you see. Come in, come in."

"And we won't keep you from your baking more than a moment," Madame Karitska told her reassuringly. "We've come to see Luis Mendez."

"Well, it's kind of you, I'm sure. A terrible business, this, I can tell you. He won't eat," said Mrs. Malone, crossing herself. "His girl friend Maria sits with him evenings but everybody else stays away. They're scared. It scares me too, frankly."

"Yes," said Madame Karitska as they began climbing steep carpeted stairs. "Does he have many friends? Is he well-liked?"

"Oh, he's very popular in the neighborhood," said Mrs. Malone. "He drives an ice-cream truck, you know, or did—and his brother too, God rest his soul—and very hard-working and personable they was too. A very nice way they had about them with children. 'Hey! Here comes Looie. *Viva* Looie,' " she said with a shift into mimicry. "Many's the time I'd hear them. The kids loved him. As for close friends," she added in a practical voice, "well, they've been here in the States only two years and more hard-working men I've never seen. Up at dawn, back late—but," she said with a twinkle, "I'm not saying there wasn't time for a few beers at the social club, or time for a girl friend. Very good men, both of 'em. Hard-working and kind."

"No enemies?" emphasized Madame Karitska.

"Enemies!" Mrs. Malone's shocked voice was reply enough. "Luis? Goodness no!" She opened the door of a room at the end of the hall and called, "Company for you, Mr. Mendez. Not that he'll hear me," she added in an aside. "Real spooky it is."

They entered a large room, sparely furnished. The walls were papered with garish climbing roses that nearly obscured two crucifixes hung on the wall. There was a huge overstuffed chair in one corner, with a lamp and magazine table beside it. The bureau was massive and bore a statue of the Virgin Mary as well as a great deal of clutter. On a double bed by the window lay a young man in a rumpled shirt and slacks, his eyes open and staring at the ceiling. He looked no more than thirty, with jet-black hair and a black stubble of beard along his jaw, but the color had been drained from his skin, leaving it gray, and there were dull blue smudges under his eyes.

The landlady withdrew, closing the door behind her, and Bill Kane stood with his back to it, like a guard. Madame Karitska walked over to the bed, looked down into the man's face and then sat on the edge of the bed and grasped one of his hands in hers. She said nothing. The man's gaze swerved to hers and he moved restlessly, rebelliously.

"Can you speak?" she asked softly.

He groaned. "*Sí*—go away." He snatched his hand away from hers and turned his face to the wall.

"He sure has the look of death on him," said Kane in a low voice. "It's uncanny."

"Yes? Well, we shall see," she said, and walked over to the bureau to glance at the many objects abandoned there. One in particular drew her attention; a black candle shaped like a man, six inches high and standing upright in a saucer. Several broken matches lay beside it. She picked up the saucer and thoughtfully examined the candle, then put it down and glanced at an elaborately framed photograph of a beautiful girl. An inscription in the corner read, "All my love, Maria."

She nodded. "We can go now," she said.

"Already?" Kane was startled. "I thought—well, frankly the lieutenant made it sound as if you could cure Luis."

Madame Karitska was amused. "I only diagnose, I cannot cure."

"Well, then," said Kane, brightening, "what did you decide about Luis?"

"That this is a case for Lieutenant Pruden and that we should call him at once," she told him crisply. "This man is being murdered, and the lieutenant handles homicides, does he not?"

"What do you mean, he's being murdered?" demanded Pruden,

climbing out of a patrol car in front of Mrs. Malone's boardinghouse. "A man decides he wants to die it's suicide, not murder."

"When you have finished losing your temper," said Madame Karitska calmly, "I will explain to you why Luis Mendez is not committing suicide. In the meantime let us walk to the Botanica around the corner and see what we can do to save his life."

"You might call a doctor first," he said irritably, falling into step beside her.

"A doctor cannot possibly help him," she told him. "This is *espiritismo*. Here we are," she added, turning the corner, and came to a stop in front of LeCruz' West Indies Botanica.

"This place?" protested Pruden. On display in the window were statues of Buddha, of the Virgin Mary, and of figures he'd never seen before, some of them grotesque, some of them appealing; holy medals lying in nests of velvet, herb-burners fashioned of pottery, and plastic bottles advertised as ritual lotions. Madame Karitska opened the door, a bell jangled, and a gnarled little man with white hair and heavily pouched eyes glanced up from the counter. "Ah, Madame Karitska," he said, brightening. "How nice to see you again."

"The pleasure is mine," Madame Karitska told him warmly, shaking his hand. "You are well? Your family is well?"

"We are all well, Madame Karitska. And you?"

"In need of help, Mr. LeCruz. I know you have several spiritists among your clientele and we urgently need the best. Can you recommend one?"

Mr. LeCruz' glance moved to Pruden and rested on him doubtfully. "For me to recommend—I am not sure this is wise."

"I can vouch for Mr. Pruden," she said with a smile. "He is no believer but I am educating him, Mr. LeCruz."

He nodded. "Okay then." He was thoughtful a moment, then brought out paper and pencil. "I give you two names with addresses."

With a nod toward the shelves Pruden said, "What's all this—uh—merchandise?"

"I'll show you," Madame Karitska said, and taking his arm guided him along the counter. "Here you see candles: red ones to attract a loved one, blue candles for healing, yellow and white when communication with the dead is wished. And here is a black Chango candle," she added, picking one up. She handed it to Pruden and he stared blankly at the shape of a male figure about six inches tall. "It's burned when one hopes for the death of an enemy," she told

him, and added casually, "I have been told Luis Mendez has no
enemies, but there is a black Chango candle like this on the bureau
in his room."

"Oh for heaven's sake," protested Pruden.

She went on, ignoring the slant of his brows. "Here you see black
rag dolls with gold-plated needles—oh dear, eight dollars now, the
price is going up. As you probably know, the needles are stuck into
the dolls to cause pain to enemies. And here are herbs, a very fine
selection, each for different purposes, and although Mr. LeCruz dis-
approves of black magic he is a man who also likes to pay his bills
and so you find here vials of snake oil, graveyard dust, and bats'
blood."

Pruden groaned. "Please. I was back at headquarters making out
reports, and you pulled me away for this? I thought—"

"Ah, Mr. LeCruz is waiting for us," she said, interrupting him,
and moved toward him with a smile.

"I've given you two names," Mr. LeCruz told her in a low voice.
"Each from different cults. Both are fine, I hear, and give good
results."

"Results are what we need. Thank you, Mr. LeCruz," she said,
and to Pruden, "Shall we go now? I'll explain outside what I discovered and then you can go back to your reports at headquarters."

"While you go to Third Street?" he said, glancing at the addresses
on the sheet of paper. "Not on your life, I'm going with you. People
like you get mugged on Third Street."

"If you go with me you will have to forget that you are a policeman," she told him sternly. "You're not dressed as one, so if you'll
not speak like one or act like one—"

"Why?"

"Because there will be nothing rational about this, my dear Lieutenant, but then there is so much in life that isn't. The important
thing—of the highest order—is to save Mendez' life. Then you must
proceed as with any attempted murder, and discover who wishes the
Mendez brothers dead."

"And the weapon?" he asked, amused.

"The mind."

"I don't think you can convict anyone on that," he told her dryly.

"Exactly," she said in her clear crisp voice. "Which makes it very
clever, do you not think so? The perfect crime."

He'd not thought of it in this light. "You really think that?" he said, his brows slanting. "Of course if it could be done, if it were possible—"

"My dear Lieutenant," she told him with a smile, "voodoo is a religion older than Christianity. You have seen far too many Hollywood movies, I think. It is as old as astronomy, and uses astronomy in its beliefs and its gods, and it has many similarities to Christianity. It is a complex, ancient, and very structured religion, with formal rites and ceremonies, a culture as well as a religion. Don't, as John Painter would say, knock it."

"Obviously I mustn't," he said meekly.

They entered Third Street, a desolate street with windows broken in many of its buildings. A few black children playing hopscotch on the sidewalk stopped and stared at them; an old man sitting on a step in the sun bowed a grayed head to them as they passed. Farther along the street rock-and-roll music poured from a delicatessen around which at least a dozen young men idled.

"Here is number 180," said Madame Karitska, and they confronted high narrow steps to an open door, beyond which rose a second flight to the floor above. "She is called Madame Souffrant."

"Madame, eh?" said Pruden with a grin.

A cardboard sign just inside the door bore the name, with a purple arrow pointing to the second floor. They climbed rickety stairs and knocked at a door. A stately West Indian woman, her skin the color of café crème, answered their knock.

Madame Karitska said briskly, "A man is dying on Fifth Street; he's possessed and needs a spiritist. He has said he will die Monday morning."

"And this is Saturday noon," the woman said, nodding. "What cult?"

"I don't know but he came here from Puerto Rico two years ago. LeCruz gave us your name and that of a Miss Loaquin. Do you think you can help him?"

"Come in," said Madame Souffrant.

They entered a room with floors that slanted alarmingly but the room itself was clean to the point of sterility; the linoleum rug shone with polish, the long couch along the wall was covered with transparent plastic and plastic roses bloomed everywhere. "Sit down," said Madame Souffrant. "I think you need look no further, but I'll go back with you first and see the man to be certain."

"You can arrange the ritual for today, perhaps?" asked Madame Karitska.

"It can be done." The woman peered into the kitchen, spoke to someone, and closed the door. "My cat," she explained, and picking up a small suitcase resembling a doctor's bag she gestured to them to precede her, and locked the door behind her.

Pruden, with the feeling that none of this could be real, escorted them back to Fifth Street.

"You will come in?" asked Madame Karitska at the steps of Mrs. Malone's boardinghouse.

Pruden shook his head. "You said it's impossible to question Luis Mendez so I'll make a few inquiries of his girl friend instead. But only," he added pointedly, "if you continue to insist this is murder."

She regarded him with sympathy but with some impatience as well. "I insist, yes."

Pruden found Luis' girl friend at the Grecian Beauty Shoppe on Seventh Street. Maria Ardizzone was her name, with a very lovely Italian face to go with it, curly hair down to her shoulders and liquid black eyes. She was plump and would run to fat in a few years, but there was poise and ambition here, he thought, as he watched her take command of the interview with the ease of a girl who knew what she wanted. What she wanted, apparently, was Luis Mendez and a number of small Mendezes, and what she most admired about Luis was his ambition and his drive.

"But his sickness I do not understand," she said, faltering for the first time. "I do not understand this at all. The men in my family, they get the flu, they break an arm, they keep working. Luis, he just lies down. It is not *like* Luis; he works hard, he has built a good business."

"Doing what?" asked Pruden.

"They own—owned—two Jack Frost ice-cream trucks."

"Ice-cream trucks," repeated Pruden, frowning.

Maria nodded, her long rippling black hair nodding with her. "They scrimp, they save, they buy one truck. That was when I first met Luis. The truck they buy from Mr. Materas, the distributor, and Luis he drove it while Arturo took any job he could get to save up and buy the second one. Luis, he made three hundred dollars a day and do you think he would spend a nickel on himself? No, every penny went to buy the second truck free and clear. One must admire a man like that, Lieutenant," she said frankly.

"Yes indeed," murmured Pruden.

"I help them with the books," she added proudly. "April to October they sold the ice cream, and last year Arturo, he made fifteen thousand dollars for the year and Luis—my Luis, he made eighteen thousand dollars."

"That's a good living on Fifth Street," put in Pruden.

She nodded. "Yes, this is very good. Luis was happy, he felt good, and then Arturo died and—" She shook her head, her luminous eyes turning into wells of sadness. "Since then everything has been bad," she said simply. "Now Luis says he too must die."

"Must?" quoted Pruden.

"That is how he said it. It is strange, isn't it?"

"Surely something must have happened to make him say that. Did anything discourage him?"

"Nothing, I tell you."

"No enemies?"

Her eyes blazed. "Luis? Luis had only *friends*."

Pruden tried a new tack. "Was there anything unusual, then, no matter how small or unimportant, that happened about that time?"

She hesitated, and he thought her eyes flickered before she shook her head. "There was nothing."

He nodded. "Then I won't keep you from your customers any longer, Miss Ardizzone, but I may come back to ask you a few more questions."

"Please—any time," she told him. "Anything that will help Luis. I would give my life for Luis," she said fiercely. "You believe he can be helped?"

"I know someone who thinks so."

"Then I will light candles for them," she said. "For them as well as Luis. I will kiss their hands and their feet."

"Yes," said Pruden, blinking at her passion. He tried to picture Madame Karitska's reaction to having her hands and feet kissed, and he left before a smile could reach his lips. He didn't return to Fifth Street, however; he went back to headquarters to see Donnelly, who had a memory like a computer bank.

"Don, I want you to tell me about ice-cream trucks."

"They sell ice cream," Donnelly pointed out sourly.

Pruden ignored this. "I'm up against a dead man and one dying man who have no enemies but happen to own and drive ice-cream trucks. It's the only lead I've got at the moment. Look, a few years ago there was some trouble, wasn't there? Muscle stuff?"

Donnelly nodded. "You bet your sweet life there was. It was over in the Dell section two years ago. Parts stolen, one driver kidnapped, ten trucks blown up. A real war over the territory."

"Who won?"

"*They* did, we think. Suddenly all the trouble stopped and nobody would talk."

"And who's 'they'?"

Donnelly regarded him laconically. " 'They' are not us, Lieutenant."

Pruden nodded. "How do I find out all the routes in the city, and who has what territory?"

"You dig," said Donnelly, giving him a faintly sympathetic smile, "and if you find yourself up against the same people who made trouble two years ago you be damned sure to carry your gun."

This was not reassuring but on the other hand it seemed infinitely remote as a possibility. Pruden returned to his office and began digging for facts, his work made easier by Maria Ardizzone's mention of the name Materas. He found it in the yellow pages: Joseph and Alice Materas, Jack Frost Ice Cream distributors, warehouse at 100 First Street, offices at 105 First Street. He was about to call them when the telephone rang at his desk: it was Madame Karitska.

"I am glad to find you," she told him. "Madame Souffrant is just beginning the voodoo ceremony and I have gained permission to watch, and for you also. This is very unusual. If you are to become Commissar of Police one day—"

He grinned. "If? I thought you were sure."

"—then this would be very good for you to see," she concluded. "We have taken Luis Mendez by taxi to 110 Third Street, to a building just behind Madame Souffrant's apartment house at 108."

Pruden considered the Materas, and he considered the voodoo ceremony, and he realized that knowing Madame Karitska was having its effect upon him: he really was curious. "I'll be there in ten minutes," he told her, and hung up.

"Where do I tell the Chief you're going?" asked Benson at the switchboard as Pruden hurried past him.

Pruden smiled. "Tell him I'm on my way to see a voodoo ceremony," he said, and was more than rewarded by the look on Benson's face.

Madame Karitska met him in the alleyway next to 108 Third Street. "It's begun," she told him, "so we must walk and speak very quietly. Madame Souffrant examined Luis and confirmed that three spirits of the dead have been sent after him and that his soul has already been given to the lord of the cemetery."

"Good God, and you believe this?" he said, his brows slanting incredulously.

She brushed this aside impatiently. "What does it matter what you or I believe? It is Luis who believes." She regarded him with exasperation. "It has been very tiring trying to find a banana tree and we have had to substitute a young willow tree instead. You think it is easy looking for a banana tree in Trafton? Also it is seven o'clock and I'm hungry. Madame Souffrant is confident, however, because her cult is very similar to Luis'."

"That's good. Where the hell are we?"

"At the *oum'phor*, or temple as you might call it. Shall we go in now?"

He followed her down the alley into the rear, where a high board fence had been erected around a dilapidated old garage. The yard inside the fence was grassless and contained what looked to be junk: stones, jugs, lamps, and innumerable drawings made in chalk or lime on the hard-beaten earth. Madame Karitska led him through a small gate at the side and they tiptoed inside the garage.

Here Luis Mendez had been laid out on the earth floor beside an intricately decorated vertical pole; he had been stripped of everything but white shorts. All kinds of delicate white designs had been drawn on the earth around him. His head was wrapped in a bandage that ran from the top of his head to his jaw, and a second bandage bound his two big toes together. His eyes were open but vacant. The garage was dark except for candles burning at various points beside Luis' body and several lanterns hanging on the wall. The air was thick with incense. Half a dozen people surrounded Madame Souffrant, who was intoning, "In the name of God the Father, God the Son, and God the Holy Ghost, in the name of Mary, in the name of Jesus, in the name of all the saints, all the dead . . ."

A strange and eerie chill rose at the nape of Pruden's neck and traveled across his scalp. That stern and declamatory voice rose and fell like a bird in the hushed and darkened room, like a hawk or an eagle, he thought, beating its wings against the walls until the walls appeared to recede, disappearing altogether, and he stood in astonishment, centuries removed from Trafton, listening to a priestess speak to the gods.

When the incantations abruptly ended he felt disoriented and confused; he discovered he was sweating profusely for reasons he couldn't understand and which his rational mind could not explain. He stole a glance at Madame Karitska and saw that her eyes were closed and her face serene. As the rituals continued he returned his attention to Madame Souffrant, but if what followed seemed to him bizarre and preposterous he didn't smile; he was unable to forget what he had felt during the incantations, unable to forget a sense of Presences, of forces appealed to and converging. . . .

Luis Mendez lay like a corpse except for an occasional twitching or shouting of what sounded like obscenities. As Pruden watched, small piles of corn and peanuts and pieces of bread were distributed at certain points of his body, and just as he wondered why in hell somebody's leftover breakfast was being heaped on Luis, two hens and a rooster were carried into the *oum'phor* and given to Madame Souffrant. She grasped the chickens, one under each arm, and held them low over Luis so that they could peck at the food on his body while at the same time she began a curious crossing and uncrossing of Luis' arms, chanting "*Ente, te, te, tete, te . . .*" When the piles of corn had been reduced in size the chickens were exchanged for the rooster, and Pruden felt a stab of alarm. The angry cock left small, bloody wounds as it moved up Luis' body, heading for his face: barely in time someone stepped forward to cover the man's eyes. After this the cock was carried away and turned loose in the yard outside, and lighted candles began to be passed over Luis from head to foot, again weaving that same strange pattern while the incantations of *Ente, te, te, tete* rose in volume.

Abruptly Madame Souffrant became silent, moved to a basin, gathered up liquid in cupped hands, and vigorously slapped Luis' face. Others moved in and began to thrash Luis with water; he was helped to a half-sitting position and whipped with small, dripping wet sacks until the bandages fell away from his dripping body. Cloves of garlic were thrust into his mouth while Madame Souffrant continued to call on the dead spirits to depart, her voice rising to a crescendo.

Suddenly Luis shuddered violently from head to foot and fell back on the earth almost unconscious.

Madame Souffrant ceased her incantations and leaned over him. "Luis," she called. "Luis Mendez. Luis, is it you?"

"Yes," he said in a calm and normal voice.

"I think the dead spirits are leaving now," whispered Madame Karitska, her eyes bright and intent.

A jar filled with something alcoholic was poured over a stone lying in a dish, and flames sprang up. The steaming dish was carried to Luis and passed over his body, again describing that same intricate pattern of movement, after which Madame Souffrant put it down, seized a bottle of fluid, lifted it to her lips, drank from it several times, and each time spat it through her teeth over Luis.

"We move out into the yard now," said Madame Karitska in a low voice, nudging Pruden, and he followed her and the others outside to a corner of the enclosure where a deep hole had been dug. To Pruden's surprise it had grown dark while they were inside, and the lamps encircling the hole sent bizarre shadows flickering up and down the fence. He turned to see Luis limp from the building on the arms of two young men, and as Luis approached the illuminated circle, Pruden saw that he looked stronger, his eyes wide open and no longer clouded. He was carefully helped down into the hole and a tree of equal stature was placed in it beside him. The rooster, protesting, was again passed over Luis' body and the incantations begun again, concluding at last with Madame Souffrant calling out in a ringing, down-to-earth voice, "I demand that you return the life of this man. . . . I, Souffrant, demand the life of this man. I buy for cash—I pay you—I owe nothing!"

With this she grasped a jug, poured its contents over Luis' head, broke it with a blow of her fist and let the pieces fall into the hole. She was still chanting as Luis was pulled out of the hole. The rooster was placed inside it instead, and buried alive at the foot of the tree.

The ritual was not over yet but Pruden's gaze was fixed on Luis now, who was being helped into a long white gown. He stood unsupported; his skin had color again and his eyes were bright, no longer haunted. It was unbelievable when Pruden remembered the prostrate, gray-faced, nearly lifeless man he'd seen lying on the earth only a little while ago.

"He will remain here now near the sacred peristyle for several days," said Madame Karitska briskly. "If the tree dies, Luis will live. If the tree lives, Luis will die. Only when this is known will he leave, dead or alive."

"Yes," said Pruden, still bemused.

"Are you all right?" she asked sharply.

He pulled himself together with an effort. "Of course I'm all right. We can leave now?"

She nodded, and they walked back to his car. As they drove away he said, "Okay, explain."

"Madame Souffrant would be the better person to ask," she pointed out. "I can only tell you what she discovered when she visited Luis in his room. She is, you know, a detective in her own way."

"Oh?" His voice was sardonic.

"She found what she called a 'disaster lamp' buried in the Malone back yard," continued Madame Karitska. "We went out, all of us, and in a corner of the yard under a tree it was obvious that digging had taken place within the last week." Madame Karitska added distastefully, "I must say the lamp was a disaster in itself when we dug it up. It smelled terribly. Madame Souffrant said it contained the gall bladder of an ox, soot, lime juice, and castor oil."

"All right, but how would Luis know it was there?" demanded Pruden.

"Exactly," said Madame Karitska. "Someone obviously had to tell him it was there, or add to it some other type of symbol that was terrifying to Luis. Madame Souffrant's guess was that graveyard dust was sent him through the mail, or left on his doorstep. It would have to be someone who knew he was a believer. In any case Luis felt he was doomed and that the gods of the cemetery had taken him."

"Well, I can't say it's nonsense any longer," Pruden admitted. "I saw how ill he was, and I saw his resurrection."

Madame Karitska said quietly, "When one believes—what is this, after all, but the demonic side of faith?"

Already the memory of the *oum'phor* was receding, releasing him from its spell so that Pruden said almost angrily, "It goes against everything believable, a man dooming himself to die."

Madame Karitska said dryly, "Yet you are witnessing precisely this. You forget that everything that makes a person human is invisible: his thoughts, his emotions, his soul. You forget that electricity is invisible, too, and can kill."

"Okay—the invisible can kill. *Maybe.*" He pulled up in front of her apartment and opened the door for her. "It's late."

She nodded. "Nearly midnight," she said with a sigh. "I left a sign on my door saying that I would be back at twelve and—*voilà*—I am back at twelve. But not the right twelve," she added, "and I shall wonder how many clients I lost today."

"Well," Pruden told her with a faint smile, "if you find your cupboard bare, give me a call and I'll take you to dinner. But a very quick one," he added, "because I'm probably losing my mind but tomorrow I plan to begin looking for someone who wants the Mendez brothers out of the way."

"Thank you," she said simply, and he watched her walk up the steps to her apartment looking as regal and grand as if she were returning from the opera.

In the morning his early call reached Mrs. Materas, the wife of the distributor. Her husband had the flu, she said, but they worked together and she knew everything that he did. She would be glad to meet him at the office if he didn't mind waiting until she'd gone to church: the church was only two blocks from their office.

Pruden was there at twelve-thirty, and he sat down with Mrs. Materas and proceeded to learn rather a lot about the ice-cream-truck business, and Jack Frost in particular. The parent company, Mrs. Materas explained, was in Rosewood Heights, New Jersey, with franchised distributors in thirty-five states. Her husband had been a vendor for years but had bought his franchise fourteen years ago. It was a good business. "Hectic but good," she said. "We have ninety-four Jack Frost trucks working Trafton. They keep the trucks in our garages down the street, and we sell them all the ingredients as well as napkins, cones, paper cups, and plastic spoons. We also help them finance their trucks."

"Any trouble lately on the routes?" Pruden asked.

"Oh no," she said, "we've never had any trouble. I know a couple of other companies had difficulties a few years ago but we've never had any."

"Any of your trucks move in the Dell section?"

She shook her head. "That's Mr. Freezee territory. Our trucks operate only in the city proper."

"Who decides all this?" he asked with interest.

She laughed. "Whoever gets there first, that's who. We happened to be first in the city, that's all, and never got around to expanding into the Dell section. Here, I'll show you." She walked over to the open door, closed it and showed him a map thumbtacked to the wall. "As you can see—"

Pruden walked over and looked at the map. The Jack Frost territories were colored in pink, the competition routes in green. He said, "The green areas, what companies have those routes?"

"Mr. Freezee."

"I thought you said Mr. Freezee had only the Dell section?"

"Oh, they started there," Mrs. Materas explained, "but over the past several years they've been expanding. Buying out other suburban territories here and there."

"For cash?"

Mrs. Materas shrugged. "I really couldn't tell you. Some of those small independents often run into debt the first year and sell out cheap."

Pruden nodded, his face thoughtful. He wondered whether Mrs. Materas had noticed lately that Jack Frost was now completely encircled by Mr. Freezee; almost, he thought, like a noose. "Well, thanks," he said. "I appreciate your help. One other question: have you many Puerto Rican drivers?"

She thought a moment. "A fair number, maybe 30 per cent. They're good workers. Ambitious. You can't explain why—?"

"Not yet," he said with a friendly smile, "but one day I will."

He went next to see Maria Ardizzone again, because he was remembering her hesitation when he'd asked if anything in particular had upset Luis just before he became ill. It had been a very slight hesitation but he'd caught it and he decided it was time to find out whether it meant anything. When he looked up her home address he found that she lived at Mrs. Malone's boardinghouse, which explained how she and Luis had met when the Mendez brothers worked such long hours.

Her room was smaller than his, and at the top of the house, and hot. It was the sort of room that he might have expected if he'd sat down first to consider her character: she had taken it ambitiously in hand, as she would Luis if he lived, and she had painted and slip-covered and decorated until it looked like one of those magazine photo stories captioned "Turning-an-Attic-Room-into-an-Apartment." There was a great deal of white shag everywhere and black-and-white flowered cloth, and fat red pillows, and little glass-topped tables. Pruden, who liked to see the bones of a room—bare floors and furniture—thought it rather suffocating but he admitted that it was as pretty as Maria.

He found her upset. "I just don't understand about this voodoo business. Luis went with me to church every Sunday," she complained in a worried voice. "I'm a Roman Catholic and he said he was too. He never mentioned any—any *voodoo* cults."

He agreed that it could be rather a shock.

"And then to hear—I can't even see him," she protested, looking suddenly very young.

"He was better last night. I saw him."

"But *I* wanted to make him better," she said simply. "I was praying hard for him."

"Then I think your prayers must have—well, brought him the people who *could* help. Do you still want to help him?"

Her eyes widened. "But of course! Oh, you mustn't think it's made any difference. It's just I don't understand why he didn't tell me."

Pruden said gently, "He might have felt a little embarrassed, you know, or thought he'd lose you. You're not Puerto Rican, are you?"

She thought about this and appeared to appreciate it. "That's true."

"So let's get down to facts." Pruden seated himself in a chair that brought his knees almost to his chin, got up and moved to the couch, which placed a more sustaining weight under him. "You hesitated when I asked if Luis had been upset by anything before he became sick."

"Oh, that," sniffed Maria. "Such a small thing, and yet—and yet you know it was the only time I've ever seen him look—well, so *changed*. Arturo's death made him sad—he cried, you know, but this—"

"Tell me."

She nodded. "It was the day after Arturo's burial and Luis had only just gone back to work. I came downstairs—we were going to go for a walk—and I saw a man on the stairs below me. Luis was standing in the door of his room watching the man leave and he had this funny look on his face, as if he'd been hit in the stomach. For about ten minutes after that he wasn't himself—very quiet, not listening—and then we went out to a movie and after that he was fine."

"Had the man been in Luis' room?"

"Yes, but Luis didn't say why. I thought it must have been a friend of Arturo's come to pay his respects."

"You don't know who the man was?"

Maria shook her head.

"Could you describe him?"

"Oh no," she said, "I saw only his back. Maybe Mrs. Malone saw him, though. She's very fussy about keeping the front door locked. Everybody has to ring the bell if they don't have a key."

"I'll go down and ask," he said, and thanked her.

Mrs. Malone, unearthed in the kitchen, wiped her hands on her apron and thought about Pruden's question. "Someone to see Luis . . ." she repeated gravely. "Well, I can't think who that would be, since Luis didn't get callers, if you know what I mean." Her brow suddenly lifted. "Oh yes, I remember. A young man, right after dinner. Asked me to tell Luis that Carlos wanted to see him. Yes, that was his name, Carlos. . . . I told him I was busy and he'd have to find Luis himself, second floor front."

"Do you remember what he looked like?"

Mrs. Malone closed her eyes. "Black hair and mustache. Good-looking young man, twenty-five or twenty-six. What I'd call a sharp dresser. Bright colors. Sharp."

"What sort of mustache?"

"Oh, the dashing kind. You know what they're wearing these days."

Pruden nodded and wrote it down. "Thanks, Mrs. Malone," he said, and went out to telephone Bill Kane, who was off duty today but had patrolled Fifth Street for three years and might recognize the description. He read it to Kane over the phone.

"Sounds like Carlos Torres," Kane said cautiously. "Hangs out a lot at the Caballeros Social Club."

This was better luck than Pruden had expected. "Any visible means of employment?"

Kane sighed into the telephone. "I don't really know, Lieutenant. At least he's never done anything antisocial, to my knowledge. Knows a lot of people. Could be a bookie, I suppose, but frankly I've never seen him up to anything suspicious. Gets around a lot, now that you mention it. Nice, polite, bright-eyed guy. Neat and sociable."

"Mmmm," murmured Pruden, and decided he would ask for a tail on Mr. Carlos Torres just to see where his getting around took him.

Twenty-four hours later, by Monday night, Pruden had a neat list of what Carlos Torres had done with his Sabbath evening and with the first day of the new week. It was an interesting list: Kane was right, the young man got around. His tail had picked him up at four-thirty on Sunday when he was walking with a girl named Esperita. He'd returned the girl to her house and stopped at the Hy-Grade Laundry, where overtime was going on in the rear section. He'd had dinner at the Grand Hotel, a decent place on Seventh Street where he lived in a rented room on the ground floor. While he'd been eating a man had stopped to talk to him for fifteen minutes, followed by another, who had coffee with him. Then Carlos had picked up another girl—a blonde this time named Carol—and had taken her to a movie. After that he'd strolled up to a shop at 1023 Broad Street, gone down an alley next to the shop, knocked on a door and gone inside. One hour later he returned to his hotel. His lights had gone out at midnight.

In the morning he'd taken the subway to the Dell section, where he'd gone to a business building and entered the offices of one Harold Robichaud, Amusement Enterprises, Inc. He'd then gone on to the office of a John Tortorelli, attorney-at-law, also in the Dell section, and at noon was back at 1023 Broad Street again, this time entering the shop (The Bazaar Curio Shop, Everything Bizarre) by the front door. After another visit to the Hy-Grade Laundry he was now at the Caballeros Social Club again, this time with a redhead named Marcia.

Bookie? thought Pruden. Messenger? Go-between? Wheeler-dealer? The name of Tortorelli was vaguely familiar. He asked for a run-down on Harold Robichaud and John Tortorelli and decided to pay a visit to 1023 Broad Street, which was one item on the list he could check out immediately.

He found the Bazaar Curio Shop a shabby but perfectly respectable little shop; in fact he'd noticed it a number of times in passing because of the carved masks displayed in a window. One window held rather good-quality secondhand books—Pruden guessed that this had been the shop's original purpose—while the right-hand window contained masks and figurines as well as a small assortment of necklaces and rings from Africa and the Orient. Small gold-leaf letters on the door announced that R. Ramon was the proprietor.

Pruden walked inside and nodded to the man who glanced up from a ledger at the counter. There was no one else in the shop. "Good morning," said Pruden.

"Morning, sir." The voice was courteous and pleasing to the ear. "Please feel free to browse, but if there's anything you wish—" He left the rest unspoken.

As he thanked the man and turned toward the masks, Pruden gave his face a quick glance and filed it away in his memory. It was a singularly homely face, he thought, yet not an unpleasant one: wire spectacles with very thick lenses, a thin wide mouth, receding chin, and receding hairline. He looked strangely like a frog with extended, magnified eyes, and in some odd way he appeared very much at home among the bizarre and the exotic, like a highly glazed, porcelain gargoyle set down among the other oddities. As Pruden examined masks, his back to the counter, he could feel the man watching him. He turned and said briskly, "Have you a card? I'm completely lost among all this but I've an uncle who collects this sort of thing. He'd go mad here."

"Oh, one hopes not," said the man gently. "Yes, I've cards." He indicated a neat stack of them beside his cash register and Pruden walked over and took one. "And you're Mr. Ramon?" he asked, reading it.

"Yes."

Pruden nodded, tucked the card in his pocket, and turned toward the books, running a finger casually over their spines like a man trying to memorize titles for a nonexistent uncle. Many of them dealt with the occult but there were also musty volumes on colonial history, herbs, theology, and American Indians. With a final nod he walked out of the store, closed the door behind him and continued up the street. So much for that, he thought, and walked back to headquarters to see what might have turned up on Robichaud and Tortorelli.

He need not have worried: there was plenty, all of it very interesting indeed.

An hour later, after digesting the reports brought to him, Pruden walked into his superior's office with a puzzled frown. He said, "Look, have there been any signs lately that the Syndicate might be moving into the Puerto Rican section in Trafton?"

Startled, the Chief said, "What have you come up with?"

"Some interesting coincidences."

His superior sighed. "That's how it usually starts: whispers, echoes, rumors and coincidences. I don't know why the hell they'd want to move in on Fifth Street, though, they had a rough enough time getting into the black section. At least five of their men turned up in alleys with knives in their backs and they ended up making a deal with Bones Jackson, didn't they?"

"Maybe they learned something," said Pruden. "Maybe they're going about this in a different way, staying out and letting Puerto Ricans take over." He slipped two sheets of paper on the Chief's desk. "I had a tail put on one Carlos Torres yesterday, for reasons so microscopic it would be embarrassing to explain, but damned if he doesn't seem to be leading me into Syndicate territory. I may be wrong but I think something's up."

He sat down and watched the Chief's face and was not surprised to see it change when he reached the second paragraph. "Tortorelli! He's certainly Syndicate—their best lawyer. And Robichaud..." He scowled. "That name rings a bell."

Pruden nodded. "You'll find him on the next page. You remember the ice-cream-truck war in the Dell section two years ago? The original distributors lost the battle, filed for bankruptcy, and Robichaud Amusement Enterprises very kindly came along, bought them out, and took over the Mr. Freezee business there."

The Chief whistled softly. "And I see that Tortorelli handled the purchase. We suspected the Syndicate connection but this Tortorelli involvement was kept damned quiet."

Pruden nodded. "Some crusading news reporter uncovered it a year ago when doing a piece on Tortorelli."

"How does this Carlos Torres fit into this?"

Pruden hesitated. "An ice-cream vendor here in Trafton died ten days ago under strange circumstances. A Jack Frost vendor, Puerto Rican, no enemies. Now his brother, who also owns a Jack Frost ice-cream truck, isn't expected to live out the week."

The Chief's brows shot up. "But he's still alive? What does he say? You've talked to him?"

"He's—uh—unconscious," said Pruden. "However, the only person to visit him at the time was Carlos Torres, which is why I had a tail put on him."

The Chief sat back, eyes narrowed in thought. "And he visits Tortorelli and Robichaud Enterprises. . . . What about the Hy-Grade Laundry?"

"I'm asking around."

The Chief nodded. "I don't like the sound of it, frankly. You'd better turn over whatever else you're working on to Benson. Go after this full-time and let me know what you need."

"I could certainly use Swope if he's available," said Pruden.

"You've got him. Anything else?"

Pruden stood up and walked to the door and then with one hand on the knob he suddenly grinned, a sense of mischief overtaking him. "Well, I wouldn't mind hearing that a certain willow tree on Third Street—that ought to be a banana tree—has shriveled up and died." He went out, gently closing the door behind him.

Leaving headquarters at five o'clock that same day, Pruden hesitated on the step and then instead of climbing into his car he turned left and began walking toward Eighth Street. He found Madame

Karitska at home, with Gavin curled up on her couch with his homework.

"My dear Lieutenant," said Madame Karitska, "you look badly in need of coffee. Nothing so anemic as your American brew but something to fortify you. I will also prepare you a cucumber sandwich."

"Aren't you supposed to be at St. Bonaventure's?" Pruden asked, throwing himself into the chair opposite Gavin.

The boy grinned. "It's okay. I came over to see Madame Karitska on Saturday but she wasn't here, so the school said I could come tonight instead. Now that I'm an orphan, you know, they give me special privileges."

"Which of course you refuse," Pruden said with a smile.

"Not if I can help it," grinned Gavin. "Have you found out who killed Arturo yet, and made Luis sick? Madame Karitska's been explaining why she wasn't here Saturday when I came."

"No, but I've been finding out a hell of a—excuse me, a heck of a lot of other things."

"Such as what, may I ask?" said Madame Karitska, returning from the kitchen with a tray.

"Well, for one thing," confessed Pruden, "I have to swallow my considerable pride and admit this isn't the small neighborhood affair I thought it would be last Saturday night. My apologies to you," he added, picking up a sandwich, "but I honestly didn't think it would amount to more than an ex-boy friend of Maria's, or a neighbor who was jealous of Arturo's success. Now it looks like the biggest case I've tackled yet."

"The Syndicate! Holy cow!" said Gavin, eyes widening. "You know about the Syndicate, don't you, Madame Karitska?"

She seated herself on the couch beside Gavin and inserted a cigarette into a long holder. "It is, I believe, very organized crime?"

"*Very* organized crime," Pruden said dryly. "And not, I might add, a group that usually dabbles in voodoo. We've been working our tails off today and it looks as if for some reason they're after the Jack Frost ice-cream business here in Trafton."

Madame Karitska laughed. "What a strange thing to be after!"

He nodded. "Both Arturo and Luis drove ice-cream trucks, remember? Here, look at the facts," he said, and brought from his pocket a condensed list of Carlos Torres' activities. Handing it to Madame Karitska he said, "Two years ago in the Dell section there was what came to be known in the media as the 'ice-cream war.' One of the vendors was kidnapped and then released, three ice-cream trucks were bombed on the streets, and the Mr. Freezee garages broken into and expensive machinery stolen or destroyed. This went on for six or eight weeks and then suddenly stopped."

"You were not told why?" asked Madame Karitska.

"No, but one looks for patterns. In this case, shortly after the turbulence ended the Mr. Freezee distributorship was taken over by Harold Robichaud of Amusement Enterprises. We know nothing about him except that he bought it, but about the attorney who handled the purchase we know a great deal. His name is John Tortorelli and he's a Syndicate man."

Madame Karitska frowned. "But you are speaking of the past, of something that happened two years ago."

"Yes, but we begin to suspect the scenario is about to be repeated."

"And this Carlos Torres?" asked Madame Karitska, glancing through the memo. "Who is this Carlos Torres?"

"He paid a call on Luis twelve hours before Luis took to his bed. In fact he was the only stranger who ever paid a call on Mendez. He lives just off Fifth Street and he's Puerto Rican."

"Ah," murmured Madame Karitska. "A link—I see . . . and he led you to these others? But this Tortorelli and Robichaud . . . do they seem to you the sort of men learned in voodoo?"

Pruden laughed. "Absolutely not, but we'll get to that eventually."

"This Carlos Torres then, perhaps he would kill by voodoo?"

"Carlos?" He shook his head. "Not likely."

Madame Karitska said with a hint of exasperation in her voice, "You are no longer investigating what has happened to the Mendez brothers, then?"

Pruden sighed. "Look, you're missing the point. This has broadened into Syndicate stuff. It's big, bigger than the Mendez brothers. It could turn into the biggest case I've uncovered."

She said gently, "On the contrary, I think *you* are missing the point, Lieutenant. You speak of patterns and scenarios and what took place two years ago but you do not see that suddenly a very original mind has become involved now. The past is *not* repeating itself. You speak of bombings and kidnappings, but someone has entered the picture who side-steps physical violence. Now there is violence against the spirit. One cannot help but admire the originality, do you not agree? The perfect crime."

"You keep saying that," he said crossly, and gave her a resentful glance. He was tired and he had expected approval, even admiration;

instead she insisted on returning him to Luis Mendez, who was only a link to something greater.

"You do not feel," she went on crisply, "that the mind of a man who could conceive of such a murder is infinitely more subtle, infinitely more sophisticated and dangerous than your Syndicate criminal?"

"We're only starting," he pointed out defensively. "It'll all unwind like a spool of thread. Luis is still alive, isn't he?"

"Yes," she said, "but so is the willow tree, and gives every evidence of remaining alive. Why do you believe they want the Jack Frost ice-cream business, or any ice-cream business?"

"We don't know yet but we'll find out."

"This Ramon," Madame Karitska said, glancing at the list. "You have looked into him too?"

"Oh yes. No record. Clean as a whistle," said Pruden, and was glad to have the subject changed. "I visited his shop first thing this morning."

"Yes?"

"You'd love it," he told her with a smile. "Books on the supernatural, books on haunted houses. Some spectacular hand-carved masks from Africa and South America."

"Hey, I'd love to have one of those," Gavin said eagerly. "Could you take me on Saturday, Madame Karitska? The kids would get a real bang out of something wild hanging on our dorm wall."

She smiled at him. "I will take you on Saturday, yes, but I think I may stop in there tomorrow to first make certain it is—how do you say?—okay for a young boy?"

"She's tough," Gavin said to Pruden, nodding. "She doesn't want me to know about porno and all that."

"She's not tough, she's cagey," said Pruden, finishing his coffee and standing up. "She'll walk in and check out Mr. Ramon for you, admire the ring he's wearing, ask to hold it, and tell us later what he eats every day for breakfast."

But it was not a ring that Madame Karitska succeeded in holding when she visited the Bazaar Curio Shop on Tuesday afternoon; it was a fountain pen, and it was only with considerable finesse that she managed this. When she arrived at the shop there were already several customers there, and Madame Karitska moved quietly among the books, from time to time glancing covertly at the man behind the counter. A strange little man, she thought. He gave every evidence of being amiable but she came to the conclusion that of all the masks on display in the shop, his was the most formidable. In the meantime she waited, and when the others had gone she moved toward the counter carrying a copy of Crowley's *Magick in Theory and Practice*. She had moved quietly and Ramon's back was turned. She reached for the pen he had been writing with and it was in her hand when he turned and looked at her. Their glances met and locked, and Madame Karitska found it necessary to steady herself against the counter.

He said softly, "You will put down my pen."

She placed the pen back on the counter.

"Thank you," he said and with an amused glance at the book in her hand he said, "Aleister Crowley, I see. . . . You're interested in black magic, perhaps?"

"Perhaps."

But he had lost interest, and his mask was back again. "It will be seven-fifty, please," he said.

She paid him, took the book, and walked out, her heart beating very quickly. She felt curiously drained of energy, as if recovering from a bout of fever that had left her nerves trembling and her body weak. She went at once to a telephone booth and dialed Pruden's number. When he answered she said, "Lieutenant, I think you should—I think you must—check out Mr. Ramon again."

"Is this Madame Karitska?" he said. "Your voice sounds changed. Look, I'm in the middle of a conference but if you can explain—"

A wave of nausea swept her; she dropped the receiver and stumbled outside, Pruden's voice following her through the open door. Outside she stood drawing in deep breaths of air, her hands trembling as she clung to the door for support. It was necessary for her to remain there several minutes before she felt well enough to return the receiver of the phone to its hook and to begin her walk back to Eighth Street.

Pruden found Madame Karitska's call frustrating, coming as it did in the middle of a planning session with the Chief, Swope, Benson, and a man named Callahan. He said, "Excuse me a minute," and called Madame Karitska back at her apartment, but when there was no answer he hung up and turned back to the others. "All right, tell me what you found out about the Hy-Grade Laundry," he asked Swope.

"Something very interesting."

"Let's hear it."

"Right." Swope picked up his reading glasses and put them on. "Back in November of last year there was an explosion at the laundry."

"Bomb?"

"No, the investigators traced it to a boiler, but the odd thing is that the owners sold out after it happened, and rather fast. It wasn't a bomb, it was a boiler blowing up and yet they sold."

"Sabotage?"

"It has that smell," said Swope. "A boiler doesn't need a bomb to blow it up—there are a dozen things you can do to accomplish the same thing—but in any case they sold. Now it's under new management, a family named Torres, and guess who the youngest son is."

Pruden felt a prickling of excitement. "Carlos?"

"You've just won the box of Crackerjacks. And," he added, "the attorney who handled the purchase was John Tortorelli."

"Good Lord," said Pruden. "The Syndicate *is* moving in."

"Looks like it. Same pattern."

"I don't get it," said Callahan, baffled. "The Syndicate goes where the money is, and I wouldn't have thought there was anything to tempt them around Fifth Street. Of course there's crime there—gambling, drugs, prostitution, numbers—but it's all small-time, petty. Nothing worth organizing."

"Looks like it's getting organized now," Pruden said grimly. "I take it the laundry is headquarters, and Carlos their bag man. What's the latest on him, by the way?"

The Chief handed him a sheet of paper. "Same pattern. He moves between his hotel, the laundry, Robichaud, Tortorelli, and the Caballeros Club."

"So what do we do?" asked Benson.

Pruden said, "I'd like to see Robichaud and Tortorelli placed on round-the-clock surveillance, informers rounded up and questioned, and a camera put on the Hy-Grade Laundry twenty-four hours a day."

"We've already got Jack the Lip downstairs," Benson said. "The guys thought you'd want to question him, although Jack insists he doesn't know anything about a Syndicate moving into Fifth Street."

Pruden nodded and rose. "I'll go down and see what I can get out of him. I don't," he said wearily, "think we're going to get much sleep for the next few days."

"So what else is new?" asked the Chief in a kindly voice.

It was seven o'clock before Pruden finished interviewing the handful of informants that had been brought in, and the only thing he'd learned was that an ice-cream vendor out in the northern section of Trafton had been taken ill and was dying. He was a Jack Frost man, and his name was Raphael Alvarez, and he was six months out of Puerto Rico. "Enough to give a guy the whammies," the informant said with a shiver. "Just says he's going to die and lies there."

Like Luis, he thought. . . . It reminded Pruden of Luis and then of Madame Karitska's aborted phone call during the afternoon. She'd said Ramon ought to be checked again—that much he'd heard, and then they'd been cut off before she could explain why. He stood on the steps at headquarters debating whether to eat, grab a few hours' sleep, or visit the Bazaar Shop.

Swope, coming up behind him, said, "Where you off to now, Lieutenant?"

Pruden made his decision. "I think I'll just take a look at the Bazaar Shop again. Look around a bit. Care to come along?"

"Why not?" said Swope affably, falling into step beside him as he began walking. "I told the wife she wouldn't be seeing much of me for a few days. Place is closed, though, isn't it?"

Pruden nodded. "Yes, but on Sunday night it was closed and Torres went around to the back. I thought—"

"I dig," said Swope. "How much farther?"

"Next block, on the left."

As they neared the store a small truck passed them and slowed down, signaling a turn to the left. Its sides were painted bright scarlet; in gold carousel script were printed the words BAZAAR CURIO SHOP—Everything Bizarre—1023 Broad Street, R. Ramon, Prop. The van turned into the alleyway beside the shop and disappeared.

"Not altogether closed," pointed out Swope.

"No," said Pruden.

Crossing the street they reached the alley in time to see the scarlet truck park in the dilapidated garage at the end of the driveway. Two young men climbed out, picked up their caps and lunch boxes and began walking down the alley toward the street. "Hey," one of them said sharply, turning and pointing, and his companion hurried back to the garage and swung the doors closed; then they continued out to Broad Street, passing Pruden and Swope, and walked up the street and turned the corner.

"They didn't lock those doors. I wouldn't mind taking a look inside," Pruden said hopefully.

"It does seem like a gift from heaven," agreed Swope. "Let's go."

The layout of the building was surprisingly simple: it had once been an old house to which the shop had been added in the front. The rear contained a yard, a side porch, a garage, and all the accouterments of a conventional frame house, including an ancient apple tree. No lights shone in the windows; the place looked deserted. They very casually swung open one unlocked garage door and slipped inside.

Swope, testing the back doors of the van, said, "Locked."

Pruden peered into the front seat of the truck. There was a bunk behind the driver's seat for sleeping on long trips, but the wall behind it was windowless and seemed to be solid, with no point of entry into the storage behind it. He decided to climb inside and make certain of this, and had one foot on the floor of the garage and the other in the cab of the truck when he lost his balance and fell against the door.

Behind him he heard Swope exclaim, "What the hell!"

Pruden, looking down, realized to his astonishment that the floor of the garage was moving. He regained his balance, looked for Swope, and found him several feet above him: the garage doors were suddenly at a level with his waist as the floor slowly descended like an elevator. Swope had jumped clear and was standing in the doorway. He shouted, "For God's sake jump, Lieutenant!"

Pruden stood paralyzed, wanting to run, wanting to join Swope, but wanting also to see what the hell lay below him. A moment later his decision was made for him as the threshold of the garage doors passed out of sight. Pruden turned back to the door of the van, climbed inside and crawled up on the sleeping shelf. There were several blankets piled in one end: he curled up in a corner and drew the blankets over him.

The descent of the truck slowed, and he and the truck emerged into a lighted room below. He heard a low murmur of voices and the clink of keys unlocking the rear of the van. Two men jumped inside; he could hear the hollow sound of their feet walking around a few feet away from him, separated only by the wall against which he lay. A dolly was wheeled up, objects began being unloaded, and then came a new sound: a hammering on the sides of the truck.

"Okay, Carlos, bring the Freezee signs," a man shouted, and the sides of the truck were assaulted again. Pruden kept himself small and quiet as he drew certain conclusions: Carlos Torres was here, and signs were being switched. An old hijacking trick, he reflected, but what did it mean? They'd mentioned Freezee signs. Presumably the Bazaar Shop truck would drive away as a Mr. Freezee delivery truck, but why, and with what?

A loud, irritating buzzer interrupted the hammering.

"Trouble at the back door," a man called sharply, and Pruden heard footsteps racing away into the distance, echoing as if in a hall of some kind. After listening for a minute he concluded that he was the only person left in the garage. He crawled gingerly down from the bunk and stuck his head out of the door and looked around him. He was in a very neat underground cement-walled room with an exit that led up a long ramp-like hall, dimly lighted, to three doors at the end. He guessed that the ramp connected with the basement of Ramon's house and shop.

Stealthily Pruden emerged and crept around to one side of the truck: it was still a blaze of scarlet, with BAZAAR CURIO SHOP emblazoned on it in gold. He walked around to the other side and was met with a blue panel and jagged white letters that read MR. FREEZEE. Neat, he thought, very neat. He moved around to the back of the truck and bent over the cartons that had been removed from the van and were stacked on the dolly. Drawing out his penknife he slit open the top of one and looked inside.

The box held Mr. Freezee popsicles.

He thought it damned careless of them to abandon the load here when ice cream melted so fast, and then he realized there was no dry ice anywhere in sight. He looked into the interior of the truck and ran a hand over its walls: this was not a refrigerated truck, and there was no sign of ice here, either. He went back to the carton and drew out a popsicle, pulled aside its blue-and-white wrapping, and examined it. It gave every evidence of being a coconut-cherry popsicle: it was red, and it was flecked with shreds of white, but it was warm to the touch, not cold. He tapped it with a finger; it was plastic.

A plastic popsicle . . . Carefully he knocked it against the side of the dolly and then slipped the wooden stick out of the plastic rectangle. The interior was a honeycomb of thin plastic: in the very center he found a cellophane envelope filled with white powder. He removed it. Tearing aside the cellophane he sniffed the white substance and then wet his finger and placed a few grains on his tongue. It was heroin, no doubt about it.

He thought he'd seen everything during his years on the force but the enormity of this numbed him. It seemed the ultimate insolence, selling drugs on the street from innocent ice-cream trucks, those Pied Pipers of the neighborhood that brought music, bells, and laughter with them on hot mucky days, the one touch of innocence left to kids. The crowds would gather, real ice cream would be exchanged for coins and then a guy with the right password, the right gesture would get this . . . this obscenity.

It filled him with a manic fury. He thought that if Carlos and his friends came back now he would delight in taking them apart one by one. At the same time all his instincts told him to leave now, look for the right switches to the hydraulic lift, crawl into the truck and ride back upstairs into the world again. But he didn't feel wise, he felt incensed and murderous. He looked at the three doors at the far end of the ramp and then he began running up the ramp toward them, not caring whether he was seen or heard. Two of the doors had small windows in them. Through the center door he saw steps leading to the upper floor; behind the left door lay a storage and workshop room with cartons of masks and a carpenter's bench. The door on his right had no windows; he opened it and walked inside.

He had entered some kind of office or study: Ramon's, he decided, because it looked like him. The walls were hung with maps and charts—astrology charts, he guessed—and fierce-looking masks. The center of the room was occupied by a huge desk covered with drawings and diagrams. A small click-click sound troubled him until he moved to the desk and saw that beside it stood a teletype machine. Ramon certainly did himself well, he thought. A second machine in the corner caught his eye and he walked over and discovered it was a computer, an honest-to-God king-sized computer with winking lights.

Then he saw the map of Trafton on the wall behind the computer, a map with every street and alley rendered in detail, and he felt a small chill. In this room incalculable plans were being made for Trafton; he'd stumbled across some kind of command post where something was being plotted and organized for his city. He went back to the desk and studied the papers and charts on its surface. Horoscopes, he saw, staring at a thick sheaf of papers with houses of the zodiac marked off. Beside these lay a pack of tarot cards and over here . . . he peered closer. A list of typed names: Arturo Mendez,

Luis Mendez, Raphael Alvarez . . . He remembered that Alvarez was the name his informant had mentioned tonight. The list was long, and Arturo's name at the top had been crossed off with red ink.

Pruden stood and thought about this. Madame Karitska had said "an original mind," and now he understood at last what she had meant. For the first time he accepted the fact that Arturo Mendez had actually been murdered and that Luis Mendez was in the process of being murdered. Not a finger had been laid on them, but here in this room a man had so clearly understood them and so accurately appraised their fears that he could manipulate their deaths without knowing anything but their history and their culture, and without ever meeting them.

"Clever," he thought, but he knew this word only concealed his unease. It was the potential behind it that disturbed him, it was the troubling sense that if this could happen to two happy, uncomplicated men, then possibly one day in the future it could reach out to him and to others.

He was lost in these thoughts when a voice spoke nearby, a voice oddly calm and almost tender. "Good evening. You realize of course, sir, that you are trespassing?"

Pruden swung around to see Ramon standing in the doorway; he had entered without a sound and stood smiling at him.

"Yes," said Pruden.

"I should, of course, be indignant or alarmed but I never waste energy on unnecessary emotion," Ramon said, the soft light glittering across the lenses of his glasses and rendering them opaque. "And I'm sure you have some suitable explanation." Was there a touch of irony in his voice? "In the meantime I'm certain we can find some practical and pragmatic solution to this confrontation if we use judgment and frankness. I've seen you before, haven't I? You were in my shop yesterday."

Pruden nodded.

"And now you are seeing what I like to think is a modern alchemist's laboratory."

The important thing, Pruden realized, was to stall for time. Swope would know what to do, Swope had seen him disappear, and thank God he'd not come alone. Calls would be going out, patrol cars rerouted, a strategy plotted. *Don't rock the boat*, he told himself, *keep it light, keep him talking.* "You're a student of the occult, I see."

Ramon laughed. "A master. How do you like my little study?"

"A bit weird," Pruden acknowledged. "Unusual, certainly." He could feel Ramon's eyes on him and it was an uncomfortable feeling because he couldn't see the man's eyes and this was even more disquieting.

"I may inquire your name, sir?" Such a gentle voice!

"Pruden."

"Ah yes. Actually, Mr. Pruden, I am a scholar and inventor. At the moment I am consultant to a group that is very interested in my research, which is highly specialized, and they are willing to pay me astronomic sums for certain research studies I've done. Absurd, of course, but I have an IQ of over two hundred, which more than makes up for the fact that I am small, almost deformed in appearance, and nearly blind." He said this softly, his eyes rooted on Pruden as he waited for his response.

"Oh?" said Pruden equally softly, and asked in a neutral voice, "And do you use your—er—research—for good or evil?"

Ramon chuckled. "A conventional question, Mr. Pruden. Power is so often used for evil, is it not? I believe it was Lord Acton who said, 'Power tends to corrupt, and absolute power corrupts absolutely.'"

"What kind of power?" asked Pruden, and decided that he must stop thinking of Swope because he had the uncanny feeling that those opaque eyes could read his mind.

"Power to destroy people." Ramon chuckled. "I could destroy you, Mr. Pruden, very easily, in less than two days. Consider that a compliment, by the way, because most people I could reduce to nothingness in hours, without violence."

"Forgive me if I'm skeptical," Pruden said.

"Oh, I can assure you it's quite possible, and entirely without physical violence of any kind. Every human being has his Achilles' heel psychologically, you see, his own self-image that he nurtures. It would take a little time to discover yours, Mr. Pruden, but you have one. Everyone does. Disturb that image, which is like the skin of a balloon, and following the loud bang there is—why, nothing at all. Or madness," he conceded modestly.

"You use drugs, of course," Pruden said harshly.

Ramon looked shocked. "My dear sir, you miss the point entirely. Of course not. You are a completely conditioned animal, Mr. Pruden, composed of habit, other people's valuations, other people's ideas, opinions, and reactions. What do you have that is yours, untouched by others? Very little. It is more likely that you have no center at all. Human beings are eternally fragmented and highly susceptible to a breakdown of the ego. Statistically, my dear sir, only one man in twenty is a leader, with the capabilities and strengths of a leader. The rest are sheep. The Chinese know this. The North Koreans discovered it for themselves when they brainwashed their captives in the fifties. Destroy that one man and the others prove no problem at all. Almost all human beings are machines, Mr. Pruden. Sleepwalkers without consciousness."

"Sleepwalkers," repeated Pruden, recognizing the phrase.

"But I think we waste time talking here," Ramon confessed with a benevolent smile. "Frankly, a small conference becomes necessary with my employees while we discuss how to solve this unexpected situation. I have never," he added with a disarming smile, "entertained a trespasser before."

"I suppose not," said Pruden.

"I would suggest that you wait in the next room while I discuss this with them. If you would be so kind—"

Pruden shrugged. "I don't mind."

"Good. The door is behind that scarlet curtain over there. You'll find cigarettes there, and a small bar. It's my living room—I can assure you I am quite civilized." Ramon walked to the curtain and drew it aside, exposing an oak door. He opened it, and flicked on the lights. "There is no trickery here, as you can see. We will keep this very brief, Mr. Pruden, with as little suspense for you as possible."

"Yes," said Pruden politely, and wondered if in passing Ramon he could get close enough to reach him but he discovered that the idea of grappling with the man filled him with ennui. He felt curiously tired, sapped of his usual energy. Anyway it had to be time for Swope, he thought. Surely now, surely any minute?

He entered a large room furnished with low couches and tables. There were no windows; instead the walls were hung with soft antique tapestries and fabric, while in the very center of the room a massive Buddha sat smiling down at him. On shelves to his right, behind glass, he saw Chinese porcelains and pieces of jade that could easily have come from a museum. It was all amazing, he thought, a sybaritic underground pied-à-terre. The theme of the room was oriental, soothing and unusual, the motif established by the Buddha, which was taller than he was, carved out of wood—teak, he realized, approaching it with curiosity—and colored with dabs of blue and red.

Abruptly he stopped, thinking *Buddha*.

Blue and red Buddha. Madame Karitska's warning . . . Buddha . . . danger from behind . . .

Pruden whirled just as Ramon fired the gun with a look of hatred and contempt distorting his face. The bullet caught Pruden sideways, he felt a stab of pain radiating through his chest, intense, grinding, unbearable pain and then he slumped to the floor and darkness crashed over him in waves.

Hours, days, weeks later Pruden opened his eyes to a bright ceiling and a feeling of dull uneasy discomfort. Slowly his eyes focused on a bouquet of yellow flowers and he thought, Somewhere between then and now I died. Beyond the flowers he saw a face that struck him as comical but also vaguely familiar: a deeply tanned face with a bristling white mustache and vivid blue eyes. The face rose and drifted nearer. "You're awake," it said. "I'll call the nurse."

"Who," began Pruden.

"Faber-Jones," the voice said. "We've been taking turns sitting with you, Madame Karitska and I."

"Karitska," repeated Pruden, and then as it all came back he said, "There was a Buddha. Tell her there was a Buddha."

"Right," said the voice, and vanished.

"A Buddha," Pruden told the nurse when she appeared in starched white cap. "There was a Buddha."

"Yes, Lieutenant, but take these capsules now. . . . You've been very, very ill, we nearly lost you."

When he swam back to consciousness again the ceiling was dark and the room was in shadow except for one light on a table. Next to the table sat Swope, wearing a rakish white hat.

"Yes, it's me, Lieutenant," Swope said, looking up from a magazine.

"What the hell," said Pruden, staring, "Hat?"

"Hat! This is no hat, it's a bandage," Swope growled. "I just got out of the hospital five days ago and I've got to wear this damn thing until Friday when the last stitches come out. We've both been out of action, Lieutenant, but you gave us a real scare. You've been here two weeks."

This galvanized Pruden. "*How* long?"

"Surgery," Swope said, nodding. "Bullet near your heart. Top man in the country took you apart and put you together again. A quarter of an inch closer and it would have been curtains."

Pruden frowned. "It was in the popsicles," he said abruptly.

Swope nodded. "If you're able to remember how it started I'll tell you how it ended. After you disappeared down that elevator I phoned in a ten-thirteen to headquarters and ran back to find you, except they were waiting for me. Damn near killed me, too. I was unconscious when the Chief got there so it took a while for them to realize you were in trouble too, and then they had to get a search warrant. That's what slowed things up. You don't have to worry about the popsicles, though, they made a clean sweep. The drugs came up from South America in the masks Ramon sold. Came in by truck, went out in popsicles."

A nurse came in and stopped Swope from saying any more. "We don't want to tire him now, do we?"

Pruden loathed her cheerful voice but was nevertheless grateful and immediately fell asleep. When he awoke again his head was clear for the first time and he felt almost himself again. It was late morning, and in the chair beside his bed sat Madame Karitska.

"Well," he said, looking at her.

"Well," she returned, her eyes twinkling at him. "You are quite a hero, Lieutenant, I actually went out and bought newspapers to read about you."

"I met your Buddha, too, you know."

"So Mr. Faber-Jones told me yesterday," she said, nodding. "I am not surprised. That Mr. Ramon—" She shook her head. "Sometime when you are better I shall tell you what I saw in him. Never," she said simply, "have I felt such evil in a man, or encountered such power, such brilliance or such a twisted soul."

"He was like you," Pruden said in a wondering voice. "I mean, he spoke of the same things you do but he had it all twisted, he'd turned it upside down. He *knew*."

"Knew?"

Pruden shivered. "Motives. Weaknesses. People. Most of all people, I think. How to bend and destroy them."

"Satanic," said Madame Karitska, nodding, "but let us not speak of him today, for the sun is shining and you are alive and I have good news for you."

"Good. What is it?"

"The willow tree has died," she said. "It died quite suddenly the morning after you were shot, and Luis is back at work driving his ice-cream truck. As a matter of fact he plans one day to come in personally to thank you, and for this he is learning a speech in English."

"Well, now," he said, pleased, "I'm certainly glad to hear that. In fact if you—" But Pruden's eyes had wandered to the window and he was abruptly silent. Someone had moved the yellow flowers to the window sill, where they were capturing the morning's brilliant sunshine in their petals and creating a blaze of gold. He thought he had never seen such color in his life, nor really looked at a flower before, and he could feel tears rising to his eyes at the impact of their beauty. A simple bouquet of daffodils in a white pottery vase. . . . He had always assumed white was colorless but in the snow-like pottery he could trace reflections of yellow, and one tender blue shadow that exactly matched the blue of the sky beyond the flowers. "My God," he said in astonishment, "I'm alive. I don't think I ever understood before what it means."

"Ah," said Madame Karitska.

"Those flowers. Did you notice them, do you see the sun in them?"

"Tell me," she said, watching him closely.

"They're alive, too, in the most incredible—" He stopped, his voice unsteady. "I sound like a nut."

She shook her head. Very softly she said, "I think the patterns in the kaleidoscope have shifted a little for you, my dear Lieutenant. You have heard the expression that to nearly lose your life is to find it? You will be changed, perhaps. Aware."

"Is that what life is?"

"It is what it *can* be," she said, "Seeing, really seeing, and then at last—at last the understanding." She rose and picked up her purse and smiled down at him. "As the French say, 'One must draw back in order to leap the better.' My French grows rusty, how do they phrase it? '*Il faut reculer pour mieux sauter.*' Rest well, my friend, I will see you again tomorrow."

The Oracle of the Dog

by G. K. Chesterton

"Yes," said Father Brown, "I always like a dog, so long as he isn't spelt backwards."

Those who are quick in talking are not always quick in listening. Sometimes even their brilliancy produces a sort of stupidity. Father Brown's friend and companion was a young man with a stream of ideas and stories, an enthusiastic young man named Fiennes, with eager blue eyes and blond hair that seemed to be brushed back, not merely with a hair-brush but with the wind of the world as he rushed through it. But he stopped in the torrent of his talk in a momentary bewilderment before he saw the priest's very simple meaning.

"You mean that people make too much of them?" he said. "Well, I don't know. They're marvelous creatures. Sometimes I think they know a lot more than we do."

Father Brown said nothing, but continued to stroke the head of the big retriever in a half-abstracted but apparently soothing fashion.

"Why," said Fiennes, warming again to his monologue, "there was a dog in the case I've come to see you about; what they call the 'Invisible Murder Case,' you know. It's a strange story, but from my point of view the dog is about the strangest thing in it. Of course, there's the mystery of the crime itself, and how old Druce can have been killed by somebody else when he was all alone in the summer-house—"

The hand stroking of the dog stopped for a moment in its rhythmic movement; and Father Brown said calmly, "Oh, it was a summer-house, was it?"

"I thought you'd read all about it in the papers," answered Fiennes. "Stop a minute; I believe I've got a cutting that will give you all the particulars." He produced a strip of newspaper from his pocket and handed it to the priest, who began to read it, holding it close to his blinking eyes with one hand while the other continued its half-conscious caresses of the dog. It looked like the parable of a man not letting his right hand know what his left hand did.

"Many mystery stories, about men murdered behind locked doors and windows, and murderers escaping without means of entrance and exit, have come true in the course of the extraordinary events at Cranston on the coast of Yorkshire, where Colonel Druce was found stabbed from behind by a dagger that has entirely disappeared from the scene, and apparently even from the neighborhood.

"The summer-house in which he died was indeed accessible at one entrance, the ordinary doorway which looked down the central walk of the garden towards the house. But by a combination of events almost to be called a coincidence, it appears that both the path and the entrance were watched during the crucial time, and there is a chain of witnesses who confirm each other. The summer-house stands at the extreme end of the garden, where there is no exit or entrance of any kind. The central garden path is a lane between two ranks of tall delphiniums, planted so close that any stray step off the path would leave its traces; and both path and plants run right up to the very mouth of the summer-house, so that no straying from that straight path could fail to be observed, and no other mode of entrance can be imagined.

"Patrick Floyd, secretary of the murdered man, testified that he had been in a position to overlook the whole garden from the time when Colonel Druce last appeared alive in the doorway to the time when he was found dead; as he, Floyd, had been on the top of a step-ladder clipping the garden hedge. Janet Druce, the dead man's daughter, confirmed this, saying that she had sat on the terrace of the house throughout that time and had seen Floyd at his work. Touching some part of the time, this is again supported by Donald Druce, her brother, who overlooked the garden standing at his bedroom window in his dressing-gown, for he had risen late. Lastly the account is consistent with that given by Dr. Valentine, a neighbor, who called for a time to talk with Miss Druce on the terrace, and by the Colonel's solicitor, Mr. Aubrey Traill, who was apparently the last to see the murdered man, presumably with the exception of the murderer.

"All are agreed that the course of events was as follows: about half-past three in the afternoon, Miss Druce went down the path to ask her father when he would like tea; but he said he did not want any and was waiting to see Traill, his lawyer, who was to be sent to him in the summer-house. The girl then came away and met Traill coming down the path; she directed him to her father and he went in as directed. About half an hour afterwards he came out again, the Colonel coming with him to the door and showing himself to all appearances in health and even high spirits. He had been somewhat annoyed earlier in the day by his son's irregular hours, but seemed to recover his temper in a perfectly normal fashion, and had been rather markedly genial in receiving other visitors, including two of his nephews who came over for the day. But as these were out walking during the whole period of the tragedy, they had no evidence to give. It is said, indeed, that the Colonel was not on very good terms with Dr. Valentine, but that gentleman only had a brief interview with the daughter of the house, to whom he is supposed to be paying serious attentions.

"Traill, the solicitor, says he left the Colonel entirely alone in the summer-house, and this is confirmed by Floyd's bird's-eye view of the garden, which showed nobody else passing the only entrance. Ten minutes later Miss Druce again went down the garden and had not reached the end of the path, when she saw her father, who was conspicuous by his white linen coat, lying in a heap on the floor. She uttered a scream which brought others to the spot, and on entering the place they found the Colonel lying dead beside his basket-chair, which was also upset. Dr. Valentine, who was still in the immediate neighborhood, testified that the wound was made by some sort of stiletto, entering under the shoulder-blade and piercing the heart. The police have searched the neighborhood for such a weapon, but no trace of it can be found."

"So Colonel Druce wore a white coat, did he?" said Father Brown as he put down the paper.

"Trick he learnt in the tropics," replied Fiennes with some wonder. "He'd had some queer adventures there, by his own account; and I fancy his dislike of Valentine was connected with the doctor coming from the tropics, too. But it's all an infernal puzzle. The account there is pretty accurate; I didn't see the tragedy, in the sense of the discovery; I was out walking with the young nephews and the dog—the dog I wanted to tell you about. But I saw the stage set for it as described: the straight lane between the blue flowers right up to the dark entrance, and the lawyer going down it in his blacks and his silk hat, and the red head of the secretary showing high above the green hedge as he worked on it with his shears. Nobody could have mistaken that red head at any distance; and if people say they saw it there all the time, you may be sure they did. This red-haired secretary Floyd is quite a character; a breathless, bounding sort of fellow, always doing everybody's work as he was doing the gardener's. I think he is an American; he's certainly got the American view of life; what they call the viewpoint, bless 'em."

"What about the lawyer?" asked Father Brown.

There was a silence and then Fiennes spoke quite slowly for him. "Traill struck me as a singular man. In his fine black clothes he was almost foppish, yet you can hardly call him fashionable. For he wore a pair of long, luxuriant black whiskers such as haven't been seen since Victorian times. He had rather a fine grave face and a fine grave manner, but every now and then he seemed to remember to smile. And when he showed his white teeth he seemed to lose a little of his dignity and there was something faintly fawning about him. It may have been only embarrassment, for he would also fidget with his cravat and his tie-pin, which were at once handsome and unusual, like himself. If I could think of anybody—but what's the good, when the whole thing's impossible? Nobody knows who did it. Nobody knows how it could be done. At least there's only one exception I'd make, and that's why I really mentioned the whole thing. The dog knows."

Father Brown sighed and then said absently: "You were there as a friend of young Donald, weren't you? He didn't go on your walk with you?"

"No," replied Fiennes smiling. "The young scoundrel had gone to bed that morning and got up that afternoon. I went with his cousins, two young officers from India, and our conversation was trivial enough. I remember the elder, whose name I think is Herbert Druce and who is an authority on horse breeding, talked about nothing but a mare he had bought and the moral character of the man who sold her; while his brother Harry seemed to be brooding on his bad luck at Monte Carlo. I only mention it to show you, in the light of what happened on our walk, that there was nothing psychic about us. The dog was the only mystic in our company."

"What sort of a dog was he?" asked the priest.

"Same breed as that one," answered Fiennes. "That's what started me off on the story, your saying you didn't believe in believing in a dog. He's a big black retriever named Nox, and a suggestive name too; for I think what he did a darker mystery than the murder. You know Druce's house and garden are by the sea; we walked about a mile from it along the sands and then turned back, going the other way. We passed a rather curious rock called the Rock of Fortune, famous in the neighborhood because it's one of those examples of one stone barely balanced on another, so that a touch would knock it over. It is not really very high, but the hanging outline of it makes it look a little wild and sinister; at least it made it look so to me, for I don't imagine my jolly young companions were afflicted with the picturesque. But it may be that I was beginning to feel an atmosphere; for just then the question arose of whether it was time to go back to tea, and even then I think I had a premonition that time counted for a good deal in the business. Neither Herbert Druce nor I had a watch, so we called out to his brother, who was some paces behind, having stopped to light his pipe under the hedge. Hence it happened that he shouted out the hour, which was twenty past four, in his big voice through the growing twilight; and somehow the loudness of it made it sound like the proclamation of something tremendous. His unconsciousness seemed to make it all the more so; but that was always the way with omens; and particular ticks of the clock were really very ominous things that afternoon. According to Dr. Valentine's testimony, poor Druce had actually died just about half-past four.

"Well, they said we needn't go home for ten minutes, and we walked a little farther along the sands, doing nothing in particular—throwing stones for the dog and throwing sticks into the sea for him to swim after. But to me the twilight seemed to grow oddly oppressive and the very shadow of the top-heavy Rock of Fortune lay on me like a load. And then the curious thing happened. Nox had just brought back Herbert's walking-stick out of the sea and his brother had thrown his in also. The dog swam out again, but just about what must have been the stroke of the half-hour, he stopped swimming. He came back again on to the shore and stood in front of us. Then he suddenly threw up his head and sent up a howl or wail of woe, if ever I heard one in the world.

" 'What the devil's the matter with the dog?' asked Herbert; but none of us could answer. There was a long silence after the brute's wailing and whining died away on the desolate shore; and then the silence was broken. As I live, it was broken by a faint and far-off shriek, like the shriek of a woman from beyond the hedges inland. We didn't know what it was then; but we knew afterwards. It was the cry the girl gave when she first saw the body of her father."

"You went back, I suppose," said Father Brown patiently. "What happened then?"

"I'll tell you what happened then," said Fiennes with a grim emphasis. "When we got back into that garden the first thing we saw was Traill the lawyer; I can see him now with his black hat and black whiskers relieved against the perspective of the blue flowers stretching down to the summer-house, with the sunset and the strange outline of the Rock of Fortune in the distance. His face and figure were in shadow against the sunset; but I swear the white teeth were showing in his head and he was smiling.

"The moment Nox saw that man, the dog dashed forward and stood in the middle of the path barking at him madly, murderously, volleying out curses that were almost verbal in their dreadful distinctness of hatred. And the man doubled up and fled along the path between the flowers."

Father Brown sprang to his feet with a startling impatience.

"So the dog denounced him, did he?" he cried. "The oracle of the dog condemned him. Did you see what birds were flying, and are you sure whether they were on the right hand or the left? Did you consult the augurs about the sacrifices? Surely you didn't omit to cut open the dog and examine his entrails. That is the sort of scientific test you heathen humanitarians seem to trust when you are thinking of taking away the life and honor of a man."

Fiennes sat gaping for an instant before he found breath to say, "Why, what's the matter with you? What have I done now?"

A sort of anxiety came back into the priest's eyes—the anxiety of a man who has run against a post in the dark and wonders for a moment whether he has hurt it.

"I'm most awfully sorry," he said with sincere distress. "I beg your pardon for being so rude; pray forgive me."

Fiennes looked at him curiously. "I sometimes think you are more of a mystery than any of the mysteries," he said. "But anyhow, if you don't believe in the mystery of the dog, at least you can't get over the mystery of the man. You can't deny that at the very moment when the beast came back from the sea and bellowed, his master's soul was driven out of his body by the blow of some unseen power that no mortal man can trace or even imagine. And as for the lawyer, I don't go only by the dog; there are other curious details too. He struck me as a smooth, smiling, equivocal sort of person; and one of his tricks seemed like a sort of hint. You know the doctor and the police were on the spot very quickly; Valentine was brought back when walking away from the house, and he telephoned instantly. That, with the secluded house, small numbers, and enclosed space, made it pretty possible to search everybody who could have been near; and everybody was thoroughly searched—for a weapon. The whole house, garden, and shore were combed for a weapon. The disappearance of the dagger is almost as crazy as the disappearance of the man."

"The disappearance of the dagger," said Father Brown, nodding. He seemed to have become suddenly attentive.

"Well," continued Fiennes, "I told you that man Traill had a trick of fidgeting with his tie and tie-pin—especially his tie-pin. His pin, like himself, was at once showy and old-fashioned. It had one of those stones with concentric colored rings that look like an eye; and his own concentration on it got on my nerves, as if he had been a Cyclops with one eye in the middle of his body. But the pin was not only large but long; and it occurred to me that his anxiety about its adjustment was because it was even longer than it looked; as long as a stiletto in fact."

Father Brown nodded thoughtfully. "Was any other instrument ever suggested?" he asked.

"There was another suggestion," answered Fiennes, "from one of the young Druces—the cousins, I mean. Neither Herbert nor Harry Druce would have struck one at first as likely to be of assistance in scientific detection; but while Herbert was really the traditional type of heavy Dragoon, caring for nothing but horses and being an ornament to the Horse Guards, his younger brother Harry had been in the Indian Police and knew something about such things. Indeed in his own way he was quite clever; and I rather fancy he had been too clever; I mean he had left the police through breaking some red-tape regulations and taking some sort of risk and responsibility of his own. Anyhow, he was in some sense a detective out of work, and threw himself into this business with more than the ardor of an amateur. And it was with him that I had an argument about the weapon—an argument that led to something new. It began by his countering my description of the dog barking at Traill; and he said that a dog at his worst didn't bark, but growled."

"He was quite right there," observed the priest.

"This young fellow went on to say that, if it came to that, he'd heard Nox growling at other people before then; and among others at Floyd the secretary. I retorted that his own argument answered itself; for the crime couldn't be brought home to two or three people, and least of all to Floyd, who was as innocent as a harum-scarum schoolboy, and had been seen by everybody all the time perched above the garden hedge with his fan of red hair as conspicuous as a scarlet cockatoo. 'I know there's difficulties anyhow,' said my colleague, 'but I wish you'd come with me down the garden a minute. I want to show you something I don't think anyone else has seen.' This was on the very day of the discovery, and the garden was just as it had been: the step-ladder was still standing by the hedge, and just under the hedge my guide stooped and disentangled something from the deep grass. It was the shears used for clipping the hedge, and on the point of one of them was a smear of blood."

There was a short silence, and then Father Brown said suddenly, "What was the lawyer there for?"

"He told us the Colonel sent for him to alter his will," answered Fiennes. "And, by the way, there was another thing about the business of the will that I ought to mention. You see, the will wasn't actually signed in the summer-house that afternoon."

"I suppose not," said Father Brown; "there would have to be two witnesses."

"The lawyer actually came down the day before and it was signed then; but he was sent for again next day because the old man had a doubt about one of the witnesses and had to be reassured."

"Who were the witnesses?" asked Father Brown.

"That's just the point," replied his informant eagerly, "the witnesses were Floyd the secretary and this Dr. Valentine, the foreign sort of surgeon or whatever he is; and the two have a quarrel. Now I'm bound to say that the secretary is something of a busybody. He's one of those hot and headlong people whose warmth of temperament has unfortunately turned mostly to pugnacity and bristling suspicion; to distrusting people instead of to trusting them. That sort of red-haired red-hot fellow is always either universally credulous or universally incredulous; and sometimes both. He was not only a Jack of all trades, but he knew better than all tradesmen. He not only knew everything, but he warned everybody against everybody. All that must be taken into account in his suspicions about Valentine; but in that particular case there seems to have been something behind it. He said the name of Valentine was not really Valentine. He said he had seen him elsewhere known by the name of De Villon. He said it would invalidate the will; of course he was kind enough to explain to the lawyer what the law was on that point. They were both in a frightful wax."

Father Brown laughed. "People often are when they are to witness a will," he said, "for one thing, it means that they can't have any legacy under it. But what did Dr. Valentine say? No doubt the universal secretary knew more about the doctor's name than the doctor did. But even the doctor might have some information about his own name."

Fiennes paused a moment before he replied.

"Dr. Valentine took it in a curious way. Dr. Valentine is a curious man. His appearance is rather striking but very foreign. He is young but wears a beard cut square; and his face is very pale, dreadfully pale and dreadfully serious. His eyes have a sort of ache in them, as if he ought to wear glasses or had given himself a headache with thinking; but he is quite handsome and always very formally dressed, with a top hat and a dark coat and a little red rosette. His manner is rather cold and haughty, and he has a way of staring at you which is very disconcerting. When thus charged with having changed his name, he merely stared like a sphinx and then said with a little laugh that he supposed Americans had no names to change. At that I think the Colonel also got into a fuss and said all sorts of angry things to the doctor; all the more angry because of the doctor's pretensions to a future place in his family. But I shouldn't have thought much of that but for a few words that I happened to hear later, early in the afternoon of the tragedy. I don't want to make a lot of them, for they weren't the sort of words on which one would like, in the ordinary way, to play the eavesdropper. As I was passing out towards the front gate with my two companions and the dog, I heard voices which told me that Dr. Valentine and Miss Druce had withdrawn for a moment into the shadow of the house, in an angle behind a row of flowering plants, and were talking to each other in passionate whisperings—sometimes almost like hissings; for it was something of a lover's quarrel as well as a lovers' tryst. Nobody repeats the sort of things they said for the most part; but in an unfortunate business like this I'm bound to say that there was repeated more than once a phrase about killing somebody. In fact, the girl seemed to be begging him not to kill somebody, or saying that no provocation could justify killing anybody; which seems an unusual sort of talk to address to a gentleman who has dropped in to tea."

"Do you know," asked the priest, "whether Dr. Valentine seemed to be very angry after the scene with the secretary and the Colonel—I mean about witnessing the will?"

"By all accounts," replied the other, "he wasn't half so angry as the secretary was. It was the secretary who went away raging after witnessing the will."

"And now," said Father Brown, "what about the will itself?"

"The Colonel was a very wealthy man, and his will was important. Traill wouldn't tell us the alteration at that stage, but I have since heard, only this morning in fact, that most of the money was transferred from the son to the daughter. I told you that Druce was wild with my friend Donald over his dissipated hours."

"The question of motive has been rather over-shadowed by the question of method," observed Father Brown thoughtfully. "At that moment, apparently, Miss Druce was the immediate gainer by the death."

"Good God! What a cold-blooded way of talking," cried Fiennes, staring at him. "You don't really mean to hint that she—"

"Is she going to marry that Dr. Valentine?" asked the other.

"Some people are against it," answered his friend. "But he is liked and respected in the place and is a skilled and devoted surgeon."

"So devoted a surgeon," said Father Brown, "that he had surgical instruments with him when he went to call on the young lady at tea-time. For he must have used a lancet or something, and he never seems to have gone home."

Fiennes sprang to his feet and looked at him in a heat of inquiry. "You suggest he might have used the very same lancet—"

Father Brown shook his head. "All these suggestions are fancies just now," he said. "The problem is not who did it or what did it, but how it was done. We might find many men and even many tools—pins and shears and lancets. But how did a man get into the room? How did even a pin get into it?"

He was staring reflectively at the ceiling as he spoke, but as he said the last words his eye cocked in an alert fashion as if he had suddenly seen a curious fly on the ceiling.

"Well, what would you do about it?" asked the young man. "You have a lot of experience, what would you advise now?"

"I'm afraid I'm not much use," said Father Brown with a sigh. "I can't suggest very much without having ever been near the place or the people. For the moment you can only go on with local inquiries. I gather that your friend from the Indian Police is more or less in charge of your inquiry down there. I should run down and see how he is getting on. See what he's been doing in the way of amateur detection. There may be news already."

As his guests, the biped and the quadruped, disappeared, Father Brown took up his pen and went back to his interrupted occupation of planning a course of lectures on the Encyclical *Rerum Novarum*. The subject was a large one and he had to re-cast it more than once, so that he was somewhat similarly employed some two days later when the big black dog again came bounding into the room and sprawled all over him with enthusiasm and excitement. The master who followed the dog shared the excitement if not the enthusiasm. He had been excited in a less pleasant fashion, for his blue eyes seemed to start from his head and his eager face was even a little pale.

"You told me," he said abruptly and without preface, "to find out what Harry Druce was doing. Do you know what he's done?"

The priest did not reply, and the young man went on in jerky tones:

"I'll tell you what he's done. He's killed himself."

Father Brown's lips moved only faintly, and there was nothing practical about what he was saying—nothing that had anything to do with this story or this world.

"You give me the creeps sometimes," said Fiennes. "Did you—did you expect this?"

"I thought it possible," said Father Brown; "that was why I asked you to go and see what he was doing. I hoped you might not be too late."

"It was I who found him," said Fiennes rather huskily. "It was the ugliest and most uncanny thing I ever knew. I went down that old garden again and I knew there was something new and unnatural about it besides the murder. The flowers still tossed about in blue masses on each side of the black entrance into the old gray summer-house; but to me the blue flowers looked like blue devils dancing before some dark cavern of the underworld. I looked all around; everything seemed to be in its ordinary place. But the queer notion grew on me that there was something wrong with the very shape of the sky. And then I saw what it was. The Rock of Fortune always rose in the background beyond the garden hedge and against the sea. And the Rock of Fortune was gone."

Father Brown had lifted his head and was listening intently.

"It was as if a mountain had walked away out of a landscape or a moon fallen from the sky; though I knew, of course, that a touch at any time would have tipped the thing over. Something possessed me and I rushed down that garden path like the wind and went crashing through that hedge as if it were a spider's web. It was a thin hedge really, though its undisturbed trimness had made it serve all the purposes of a wall. On the shore I found the loose rock fallen from its pedestal; and poor Harry Druce lay like a wreck underneath it. One arm was thrown round it in a sort of embrace as if he had pulled it down on himself; and on the broad brown sands beside it, in large crazy lettering, he had scrawled the words, 'The Rock of Fortune falls on the Fool.' "

"It was the Colonel's will that did that," observed Father Brown. "The young man had staked everything on profiting himself by Donald's disgrace, especially when his uncle sent for him on the same day as the lawyer, and welcomed him with so much warmth. Otherwise he was done; he'd lost his police job; he was beggared at Monte Carlo. And he killed himself when he found he'd killed his kinsman for nothing."

"Here, stop a minute!" cried the staring Fiennes. "You're going too fast for me."

"Talking about the will, by the way," continued Father Brown calmly, "before I forget it, or we go on to bigger things, there was a simple explanation, I think, of all that business about the doctor's name. I rather fancy I have heard both names before somewhere. The doctor is really a French nobleman with the title of the Marquis de Villon. But he is also an ardent Republican and has abandoned his title and fallen back on the forgotten family surname. 'With your Citizen Riquetti you have puzzled Europe for ten days.' "

"What is that?" asked the young man blankly.

"Never mind," said the priest. "Nine times out of ten it is a rascally thing to change one's name; but this was a piece of fine fanaticism. That's the point of his sarcasm about Americans having no names—that is, no titles. Now in England the Marquis of Hartington is never called Mr. Hartington; but in France the Marquis de Villon is called M. de Villon. So it might well look like a change of name. As for the talk about killing, I fancy that also was a point of French etiquette. The doctor was talking about challenging Floyd to a duel, and the girl was trying to dissuade him."

"Oh, I *see*," cried Fiennes slowly. "Now I understand what she meant."

"And what is that about?" asked his companion, smiling.

"Well," said the young man, "it was something that happened to me just before I found that poor fellow's body; only the catastrophe drove it out of my head. I suppose it's hard to remember a little romantic idyll when you've just come on top of a tragedy. But as I went down the lanes leading to the Colonel's old place, I met his daughter walking with Dr. Valentine. She was in mourning of course, and he always wore black as if he were going to a funeral; but I can't say that their faces were very funereal. Never have I seen two people looking in their own way more respectably radiant and cheerful. They stopped and saluted me and then she told me they were married and living in a little house on the outskirts of the town, where the doctor was continuing his practise. This rather surprised me, because I knew that her old father's will had left her his property; and I hinted at it delicately by saying I was going along to her father's old place and had half expected to meet her there. But she only laughed and said, 'Oh, we've given up all that. My husband doesn't like heiresses.' And I discovered with some astonishment they really had insisted on restoring the property to poor Donald; so I hope he's had a healthy shock and will treat it sensibly. There was never much really the matter with him; he was very young and his father was not very wise. But it was in connection with that that she said something I didn't understand at the time; but now I'm sure it must be as you say. She said with a sort of sudden and splendid arrogance that was entirely altruistic:

" 'I hope it'll stop that red-haired fool from fussing any more about the will. Does he think my husband, who has given up a crest and a coronet as old as the Crusades for his principles, would kill an old man in a summer-house for a legacy like that?' Then she laughed again and said, 'My husband isn't killing anybody except in the way of business. Why, he didn't even ask his friends to call on the secretary.' Now, of course, I see what she meant."

"I see part of what she meant, of course," said Father Brown. "What did she mean exactly by the secretary fussing about the will?"

Fiennes smiled as he answered. "I wish you knew the secretary, Father Brown. It would be a joy to you to watch him make things hum, as he calls it. He made the house of mourning hum. He filled the funeral with all the snap and zip of the brightest sporting event. There was no holding him, after something had really happened. I've told you how he used to oversee the gardener as he did the garden, and how he instructed the lawyer in the law. Needless to say, he also instructed the surgeon in the practise of surgery; and as the surgeon was Dr. Valentine, you may be sure it ended in accusing him of something worse than bad surgery. The secretary got it fixed in his red head that the doctor had committed the crime;

and when the police arrived he was perfectly sublime. Need I say that he became on the spot the greatest of all amateur detectives? Sherlock Holmes never towered over Scotland Yard with more Titanic intellectual pride and scorn than Colonel Druce's private secretary over the police investigating Colonel Druce's death. I tell you it was a joy to see him. He strode about with an abstracted air, tossing his scarlet crest of hair and giving curt impatient replies. Of course it was his demeanor during these days that made Druce's daughter so wild with him. Of course he had a theory. It's just the sort of theory a man would have in a book; and Floyd is the sort of man who ought to be in a book. He'd be better fun and less bother in a book."

"What was his theory?" asked the other.

"Oh, it was full of pep," replied Fiennes gloomily. "It would have been glorious copy if it could have held together for ten minutes longer. He said the Colonel was still alive when they found him in the summer-house and the doctor killed him with the surgical instrument on pretense of cutting the clothes."

"I see," said the priest. "I suppose he was lying flat on his face on the mud floor as a form of siesta."

"It's wonderful what hustle will do," continued his informant. "I believe Floyd would have got his great theory into the papers at any rate, and perhaps had the doctor arrested, when all these things were blown sky high as if by dynamite by the discovery of that dead body lying under the Rock of Fortune. And that's what we come back to after all. I suppose the suicide is almost a confession. But nobody will ever know the whole story."

There was a silence, and then the priest said modestly, "I rather think I know the whole story."

Fiennes stared. "But look here," he cried, "how do you come to know the whole story, or to be sure it's the true story? You've been sitting here a hundred miles away writing a sermon; do you mean to tell me you really know what happened already? If you've really come to the end, where in the world do you begin? What started you off with your own story?"

Father Brown jumped up with a very unusual excitement and his first exclamation was like an explosion.

"The dog!" he cried. "The dog, of course! You had the whole story in your hands in the business of the dog on the beach, if you'd only noticed the dog properly."

Fiennes stared still more. "But you told me before that my feelings about the dog were all nonsense, and the dog had nothing to do with it."

"The dog had everything to do with it," said Father Brown, "as you'd have found out if you'd only treated the dog as a dog and not as God Almighty judging the souls of men."

He paused in an embarrassed way for a moment, and then said, with a rather pathetic air of apology:

"The truth is, I happen to be awfully fond of dogs. And it seemed to me that in all this lurid halo of dog superstitions nobody was really thinking about the poor dog at all. To begin with a small point, about his barking at the lawyer or growling at the secretary. You asked how I could guess things a hundred miles away; but honestly it's mostly to your credit, for you described people so well that I know the types. A man like Traill who frowns unusually and smiles suddenly, a man who fiddles with things, especially at his throat, is a nervous, easily embarrassed man. I shouldn't wonder if Floyd, the efficient secretary, is nervy and jumpy too; those Yankee hustlers often are. Otherwise he wouldn't have cut his fingers on the shears and dropped them when he heard Janet Druce scream.

"Now dogs hate nervous people. I don't know whether they make the dog nervous too; or whether, being after all a brute, he is a bit of a bully; or whether his canine vanity (which is colossal) is simply offended at not being liked. But anyhow there was nothing in poor Nox protesting against those people, except that he disliked them for being afraid of him. Now I know you're awfully clever, and nobody of sense sneers at cleverness. But I sometimes fancy, for instance, that you are too clever to understand animals. Sometimes you are too clever to understand men, especially when they act almost as simply as animals. Animals are very literal; they live in a world of truisms. Take this case; a dog barks at a man and a man runs away from a dog. Now you do not seem to be quite simple enough to see the fact; that the dog barked because he disliked the man and the man fled because he was frightened of the dog. They had no other motives and they needed none. But you must read psychological mysteries into it and suppose the dog had super-normal vision, and was a mysterious mouthpiece of doom. You must suppose the man was running away, not from the dog but from the hangman. And yet, if you come to think of it, all this deeper psychology is exceedingly improbable. If the dog really could completely and consciously realize the murderer of his master, he wouldn't stand yapping as he might at a curate at a tea-party; he's much more likely to fly at his throat. And on the other hand, do you really think a man who had hardened his heart to murder an old friend and then walk about smiling at the old friend's family, under the eyes of his old friend's daughter and postmortem doctor—do you think a man like that would be doubled up by mere remorse because a dog barked? He might feel the tragic irony of it; it might shake his soul, like any other tragic trifle. But he wouldn't rush madly the length of a garden to escape from the only witness whom he knew to be unable to talk. People have a panic like that when they are frightened, not of tragic ironies, but of teeth. The whole thing is simpler than you can understand.

"But when we come to that business by the seashore, things are much more interesting. As you stated then, they were much more puzzling. I didn't understand that tale of the dog going in and out of the water; it didn't seem to me a doggy thing to do. If Nox had been very much upset about something else, he might possibly have refused to go after the stick at all. He'd probably go off nosing in whatever direction he suspected the mischief. But when once a dog is actually chasing a thing, a stone or a stick or a rabbit, my experience is that he won't stop for anything but the most peremptory command, and not always for that. That he should turn around because his mood changed seems to me unthinkable."

"But he did turn around," insisted Fiennes, "and came back without the stick."

"He came back without the stick for the best reason in the world," replied the priest. "He came back because he couldn't find it. He whined because he couldn't find it. That's the sort of thing a dog really does whine about. A dog is a devil of a ritualist. He is as particular about the precise routine of a game as a child about the precise repetition of a fairy-tale. In this case something had gone wrong with the game. He came back to complain seriously of the conduct of the stick. Never had such a thing happened before. Never had an eminent and distinguished dog been so treated by a rotten old walking-stick."

"Why, what had the walking-stick done?" inquired the young man.

"It had sunk," said Father Brown.

Fiennes said nothing, but continued to stare, and it was the priest who continued:

"It had sunk because it was not really a stick, but a rod of steel with a very thin shell of cane and a sharp point. In other words, it was a sword-stick. I suppose a murderer never got rid of a bloody weapon so oddly and yet so naturally as by throwing it into the sea for a retriever."

"I begin to see what you mean," admitted Fiennes; "but even if a sword-stick was used, I have no guess of how it was used."

"I had a sort of guess," said Father Brown, "right at the beginning when you said the word summer-house. And another when you said that Druce wore a white coat. As long as everybody was looking for a short dagger, nobody thought of it; but if we admit a rather long blade like a rapier, it's not so impossible."

He was leaning back, looking at the ceiling, and began like one going back to his own first thoughts and fundamentals.

"All that discussion about detective stories like the Yellow Room, about a man found dead in sealed chambers which no one could enter, does not apply to the present case, because it is a summer-house. When we talk of a Yellow Room, or any room, we imply walls that are really homogeneous and impenetrable. But a summer-house is not made like that; it is often made, as it was in this case, of closely interlaced but still separate boughs and strips of wood, in which there are chinks here and there. There was one of them just behind Druce's back as he sat in his chair up against the wall. But just as the room was a summer-house, so the chair was a basket-chair. That also was a lattice of loopholes. Lastly, the summer-house was close up under the hedge; and you have just told me that it was really a thin hedge. A man standing outside it could easily see, amid a network of twigs and branches and canes, one white spot of the Colonel's coat as plain as the white of a target.

"Now, you left the geography a little vague; but it was possible to put two and two together. You said the Rock of Fortune was not really high; but you also said it could be seen dominating the garden like a mountain-peak. In other words, it was very near the end of the garden, though your walk had taken you a long way round to it. Also, it isn't likely the young lady really howled so as to be heard half a mile. She gave an ordinary involuntary cry, and yet you heard it on the shore. And among other interesting things that you told me, may I remind you that you said Harry Druce had fallen behind to light his pipe under a hedge."

Fiennes shuddered slightly. "You mean he drew his blade there and sent it through the hedge at the white spot. But surely it was a very odd chance and a very sudden choice. Besides, he couldn't be certain the old man's money had passed to him, and as a fact it hadn't."

Father Brown's face became animated.

"You misunderstand the man's character," he said, as if he himself had known the man all his life. "A curious but not unknown type of character. If he had really *known* the money would come to him, I seriously believe he wouldn't have done it. He would have seen it as the dirty thing it was."

"Isn't that rather paradoxical?" asked the other.

"This man was a gambler," said the priest, "and a man in disgrace for having taken risks and anticipated orders. It was probably for something pretty unscrupulous, for every imperial police is more like a Russian secret police than we like to think. But he had gone beyond the line and failed.

"Now, the temptation of that type of man is to do a mad thing precisely because the risk will be wonderful in retrospect. He wants to say, 'Nobody but I could have seized that chance or seen that it was then or never. What a wild and wonderful guess it was, when I put all those things together; Donald in disgrace; and the lawyer being sent for; and Herbert and I sent for at the same time—and then nothing more but the way the old man grinned at me and shook hands. Anybody would say I was mad to risk it; but that is how fortunes are made, by the man mad enough to have a little foresight.'

"In short, it is the vanity of guessing. It is the megalomania of the gambler. The more incongruous the coincidence, the more instantaneous the decision, the more likely he is to snatch the chance. The accident, the very triviality, of the white speck and the hole in the hedge intoxicated him like a vision of the world's desire. Nobody clever enough to see such a combination of accidents could be cowardly enough not to use them! That is how the devil talks to the gambler. But the devil himself would hardly have induced that unhappy man to go down in a dull, deliberate way and kill an old uncle from whom he'd always had expectations. It would be too respectable."

He paused a moment; and then went on with a certain quiet emphasis.

"And now try to call up the scene, even as you saw it yourself. As he stood there, dizzy with his diabolical opportunity, he looked up and saw that strange outline that might have been the image of his own tottering soul; the one great crag poised perilously on the other like a pyramid on its point and remembered that it was called the Rock of Fortune. Can you guess how such a man at such a moment would read such a signal? I think it strung him up to action and even to vigilance. He who would be a tower must not fear to be a toppling tower. Anyhow, he acted; his next difficulty was to cover his tracks. To be found with a sword-stick, let alone a blood-stained sword-stick, would be fatal in the search that was certain to follow. If he left it anywhere, it would be found and probably traced. Even if he threw it into the sea the action might be noticed, and thought noticeable—unless indeed he could think of some more natural way of covering the action. As you know, he did think of one, and a very good one. Being the only one of you with a watch, he told you it was not yet time to return, strolled a little farther and started the game of throwing in sticks for the retriever. But how his eyes must have rolled darkly over all that desolate seashore before they alighted on the dog!"

Fiennes nodded, gazing thoughtfully into space. His mind seemed to have drifted back to a less practical part of the narrative.

"It's queer," he said, "that the dog really was in the story after all."

"The dog could almost have told you the story, if he could talk," said the priest. "All I complain of is that because he couldn't talk, you made up his story for him, and made him talk with the tongues of men and angels. It's part of something I've noticed more and more in the modern world, appearing in all sorts of newspaper rumors and conversational catch-words; something that's arbitrary without being authoritative. People readily swallow the untested claims of this, that, or the other. It's drowning all your old rationalism and scepticism, it's coming in like a sea; and the name of it is superstition."

He stood up abruptly, his face heavy with a sort of frown, and went on talking almost as if he were alone. "It's the first effect of not believing in God that you lose your common sense, and can't see things as they are. Anything that anybody talks about, and says there's a good deal in it, extends itself indefinitely like a vista in a nightmare. And a dog is an omen and a cat is a mystery and a pig is a mascot and a beetle is a scarab, calling up all the menagerie of polytheism from Egypt and old India; Dog Anubis and great green-eyed Pasht and all the holy howling Bulls of Bashan; reeling back to the bestial gods of the beginning, escaping into elephants and snakes and crocodiles; and all because you are frightened of four words: 'He was made Man.' "

The young man got up with a little embarrassment, almost as if he had overheard a soliloquy.

He called to the dog and left the room with vague but breezy farewells. But he had to call the dog twice, for the dog had remained behind quite motionless for a moment, looking up steadily at Father Brown as the wolf looked at St. Francis.

The Dream-Woman

by Wilkie Collins

I

I had not been settled much more than six weeks in my country practice, when I was sent for to a neighboring town, to consult with the resident medical man there on a case of very dangerous illness.

My horse had come down with me at the end of a long ride the night before, and had hurt himself, luckily, much more than he had hurt his master. Being deprived of the animal's services, I started for my destination by the coach (there were no railways at that time), and I hoped to get back again, towards the afternoon, in the same way. After the consultation was over, I went to the principal inn of the town to wait for the coach. When it came up it was full inside and out. There was no resource left me but to get home as cheaply as I could by hiring a gig. The price asked for this accommodation struck me as being so extortionate that I determined to look out for an inn of inferior pretensions, and to try if I could not make a better bargain with a less prosperous establishment.

I soon found a likely-looking house, dingy and quiet, with an old-fashioned sign, that had evidently not been repainted for many years past. The landlord, in this case, was not above making a small profit, and as soon as we came to terms he rang the yard bell to order the gig.

"Has Robert not come back from that errand?" asked the landlord, appealing to the waiter who answered the bell.

"No, sir, he hasn't."

"Well, then, you must wake up Isaac."

"Wake up Isaac!" I repeated: "that sounds rather odd. Do your ostlers go to bed in the daytime?"

"This one does," said the landlord, smiling to himself in rather a strange way.

"And dreams, too," added the waiter; "I shan't forget the turn it gave me the first time I heard him."

"Never you mind about that," retorted the proprietor; "you go and rouse Isaac up. The gentleman's waiting for his gig."

The landlord's manner and the waiter's manner expressed a great deal more than they either of them said. I began to suspect that I might be on the track of something professionally interesting to me as a medical man, and I thought I should like to look at the ostler before the waiter awakened him.

"Stop a minute," I interposed: "I have rather a fancy for seeing this man before you wake him up. I'm a doctor: and if this queer sleeping and dreaming of his comes from anything wrong in his brain, I may be able to tell you what to do with him."

"I rather think you will find his complaint past all doctoring, sir," said the landlord; "but if you would like to see him, you're welcome, I'm sure."

He led the way across a yard and down a passage to the stables, opened one of the doors, and, waiting outside himself, told me to look in.

I found myself in a two-stall stable. In one of the stalls a horse was munching his corn; in the other an old man was lying asleep on the litter.

I stooped and looked at him attentively. It was a withered, woebegone face. The eyebrows were painfully contracted; the mouth was fast set, and drawn down at the corners. The hollow wrinkled cheeks, and the scanty grizzled hair, told their own tale of some past sorrow or suffering. He was drawing his breath convulsively when I first looked at him, and in a moment more he began to talk in his sleep.

"Wake up!" I heard him say, in a quick whisper, through his clenched teeth. "Wake up there! Murder!"

He moved one lean arm slowly till it rested over his throat, shuddered a little, and turned on his straw. Then the arm left his throat, the hand stretched itself out, and clutched at the side towards which he had turned, as if he fancied himself to be grasping at the edge of something. I saw his lips move, and bent lower over him. He was still talking in his sleep.

"Light grey eyes," he murmured, "and a droop in the left eyelid; flaxen hair, with a gold-yellow streak in it—all right, Mother—fair white arms, with a down on them—little lady's hand, with a reddish look under the fingernails. The knife—always the cursed knife—first on one side, then on the other. Aha! you she-devil, where's the knife?"

At the last word his voice rose, and he grew restless on a sudden. I saw him shudder on the straw; his withered face became distorted, and he threw up both his hands with a quick hysterical gasp. They struck against the bottom of the manger under which he lay, and the blow awakened him. I had just time to slip through the door and close it before his eyes were fairly open, and his senses his own again.

"Do you know anything about that man's past life?" I said to the landlord.

"Yes, sir. I know pretty well all about it," was the answer, "and an uncommon queer story it is. Most people don't believe it. It's true, though, for all that. Why, just look at him," continued the landlord, opening the stable door again. "Poor devil! he's so worn out with his restless nights that he's dropped back into his sleep already."

"Don't wake him," I said; "I'm in no hurry for the gig. Wait till the other man comes back from his errand; and, in the meantime, suppose I have some lunch and a bottle of sherry, and suppose you come and help me to get through it?"

The heart of mine host, as I had anticipated, warmed to me over his own wine. He soon became communicative on the subject of the man asleep in the stable, and by little and little I drew the whole story out of him. Extravagant and incredible as the events must appear to everybody, they are related here just as I heard them and just as they happened.

II

Some years ago there lived in the suburbs of a large seaport town on the west coast of England a man in humble circumstances, by name Isaac Scatchard. His means of subsistence were derived from any employment that he could get as an ostler, and occasionally when times went well with him, from temporary engagements in service as stable helper in private houses. Though a faithful, steady, and honest man, he got on badly in his calling. His ill luck was proverbial among his neighbors. He was always missing good opportunities by no fault of his own, and always living longest in service with amiable people who were not punctual payers of wages. "Unlucky Isaac" was his nickname in his own neighborhood, and no one could say that he did not richly deserve it.

With far more than one man's fair share of adversity to endure,

Isaac had but one consolation to support him, and that was of the dreariest and most negative kind. He had no wife and children to increase his anxieties and add to the bitterness of his various failures in life. It might have been from mere insensibility, or it might have been from generous unwillingness to involve another in his own unlucky destiny; but the fact undoubtedly was, that he had arrived at the middle term of life without marrying, and, what is much more remarkable, without once exposing himself, from eighteen to eight-and-thirty, to the genial imputation of ever having had a sweetheart.

When he was out of service he lived alone with his widowed mother. Mrs. Scatchard was a woman above the average in her lowly station as to capacity and manners. She had seen better days, as the phrase is, but she never referred to them in the presence of curious visitors; and, though perfectly polite to everyone who approached her, never cultivated any intimacies among her neighbors. She contrived to provide, hardly enough, for her simple wants by doing rough work for the tailors, and always managed to keep a decent home for her son to return to whenever his ill luck drove him out helpless into the world.

One bleak autumn, when Isaac was getting on fast towards forty, and when he was, as usual, out of place through no fault of his own, he set forth from his mother's cottage on a long walk inland to a gentleman's seat where he had heard that a stable helper was required.

It wanted then but two days of his birthday; and Mrs. Scatchard, with her usual fondness, made him promise, before he started, that he would be back in time to keep that anniversary with her, in as festive a way as their poor means would allow. It was easy for him to comply with this request, even supposing he slept a night each way on the road.

He was to start from home on Monday morning, and, whether he got the new place or not, he was to be back for his birthday dinner on Wednesday at two o'clock.

Arriving at his destination too late on the Monday night to make application for the stable helper's place, he slept at the village inn, and in good time on the Tuesday morning presented himself at the gentleman's house to fill the vacant situation. Here again his ill luck pursued him as inexorably as ever. The excellent written testimonials to his character which he was able to produce availed him nothing; his long walk had been taken in vain; only the day before the stable helper's place had been given to another man.

Isaac accepted this new disappointment resignedly and as a matter of course. Naturally slow in capacity, he had the bluntness of sensibility and phlegmatic patience of disposition which frequently distinguish men with sluggishly working mental powers. He thanked the gentleman's steward with his usual quiet civility for granting him an interview, and took his departure with no appearance of unusual depression in his face or manner.

Before starting on his homeward walk, he made some inquiries at the inn, and ascertained that he might save a few miles on his return by following a new road. Furnished with full instructions, several times repeated, as to the various turnings he was to take, he set forth on his homeward journey, and walked on all day with only one stoppage for bread and cheese. Just as it was getting towards dark, the rain came on and the wind began to rise, and he found himself, to make matters worse, in a part of the country with which he was entirely unacquainted, though he knew himself to be some fifteen miles from home. The first house he found to inquire at was a lonely roadside inn standing on the outskirts of a thick wood. Solitary as the place looked, it was welcome to a lost man who was also hungry, thirsty, footsore, and wet. The landlord was civil and respectable-looking, and the price he asked for a bed was reasonable enough. Isaac therefore decided on stopping comfortably at the inn for that night.

He was constitutionally a temperate man. His supper consisted of two rashers of bacon, a slice of home-made bread, and a pint of ale. He did not go to bed immediately after this moderate meal, but sat up with the landlord, talking about his bad prospects and his long run of ill luck, and diverging from these topics to the subjects of horseflesh and racing. Nothing was said either by himself, his host, or the few laborers who strayed into the taproom, which could, in the slightest degree, excite the very small and very dull imaginative faculty which Isaac Scatchard possessed.

At a little after eleven the house was closed. Isaac went around with the landlord and held the candle while the doors and lower windows were being secured. He noticed with surprise the strength of the bolts and bars, and iron-sheathed shutters.

"You see, we are rather lonely here," said the landlord. "We never have had any attempts made to break in yet, but it's always as well to be on the safe side. When nobody is sleeping here, I am the only man in the house. My wife and daughter are timid, and the servant girl takes after her missuses. Another glass of ale before you turn in? No! Well, how such a sober man as you comes to be out of place is more than I can make out, for one. Here's where you're to sleep. You're our only lodger tonight, and I think you'll say my missus has done her best to make you comfortable. You're quite sure you won't have another glass of ale? Very well. Good night."

It was half past eleven by the clock in the passage as they went upstairs to the bedroom, the window of which looked on to the wood at the back of the house.

Isaac locked the door, set his candle on the chest of drawers, and wearily got ready for bed. The bleak autumn wind was still blowing, and the solemn, monotonous surging moan of it in the wood was dreary and awful to hear through the night-silence. Isaac felt strangely wakeful. He resolved, as he lay down in bed, to keep the candle alight until he began to grow sleepy, for there was something unendurably depressing in the bare idea of lying awake in the darkness, listening to the dismal, ceaseless moaning of the wind in the wood.

Sleep stole on him before he was aware of it. His eyes closed, he fell off insensibly to rest without having so much as a thought of extinguishing the candle.

The first sensation of which he was conscious after sinking into slumber was a strange shivering that ran through him suddenly from head to foot, and a dreadful sinking pain at the heart, such as he had never felt before. The shivering only disturbed his slumbers; the pain woke him instantly. In one moment he passed from a state of sleep to a state of wakefulness—his eyes wide open—his mental perceptions cleared suddenly, as if by a miracle.

The candle had burnt down nearly to the last morsel of tallow, but the top of the unsnuffed wick had just fallen off, and the light in the little room was, for the moment, fair and full.

Between the foot of his bed and the closed door there stood a woman with a knife in her hand, looking at him.

He was stricken speechless with terror, but he did not lose the preternatural clearness of his faculties, and he never took his eyes off the woman. She said not a word as they stared each other in the face; she began to move slowly towards the left-hand side of the bed.

His eyes followed her. She was a fair, fine woman, with yellowish flaxen hair and light grey eyes, with a droop in the left eyelid. He noticed those things and fixed them on his mind before she was around at the side of the bed. Speechless, with no expression in her face, with no noise following her footfall, she came closer and closer—stopped—and slowly raised the knife. He laid his right arm over his throat to save it; but, as he saw the knife coming down, threw his hand across the bed to the right side, and jerked his body over that way just as the knife descended on the mattress within an inch of his shoulder.

His eyes fixed on her arm and hand as she slowly drew her knife out of the bed; a white, well-shaped arm, with a pretty down lying lightly over the fair skin—a delicate lady's hand, with the crowning beauty of a pink flush under the round fingernails.

She drew the knife out, and passed back again slowly to the foot of the bed; stopped there for a moment looking at him; then came on—still speechless, still with no expression on the blank beautiful face, still with no sound following the stealthy footfalls—came on to the right side of the bed, where he now lay.

As she approached she raised the knife again, and he drew himself away to the left side. She struck, as before, right into the mattress, with a deliberate perpendicularly downward action of the arm. This time his eyes wandered from her to the knife. It was like the large clasp knives which he had often seen laboring men use to cut their bread and bacon with. Her delicate little fingers did not conceal more than two thirds of the handle; he noticed that it was made of buckhorn, clean and shining as the blade was, and looking like new.

For the second time she drew the knife out, concealed it in the wide sleeve of her gown, then stopped by the bedside, watching him. For an instant he saw her standing in that position, then the wick of the spent candle fell over into the socket; the flame diminished to a little blue point, and the room grew dark.

A moment, or less, if possible, passed so, and then the wick flamed up, smokingly, for the last time. His eyes were still looking eagerly over the right-hand side of the bed when the final flash of light came, but they discerned nothing. The fair woman with the knife was gone.

The conviction that he was alone again weakened the hold of the terror that had struck him dumb up to this time. The preternatural sharpness which the very intensity of his panic had mysteriously imparted to his faculties left them suddenly. His brain grew confused—his heart beat wildly—his ears opened for the first time since the appearance of the woman to a sense of the woeful ceaseless moaning of the wind among the trees. With the dreadful conviction of the reality of what he had seen still strong within him, he leaped out of bed, and screaming "Murder! Wake up, here! wake up!" dashed headlong through the darkness to the door.

It was fast locked, exactly as he had left it on going to bed.

His cries on starting up had alarmed the house. He heard the terrified, confused exclamations of women; he saw the master of the house approaching along the passage with his burning rush candle in one hand and his gun in the other.

"What is it?" asked the landlord breathlessly.

Isaac could only answer in a whisper. "A woman, with a knife in her hand," he gasped out. "In my room—a fair yellow-haired woman; she jabbed at me with the knife twice over."

The landlord's pale cheeks grew paler. He looked at Isaac eagerly by the flickering light of his candle, and his face began to get red again; his voice altered, too, as well as his complexion. "She seems to have missed you twice," he said.

"I dodged the knife as it came down," Isaac went on, in the same scared whisper. "It struck the bed each time."

The landlord took his candle into the bedroom immediately. In less than a minute he came out again into the passage in a violent passion.

"The devil fly away with you and your woman with the knife! There isn't a mark in the bedclothes anywhere. What do you mean by coming into a man's place, and frightening his family out of their wits about a dream?"

"I'll leave your house," said Isaac faintly. "Better out on the road, in rain and dark, on my road home, than back again in that room, after what I've seen in it. Lend me a light to get my clothes by, and tell what I'm to pay."

"Pay!" cried the landlord, leading the way with his light sulkily into the bedroom. "You'll find your score on the slate when you go downstairs. I wouldn't have taken you in for all the money you've got about you if I'd known your dreaming, screeching ways beforehand. Look at the bed. Where's the cut of a knife in it? Look at the window—is the lock busted? Look at the door (which I heard you fasten yourself)—is the lock busted? A murdering woman with a knife in my house! You ought to be ashamed of yourself!"

Isaac answered not a word. He huddled on his clothes, and then they went downstairs together.

"Nigh on twenty minutes past two!" said the landlord, as they passed the clock. "A nice time in the morning to frighten honest people out of their wits!"

Isaac paid his bill, and the landlord let him out at the front door, asking, with a grin of contempt, as he undid the strong fastenings, whether "the murdering woman got in that way."

They parted without a word on either side. The rain had ceased, but the night was dark, and the wind bleaker than ever. Little did the darkness, or the cold, or the uncertainty about the way home matter to Isaac. If he had been turned out into a wilderness in a thunderstorm, it would have been a relief after what he had suffered in the bedroom of the inn.

What was the fair woman with the knife? The creature of a dream, or that other creature from the unknown world called among men by the name of ghost? He could make nothing of the mystery—had made nothing of it, even when it was midday on Wednesday, and when he stood, at last, after many times missing his road, once more on the doorstep of home.

III

His mother came out eagerly to receive him. His face told her in a moment that something was wrong.

"I've lost the place; but that's my luck. I dreamed an ill dream last night, Mother—or maybe I saw a ghost. Take it either way, it scared me out of my senses, and I'm not my own man again yet."

"Isaac, your face frightens me. Come in to the fire—come in, and tell mother all about it.

He was as anxious to tell as she was to hear; for it had been his hope all the way home, that his mother, with her quicker capacity and superior knowledge, might be able to throw some light on the mystery which he could not clear up for himself. His memory of the dream was still mechanically vivid, though his thoughts were entirely confused by it.

His mother's face grew paler and paler as he went on. She never interrupted him by so much as a single word; but when he had done, she moved her chair close to his, put her arm around his neck and said to him.

"Isaac, you dreamed your ill dream on this Wednesday morning. What time was it when you saw the fair woman with the knife in her hand?"

Isaac reflected on what the landlord had said when they had passed the clock on his leaving the inn; allowed as nearly as he could

for the time that must have elapsed between the unlocking of his
bedroom door and the paying of his bill just before going away, and
answered.

"Somewhere about two o'clock in the morning."

His mother suddenly quitted her hold on his neck, and struck her
hands together in a gesture of despair.

"This Wednesday is your birthday, Isaac, and two o'clock in the
morning was the time when you were born."

Isaac's capacities were not quick enough to catch the infection of
his mother's superstitious dread. He was amazed, and a little startled
also, when she suddenly rose from her chair, opened her old writing-
desk, took pen, ink, and paper and then said to him: "Your memory
is but a poor one, Isaac, and now I'm an old woman, mine's not much
better. I want all about this dream of yours to be as well known to
both of us, years hence, as it is now. Tell me over again all you told
me a minute ago, when you spoke of what the woman with the knife
looked like."

Isaac obeyed, and marvelled much as he saw his mother carefully
set down on paper the very words he was saying.

"Light grey eyes," she wrote, as they came to the descriptive part,
"with a droop in the left eyelid; flaxen hair, with a gold-yellow streak
in it; white arms, with a down upon them; little lady's hand, with
a reddish look about the fingernails; clasp knife with a buckhorn
handle, that seemed as good as new." To these particulars Mrs.
Scatchard added the year, month, day of the week, and time in the
morning when the woman of the dream appeared to her son. She
then locked up the paper carefully in her writing desk.

Neither on that day nor on any day after could her son induce her
to return to the matter of the dream. She obstinately kept her
thoughts about it to herself, and even refused to refer again to the
paper in her writing desk. Ere long Isaac grew weary of attempting
to make her break her resolute silence; and time, which sooner or
later wears out all things, gradually wore out the impression produced on him by the dream. He began by thinking of it carelessly,
and he ended by not thinking of it at all.

The result was the more easily brought about by the advent of
some important changes for the better in his prospects which commenced not long after his terrible night's experience at the inn. He
reaped at last the reward of his long and patient suffering under
adversity by getting an excellent place, keeping it for seven years,
and leaving it, on the death of his master, not only with an excellent

character, but also with a comfortable annuity bequeathed to him as a reward for saving his mistress's life in a carriage accident. Thus it happened that Isaac Scatchard returned to his old mother, seven years after the time of the dream at the inn, with an annual sum of money at his disposal sufficient to keep them both in ease and independence for the rest of their lives.

The mother, whose health had been bad of late years, profited so much by the care bestowed on her and by freedom from money anxieties, that when Isaac's birthday came round she was able to sit up comfortably at a table and dine with him.

On that day, as the evening drew on, Mrs. Scatchard discovered that a bottle of tonic medicine which she was accustomed to take, and in which she had fancied that a dose or more was still left, happened to be empty. Isaac immediately volunteered to go to the chemist's and get it filled again. It was as rainy and bleak an autumn night as on the memorable past occasion when he lost his way and slept at the roadside inn.

On going to the chemist's shop he was passed hurriedly by a poorly dressed woman coming out of it. The glimpse he had of her face struck him, and he looked back after her as she descended the doorstep.

"You're noticing that woman?" said the chemist's apprentice behind the counter. "It's my opinion there's something wrong with her. She's been asking for laudanum to put on a bad tooth. Master's out for half an hour, and I told her I wasn't allowed to sell poison to strangers in his absence. She laughed in a queer way, and said she would come back in half an hour. If she expects master to serve her, I think she'll be disappointed. It's a case of suicide, sir, if ever there was one yet."

These words added immeasurably to the sudden interest in the woman which Isaac had felt at the first sight of her face. After he had got the medicine bottle filled, he looked about anxiously for her as soon as he was out in the street. She was walking slowly up and down on the opposite side of the road. With his heart, very much to his own surprise, beating fast, Isaac crossed over and spoke to her.

He asked if she was in any distress. She pointed to her torn shawl, her scanty dress, her crushed, dirty bonnet, then moved under the lamp so as to let the light fall on her stern, pale but still most beautiful face.

"I look like a comfortable, happy woman, don't I?" she said, with a bitter laugh.

She spoke with a purity of intonation which Isaac had never heard before from other than ladies' lips. Her slightest actions seemed to have the easy, negligent grace of a thoroughbred woman. Her skin, for all its poverty-stricken paleness, was as delicate as if her life had been passed in the enjoyment of every social comfort that wealth can purchase. Even her small, finely shaped hands, gloveless as they were, had not lost whiteness.

Little by little, in answer to his questions, the sad story of the woman came out. There is no need to relate it here; it is told over and over again in police reports and paragraphs about attempted suicides.

"My name is Rebecca Murdoch," said the woman, as she ended. "I have ninepence left, and I thought of spending it at the chemist's over the way in securing a passage to the other world. Whatever it is, it can't be worse to me than this, so why should I stop here?"

Besides the natural compassion and sadness moved in his heart by what he heard, Isaac felt within him some mysterious influence at work all the time the woman was speaking which utterly confused his ideas and almost deprived him of his powers of speech. All he could say in answer to her last reckless words was that he would prevent her from attempting her own life, if he followed her about all night to do it. His rough, trembling earnestness seemed to impress her.

"I won't occasion you that trouble," she answered, when he repeated his threat. "You have given me a fancy for living by speaking kindly to me. No need for the mockery of protestations and promises. You may believe me without them. Come to Fuller's Meadow tomorrow at twelve, and find me alive, to answer for myself—No!—no money. My ninepence will do to get me as good a night's lodging as I want."

She nodded and left him. He made no attempt to follow—he felt no suspicion that she was deceiving him.

"It's strange, but I can't help believing her," he said to himself, and walked away, bewildered, towards home.

On entering the house, his mind was still so completely absorbed by its new subject of interest that he took no notice of what his mother was doing when he came in with the bottle of medicine. She had opened her old writing desk in his absence, and was now reading a paper attentively that lay inside it. On every birthday of Isaac's since she had written down the particulars of his dream from his own lips, she had been accustomed to read the same paper, and ponder over it in private.

The next day he went to Fuller's Meadow.

He had done only right in believing her so implicitly. She was there, punctual to a minute, to answer for herself. The last-left faint defences in Isaac's heart against the fascination which a word or look from her began inscrutably to exercise over him sank down and vanished before her forever on that memorable morning.

When a man previously insensible to the influence of women forms an attachment in middle life, the instances are rare indeed, let the warning circumstances be what they may, in which he is found capable of freeing himself from the tyranny of the new ruling passion. The charm of being spoken to familiarly, fondly, and gratefully by a woman whose language and manners still retain enough of their early refinement to hint at a high social station that she had lost would have been a dangerous luxury to a man of Isaac's rank at the age of twenty. But it was far more than that—it was certain ruin to him—now that his heart was opening strong feelings of all kinds that, once implanted, strike root most stubbornly in a man's moral nature. A few more stolen interviews after the first morning in Fuller's Meadow completed his infatuation. In less than a month from the time when he first met her, Isaac Scatchard had consented to give Rebecca Murdoch a new interest in existence, and a chance of recovering the character she had lost by promising to make her his wife.

She had taken possession, not of his passions only, but of his faculties as well. All the mind he had he put into her keeping. She directed him on every point—even instructing him how to break the news of his approaching marriage in the safest manner to his mother.

"If you tell her how you met me and who I am at first," said the cunning woman, "she will move heaven and earth to prevent our marriage. Say I am the sister of one of your fellow servants—ask her to see me before you go into any more particulars—and leave it to me do the rest. I mean to make her love me next best to you, Isaac, before she knows anything of who I really am."

The motive of the deceit was sufficient to sanctify it to Isaac. The stratagem proposed relieved him of his one great anxiety, and quieted his uneasy conscience on the subject of his mother. Still, there was something wanting to perfect his happiness, something that he could not realize, something mysteriously untraceable, and yet something that perpetually made itself felt; not when he was absent from Rebecca Murdoch, but, strange to say, when he was actually in her presence! She was kindness itself with him. She never made him feel his inferior capacities and inferior manners. She showed the sweetest anxiety to please him in the smallest trifles; but, in spite of all these attractions, he never could feel quite at ease with her. At their first meeting, there had mingled with his admiration, when he looked in her face, a faint, involuntary feeling of doubt whether that face was entirely strange to him. No after familiarity had the slightest effect on his inexplicable, wearisome uncertainty.

Concealing the truth as he had been directed, he announced his marriage engagement precipitately and confusedly to his mother on the day when he contracted it. Poor Mrs. Scatchard showed her perfect confidence in her son by flinging her arms around his neck, and giving him joy of having found at last, in the sister of one of his fellow servants, a woman to comfort and care for him after his mother was gone. She was all eagerness to see the woman of her son's choice, and the next day was fixed for the introduction.

It was a bright sunny morning, and the little cottage parlor was full of light as Mrs. Scatchard, happy and expectant, dressed for the occasion in her Sunday gown, sat waiting for her son and her future daughter-in-law.

Punctual to the appointed time, Isaac hurriedly and nervously led his promised wife into the room. His mother rose to receive her—advanced a few steps, smiling—looked Rebecca full in the eyes, and suddenly stopped. Her face, which had been flushed the moment before, turned white in an instant; her eyes lost their expression of softness and kindess, and assumed a blank look of terror; her outstretched hands fell to her sides, and she staggered back a few steps with a low cry to her son.

"Isaac," she whispered, clutching him fast by the arm when he asked alarmedly if she had taken ill. "Isaac, does that woman's face remind you of nothing?"

Before he could answer—before he could look round to where Rebecca stood, astonished and angered by her reception, at the lower end of the room—his mother pointed impatiently to her writing desk, and gave him the key.

"Open it," she said, in a quick, breathless whisper.

"What does this mean? Why am I treated as if I had no business here? Does your mother want to insult me?" asked Rebecca angrily.

"Open it, and give me the paper in the left-hand drawer. Quick! quick, for Heaven's sake!" said Mrs. Scatchard, shrinking farther back in terror.

Isaac gave her the paper. She looked it over eagerly for a moment, then followed Rebecca, who was now turning away haughtily to leave the room, and caught her by the shoulder—abruptly raised the long, loose sleeve of her gown, and glanced at her hand and arm. Something like fear began to steal over the angry expression of Rebecca's face as she shook herself free from the old woman's grasp. "Mad!" she said to herself; "and Isaac never told me." With these few words she left the room.

Isaac was hastening after her when his mother turned and stopped his farther progress. It wrung his heart to see the misery and terror in her face as she looked at him.

"Light grey eyes," she said, in low, mournful, awestruck tones, pointing towards the open door; "a droop in the left eyelid; flaxen hair, with a gold-yellow streak in it; white arms, with a down upon them; little lady's hand, with a reddish look under the finger-nails—*The Dream-Woman*. Isaac, the Dream-Woman!"

The faint cleaving doubt which he had never been able to shake off in Rebecca Murdoch's presence was fatally set at rest forever. He *had* seen her face, then, before—seven years before, on his birthday, in the bedroom of the lonely inn.

"Be warned! oh, my son, be warned! Isaac, let her go, and do you stop with me!"

Something darkened the parlor window as those words were said. A sudden chill ran through him, and he glanced sidelong at the shadow. Rebecca Murdoch had come back. She was peering in curiously at them over the low window blind.

"I have promised to marry, Mother," he said, "and marry I must."

The tears came into his eyes as he spoke and dimmed his sight, but he could just discern the fatal face outside moving away again from the window.

His mother's head sank lower.

"Are you faint?" he whispered.

"Broken hearted, Isaac."

He stooped down and kissed her. The shadow, as he did so, returned to the window, and the fatal face peered in curiously once more.

IV

Three weeks after that day Isaac and Rebecca were man and wife.
All that was hopelessly dogged and stubborn in the man's moral
nature seemed to have closed round his fatal passion, and to have
fixed it unassailably in his heart.

After that first interview in the cottage parlor no consideration
would induce Mrs. Scatchard to see her son's wife again, or even to
talk of her when Isaac tried hard to plead her cause after their
marriage.

This course of conduct was not in any degree occasioned by a
discovery of the degradation in which Rebecca had lived. There was
no question of that between mother and son.

There was no question of anything but the fearfully exact resem-
blance between the living, breathing woman, and the spectre-woman
of Isaac's dream.

Rebecca, on her side, neither felt nor expressed the slightest sorrow at the estrangement between herself and her mother-in-law.
Isaac, for the sake of peace, had never contradicted her first idea
that age and long illness had affected Mrs. Scatchard's mind. He
even allowed his wife to upbraid him for not having confessed this
to her at the time of their marriage engagement, rather than risk
anything by hinting at the truth. The sacrifice of his integrity before
his one all-mastering delusion seemed but a small thing, and cost
his conscience but little after the sacrifices he had already made.

The time of waking from this delusion—the cruel and rueful
time—was not far off. After some quiet months of married life, as
the summer was ending, and the year was getting on towards the
month of his birthday, Isaac found his wife altering towards him.
She grew sullen and contemptuous; she formed acquaintances of the
most dangerous kind in defiance of his objections, his entreaties,
and his commands; and, worst of all, she learned, ere long, after
every fresh difference with her husband, to seek the deadly self-
oblivion of drink. Little by little, after the first miserable discovery
that his wife was keeping company with drunkards, the shocking
certainty forced itself on Isaac that she had grown to be a drunkard
herself.

He had been in a sadly desponding state for some time before the
occurrence of these domestic calamities. His mother's health, as he
could but too plainly discern every time he went to see her at the

cottage, was failing fast, and he upbraided himself in secret as the cause of the bodily and mental suffering she endured. When to his remorse on his mother's account was added the shame and misery occasioned by the discovery of his wife's degradation, he sank under the double trial—his face began to alter fast, and he had looked what he was, a spirit-broken man.

His mother, still struggling bravely against the illness that was hurrying her to the grave, was the first to notice the sad alteration in him, and the first to hear of his last worst trouble with his wife. She could only weep bitterly on the day when he made his humiliating confession, but on the next occasion when he went to see her she had taken a resolution in reference to his domestic afflictions which astonished and even alarmed him. He found her dressed to go out, and on asking the reason received this answer:

"I am not long for this world, Isaac," she said, "and I shall not feel easy on my deathbed unless I have done my best to the last to make my son happy. I mean to put my own fears and my own feelings out of the question, and go with you to your wife, and try what I can do to reclaim her. Give me your arm, Isaac, and let me do the last thing I can in this world to help my son before it is too late."

He could not disobey her, and they walked together slowly towards his miserable home.

It was only one o'clock in the afternoon when they reached the cottage where he lived. It was their dinner hour, and Rebecca was in the kitchen. He was thus able to take his mother quietly into the parlor, and then prepare his wife for the interview. She had fortunately drunk but little at that early hour, and she was less sullen and capricious than usual.

He returned to his mother with his mind tolerably at ease. His wife soon followed him into the parlor, and the meeting between her and Mrs. Scatchard passed off better than he had ventured to anticipate, though he observed with secret apprehension that his mother, resolutely as she controlled herself in other respects, could not look his wife in the face when she spoke to her. It was a relief to him, therefore, when Rebecca began to lay the cloth.

She laid the cloth, brought the bread tray, and cut a slice from the loaf for her husband, then returned to the kitchen. At that moment, Isaac, still anxiously watching his mother, was startled by seeing the same ghastly change pass over her face which had altered it so awfully on the morning when Rebecca and she first met. Before he could say a word, she whispered, with a look of horror, "Take me back—home, home again, Isaac. Come with me, and never go back again."

He was afraid to ask for an explanation; he could only sign to her to be silent, and help her quickly to the door. As they passed the bread tray on the table she stopped and pointed to it. "Did you see what your wife cut your bread with?" she asked, in a low whisper.

"No, Mother—I was not noticing—what was it?"

"Look!"

He did look. A new clasp knife, with a buckhorn handle, lay with the loaf in the bread tray. He stretched out his hand shudderingly to possess himself of it; but, at the same time, there was a noise in the kitchen, and his mother caught at his arm.

"The knife of the dream! Isaac, I'm faint with fear. Take me away before she comes back."

He was hardly able to support her. The visible, tangible reality of the knife struck him with a panic, and utterly destroyed any faint doubts that he might have entertained up to this time in relation to the mysterious dream-warning of nearly eight years before. By a last desperate effort, he summoned self-possession enough to help his mother out of the house—so quietly that the "Dream-Woman" (he thought of her by that name now) did not hear them departing from the kitchen.

"Don't go back, Isaac—don't go back!" implored Mrs. Scatchard, as he turned to go away, after seeing her safely seated again in her own room.

"I must get the knife," he answered, under his breath. His mother tried to stop him again, but he hurried out without another word.

On his return he found that his wife had discovered their secret departure from the house. She had been drinking, and was in a fury of passion. The dinner in the kitchen was flung under the grate; the cloth was off the parlour table. Where was the knife?

Unwisely, he asked for it. She was only too glad of the opportunity of irritating him which the request afforded her. He wanted the knife, did he? Could he give her a reason why? No! Then he should not have it—not if he went down on his knees and asked for it. Further recriminations elicited the fact that she had bought it at a bargain, and that she considered it her own especial property. Isaac saw the uselessness of attempting to get the knife by fair means, and determined to search for it, later in the day, in secret. The search was unsuccessful. Night came on, and he left the house to walk about the streets. He was afraid now to sleep in the same room with her.

Three weeks passed. Still sullenly enraged with him, she would not give up the knife; and still that fear of sleeping in the same room with her possessed him. He walked about at night, or dozed in the parlor, or sat watching by his mother's bedside. Before the expiration of the first week in the new month his mother died. It wanted then but ten days of her son's birthday. She had longed to live till that anniversary. Isaac was present at her death, and her last words in this world were addressed to him:

"Don't go back, my son, don't go back!"

He was obliged to go back, if it were only to watch his wife. Exasperated to the last degree by his distrust of her, she had revengefully sought to add a sting to his grief, during the last days of his mother's illness, by declaring that she would assert her right to attend the funeral. In spite of all that he could do or say, she held with wicked pertinacity to her word, and on the day appointed for the burial forced herself—inflamed and shameless with drink—into her husband's presence, and declared that she would walk in the funeral procession to his mother's grave.

This last worst outrage, accompanied by all that was most insulting in word and look, maddened him for a moment. He struck her.

The instant the blow was dealt he repented it. She crouched down, silent, in a corner of the room, and eyed him steadily; it was a look that cooled his hot blood and made him tremble. But there was no time now to think of a means of making atonement. Nothing remained but to risk the worst till the funeral was over. There was but one way of making sure of her. He locked her into her bedroom.

When he came back some hours after, he found her sitting, very much altered in look and bearing, by the bedside, with a bundle on her lap. She rose, and faced him quietly, and spoke with a strange stillness in her voice, a strange repose in her eyes, a strange composure in her manner.

"No man has ever struck me twice," she said, "and my husband shall have no second opportunity. Set the door open and let me go. From this day forth we see each other no more."

Before he could answer she passed him and left the room. He saw her walk away up the street.

Would she return?

All that night he watched and waited, but no footsteps came near the house. The next night, overpowered by fatigue, he lay down in his clothes, with the door locked, the key on the table, and the candle burning. His slumber was not disturbed. The third night, the fourth, the fifth, the sixth passed, and nothing happened. He lay down on the seventh, still in his clothes, still with the door locked, the key on the table, and the candle burning, but easier in his mind.

Easier in his mind, and in perfect health and body when he fell off to sleep. But his rest was disturbed. He woke twice without any sensation of uneasiness. But the third time it was that never-to-be-forgotten shivering of the night at the lonely inn, that dreadful sinking pain at heart, which once more aroused him in an instant.

His eyes opened towards the left-hand side of the bed, and there stood—

The Dream-Woman again? No! His wife: the living reality, with the dream-spectre's attitude; the fair arm up, the knife clasped in the delicate white hand.

He sprang upon her almost at the instant of seeing her, and yet not quickly enough to prevent her from hiding the knife. Without a word from him—without a cry from her—he pinioned her in a chair. With one hand he felt up her sleeve, and there, where the Dream-Woman had hidden the knife, his wife had hidden it—the knife with the buckhorn handle, that looked like new.

In the despair of that fearful moment his brain was steady, his heart was calm. He looked at her fixedly with the knife in his hand, and said these last words.

"You told me we should see each other no more, and you have come back. It is my turn now to go, and to go forever. I say that we shall see each other no more, and *my* word shall not be broken."

He left her, and set forth into the night. There was a bleak wind abroad, and the smell of recent rain was in the air. The distant church clocks chimed the quarter as he walked rapidly beyond the last houses in the suburb. He asked the first policeman he met what the hour that was of which the quarter past had just struck.

The man referred sleepily to his watch, and answered, "Two o'clock." Two in the morning. What day of the month was this day that had just begun? He reckoned it up from the date of his mother's funeral. The fatal parallel was complete; it was his birthday!

Had he escaped the mortal peril which his dream foretold? Or had he only received a second warning?

As that ominous doubt forced itself on his mind, he stopped, reflected, and turned back towards the city. He was still resolute to hold to his word, and never to let her see him more, but there was thought now in his mind of having her watched and followed. The knife was in his possession; the world was before him; but a new distrust of her—vague, unspeakable, superstitious dread—had overcome him.

"I must know where she goes, now she thinks I have left her," he said to himself, as he stole back wearily to the precincts of his house.

It was still dark. He had left the candle burning in the bedchamber; but when he looked up at the window of the room above, there was no light in it. He crept cautiously to the house door. On going away, he remembered to have closed it; on trying it now, he found it open.

He waited outside, never losing sight of the house, till daylight. Then he ventured indoors—listened, and heard nothing—looked into the kitchen, scullery, parlor, and found nothing; went up, at last into the bedroom—it was empty. A picklock lay on the floor, betraying how she had gained entrance in the night, and that was the only trace of her.

Whither had she gone? That no mortal tongue could tell him. The darkness had covered her flight; and when the day broke, no man could say where the light found her.

Before leaving the house and the town forever, he gave instructions to a friend and neighbor to sell his furniture for anything that it would fetch, and apply the proceeds to employing the police to trace her. The directions were honestly followed and the money was all spent, but the inquiries led to nothing. The picklock in the bedroom remained the one last useless trace of the Dream-Woman.

At this point of the narrative the landlord paused, and, turning towards the window of the room in which we were sitting, looked in the direction of the stableyard.

"So far," he said, "I tell you what was told me. The little that remains to be added lies within my own experience. Between two and three months after the events I have just been relating, Isaac Scatchard came to me, withered and old-looking before his time, just as you saw him today. He had his testimonials to character with him, and he asked for employment here. Knowing that my wife and he were distantly related, I gave him a trial in consideration of that relationship, and liked him in spite of his queer habits. He is as sober, honest, and willing a man as there is in England. As for his restlessness at night, and his sleeping away his leisure time in the day, who can wonder at it after hearing his story? Besides, he never objects to being roused up when he's wanted, so there's not much inconvenience to complain of, after all."

"I suppose he is afraid to return to that dreadful dream, and of walking out of it in the dark?" said I.

"No," returned the landlord. "The dream comes back to him so often that he has got to bear with it by time resignedly enough. It's his wife keeps him waking at night, as he has often told me."

"What! Has she never been heard of yet?"

"Never. Isaac himself has the one perpetual thought about her, that she is alive and looking for him. I believe he wouldn't let himself drop off to sleep towards two in the morning for a king's ransom. Two in the morning, he says, is the time she will find him, one of these days. Two in the morning is the time all the year round when he likes to be most certain that he has got that clasp knife safe about him. He does not mind being alone as long as he is awake, except on the night before his birthday, when he firmly believes himself to be in peril of his life. The birthday has only come round once since he has been here, and then he sat up along with the nightporter. "She's looking for me," is all he says when anybody speaks to him about the one anxiety of his life; "she's looking for me." He may be right. She *may* be looking for him. Who can tell?"

"Who can tell?" said I.

The Stolen Rubens

by Jacques Futrelle

Matthew Kale made fifty million dollars out of axle grease, after which he began to patronize the high arts. It was simple enough: He had the money, and Europe had the old masters. His method of buying was simplicity itself. There were five thousand square yards, more or less, in the huge gallery of his marble mansion which were to be covered, so he bought five thousand yards, more or less, of art. Some of it was good, some of it fair, and much of it bad. The chief picture of the collection was a Rubens, which he had picked up in Rome for fifty thousand dollars.

Soon after acquiring his collection, Kale decided to make certain alterations in the vast room where the pictures hung. They were all taken down and stored in the ballroom, equally vast, with their faces toward the wall. Meanwhile Kale and his family took refuge in a nearby hotel.

It was at this hotel that Kale met Jules de Lesseps. De Lesseps was distinctly the sort of Frenchman whose conversation resembles calisthenics. He was nervous, quick, and agile, and he told Kale in confidence that he was not only a painter himself, but a connoisseur in the high arts. Pompous in the pride of possession, Kale went to a good deal of trouble to exhibit his private collection for de Lesseps' delectation. It happened in the ballroom, and the true artist's delight shone in the Frenchman's eyes as he handled the pieces which were good. Some of the others made him smile, but it was an inoffensive sort of smile.

With his own hands Kale lifted the precious Rubens and held it before the Frenchman's eyes. It was a "Madonna and Child," one of those wonderful creations which have endured through the years with all the sparkle and color beauty of their pristine days. Kale seemed disappointed because de Lesseps was not particularly enthusiastic about this picture.

"Why, it's a Rubens!" he exclaimed.

"Yes, I see," replied de Lesseps.

"It cost me fifty thousand dollars."

"It is perhaps worth more than that," and the Frenchman shrugged his shoulders as he turned away.

Kale looked at him in chagrin. Could it be that de Lesseps did not understand that it was a Rubens, and that Rubens was a painter? Or was it that he had failed to hear him say that it cost him fifty thousand dollars? Kale was accustomed to seeing people bob their heads and open their eyes when he said fifty thousand dollars; therefore, "Don't you like it?" he asked.

"Very much indeed," replied de Lesseps; "but I have seen it before. I saw it in Rome just a week or so before you purchased it."

They rummaged on through the pictures, and at last a Whistler was turned up for their inspection. It was one of the famous Thames series, a water color. De Lesseps' face radiated excitement, and several times he glanced from the water color to the Rubens as if mentally comparing the exquisitely penciled and colored newer work with the bold, masterly technic of the older painting.

Kale misunderstood his silence. "I don't think much of this one myself," he explained apologetically. "It's a Whistler, and all that, and it cost me five thousand dollars, and I sort of had to have it, but still it isn't just the kind of thing that I like. What do you think of it?"

"I think it is perfectly wonderful!" replied the Frenchman enthusiastically. "It is the essence, the superlative, of Whistler's work. I wonder if it would be possible," and he turned to face Kale, "for me to make a copy of that? I have some slight skill in painting myself, and dare say I could make a fairly creditable copy of it."

Kale was flattered. He was more and more impressed each moment with the picture. "Why certainly," he replied. "I will have it sent up to the hotel, and you can—"

"No, no, no!" interrupted de Lesseps quickly. "I wouldn't care to accept the responsibility of having the picture in my charge. There is always danger of fire. But if you would give me permission to come here—this room is large and airy and light—and besides it is quiet—"

"Just as you like," said Kale magnanimously. "I merely thought the other way would be most convenient for you."

De Lesseps laid one hand on the millionaire's arm. "My dear friend," he said earnestly, "if these pictures were my pictures, I shouldn't try to accommodate anybody where they were concerned. I dare say the collection as it stands cost you—"

"Six hundred and eighty-seven thousand dollars," volunteered Kale proudly.

"And surely they must be well protected here in your house during your absence?"

"There are about twenty servants in the house, while the workmen are making the alterations," said Kale, "and three of them don't do anything but watch this room. No one can go in or out except by the door we entered—the others are locked and barred—and then only with my permission, or a written order from me. No, sir, nobody can get away with anything in this room."

"Excellent—excellent!" said de Lesseps admiringly. He smiled a little. "I am afraid I did not give you credit for being the farsighted businessman that you are." He turned and glanced over the collection of pictures abstractedly. "A clever thief, though," he ventured, "might cut a valuable painting, for instance the Rubens, out of the frame, roll it up, conceal it under his coat, and escape."

Kale laughed and shook his head.

It was a couple of days later at the hotel that de Lesseps brought up the subject of copying the Whistler. He was profuse in his thanks when Kale volunteered to accompany him into the mansion and witness the preliminary stages of the work. They paused at the ballroom door.

"Jennings," said Kale to the liveried servant there, "this is Mr. De Lesseps. He is to come and go as he likes. He is going to do some work in the ballroom here. See that he isn't disturbed."

De Lesseps noticed the Rubens leaning carelessly against some other pictures, with the holy face of the Madonna turned toward them. "Really, Mr. Kale," he protested, "that picture is too valuable to be left about like that. If you will let your servants bring me some canvas, I shall wrap it and place it up on this table off the floor. Suppose there were mice here!"

Kale thanked him. The necessary orders were given, and finally the picture was carefully wrapped and placed beyond harm's reach, whereupon de Lesseps adjusted himself, paper, easel, stool, and all, and began his work. There Kale left him.

Three days later Kale found the artist still at his labor.

"I just dropped by," he explained, "to see how the work in the gallery was getting along. It will be finished in another week. I hope I am not disturbing you?"

"Not at all," said de Lesseps; "I have nearly finished. See how I am getting along?" He turned the easel toward Kale.

The millionaire gazed from that toward the original which stood on a chair nearby, and frank admiration for the artist's efforts was in his eyes. "Why, it's fine!" he exclaimed. "It's just as good as the other one, and I bet you don't want any five thousand dollars for it—eh?"

That was all that was said about it at the time. Kale wandered about the house for an hour or so, then dropped into the ballroom where de Lesseps was getting his paraphernalia together, and they walked back to the hotel. The artist carried under one arm his copy of the Whistler, loosely rolled up.

Another week passed, and the workmen who had been engaged in refinishing and decorating the gallery had gone. De Lesseps volunteered to assist in the work of rehanging the pictures, and Kale gladly turned the matter over to him. It was in the afternoon of the day this work began that de Lesseps, chatting pleasantly with Kale, ripped loose the canvas which enshrouded the precious Rubens. Then he paused with an exclamation of dismay. The picture was gone; the frame which had held it was empty. A thin strip of canvas around the inside edge showed that a sharp penknife had been used to cut out the painting.

All of these facts came to the attention of Professor Augustus S.F.X. Van Dusen—The Thinking Machine. This was a day or so after Kale had rushed into Detective Mallory's office at police headquarters with the statement that his Rubens had been stolen. He banged his fist down on the detective's desk, and roared at him.

"It cost me fifty thousand dollars! Why don't you do something? What are you sitting there staring at me for?"

"Don't excite yourself, Mr. Kale," the detective advised. "I will put my men at work right now to recover the—the—What is a Rubens, anyway?"

"It's a picture!" bellowed Kale. "A piece of canvas with some paint on it, and it cost me fifty thousand dollars—don't you forget that!"

So the police machinery was set in motion to recover the picture. And in time the matter fell under the watchful eye of Hutchinson Hatch, reporter. He learned the facts preceding the disappearance of the picture and then called on de Lesseps. He found the artist in a state of excitement bordering on hysteria; an intimation from the reporter of the object of his visit caused de Lesseps to burst into words.

"Mon Dieu! It is outrageous! What can I do? I was the only one

in the room for several days. I was the one who took such pains to protect the picture. And now it is gone! The loss is irreparable. What can I do?"

Hatch didn't have any very definite idea as to just what he could do, so he let him go on. "As I understand it, Mr. de Lesseps," he interrupted at last, "no one else was in the room, except you and Mr. Kale, all the time you were there?"

"No one else."

"And I think Mr. Kale said that you were making a copy of some famous water color; weren't you?"

"Yes, a Thames scene by Whistler," was the reply. "That is it, hanging over the fireplace."

Hatch glanced at the picture admiringly. It was an exquisite copy, and showed the deft touch of a man who was himself an artist of great ability.

De Lesseps read the admiration on his face. "It is not bad," he said modestly. "I studied with Carolus Duran."

With all else that was known, and this little additional information, which seemed of no particular value to the reporter, the entire matter was laid before The Thinking Machine. That distinguished man listened from beginning to end without comment.

"Who had access to the room?" he asked finally.

"That is what the police are working on now," said Hutchinson Hatch. "There are a couple of dozen servants in the house, and I suppose, in spite of Kale's rigid orders, there was a certain laxity in their enforcement."

"Of course that makes it more difficult," said The Thinking Machine in the perpetually irritated voice which was so characteristic a part of himself. "Perhaps it would be best for us to go to Mr. Kale's home and personally investigate."

Kale received them with the reserve which rich men usually show in the presence of representatives of the press. He stared frankly and somewhat curiously at the diminutive figure of the scientist, who explained the object of their visit.

"I guess you fellows can't do anything with this," the millionaire assured them. "I've got some regular detectives on it."

"Is Mr. Mallory here now?" asked The Thinking Machine curtly.

"Yes, he is upstairs in the servants' quarters."

"May we see the room from which the picture was taken?" inquired the scientist, with a suave intonation which Hatch knew well.

Kale granted the permission with a wave of the hand, and ushered them into the ballroom, where the pictures had been stored. From the center of this room The Thinking Machine surveyed it all. The windows were high. Half a dozen doors leading out into the hallways, the conservatory, quiet nooks of the mansion offered innumerable possibilities of access. After this one long comprehensive squint, The Thinking Machine went over and picked up the frame from which the Rubens had been cut. For a long time he examined it. Kale's impatience was evident. Finally the scientist turned to him.

"How well do you know M. de Lesseps?"

"I've known him for only a month or so. Why?"

"Did he bring you letters of introduction, or did you meet him merely casually?"

Kale regarded him with displeasure. "My own personal affairs have nothing whatever to do with this matter! Mr. de Lesseps is a gentleman of integrity, and certainly he is the last whom I would suspect of any connection with the disappearance of the picture."

"That is usually the case," remarked The Thinking Machine tartly. He turned to Hatch. "Just how good a copy was that he made of the Whistler picture?"

"I have never seen the original," Hatch replied; "but the workmanship was superb. Perhaps Mr. Kale wouldn't object to us seeing—"

"Oh, of course not," said Kale resignedly. "Come in; it's in the gallery."

Hatch submitted the picture to a careful scrutiny. "I should say the copy is well-nigh perfect," was his verdict. "Of course, in its absence, I can't say exactly; but it is certainly a superb work."

The curtains of a wide door almost in front of them were thrown aside suddenly, and Dectective Mallory entered. He carried something in his hand, but at sight of them concealed it behind him. Unrepressed triumph was in his face.

"Ah, professor, we meet often; don't we?" he said.

"This reporter here and his friend seem to be trying to drag de Lesseps into this affair somehow," Kale complained to the detective. "I don't want anything like that to happen. He is liable to go out and print anything. They always do."

The Thinking Machine glared at him unwaveringly for an instant, then extended his hand toward Mallory. "Where did you find it?" he asked.

"Sorry to disappoint you, professor," said the detective sarcastically, "but this is the time when you were a little late," and he produced the object which he held behind him. "Here is your picture, Mr. Kale."

Kale gasped in relief and astonishment, and held up the canvas with both hands to examine it. "Fine!" he told the detective. "I'll see that you don't lose anything by this. Why, that thing cost me fifty thousand dollars."

The Thinking Machine leaned forward to squint at the upper righthand corner of the canvas. "Where did you find it?" he asked again.

"Rolled up tight, and concealed in the bottom of a trunk in the room of one of the servants," explained Mallory. "The servant's name is Jennings. He is now under arrest."

"Jennings!" exclaimed Kale. "Why, he has been with me for years."

"Did he confess?" asked the scientist imperturbably.

"Of course not," said Mallory. "He says some of the other servants must have hidden it there."

The Thinking Machine nodded at Hatch. "I think perhaps that is all," he remarked. "I congratulate you, Mr. Mallory, upon bringing the matter to such a quick and satisfactory conclusion."

Ten minutes later they left the house and took a taxi for the scientist's home. Hatch was a little chagrined at the unexpected termination of the affair.

"Mallory does show an occasional gleam of human intelligence, doesn't he?"

"Not that I ever noticed," remarked The Thinking Machine crustily.

"But he found the picture," Hatch insisted.

"Of course he found it. It was put there for him to find."

"Put there for him to find!" repeated the reporter. "Didn't Jennings steal it?"

"If he did, he's a fool."

"Well, if he didn't steal it, who put it there?"

"De Lesseps."

"De Lesseps!" echoed Hatch. "Why the deuce did he steal a fifty-thousand-dollar picture and put it in a servant's trunk to be found?"

The Thinking Machine twisted around in his seat and squinted at him coldly for a moment. "At times, Mr. Hatch, I am absolutely amazed at your stupidity. I can understand it in a man like Mallory, but I have always given you credit for being an astute, quick-witted man."

Hatch smiled at the reproach. It was not the first time he had heard it. But nothing bearing on the problem in hand was said until they reached The Thinking Machine's house.

"The only real question in my mind, Mr. Hatch," said the scientist then, "is whether or not I should take the trouble to restore Mr. Kale's picture at all. He is perfectly satisfied, and will probably never know the difference. So—"

Suddenly Hatch saw something. "Great Scott!" he exclaimed. "Do you mean that the picture Mallory found was—"

"A copy of the original," snapped the scientist. "Personally I know nothing whatever about art; therefore, I could not say from observation that it is a copy, but I know it from the logic of the thing. When the original was cut from the frame, the knife swerved a little at the upper right-hand corner. The canvas remaining in the frame told that. The picture that Mr. Mallory found did not correspond in this detail with the canvas in the frame. The conclusion is obvious."

"And de Lesseps has the original?"

"De Lesseps has the original. How did he get it? In any one of a dozen ways. He might have rolled it up and stuck it under his coat. He might have had a confederate. But I don't think that any ordinary method of theft would have appealed to him. I am giving him credit for being clever, as I must when we review the whole case.

"For instance, he asked for permission to copy the Whistler, which you saw was the same size as the Rubens. It was granted. He copied it practically under guard, always with the chance that Mr. Kale himself would drop in. It took him three days to copy it, so he says. He was alone in the room all that time. He knew that Mr. Kale had not the faintest idea of art. Taking advantage of that, what would have been simpler than to have copied the Rubens in oil? He could have removed it from the frame immediately after he canvased it over, and kept it in a position near him where it could be quickly concealed if he was interrupted. Remember, the picture is worth fifty thousand dollars; therefore, was worth the trouble.

"De Lesseps is an artist—we know that—and dealing with a man who knew nothing whatever of art, he had no fears. We may suppose his idea all along was to use the copy of the Rubens as a sort of decoy after he got away with the original. You saw that Mallory didn't know the difference, and it was safe for him to suppose that Mr. Kale wouldn't. His only danger until he could get away gracefully was of some critic or connoisseur, perhaps, seeing the copy. His boldness we see readily in the fact that he permitted himself to discover the theft; that he discovered it after he had volunteered to assist Mr. Kale in the general work of rehanging the pictures in the gallery. Just how he put the picture in Jennings' trunk I don't happen to know. We can imagine many ways." He lay back in his chair for a minute without speaking, eyes steadily turned upward, fingers placed precisely tip to tip.

"But how did he take the picture from the Kale home?" asked Hatch.

"He took it with him probably under his arm the day he left the house with Mr. Kale," was the astonishing reply.

Hatch was staring at him in amazement. After a moment the scientist rose and passed into the adjoining room, and the telephone bell there jingled. When he joined Hatch again he picked up his hat and they went out together.

De Lesseps was in when their cards were sent up, and received them. They conversed about the case generally for ten minutes, while the scientist's eyes were turned inquiringly here and there about the room. At last there came a knock on the door.

"It is Detective Mallory, Mr. Hatch," remarked The Thinking Machine. "Open the door for him."

De Lesseps seemed startled for just one instant, then quickly recovered. Mallory's eyes were full of questions when he entered.

"I should like, Mr. Mallory," began The Thinking Machine quietly, "to call your attention to this copy of Mr. Kale's picture by Whistler—over the mantel here. Isn't it excellent? You have seen the original?"

Mallory grunted. De Lesseps' face, instead of expressing appreciation of the compliment, blanched, and his hands closed tightly. Again he recovered himself and smiled.

"The beauty of this picture lies not only in its faithfulness to the original," the scientist went on, "but also in the fact that it was painted under extraordinary circumstances. For instance, I don't know if you know, Mr. Mallory, that it is possible so to combine glue and putty and a few other commonplace things into a paste which will effectually blot out an oil painting, and offer at the same time an excellent surface for water color work!"

There was a moment's pause, during which the three men stared at him silently—with conflicting emotions.

"This water color—this copy of Whistler," continued the scientist evenly—"is painted on such a paste as I have described. That paste in turn covers the original Rubens picture. It can be removed with water without damage to the picture, which is in oil, so that instead of a copy of the Whistler painting, we have an original by Rubens, worth fifty thousand dollars. That is true; isn't it, M. De Lesseps?"

There was no reply to the question—none was needed.

It was an hour later, after de Lesseps was safely in his cell, that Hatch called up The Thinking Machine and asked one question.

"How did you know that the water color was painted over the Rubens?"

"Because it was the only absolutely safe way in which the Rubens could be hopelessly lost to those who were looking for it, and at the same time perfectly preserved," was the answer. "I told you de Lesseps was a clever man, and a little logic did the rest. Two and two always make four, Mr. Hatch, not sometimes, but all the time."

The Story of the Bagman's Uncle

by Charles Dickens

"My uncle, gentlemen," said the bagman, "was one of the merriest, pleasantest, cleverest fellows that ever lived. I wish you had known him, gentlemen. On second thoughts, gentlemen, I *don't* wish you had known him, for if you had, you would have been all, by this time, in the ordinary course of nature, if not dead, at all events so near it as to have taken to stopping at home and giving up company: which would have deprived me of the inestimable pleasure of addressing you at this moment. Gentlemen, I wish your fathers and mothers had known my uncle. They would have been amazingly fond of him, especially your respectable mothers; I know they would. If any two of his numerous virtues predominated over the many that adorned his character, I should say they were his mixed punch, and his after-supper song. Excuse my dwelling on these melancholy recollections of departed worth; you won't see a man like my uncle every day in the week.

"I have always considered it a great point in my uncle's character, gentlemen, that he was the intimate friend and companion of Tom Smart, of the great house of Bilson and Slum, Cateaton Street, City. My uncle collected for Tiggin and Welps, but for a long time he went pretty near the same journey as Tom; and the very first night they met, my uncle took a fancy for Tom, and Tom took a fancy for my uncle. They made a bet of a new hat, before they had known each other half an hour, who should brew the best quart of punch and drink it the quickest. My uncle was judged to have won the making, but Tom Smart beat him in the drinking by about half a salt-spoonful. They took another quart apiece to drink each other's health in, and were staunch friends ever afterwards. There's a destiny in these things, gentlemen; we can't help it.

"In personal appearance, my uncle was a trifle shorter than the middle size; he was a thought stouter, too, than the ordinary run of people, and perhaps his face might be a shade redder. He had the

333

jolliest face you ever saw, gentlemen: something like Punch, with a handsomer nose and chin; his eyes were always twinkling and sparkling with good-humour; and a smile—not one of your un-meaning, wooden grins, but a real merry, hearty, good-tempered smile—was perpetually on his countenance. He was pitched out of his gig once, and knocked, head first, against a milestone. There he lay, stunned, and so cut about the face with some gravel which had been heaped up alongside it, that, to use my uncle's own strong expression, if his mother could have revisited the earth, she wouldn't have known him. Indeed, when I come to think of the matter, gentle-men, I feel pretty sure she wouldn't, for she died when my uncle was two years and seven months old, and I think it's very likely that, even without the gravel, his top-boots would have puzzled the good lady not a little: to say nothing of his jolly red face. However, there he lay, and I have heard my uncle say, many a time, that the man said who picked him up that he was smiling as merrily as if he had tumbled out for a treat, and that after they had bled him, the first faint glimmerings of returning animation were, his jumping up in bed, bursting out into a loud laugh, kissing the young woman who held the basin, and demanding a mutton chop and a pickled walnut instantly. He was very fond of pickled walnuts, gentlemen. He said he always found that, taken without vinegar, they relished the beer.

"My uncle's great journey was in the fall of the leaf, at which time he collected debts, and took orders, in the north: going from London to Edinburgh, from Edinburgh to Glasgow, from Glasgow back to Edinburgh, and thence to London by the smack. You are to under-stand that his second visit to Edinburgh was for his own pleasure. He used to go back for a week, just to look up his old friends; and what with breakfasting with this one, lunching with that, dining with a third, and supping with another, a pretty tight week he used to make of it. I don't know whether any of you gentlemen ever partook of a real substantial hospitable Scotch breakfast, and then went out to a slight lunch of a bushel of oysters, a dozen or so of bottled ale, and a noggin or two of whiskey to close up with. If you ever did, you will agree with me that it requires a pretty strong head to go out to dinner and supper afterwards.

"But bless your hearts and eyebrows, all this sort of thing was nothing to my uncle! He was so well seasoned, that it was mere child's play. I have heard him say that he could see the Dundee people out any day, and walk home afterwards without staggering; and yet the Dundee people have as strong heads and as strong punch, gentlemen, as you are likely to meet with between the poles. I have heard of a Glasgow man and a Dundee man drinking against each other for fifteen hours at a sitting. They were both suffocated, as nearly as could be ascertained, at the same moment, but with this trifling exception, gentlemen, they were not a bit the worse for it.

"One night, within four-and-twenty hours of the time when he had settled to take shipping for London, my uncle supped at the house of a very old friend of his, a Baillie Mac something, and four syllables after it, who lived in the old town of Edinburgh. There were the baillie's wife and the baillie's three daughters, and the baillie's grown-up son, and three or four stout, bushy-eyebrowed, canty old Scotch fellows, that the baillie had got together to do honour to my uncle, and help to make merry. It was a glorious supper. There were kippered salmon, and Finnan haddocks, and a lamb's head, and a haggis—a celebrated Scotch dish, gentlemen, which my uncle used to say always looked to him, when it came to table, very much like a cupid's stomach—and a great many other things besides, that I forget the names of, but very good things notwithstanding. The lassies were pretty and agreeable; the baillie's wife, one of the best creatures that ever lived; and my uncle in thoroughly good cue: the consequence of which was, that the young ladies tittered and giggled, and the old lady laughed out loud, and the baillie and the other old fellows roared till they were red in the face, the whole mortal time. I don't quite recollect how many tumblers of whiskey toddy each man drank after supper; but this I know, that about one o'clock in the morning, the baillie's grown-up son became insensible while attempting the first verse of 'Willie brewed a peck o' maut;' and he having been, for half an hour before, the only other man visible above the mahogany, it occurred to my uncle that it was almost time to think about going: especially as drinking had set in at seven o'clock, in order that he might get home at a decent hour. But, thinking it might not be quite polite to go just then, my uncle voted himself into the chair, mixed another glass, rose to propose his own health, addressed himself in a neat and complimentary speech, and drank the toast with great enthusiasm. Still nobody woke; so my uncle took a little drop more—neat this time, to prevent the toddy disagreeing with him—and, laying violent hands on his hat, sallied forth into the street.

"It was a wild gusty night when my uncle closed the baillie's door, and setting his hat firmly on his head, to prevent the wind from taking it, thrust his hands into his pockets, and looking upwards, took a short survey of the state of the weather. The clouds were drifting over the moon at their giddiest speed: at one time wholly obscuring her: at another, suffering her to burst forth in full splendour and shed her light on all the objects around: anon, driving over her again with increased velocity, and shrouding everything in darkness. 'Really, this won't do,' said my uncle, addressing himself to the weather, as if he felt himself personally offended. 'This is not at all the kind of thing for my voyage. It will not do at any price,' said my uncle very impressively. Having repeated this several times, he recovered his balance with some difficulty—for he was rather giddy with looking up into the sky so long—and walked merrily on.

"The baillie's house was in the Canongate, and my uncle was going to the other end of Leith Walk, rather better than a mile's journey. On either side of him, there shot up against the dark sky, tall, gaunt, straggling houses, with time-stained fronts, and windows that seemed to have shared the lot of eyes in mortals, and to have grown dim and sunken with age. Six, seven, eight stories high, were the houses; story piled above story, as children build with cards—throwing their dark shadows over the roughly paved road, and making the dark night darker. A few oil lamps scattered at long distances, but they only served to mark the dirty entrance to some narrow close, or to show where a common stair communicated, by steep and intricate windings, with the various flats above. Glancing at all these things with the air of a man who had seen them too often before to think them worthy of much notice now, my uncle walked up the middle of the street, with a thumb in each waistcoat pocket, indulging, from time to time, in various snatches of song, chanted forth with such good-will and spirit, that the quiet honest folk started from their first sleep, and lay trembling in bed till the sound died away in the distance; when, satisfying themselves that it was only some drunken ne'er-do-weel finding his way home, they covered themselves up warm and fell asleep again.

"I am particular in describing how my uncle walked up the middle of the street, with his thumbs in his waistcoat pockets, gentlemen, because, as he often used to say (and with great reason too), there is nothing at all extraordinary in this story, unless you distinctly understand at the beginning that he was not by any means of a marvellous or romantic turn.

"Gentlemen, my uncle walked on with his thumbs in his waistcoat pockets, taking the middle of the street to himself, and singing, now a verse of a love song, and then a verse of a drinking one, and when he was tired of both, whistling melodiously, until he reached the North Bridge, which, at this point, connects the old and new towns of Edinburgh. Here he stopped for a minute, to look at the strange irregular clusters of lights piled one above the other, and twinkling afar off, so high in the air, that they looked like stars, gleaming from the castle walls on the one side, and the Calton Hill on the other, as if they illuminated veritable castles in the air: while the old picturesque town slept heavily on, in gloom and darkness below: its palace and chapel of Holyrood, guarded day and night, as a friend of my uncle's used to say, by old Arthur's Seat, towering, surly and dark, like some gruff genius, over the ancient city he has watched so long. I say, gentlemen, my uncle stopped here, for a minute, to look about him; and then paying a compliment to the weather, which had a little cleared up, though the moon was sinking, walked on again, as royally as before: keeping the middle of the road with great dignity, and looking as if he should very much like to meet with somebody who would dispute possession of it with him. There was nobody at all disposed to contest the point, as it happened; and so, on he went, with his thumbs in his waistcoat pockets, like a lamb.

"When my uncle reached the end of Leith Walk, he had to cross a pretty large piece of waste ground, which separated him from a short street which he had to turn down, to go direct to his lodging. Now, in this piece of waste ground, there was, at that time, an enclosure belonging to some wheelwright, who contracted with the Post Office for the purchase of old worn-out mail-coaches; and my uncle, being very fond of coaches, old, young, or middle-aged, all at once took it into his head to step out of his road for no other purpose than to peep between the palings at these mails: about a dozen of which he remembered to have seen, crowded together in a very forlorn and dismantled state, inside. My uncle was a very enthusiastic, emphatic sort of person, gentlemen; so, finding that he could not obtain a good peep between the palings, he got over them, and sitting himself quietly down on an old axletree, began to contemplate the mail-coaches with a deal of gravity.

"There might be a dozen of them, or there might be more—my uncle was never quite certain on this point, and being a man of very scrupulous veracity about numbers, didn't like to say—but there they stood, all huddled together in the most desolate condition imaginable. The doors had been torn from their hinges and removed; the linings had been stripped off: only a shred hanging here and there by a rusty nail; the lamps were gone, the poles had long since vanished, the iron-work was rusty, the paint worn away; the wind whistled through the chinks in the bare wood-work; and the rain which had collected on the roofs, fell, drop by drop, into the insides with a hollow and melancholy sound. They were the decaying skeletons of departed mails, and in that lonely place, at that time of night, they looked chill and dismal.

"My uncle rested his head upon his hands, and thought of the busy bustling people who had rattled about, years before, in the old coaches, and were now as silent and changed: he thought of the numbers of people to whom one of those crazy, mouldering vehicles had borne, night after night, for many years, and through all weathers, the anxiously expected intelligence, the eagerly looked-for remittance, the promised assurance of health and safety, the sudden announcement of sickness and death. The merchant, the lover, the wife, the widow, the mother, the schoolboy, the very child who tottered to the door at the postman's knock—how had they all looked forward to the arrival of the old coach! And where were they all now?

"Gentlemen, my uncle used to *say* that he thought all this at the time, but I rather suspect he learnt it out of some book afterwards, for he distinctly stated that he fell into a kind of doze as he sat on the old axletree looking at the decayed mail-coaches, and that he was suddenly awakened by some deep church bell striking two. Now, my uncle was never a fast thinker, and if he had thought all these things, I am quite certain it would have taken him till full half-past two o'clock, at the very least. I am, therefore, decidedly of opinion, gentlemen, that my uncle fell into a kind of doze, without having thought about anything at all.

"Be this as it may, a church bell struck two. My uncle woke, rubbed his eyes, and jumped up in astonishment.

"In one instant after the clock struck two, the whole of this deserted and quiet spot had become a scene of most extraordinary life and animation. The mail-coach doors were on their hinges, the lining was replaced, the iron-work was as good as new, the paint was restored, the lamps were alight, cushions and great-coats were on every coach-box, porters were thrusting parcels into every boot, guards were stowing away letter-bags, hostlers were dashing pails of water against the renovated wheels; numbers of men were rushing about, fixing poles into every coach; passengers arrived, portmanteaus were handed up, horses were put to; and, in short, it was perfectly clear that every mail there was to be off directly. Gentlemen, my uncle opened his eyes so wide at all this, that, to the very last moment of his life, he used to wonder how it fell out that he had ever been able to shut 'em again.

" 'Now then!' said a voice, as my uncle felt a hand on his shoulder. 'You're booked for one inside. You'd better get in.'

" '*I* booked!' said my uncle, turning round.

" 'Yes, certainly.'

"My uncle, gentlemen, could say nothing; he was so very much astonished. The queerest thing of all was, that although there was such a crowd of persons, and although fresh faces were pouring in every monent, there was no telling where they came from; they seemed to start up, in some strange manner, from the ground or the air, and disappear in the same way. When a porter had put his luggage in the coach, and received his fare, he turned round and was gone; and before my uncle had well begun to wonder what had become of him, half-a-dozen fresh ones started up, and staggered along under the weight of parcels which seemed big enough to crush them. The passengers were all dressed so oddly too—large, broad-skirted, laced coats with great cuffs, and no collars; and wigs, gentlemen,—great formal wigs and a tie behind. My uncle could make nothing of it.

" 'Now, *are* you going to get in?' said the person who had addressed my uncle before. He was dressed as a mail guard, with a wig on his head, and most enormous cuffs to his coat, and had a lantern in one hand, and a huge blunderbuss in the other, which he was going to stow away in his little arm-chest. '*Are* you going to get in, Jack Martin?' said the guard, holding the lantern to my uncle's face.

" 'Hallo!' said my uncle, falling back a step or two. 'That's familiar!'

" 'It's so on the way-bill,' replied the guard.

" 'Isn't there a "Mister" before it?' said my uncle—for he felt, gentlemen, that for a guard he didn't know to call him Jack Martin, was a liberty which the Post Office wouldn't have sanctioned if they had known it.

" 'No; there is not,' rejoined the guard coolly.

" 'Is the fare paid?' inquired my uncle.

" 'Of course it is,' rejoined the guard.

" 'It is, is it?' said my uncle. 'Then here goes—which coach?'

" 'This,' said the guard, pointing to an old-fashioned Edinburgh and London Mail, which had the steps down, and the door open. 'Stop—here are the other passengers. Let them get in first.'

"As the guard spoke, there all at once appeared, right in front of my uncle, a young gentleman in a powdered wig, and a sky-blue coat trimmed with silver, made very full and broad in the skirts, which were lined with buckram. Tiggin and Welps were in the printed calico and waistcoat-piece line, gentlemen, so my uncle knew all the materials at once. He wore knee breeches, and a kind of leggings rolled up over his silk stockings, and shoes with buckles; he had ruffles at his wrists, a three-cornered hat on his head, and a long taper sword by his side. The flaps of his waistcoat came half-way down his thighs, and the ends of his cravat reached to his waist. He stalked gravely to the coach door, pulled off his hat, and held it above his head at arm's length: cocking his little finger in the air at the same time, as some affected people do when they take a cup of tea. Then he drew his feet together, and made a low grave bow, and then put out his left hand. My uncle was just going to step forward, and shake it heartily, when he perceived that these attentions were directed, not towards him, but to a young lady, who just then appeared at the foot of the steps, attired in an old-fashioned green velvet dress, with a long waist and stomacher. She had no bonnet on her head, gentlemen, which was muffled in a black silk hood, but she looked round for an instant as she prepared to get into the coach, and such a beautiful face as she discovered, my uncle had never seen—not even in a picture. She got into the coach, holding up her dress with one hand; and, as my uncle always said with a round oath, when he told the story, he wouldn't have believed it possible that legs and feet could have been brought to such a state of perfection, unless he had seen them with his own eyes.

"But, in this one glimpse of the beautiful face, my uncle saw that the young lady had cast an imploring look upon him, and that she appeared terrified and distressed. He noticed, too, that the young fellow in the powdered wig, notwithstanding his show of gallantry, which was all very fine and grand, clasped her tight by the wrist when she got in, and followed himself immediately afterwards. An uncommonly ill-looking fellow in a close brown wig and a plum-coloured suit, wearing a very large sword, and boots up to his hips, belonged to the party; and when he sat himself down next to the young lady, who shrunk into a corner at his approach, my uncle was confirmed in his original impression that something dark and mysterious was going forward, or, as he always said himself, that 'there was a screw loose somewhere.' It's quite surprising how quickly he made up his mind to help the lady at any peril, if she needed help.

" 'Death and lightning!' exclaimed the young gentleman, laying his hand upon his sword, as my uncle entered the coach.

" 'Blood and thunder!' roared the other gentleman. With this, he whipped his sword out, and made a lunge at my uncle without further ceremony. My uncle had no weapon about him, but with great dexterity he snatched the ill-looking gentleman's three-cornered hat from his head, and receiving the point of his sword right through the crown, squeezed the sides together, and held it tight.

" 'Pink him behind!' cried the ill-looking gentleman to his companion, as he struggled to regain his sword.

" 'He had better not,' cried my uncle, displaying the heel of one of his shoes in a threatening manner. 'I'll kick his brains out if he has any, or fracture his skull if he hasn't.' Exerting all his strength at this moment, my uncle wrenched the ill-looking man's sword from his grasp, and flung it clean out of the coach window; upon which the younger gentleman vociferated 'Death and lightning!' again, and laid his hand upon the hilt of his sword in a very fierce manner, but didn't draw it. Perhaps, gentlemen, as my uncle used to say, with a smile, perhaps he was afraid of alarming the lady.

" 'Now, gentlemen,' said my uncle, taking his seat deliberately, 'I don't want to have any death, with or without lightning, in a lady's presence, and we have had quite blood and thundering enough for one journey; so, if you please, we'll sit in our places like quiet insides. Here, guard, pick up that gentleman's carving-knife.'

"As quickly as my uncle said the words, the guard appeared at the coach window, with the gentleman's sword in his hand. He held up his lantern and looked earnestly in my uncle's face, as he handed it in: when, by its light, my uncle saw, to his great surprise, that an immense crowd of mail-coach guards swarmed round the window, every one of whom had his eyes earnestly fixed upon him too. He had never seen such a sea of white faces, and red bodies, and earnest eyes, in all his born days.

" 'This is the strangest sort of thing I ever had anything to do with,' thought my uncle. 'Allow me to return you your hat, sir.'

"The ill-looking gentleman received his three-cornered hat in silence; looked at the hole in the middle with an inquiring air; and finally stuck it on the top of his wig, with a solemnity the effect of which was a trifle impaired by his sneezing violently at the moment, and jerking it off again.

" 'All right!' cried the guard with the lantern, mounting into his little seat behind. Away they went. My uncle peeped out of the coach window as they emerged from the yard, and observed that the other mails, with coachmen, guards, horses, and passengers, complete, were driving round and round in circles, at a slow trot of about five miles an hour. My uncle burnt with indignation, gentlemen. As a commercial man, he felt that the mail-bags were not to be trifled with, and he resolved to memorialise the Post Office on the subject, the very instant he reached London.

"At present, however, his thoughts were occupied with the young lady who sat in the farthest corner of the coach, with her face muffled closely in her hood: the gentleman with the sky-blue coat sitting opposite to her: and the other man in the plum-coloured suit at her side: and both watching her intently. If she so much as rustled the folds of her hood, he could hear the ill-looking man clap his hand upon his sword, and could tell by the other's breathing (it was so dark he couldn't see his face) that he was looking as big as if he were going to devour her at a mouthful. This roused my uncle more and more, and he resolved, come what might, to see the end of it. He had a great admiration for bright eyes, and sweet faces, and pretty legs and feet; in short, he was fond of the whole sex. It runs in our family, gentlemen—so am I.

"Many were the devices which my uncle practised to attract the lady's attention, or, at all events, to engage the mysterious gentleman in conversation. They were all in vain; the gentleman wouldn't talk, and the lady didn't dare. He thrust his head out of the coach window at intervals, and bawled out to know why they didn't go faster. But he called till he was hoarse—nobody paid the least attention to him. He leant back in the coach, and thought of the beautiful face, and the feet, and legs. This answered better; it whiled away the time, and kept him from wondering where he was going, and how it was he found himself in such an odd situation. Not that this would have worried him much, anyway—he was a mighty free and easy, roving, devil-may-care sort of person, was my uncle, gentlemen.

"All of a sudden the coach stopped. 'Hallo!' said my uncle, 'what's in the wind now?'

" 'Alight here,' said the guard, letting down the steps.

" 'Here!' cried my uncle.

" 'Here,' rejoined the guard.

" 'I'll do nothing of the sort,' said my uncle.

" 'Very well, then stop where you are,' said the guard

" 'I will,' said my uncle.

" 'Do,' said the guard.

"The other passengers had regarded this colloquy with great attention; and, finding that my uncle was determined not to alight, the younger man squeezed past him, to hand the lady out. At this moment, the ill-looking man was inspecting the hole in the crown of his three-cornered hat. As the young lady brushed past, she dropped one of her gloves into my uncle's hand, and softly whispered with her lips so close to his face, that he felt her warm breath on his nose, the single word 'Help!' Gentlemen, my uncle leaped out of the coach at once, with such violence that it rocked on the springs again.

" 'Oh! you've thought better of it, have you?' said the guard, when he saw my uncle standing on the ground.

"My uncle looked at the guard for a few seconds, in some doubt whether it wouldn't be better to wrench his blunderbuss from him, fire it in the face of the man with the big sword, knock the rest of the company over the head with the stock, snatch up the young lady, and go off in the smoke. On second thoughts, however, he abandoned this plan, as being a shade too melodramatic in the execution, and followed the two mysterious men, who, keeping the lady between them, were now entering an old house, in front of which the coach had stopped. They turned into the passage, and my uncle followed.

"Of all the ruinous and desolate places my uncle had ever beheld, this was the most so. It looked as if it had once been a large house of entertainment; but the roof had fallen in in many places, and the stairs were steep, rugged, and broken. There was a huge fire-place in the room into which they walked, and the chimney was blackened with smoke; but no warm blaze lighted it up now. The white feathery dust of burnt wood was still strewed over the hearth, but the stove was cold, and all was dark and gloomy.

" 'Well,' said my uncle, as he looked about him, 'a mail travelling at the rate of six miles and a half an hour, and stopping for an indefinite time at such a hole as this, is rather an irregular sort of proceeding, I fancy. This shall be made known; I'll write to the papers.'

"My uncle said this in a pretty loud voice, and in an open unreserved sort of manner, with the view of engaging the two strangers in conversation if he could. But, neither of them took any more notice of him than whispering to each other, and scowling at him as they did so. The lady was at the farther end of the room, and once she ventured to wave her hand, as if beseeching my uncle's assistance.

"At length the two strangers advanced a little, and the conversation began in earnest.

" 'You don't know this is a private room, I suppose, fellow?' said the gentleman in sky-blue.

" 'No, I do not, fellow,' rejoined my uncle. 'Only if this is a private room specially ordered for the occasion, I should think the public room must be a *very* comfortable one.' With this my uncle sat himself down in a high-backed chair, and took such an accurate measure of the gentlemen with his eyes, that Tiggin and Welps could have supplied him with printed calico for a suit, and not an inch too much or too little, from that estimate alone.

" 'Quit this room,' said both the men together, grasping their swords.

" 'Eh?' said my uncle, not at all appearing to comprehend their meaning.

" 'Quit the room, or you are a dead man,' said the ill-looking fellow with the large sword, drawing it at the same time, and flourishing it in the air.

" 'Down with him!' cried the gentleman in sky-blue, drawing his sword also, and falling back two or three yards. 'Down with him!' The lady gave a loud scream.

"Now, my uncle was always remarkable for great boldness, and great presence of mind. All the time that he had appeared so indifferent to what was going on, he had been looking slily about for some missile or weapon of defence, and at the very instant when the swords were drawn, he espied, standing in the chimney-corner, an old basket-hilted rapier in a rusty scabbard. At one bound, my uncle caught it in his hand, drew it, flourished it gallantly above his head, called aloud to the lady to keep out of the way, hurled the chair at the man in sky-blue, and the scabbard at the man in plum-colour, and taking advantage of the confusion, fell upon them both, pell-mell.

"Gentlemen, there is an old story—none the worse for being true—regarding a fine young Irish gentleman, who, being asked if he could play the fiddle, replied he had no doubt he could, but he couldn't exactly say for certain, because he had never tried. This is not inapplicable to my uncle and his fencing. He had never had a sword in his hand before, except once when he played Richard the Third at a private theatre: upon which occasion it was arranged with Richmond that he was to be run through from behind, without showing fight at all; but here he was, cutting and slashing with two experienced swordsmen, thrusting, and guarding, and poking, and slicing, and acquitting himself in the most manful and dexterous manner possible, although up to that time, he had never been aware that he had the least notion of the science. It only shows how true the old saying is, that a man never knows what he can do till he tries, gentlemen.

"The noise of the combat was terrific; each of the three combatants swearing like troopers, and their swords clashing with as much noise as if all the knives and steels in Newport Market were rattling together at the same time. When it was at its very height, the lady, to encourage my uncle most probably, withdrew her hood entirely from her face, and disclosed a countenance of such dazzling beauty, that he would have fought against fifty men, to win one smile from it, and die. He had done wonders before, but now he began to powder away like a raving mad giant.

"At this very moment, the gentleman in sky-blue turning round, and seeing the young lady with her face uncovered, vented an exclamation of rage and jealousy; and turning his weapon against her beautiful bosom, pointed a thrust at her heart, which caused my uncle to utter a cry of apprehension that made the building ring. The lady stepped lightly aside, and snatching the young man's sword from his hand before he had recovered his balance, drove him to the wall, and running it through him, and the panelling, up to the very hilt, pinned him there, hard and fast. It was a splendid example. My uncle, with a loud shout of triumph, and a strength that was irresistible, made his adversary retreat in the same direction, and plunging the old rapier into the very centre of a large red flower in the pattern of his waistcoat, nailed him beside his friend. There they both stood, gentlemen: jerking their arms and legs about in agony, like the toy-shop figures that are moved by a piece of packthread. My uncle always said, afterwards, that this was one of the surest means he knew of for disposing of an enemy; but it was liable to one objection on the ground of expense, inasmuch as it involved the loss of a sword for every man disabled.

" 'The mail, the mail!' cried the lady, running up to my uncle and throwing her beautiful arms around his neck; 'we may yet escape.'

" '*May!*' cried my uncle; 'why, my dear, there's nobody else to kill, is there?' My uncle was rather disappointed, gentlemen, for he thought a little quiet bit of love-making would be agreeable after the slaughtering, if it were only to change the subject.

" 'We have not an instant to lose here,' said the young lady. 'He (pointing to the young gentleman in sky-blue) is the only son of the powerful Marquess of Filletoville.'

" 'Well, then, my dear, I'm afraid he'll never come to the title,' said my uncle, looking coolly at the young gentleman as he stood fixed up against the wall, in the cockchafer fashion I have described. 'You have cut off the entail, my love.'

" 'I have been torn from my home and friends by these villains,' said the young lady, her features glowing with indignation. 'That wretch would have married me by violence in another hour.'

" 'Confound his impudence!' said my uncle, bestowing a very contemptuous look on the dying heir of Filletoville.

" 'As you may guess from what you have seen,' said the young lady, 'the party were prepared to murder me if I appealed to anyone for assistance. If their accomplices find us here, we are lost. Two minutes hence may be too late. The mail!' With these words, overpowered by her feelings, and the exertion of sticking the young Marquess of Filletoville, she sunk into my uncle's arms. My uncle caught her up, and bore her to the house-door. There stood the mail, with four long-tailed, flowing-maned, black horses, ready harnessed; but no coachman, no guard, no hostler even, at the horses' heads.

"Gentlemen, I hope I do no injustice to my uncle's memory, when I express my opinion, that although he was a bachelor, he *had* held some ladies in his arms before this time; I believe, indeed, that he had rather a habit of kissing barmaids; and I know that, in one or two instances, he had been seen by credible witnesses to hug a landlady in a very perceptible manner. I mention the circumstance to show what a very uncommon sort of person this beautiful young lady must have been, to have affected my uncle in the way she did; he used to say, that as her long dark hair trailed over his arm, and her beautiful dark eyes fixed themselves upon his face when she recovered, he felt so strange and nervous, that his legs trembled beneath him. But, who can look in a sweet soft pair of dark eyes without feeling queer? *I* can't, gentlemen. I am afraid to look at some eyes I know, and that's the truth of it.

" 'You will never leave me,' murmured the young lady.

" 'Never,' said my uncle. And he meant it too.

" 'My dear preserver!' exclaimed the young lady. 'My dear, kind, brave preserver!'

" 'Don't,' said my uncle, interrupting her.

" 'Why?' inquired the young lady.

" 'Because your mouth looks so beautiful when you speak,' rejoined my uncle, 'that I am afraid I shall be rude enough to kiss it.'

"The young lady put up her hand as if to caution my uncle not to do so, and said—no, she didn't say anything—she smiled. When you are looking at a pair of the most delicious lips in the world, and see them gently break into a roguish smile—if you are very near them, and nobody else by—you cannot better testify your admiration of their beautiful form and colour than by kissing them at once. My uncle did so, and I honour him for it.

" 'Hark!' cried the young lady, starting. 'The noise of wheels and horses!'

" 'So it is,' said my uncle, listening. He had a good ear for wheels and the tramping of hoofs; but there appeared to be so many horses and carriages rattling towards them from a distance, that it was impossible to form a guess at their number. The sound was like that of fifty brakes, with six blood cattle in each.

" 'We are pursued!' cried the young lady, clasping her hands. 'We are pursued. I have no hope but in you!'

"There was such an expression of terror in her beautiful face, that my uncle made up his mind at once. He lifted her into the coach, told her not to be frightened, pressed his lips to hers once more, and then advising her to draw up the window to keep the cold air out, mounted to the box. 'Stay, love,' cried the young lady.

" 'What's the matter?' said my uncle, from the coach-box.

" 'I want to speak to you,' said the young lady; 'only a word—only one word, dearest.'

" 'Must I get down?' inquired my uncle. The lady made no answer, but she smiled again. Such a smile, gentlemen!—it beat the other one all to nothing. My uncle descended from his perch in a twinkling.

" 'What is it, my dear?' said my uncle, looking in at the coach window. The lady happened to bend forward at the same time, and my uncle thought she looked more beautiful than she had done yet. He was very close to her just then, gentlemen, so he really ought to know. 'What is it, my dear?' said my uncle.

" 'Will you never love any one but me—never marry any one besides?' said the young lady.

"My uncle swore a great oath that he never would marry anybody else, and the young lady drew in her head, and pulled up the window. He jumped upon the box, squared his elbows, adjusted the ribbons, seized the whip which lay on the roof, gave one flick to the off leader, and away went the four long-tailed, flowing-maned black horses, at fifteen good English miles an hour, with the mail-coach behind them. Whew! how they tore along!

"The noise behind grew louder. The faster the old mail went, the faster came the pursuers—men, horses, dogs, were leagued in the pursuit. The noise was frightful, but, above all, rose the voice of the young lady, urging my uncle on, and shrieking 'Faster! faster!'

"They whirled past the dark trees, as feathers would be swept before a hurricane. Houses, gates, churches, haystacks, objects of every kind they shot by, with a velocity and noise like roaring waters suddenly let loose. Still the noise of pursuit grew louder, and still my uncle could hear the young lady wildly screaming 'Faster! faster!'

"My uncle plied whip and rein; and the horses flew onward till they were white with foam; and yet the noise behind increased; and yet the young lady cried 'Faster! faster!' My uncle gave a loud stamp on the boot in the energy of the moment, and found that it was grey morning, and he was sitting in the wheelwright's yard, on the box of an old Edinburgh mail, shivering with the cold and wet, and stamping his feet to warm them! He got down, and looked eagerly inside for the beautiful young lady. Alas! there was neither door nor seat to the coach—it was a mere shell.

"Of course, my uncle knew very well that there was some mystery in the matter, and that everything had passed exactly as he used to relate it. He remained staunch to the great oath he had sworn to the beautiful young lady: refusing several eligible landladies on her account, and dying a bachelor at last. He always said, what a curious thing it was that he should have found out, by such a mere accident as his clambering over the palings, that the ghosts of mail-coaches and horses, guards, coachmen, and passengers, were in the habit of making journeys regularly every night; he used to add, that he believed he was the only living person who had ever been taken as a passenger on one of these excursions; and I think he was right, gentlemen—at least I never heard of any other."

"I wonder what these ghosts of mail-coaches carry in their bags," said the landlord, who had listened to the whole story with profound attention.

"The dead letters, of course," said the bagman.

"Oh, ah—to be sure," rejoined the landlord. "I never thought of that."